37

A NOVEL

GUERNICA WORLD EDITIONS 37

37

A NOVEL

Joy Cohen

GUERNICA
World
EDITIONS

TORONTO—CHICAGO—BUFFALO—LANCASTER (U.K.)
2021

Michael Mirolla, general editor
Julie Roorda, editor
Cover design: Allen Jomoc Jr.
Interior layout: Jill Ronsley, suneditwrite.com
Guernica Editions Inc.
287 Templemead Drive, Hamilton (ON), Canada L8W 2W4
2250 Military Road, Tonawanda, N.Y. 14150-6000 U.S.A.
www.guernicaeditions.com

Distributors:
Independent Publishers Group (IPG)
600 North Pulaski Road, Chicago IL 60624
University of Toronto Press Distribution (UTP)
5201 Dufferin Street, Toronto (ON), Canada M3H 5T8
Gazelle Book Services, White Cross Mills
High Town, Lancaster LA1 4XS U.K.

First edition.
Printed in Canada.

Legal Deposit—Third Quarter
Library of Congress Catalog Card Number: 2021933085
Library and Archives Canada Cataloguing in Publication
Title: 37 : a novel / Joy Cohen.
Other titles: Thirty-seven
Names: Cohen, Joy, author.
Series: Guernica world editions ; 37.
Description: First edition. | Series statement: Guernica world editions ; 37
Identifiers: Canadiana (print) 20210141387 | Canadiana (ebook)
20210143045 | ISBN 9781771836432 (softcover) | ISBN 9781771836449
(EPUB) | ISBN 9781771836456 (Kindle)
Classification: LCC PS3603.O4415 A137 2021 | DDC 813/.6—dc23

for Dylana and Ezra
with deep gratitude and love
thank you for being a wellspring of kindness, strength,
and inspiration
thank you for being

In mayne oygn bistu sheyn, sheyn vi di velt.

We tell so many stories about ourselves, and others. It's when we dig beneath the words and burrow between the sighs, that's where the true stories lie.

P.A. Stern

Contents

Prologue

You have to make love to the stories. Treat them with tenderness, take time, pay attention to their needs. You know what I mean, she said, as they walked along the frosted road. Otherwise, the tellers can shut down, or the words might drift away disheartened, another possibility lost.

Pale snowflakes, powdering the sky, melted on their eyelashes. There was no sunshine. There were no shadows, just a uniform graininess right out of a black-and-white movie. He said maybe they never do vanish completely. Maybe, like old lovers, they simply swirl until they land somewhere new. Recycled, yet everlasting, only the form changing.

She drew him closer to her side. Dust kicked up where patches of the dirt lane had thawed. She thought of Anthony and Cleopatra, Genghis Khan and Börte, Zipporah and Moses, long dead, their molecules still floating along divine winds, some buried deep in the earth, others mixed into fresh-ground coffee beans at the corner café.

We tend to tell stories that set people and places in a string of events, she went on. Didn't you think life was going to be like that path along the Candy Land track: linear, moving ahead step by step? Our days spent winding through Gumdrop Mountains and skipping across the Molasses Swamp?

He stopped walking. They were holding hands, and he, like a confident dance partner, spun her to face him. She didn't resist. He gently tilted her chin up toward his. That game doesn't require much—or any—strategy, he said. It has a preordained outcome, which depends only upon how the deck's been shuffled. Not sure life is like that, but maybe it is. Look at us.

Buddhists say the way we experience time—flowing on a chronological path—is an illusion. Time is timeless. To Jewish mystics, time also has no sequence: really, it's kind of a mind game, the way our brain senses and interprets motion, then turns those movements into moments. Even physicists describe the concept of time as fabricated. Tiny, vibrating loops harmoniously unite space, time, and matter—every instant happening simultaneously. Picture an unrolled filmstrip laid out end to end; all the frames and all the moments occur at the same time.

Thoughts whirled around, punctuated by each step that fell on the frozen dirt road. A gust of wind blew off the lake and rushed east. The cows startled and took off across the snow-covered field in a frenzied dance. They both laughed and kept walking, frigid wind biting their exposed skin, like an unexpected kiss.

Chapter 1

When the phone rings in the middle of the night, it's never good news. My cell phone occupied the empty pillow next to mine, and had created a permanent, rectangular dent in the blush linen. The ringing triggered a surge of adrenaline, which tried to wake my sleepy brain. Hearing Gregg's addled tone was all I needed to snap alert. Something must have happened to our daughter.

"Is Nebi okay? Where is she? Please just tell me she's—"

"It's not about Nebi. Sorry to be calling this late—uh, this early," he said.

"Then what do you want?" I was the first to admit I wasn't the most pleasant when my sleep was disturbed.

"Ahhhh …"

Really? You're annoyed with me?

"Polly, I kind of landed in jail," he said.

"Jail?" My ex-husband was a putz sometimes, but he was no criminal.

"I'm in New Hampshire. I was driving back to Vermont, and got stopped for speeding. Looks like I forgot to pay some tickets ten years ago, and here I am."

A PhD might signify you're brilliant or studious; it doesn't necessarily mean you can handle the mundane. It's not easy being married to an absent-minded scientist. Try being divorced from one.

"Gregg."

"Yeah, yeah, I know. I'm so damned predicta—"

"You manage to conduct research and publish articles, but somehow you can't get it together to pay bills, or do taxes, or …" My brain was now firing just fine. So was my tongue.

"You're better at those things."

Come on. You still expect me to fall for that line?

"Okay, Pol, could you please, please just do me a favor and bring a certified check so I can get out of here? I'm so sorry to ask, but …"

It was a two-hour trip to cross the state border. Well, plus the time at the bank. I didn't tell Gregg, but I needed to drive in that direction anyway, to pick up a report at the Department of Water Resources. I'd stop on the way to New Hampshire. Gregg could wait.

One of the 613 holy commandments found in the Torah directs us "… to relieve a neighbor of his burden and help unload his beast." It doesn't say how quickly you have to do it.

We sat in the chilly police station for hours, waiting for the release papers. The khaki polyester sofa reeked of boozy sweat. Anemic pink walls and canned elevator music were supposed to be calming. Each guitar strum ended with an echo, and even as it faded, as a new chord was played, the last notes continued to sound, like the songs and stories we play over and over in our minds. I couldn't tell whether I was hearing it or remembering it … an acoustic relic.

I tried to be silent—gloating is more effective that way—but Gregg insisted on giving me the *my night in prison* blow-by-blow. I could see through his clinical anthropological analysis of incarceration. He quoted some statistics about penal system ethnography before his voice broke—"the kid in the drunk tank was sobbing"—then he cleared his throat and filled me in on his last conversation with Nebi.

"She loves her job."

"I know. The Embassy's calling her a Cultural Ambassador."

"Told you those Spanish lessons would pay off someday."

"Wonder how long she'll stay in Madrid."

"She's something, huh? Kind of got the best of both of us—super smart, but also organized and responsible," he said.

The master of left-handed compliments.

I put my hands on his shoulders. "You're responsible, Gregg. Whenever something goes wrong, you're responsible."

Outside, we stood next to our matching grey Priuses. He lifted me off my feet and gave me a long, pressing hug. Even after a night in the lockup, he smelled good, like amber and wood shavings. I wasn't going to fall for that, either.

"Thanks, Pol. I really owe you one."

"Just one?" I laughed.

As I settled into the worn driver's seat, I turned to remind him he also owed me the bail money, but he was already driving away.

The three-story newspaper building was one of the oldest—and tallest—in town, its red brick façade complete with stately white Doric columns and detailed moulding along the portico—refinement from another time. The paint job was immaculate, and the boxwood hedge had been trimmed, mulched, and manicured into submission.

I parked behind the building in my unofficial spot. The back entrance was a peeling metal door next to an overflowing recycling dumpster. This less-than-grand access was a better fit for my newshound identity. Gritty, not pretty.

It takes a lot of raw mettle to interview the Ladies' Quilt League.

I still had the manure runoff piece to finish. The road trip to rescue Gregg hadn't quite paid off; that water resources report had turned out to be useless. My new assignment was to write an article about the changing Vermont economy, what with green energy transformation, the locavore movement, and the diversification of agribusiness. I stood in my cubicle and tickled the keyboard, searching for inspiration in pretend Morse code.

...upposed to be working today. My vacation had
...ning, but I had come in just to wrap up a few
...aving. Digital recorder in carrying case. Fresh sup-
...ned pencils. Time card in.

...a short walk down the hall to grab some reference
...in the research library. My light vacation reading.

...nputer off. And the unavoidable co-worker platitudes as I
...d out the door.

"Have a good break, Polly!"

Followed by, "Don't work too hard!"

They knew me too well.

Back at home, I lined up the pencils and stacked the reference
books—in size order. Centered on my old oak desk was the most
recent piece I'd written, "Quilts of Valor," yet another article in
which there'd been no need to use my reporter's moral compass.
Before filing away my notes from that assignment, I glanced over
my cryptic jottings. Dozens of pages, and not a controversial word.
What more would I expect from women who volunteered hundreds of hours to hand-stitch together thousands of tiny pieces of
cloth to make quilts for wounded veterans? "Oh, my, it's all just
a labor of love." A fascinating oxymoron to ponder as I readied
myself for my working vacation.

First, I needed to call Dad. For whatever good that would
do. If Mark would just keep me up to date about Dad, I wouldn't
have to go through this … but no. My brother barely talked to me.

I took a deep breath, tried to unlock my jaw, and dialed.

They connected me to Dad's room. The aide must have been
away. The ringing stopped, and Dad *hmphed* and *huhed* as the
phone banged around. I could just picture him staring at the re-
ceiver, trying to figure out what in the world he was supposed to
do with it. It could as easily have been a boat as a phone.

"Dad?" I said. "Dad, it's me, Polly, on the phone."

It took minutes until he finally spoke. The delay smelled like
moldy meat and old skin.

"Hello?" The questioning was more a desperate attempt to figure out what that word meant than to find out who was on the line.

"Hi. How are you?" A forced smile in my voice.

"Miriam, is that you?" He thought I was his dead sister, and he sounded so happy.

"No, Dad, it's me."

"Who is this?" He became immediately agitated.

"It's Polly."

"Oh."

"Hey, Dad. What you been up to?"

Silence.

"Lie … er, Li, uh, er," he stammered and puffed.

"I'm sorry, but I don't know what you want."

"Errrrrrrr," he growled.

"Dad, it's okay. Take it easy."

"You. Lieerrrrrrrrrrrrr."

"Dad, calm down. I only wanted to tell you—"

"Liiiiiiiiiiiiie, errrr, I'm telling you. Listen to me, you stupid girl!"

Then he yelled louder.

A woman's voice took over. "I'm sorry. Can you please call back later? Mr. Stern can't talk right now."

She hung up on me.

I was still shaking when I grabbed a cup of coffee. I should have known better than to try to make a quick call to my father.

How could a brain change that fast? It had been less than a year since his tangled neurons and thickened plaque had shown up as memory loss and erratic outbursts. Supposedly, it can take twenty years before the Alzheimer's symptoms appear, though the disease's damage can be lurking all that time. Damned sneaky bastard.

You'd think all the alcohol my father consumed might have preserved his brain cells a little better.

I wanted to go see Dad, but the last time I had talked to Mark, he'd said he and his partner Stephen were already in the city visiting Dad, and he was planning to go back soon.

"You don't need to come right away. Dad's fine until I come back. Waiting a few more weeks won't matter."

He probably meant that it did matter to him if I didn't come right away. Then our paths wouldn't cross.

When Mom died last summer, Mark cut me off. I never imagined what it would be like to bury Mom, but having my big brother—my best friend—shun me at the funeral would not have been part of the picture. We watched the pine coffin lower, felt the thud as it landed. The sun beat down on us, searing. We were holding hands, and Mark pulled his away from mine.

"You're too sweaty," he said.

While we sat *shiva*, seven days of mourning through non-stop company and deli platters, he avoided me. The more I reached out to him, the more he withdrew. Right when I was in the middle of a sizeable bite of chocolate-covered marble halvah, Mark announced that he and Stephen were moving away. Across the country.

"What do you mean?" It came out in a sesame-paste garble.

"I, we, just want to, to live in California," he said.

"You just want to?" I couldn't avoid the unflattering shriek. "Just want to."

"When do you leave? Why didn't you tell me? How can—"

"We're heading out tomorrow."

When *shiva* ended, I removed the torn black ribbon that had covered my heart. Mark shed his ribbon, like he had shed me.

I still wasn't clear why.

We all grieve in different ways. Dealing with grief can be like solving one of those sliding-tile puzzles. Most likely, Mark just needed a little extra space to be able to unscramble the tiles. Hopefully, whatever had gone wrong between us would soon be sorted out.

Hope can be a beacon—or a fool's paradise.

I topped off my coffee and walked into the living room. It wouldn't do anybody any good to worry about Dad; I'd take care

of him when I saw him. I'd take care o:
sure about that. Time to water the h
might as well dust off the lyrebird t
Someone at the turn of the century h
to rip the tail feathers off of a lyrebird,
frame it with gold-leafed bamboo. Its
century Japanese export bamboo-frame

A gift from Dad to Mom after r
prominent spot in their formal living room for as long as I could
remember. When I was a kid, the fact that it was just the tail—even
though it was supposed to resemble an actual lyre, the musical instrument—had made me sick to my stomach. For some twisted
reason, Mom had left it to me. Why the hell did I have to end up
with it? Why had I kept it? I tried to hide it behind the ficus, but
it was hard to cover up something that perverse.

Between the phone call with Dad and the repulsive bird rump,
I felt … green. Can you feel nauseated, but in your heart? Maybe
my morning routine would allay the queasiness.

I checked my email. Nothing worth opening, except the one
with the subject *¡Hola!* I'd recently begun communicating with
a man down in the Dominican Republic. Let me clarify: he was
ninety-nine years old, and it was purely a professional affair. Ah,
not the best word choice. Not that I would have minded a long-
overdue romantic liaison. Divorce does have its disadvantages.

Something the *señor* wrote got me thinking of a possible new
slant for the Vermont story.

*You asked why I never moved to the States after the war. I'm sorry
to say this, but I had a bad taste in my mouth ever since FDR. How
could America's leader not accept European Jews who sought refuge?
How could America itself ignore us?*

Traces of bile lasting all the way back to the 1930s. It's said
that it is easier to forgive than forget. Maybe both are equally difficult. I was about to email back, to ask some follow-up questions,
when something struck me about his message.

*But during the same time that FDR was ignoring the impending
holocaust, he was also implementing innovative ways to shore up the*

help American families. And help the environment. Ah,
y of life.

did an Internet search with the keywords Franklin Delano osevelt and 1930s, and of course, the New Deal kept turning up. I needed to read more about the Works Progress Administration and the Civilian Conservation Corps, and their presence in Vermont. Possibly there'd be something I could use.

I took my coffee and newspaper and went to the porch. The morning had started off rotten, but I always considered it a good day when I turned the pages of the *Free Press* and didn't know anyone on the Day in Court list. Or when I wasn't on the obituary page. After reading the not-so-funny funnies (seriously, how is Rex Morgan, M.D. considered comic?), I turned to the calendar section, and a listing threw itself at me like one of Mark Trail's salmon running to spawn. Splash. Smash.

Ten o'clock in the morning, Tuesday, September 25, 2007. Combined meeting of something called the Vermont Youth Conservation Corps with the seventieth reunion of the Vermont branch of the—what else?—Civilian Conservation Corps. CCC Boys who had to be in their late eighties. They'd be at the old Round Barn in Jonesville tomorrow.

This could be just the angle I needed to look at the changing Vermont economy, from a historical perspective. One quick call to invite myself, and I had a valid excuse to spend the day immersed in work, busying my mind. I was looking forward to being lost in time, including a trip to one of my favorite places: the Vermont Historical Society, which I, like so many others, affectionately call the Hysterical Society.

The drive there was along one of those routes that tends to happen on autopilot. Sometimes, I was fine with the fact that I'd driven a 3,000-pound vehicle across interstate highways without any awareness. Other times, the fact that I'd disassociated and zoned out entire sections of geography and portions of time was slightly unsettling. But there I was.

The reflection in my rearview mirror shouted that I hadn't looked at myself once in the past day or so. *Ma nashtinah?* A few gentle whacks on my face flushed some pink into my olive cheeks. A little spit tamed the errant frizz. Now I knew why older women cut their hair short. My dark mane was wild enough, but new coarse grey hairs stuck out, coiled and uncooperative, like desperate pea tendrils grasping for a pole. I was as presentable as possible, given the remedial cosmetic attempt. Nebi would have given me such grief.

As I sat on the cold State Building floor surrounded by musty boxes and folders of old documents and letters, the photos and papers conjured up images, tastes, ideas, warming me with their histories. The grainy postcard of people picnicking along the river bank. That *Pennysaver* advertisement of a local family buying a 1937 Hudson Terraplane: "The Thompsons Discover The New Way To Drive! A flick of a finger … A touch of a toe … TO SHIFT! TO STOP! TO GO!" The yellowing, tissue-thin receipt, handwritten with an ink fountain pen from a cobbler to a customer: "Four pair of new leather school shoes. $1.34 each. To be paid when Mr. Pell gets back to work." Who were these people? What had life been like back then? The rest of the day, I was in and out of the 1930s, imagining the landscape then and now. Meeting the characters. Finding the connections. Forming the questions.

For a moment, I'd almost forgotten about Dad, and how upset he had sounded on the phone. I had to get my head back into focus. I was supposed to be researching Roosevelt, the New Deal, and the Civilian Conservation Corps.

Actually, I was supposed to be on vacation.

I read about CCC projects that had happened all around Vermont. It was sad how little I knew, sad that I could enter buildings or cross bridges and never consider the people who had built them. So many hands and backs, so many stories swinging from the rafters and holding up the foundations. I also did not know that a newer version of the CCC, the Youth Conservation Corps, was being resurrected throughout Vermont, with similar goals, and out of similar necessity: to conserve and develop natural resources, and to provide jobs for young people struggling through tough economic times. The unintended results—back in the 30s, as well as today—were measured neither in dollars earned nor numbers of trees planted, but in invaluable relationships and rebuilt morale.

That night, I could barely sleep, and when I did, my dreams were filled with snippets of how the story might play out. I awoke curious and eager. I did a series of yoga asanas to center my breathing—when the breath is steady and still, so is the mind—and I headed for Jonesville.

At the CCC reunion, a roundtable discussion compared the experiences of old-timers with the current participants. Faded, sepia-toned photographs glued into albums contrasted with highly pixilated, full-spectrum digital displays. A twenty-something man shook his purple dreadlocks in empathy as the wife of a former CCC boy recounted an incident her deceased husband had shared. They hugged like old friends. A balding octogenarian squirmed when he realized that a young woman was, in fact, one of the group leaders, not the waitress. *Sorry about that, honey. Times sure have changed.*

The participants gave me details of their personal stories: who they were, how and why they had joined the Corps, and what it meant to be involved in that type of service. They also gave me a sense of what it felt like to be part of an extended family, closer than many families tied by blood.

I left the gathering with lots of interesting material, but skeptical about how relevant anything was for the article I wanted to write. Before I even exited the Round Barn, I noticed two people huddled together in a gazebo at the edge of a hayfield. One of them was a trim young woman with shoulder-length, dirty blonde hair. The other was an elderly man; his profile reminded me of Dad. Hopefully, the people in the pavilion wouldn't think I was frowning at them as I looked their way.

They were in the middle of an animated conversation and, though I didn't want to interrupt them, it seemed that this might be a good chance for a last interview. One path led to the parking lot. The other path led to the gazebo. Robert Frost guided my heart. When I approached to introduce myself—recorder, notebook, and primed questions at the ready—I had no idea of the story about to unfold. I had no idea that choosing this path would make all the difference.

The two of them spoke freely about what they'd been through, asking each other questions more poignant than the ones I had prepared. In sync, they described how a moss-covered stone had become a confidant, an eagle their muse.

"It circled right above me, at that rock," she said.

"Me, too. It flew really low, and then stared at me," he said.

They paused, and I could only imagine where they had gone. These two unlikely friends had a good sixty years between them, and they hadn't known each other very long, yet they were finishing each other's thoughts like a married couple. The young woman pulled out her journal to show the sketches she'd made on the mountain. The old man showed me the faded letters his mother had saved all these years.

As I listened to their stories, my mind was all over the place. Unlike this former CCC boy, my mom had kept hardly anything from her childhood, or mine. She hadn't had a sentimental bone in her body.

I felt inspired by their insights, ready to write their story. I felt pangs of loss that my dad could no longer tell his story to me, or anyone. And I was overwhelmed by the kind of sorrow that makes your arms droop, like they're full of wet cement. I'd dismissed Dad without realizing our time was short.

How many times had my dad tried to connect with me through all those incessant lectures about budgeting and finance and retirement? Though he was frivolous with money in his personal life, he was a very smart businessman. His corner was filled with yellow legal pads of numbers and figures and endless accounting. He'd tried to show me, and I had brushed him off. Why the hell would I have listened to his slurred words? I became the monkey with covered ears: *hear no evil*. And I certainly wouldn't look into his bloodshot eyes. My own eyes glazed over as he rambled on. All he cared about was money. And booze.

Did the CCC boys, now elderly men, have children who judged them, who did not listen? Too often, the dad is always greener on the other side.

When the pair of interviewees ran out of words, we sat in the leftover silence. It was as if I had just watched a movie—and, deep in contemplation, stayed in my seat as the credits rolled. The gazebo held us like a cradle until the crowd poured out of the barn, their goodbyes booming across the field, rocking us back to reality. It was difficult to leave, to part ways with these two new friends, but I had a job to do.

I drove away from the Round Barn and tried to sieve through all the personal confusion that had been mucked up in my virtual moat. I began to let the drawbridge lower. Ah, but if I took a few steps, perhaps I'd have to see myself as the cause of most of my childhood disappointments. That was a big fat ball of awakening, and one I wasn't quite ready to tackle. Drawbridge up!

I spent the rest of the afternoon, and all through the night, writing. As I reviewed my notes and listened to the recordings, I realized there was really nothing left to research, nothing to invent. "Three Cs" seemed like the right title for the story, since the Civilian Conservation Corps was the gossamer that wove these two people together. I'd never finished a story so quickly, without hesitation or doubt. I didn't quite follow standard journalistic technique, but I was done simply reporting about town meetings or development review boards. Done. And done.

I'd finally—and finely—been able to take threads of factual information and entwine them into a compelling tale, one in which it would be difficult to discern whether the story, the characters, the plot—even the setting—were real or imagined. "Three Cs" managed to blur the boundaries, landing somewhere between historical fiction and creative nonfiction. This was the form I'd been aspiring to perfect. Not that perfection was possible. Hmm, maybe all those Adult Children of Alcoholics meetings *had* done some good.

THREE Cs

BY P.A. STERN

Just another day begun by climbing the grungy, black rubber steps onto the school bus. Little bits of gum and who-knows-what-else stuck to the treads. Her legs felt like iron pipes. She was in a daze from yet another sleepless night. She had slept, but with one eye open. So, a half-sleep. The other half, never finished. Dangling dreams and unrested thoughts led her to constant exhaustion. She arrived at the top step, and the bus driver welcomed her on board in the same hokey way she greeted all the other kids. "Good morning, Miss Hale. And how are you today?" Emma didn't respond. *Who the hell are you to act all friendly? So two-faced. Go ahead, mock all you want, and pretend to care. Just like all of them. What a joke.*

Head hung down, Emma slogged to the back of the bus. She passed a group of three classmates. They snickered when she walked by. One of the girls feigned interest. "Hey, Emma. Ready for that bio test? I know you got the guts!" The other girls giggled. Emma didn't respond. Last week, the girl had been assigned to be Emma's lab partner, and she had flung frog intestines all over Emma's shirt. On purpose. When Emma had complained, the teacher had stifled a laugh, and—in front of the whole class—all she said was, "That's not very nice. Emma, go clean yourself up." Now the girl wouldn't let up. "I'm talking to you, bitch," she goaded. Emma seethed, but continued to her seat. Her jaw was throbbing as she clenched it, preventing herself from responding. The girls continued to whisper and snicker, glancing toward the back of the bus.

Emma pulled out her journal. May 18, 2007. She wrote non-stop, stabbing the pages with the point of her mechanical pencil.

There were more rips than words. *They can all go fuck themselves.*
Screw that biatch. I will not let them get to me. I will not let them get
to me. I will not let them get to me.

The bus passed her old school, Shaughnessy Elementary.
Emma managed a slight smile at the memory of her fourth-grade
teacher, Mr. Kaufmann. He was always so nice. To everybody. All
of those teachers were. They sang a lot and smiled all the time,
and learning was exciting and easy and fun back then. Everything
was. All conflicts were settled with rock, paper, scissors. So simple.
What more do you need?

The old monkey bars were still up. She thought they were going to tear them down when they put on the new addition. They
were kind of rusty and unsafe. One little girl was hanging on them
now, swinging from bar to bar. *Why is she at the playground so early,*
alone, way before school opens? She probably has parents who don't
care, Emma thought.

The bus picked up speed, because they were running a little
late. Road construction on 3A in front of the strip mall had been
going on for months, and it seemed like nothing had gotten done.
They just kept moving the cones around, the flag hags talking
back and forth on their radios while the road workers stood in
groups, drinking coffee, discussing bullshit. The whole summer
could go by, and they probably wouldn't get this stretch done by
fall. Emma's dad would have had it done in a month. *Too many*
people just strive for mediocrity. His words.

A few of the younger boys in the front of the bus were goofing
around, and the driver yelled at them to shut up. Everyone says
adults aren't supposed to talk to kids like that, but they always
do. When no other adult is listening. Right after they passed the
strip mall, the driver stopped the bus short. She put on the emergency brake, stood up, turned around, and gave the boys her evil
eye. They settled down immediately. The three girls cackled some
more; anyone was fair game.

Right out Emma's window was the entrance to St. Patrick's
Cemetery. She pushed her dark blonde bangs aside and glanced

up for just a second, then continued drawing in her journal. Three-dimensional boxes. *Draw two vertical lines. Cross with two horizontal lines to form a square. Two more vertical lines, shadows of the first two. Then form another square, a little behind the first. Four angled lines, connecting the two squares.* A perfect box that looked like it stuck out of the paper, but it was just a bunch of flat lines. *Repeat. Over and over and over.* She covered page after page with boxes. All optical illusions.

Emma was lost in the boxes as they pulled away from the cemetery, but she found her way back long enough to take one more quick look out the window. Behind the sprawling forsythia in full bloom, she could just barely make out the two granite tombstones. She was glad they had put them side by side, even though a lot of people told her they thought it was *awful, just awful*, and should never have been done. As she looked back down at her drawings, Emma noticed that the three girls had been watching her.

Don't look at me, she thought. She stared at them, and they stared back. *Don't look at me*, she thought. Harder. They continued to look. She screamed aloud, "Don't look at me!" The sudden outburst surprised everyone, even her. The girls rolled their eyes and peered at her—intense, glaring barbs aimed for the jugular.

"I told you to stop talking about me," Emma yelled.

"We're not saying anything," the queen bee enunciated slowly, her superiority evident in her vocal self-control.

"I can hear you thinking," Emma replied, knowing it sounded stupid coming out of her mouth but made perfect sense inside her head.

"You crazy-ass pathetic orphan," the girl spat back, quietly enough to ensure that the bus driver could not hear, but loudly enough that the words shot down the aisle for everyone else's ears landing smack on Emma's face, a face already blistering from years of so many slights, both perceived and real.

Emma was on her immediately, a tsunami in full force. Screams and cheers erupted. The bus stopped short again. This time, kids flew forward—momentum does not cease just because a driver slams on the brakes.

The driver stormed past students fallen to the floor and banged against seat backs, ignoring their whines and moans. She ripped Emma off the girls. Handfuls of hair remained in Emma's grip.

The woman cursed at Emma, her words streaming out coated in suppressed venom. "You just never learn, do you? Bad blood is bad blood. Shoulda never even bothered with the likes of you. But now we're done. You did it. You finally did it. Wonder what took you so long, you piece of shit."

The blue lights showed up pretty quickly. Flashes of her past blazoned through her mind; time to shut down. She still went to that place of darkness whenever the trigger appeared. An out-of-luck driver getting a speeding ticket on the side of the road. Emergency vehicles on their way to some fateful event. Pulsating lights meant time to get small, stop thinking, feel nothing. Numb.

Emma was removed from the bus and sat alone in the back of the police car, waiting to hear what they'd do with her. All the other kids were on their way to school. Even the vitriolic triumvirate had been released, after hugs of sympathy, voices of concern. Perfect. She wrote in the margins of pages that were already filled with boxes. *They get hugs. I end up here. Yeah, like that's fucking fair.*

It was the third time, so being expelled from school wouldn't be enough. The first time she had gotten into a fight with one of the girls on the bus, the police had come to the bus stop and reprimanded her, and she had been released at the scene. She was given a three-day, in-school suspension. The next time, she attacked a group of girls in the school stairwell—*yeah, that makes a lot of sense, I attacked the whole group of them*—and they brought her to the station house. The officer gave her a formal written reprimand, and she was released. She was suspended from school for five days. This time, they cuffed her. This time, she was arrested. Seventeen years old and behind bars. In custody at the juvenile center.

How the hell had her life turned out like this? She must have done something really bad in a past life to end up in this pile of shit. Or maybe she had led an extremely charmed past life, and this was payback for the good fortune of family and love and comfort and warmth and respect. *This time around, strip her of all of those things.* At least she'd had them for the first nine years.

The day Emma turned nine, her dad stepped out of his car with a strange, blank look on his face, walked robotically past where she was playing in the yard, and went straight into the house. Emma couldn't figure out why he didn't come grab her and kiss her and whip her around like he did every other time he got home from work. She ran over to the back-door window and watched him walk into the kitchen, watched her mom look at him with a curious, concerned expression on her face, and watched her dad take out a gun and fatally shoot her mom and then himself.

Emma's foster mom showed up at juvy, but the probation officer wouldn't let Emma leave because her foster mom—her legal guardian—refused to sign court documentation declaring that, as the responsible adult, she would follow all of the conditions of release. Emma was left in the juvenile hall. It was a Friday, and she had to spend three nights in jail before she could appear before the court. The probation officer suggested that the district attorney file charges. Aggravated battery with intent to harm. There was a detention hearing in which the court appointed Emma a lawyer because her foster parents refused to pay.

Emma sat in juvenile detention for ten days before the disposition hearing. During this time, she drew and wrote in her journal, and read *God Bless You, Mr. Rosewater*, *On the Road*, and a collection of Faulkner's short stories. Emma kept to herself most of the time, as much as she was able. They held counseling groups, and she was supposed to open up and learn about herself from listening to and sharing with the other juvies. Group after group, Emma just sat there. They couldn't force her to talk. And she did not have to listen to the mentor she was assigned, nor to the caseworker. They weren't listening to her. Like they would make any difference anyway.

She spent as much time outside as they would allow her. Even though the detention hall was in the center of the developed part of town, in the middle of an old industrial park, surrounded by abandoned, dilapidated textile mills, there were still trees and remnants of fields—empty, overgrown lots, really—that she could look at while she walked around the penned-in area. The leaves danced and reflected sunshine. Birds flew over, but never landed on the razor-wire security fence. Emma gazed at the drifting clouds passing by the sharp barbs, and she floated on the soft spring breezes. The winds did not know they were incarcerated.

On the day of her hearing, Emma was led into court. Her dark green coveralls were stiff and made loud *swooshing* noises as she walked toward her seat. She looked around and saw no one she knew among the spectators. What did she expect? This was her fifth foster home in eight years. None of them cared about anything other than the extra $22.15 per day they were paid to let her stay in their home. They were supposed to use that money to buy her clothing and food and school supplies, but she was never given anything but hand-me-downs. Her backpacks were filled with notebooks and pens that were always donated by some bleeding-heart teacher, and the food was usually Spam or ramen noodles or whatever else was the cheapest way to feed her without making it seem like she was being neglected.

As far as care went, she was usually crammed into a bedroom to share with some other unfortunate, damaged kids. Just for fun, they'd cut up her clothes. Just to get a rise out of her, they'd steal her things, the few she had. If they made it through the week without fighting or drinking or getting high or sneaking out or getting laid—or complaining—they were allowed to sit in the "family room" and enjoy the companionship of the foster family, complete with the faux-kind mom and her real children, along with her latest grubby, creepy boyfriend, *call me Daddy*.

Each foster home was basically the same scenario: only the number of kids they roped in and the state of cleanliness differed. During the infrequent Child Protective Services inspections, there were always the requisite board games on the shelves and the simmering stew or baking cookies—only for these rare occasions—signaling to the authorities that this was a nice home. Emma wasn't sure what it was they were supposed to be fostering, but it certainly wasn't a happy family, laughing and loving and living in some pretty house with a white picket fence. She figured it was better to be ignored than abused, so at least she had that going for her.

Each time she moved, it was the foster parents who made the request. They said she was too much trouble. She's very cold, they'd say. She won't let us in, they'd complain. She's too aggressive with the other kids. Sometimes, she'd hear them whispering, *I think she has post-traumatic stress disorder or something. You can hardly blame the poor girl, but really, we just can't handle her flashbacks or blackouts or whatever it is that makes her act like she does. She never smiles. We just can't reach her. It's too disturbing to have her in our home. She's too much trouble.*

Emma's lawyer shuffled some papers and sniggered with the DA about some party they had both attended the night before. Emma sat between the two of them. Monkey in the middle, only no one was trying to involve her or keep anything away from her—they barely noticed she was there.

The wall behind the judge's bench was covered with a mural that looked as if it could have been from one of Faulkner's stories. Emma squinted to see the plaque, and read, "The mural represents the theme Law and Culture, painted as part of the Works Progress Administration, funded by the United States Treasury Department's Section of Painting and Sculpture." One of the panels showed a homesteading couple hard at work on their farm. The man was plowing the field with two oxen, while the woman pulled weeds and roots from the soil. Geese flew overhead. Forest-covered mountains rose in the background. That would be a nice

life. Where were their children? What were they doing while their
mom and dad worked the fields?

Judge MacNamara entered and everyone rose, and then they
were seated again. Like church services when her mom had taken
her. Her dad didn't like to go with them. Emma's mom never
seemed to mind; it was Sunday, and he worked hard all week.
Her mom said he deserved some time to himself. On the way
back from church, they'd often stop at Ye Olde Donut Shoppe to
pick up a maple-frosted donut for her dad—his favorite. "You two
been to the shoppy?" he'd tease.

Emma's stomach spasmed, but the pain disappeared as she
wondered what kind of donuts the judge liked. Did his children
bring him his favorite? Maybe his grandchildren? The judge
had a head full of thick, smoky-grey hair, and his face was covered in deep wrinkles. He must have been old enough to be her
great-grandfather, but she didn't have any grandparents, or great-
grandparents. The judge was so old, she couldn't understand how
he was still practicing.

Between these manic, random thoughts—one of her tactics
to ease herself in anxious situations—Emma kept dozing off, another survival technique. It was almost summer, the courthouse
was hot and musty, the air was dead, and Emma's coveralls were
made of thick, heavy fabric, but still, she felt cold to the core. She
was shaking inside from the chill and from her worry, but she
sat still as a stone and stared straight through the judge, past the
bench and into the fresh-tilled pasture, where the churned earth
smelled like rain.

The preliminary statements were made. Emma paid no attention. Until she heard the judge ask her to stand, Emma wandered
in the painted fields.

"Okay, miss, I understand you've gotten yourself into a bit of
trouble these past few years."

Emma did not reply. Her attorney prodded her and she came
out of her haze. "Uh, yes, Your Honor. That is the truth."

The judge flipped through a three-inch-thick folder of papers: the complete, unabridged history of Emma Hale.

"Humph," he grunted, loudly enough for them all to hear. She wondered which chapter he was on, if he'd gotten to any good parts yet. The rising action. The climax. The dénouement. The unexpected twist: *Emma was born with a sweet nature, but at the moment she witnessed her parents' death, the sweetness melted away and formed a hard coating that was impossible to break through.*

"It looks like you're a smart girl. I want to ask you a question," he said.

"Okay."

"Why? Why have you been acting the way you have?"

Emma was unprepared for this sucker-punch, and needed to find her breath. Never once had anyone ever, ever asked her that question. Why? They all thought they knew her, knew her past, knew what she was doing, why she was doing it. Mostly, they didn't really care. And no one took time to listen. She did bad things, and she needed consequences. Reality therapy, they called it. In-school detention. Being grounded. Put on probation. Kicked out of foster home after home after home after …

Now it seemed remarkable that no one, in eight years, had ever asked her the simplest of questions: Why?

She was stunned. In the smallest of moments, something had shifted. *Why?* Emma let out a laugh, first loudly, then in quiet gasps of air she couldn't control. Her attorney tried to stop her. He looked worried, but she could see the judge, could read his face. His soft eyes were kind and wise and patient. She had offended lots of people before, and she knew all the variations of what that looked like. Maybe his long life had been full of trials, both in and out of the courtroom. Surely, he knew her laughter was not aimed at him. The warped humor came from her realization that she, too, had never asked herself that question before.

The court was as silent as the hollow of an old-growth tree in the deep woods. The DA began to speak.

"Not now," the judge told him.

The silence continued. Emma finally took in a deep breath and let out a big sigh.

"Your Honor, that's a very good question. I suppose … I suppose I've been acting this way because my life is shit, and I am angry, and—to be perfectly honest—when I'm not a walking zombie, I'm scared to death."

The DA stood up again. "Your Honor, this is most inappropriate, and totally irrelevant to—"

"That's enough," the judge pronounced. He continued, speaking directly to Emma. "Despite your unimpressive record, and despite the recommendations of the prosecution, I am inclined to give you one more chance."

"Your Honor, she's already been given chance after chance, and look where she's ended up."

The judge once again put up his hand to silence the persistent attorney. "I understand your position quite clearly. Sit down and stop talking. Now.

"Young lady, I am not big on the whole 'you're depraved on account of you were deprived' rationale, but in your case, I feel you have been dealt a pretty lousy hand. That gives you no excuse for your behaviors. But it is difficult to change one's behavior, or to learn the proper conduct in the first place, if you have never been exposed to it or had someone teach you."

"My parents taught me," Emma responded. *Here we go again.*

"I understand they were very good parents, but there have been a lot of years and experiences to corrode that foundation. There's a program I feel might benefit you greatly, that might lead you in the right direction. So, I am offering you these two choices. Option one: I accept the prosecution's recommendation, and you spend the next year and a day in our lovely juvenile facility, and then you will be on probation for three years once you are no longer a minor. Option two: You attend eight weeks in the Vermont Youth Conservation Corps—under strict supervision. At the end of that period, we will reassess the terms of your release. Your choice: hard work and stale prison air, or harder work and fresh mountain air. What do you think, Miss Hale?"

She left two days later. The bus ride took four hours. Emma watched the mill towns and train yards pass by, quickly replaced by open fields and verdant foothills. Trees that had been dormant the long winter past were in peak bloom, infant buds spraying infinite shades of green across the countryside. How was it possible that there were so many kinds of green? Emma's eyes began to hurt from the bright sun rays. She couldn't stop looking, though. It was a world she had only imagined, now right in front of her. The bus ride ended in Windsor, a small town in southern Vermont in the middle of the Green Mountains.

An older man and two young women sat outside a dark green van with the letters VYCC printed on its side. They were soaking up the warm rays, licking their ice cream cones. Creemees, they called them. A favorite Vermont summer tradition, especially the maple creemees. Emma felt a cramp deep in her gut. Her dad would have loved those. The three of them were waiting to pick up Emma. They were cheerful and energetic and overwhelming.

"Oh, I remember the first time I came to Vermont. Thought I'd stepped into a 1950s postcard."

"I couldn't believe that smell … fresh eau de manure!"

"I actually stopped at a Moose Crossing sign and pulled out my camera, thinking one would just show up."

Emma managed a meek nod. What had she gotten herself into?

People walked by and waved, or stopped to talk to passersby. Many had dogs or children in tow. The sun was shining, people were smiling, the air was full of pleasantries. A goddamned Norman Rockwell painting come to life. When the VYCC team was done visiting with some apparent friends, they led Emma to the van and introduced the vehicle as "a very artistic soul with the name Van Go." The three of them had a good chuckle, even though they must have told the same corny pun many times before. Emma threw her backpack in the rear of the van, but clutched tightly to the small satchel that held her journal and personal belongings, of which there were few.

The man was Tom, and he was the head of the Vermont Youth Conservation Corps, the VYCC. He had actually been instrumental in starting the program about thirty years ago, modeled after something he kept referring to as the CCC, a program from the 1930s.

"This is Laura. She'll be your crew leader," Tom said.

"Hey," Laura said. She looked really young. No makeup, no pretense.

"And this is Gracie, our driver and crew leader of one of the roving crews."

Tom, Gracie, and Laura chatted constantly and tried to engage Emma, but Emma kept as quiet as possible without appearing rude. She had learned her lesson well in juvy. Keep a low profile, and don't ask questions. Her hosts did not seem fazed by Emma's behavior.

They made a quick stop at the local co-op to pick up a few burlap bags of oats, something called quinoa—*keeeeenwhahhhhh,* Tom kept repeating, apparently enjoying the sound coming from his mouth—and a few other grains. She wondered what she'd be eating over the next months. She hoped they weren't all hippie vegetarians. There had been a few crunchy kids back in her last school and she never got friendly with them, though they approached her a few times. She sometimes thought they might not be so bad. Outcasts understand misfits.

Before they left the co-op parking lot, Laura turned to Emma and handed her a small pouch that seemed to be filled with herbs. *Shit,* thought Emma. *I know what they say about Vermont and its number-one crop, but I can't believe they're handing out weed. I don't even use the stuff, and I sure can't afford to get busted.* Laura said, "Smell it." Hesitantly, Emma lifted the pouch to her nose and breathed in the pleasing aroma. She felt calm at once. "Lavender,"

Laura said. "From the Latin root *lavare*, which means *to wash*. The scent's good for washing away your worries." Emma's jaw tightened, negating the effects of the lavender and guarding against Laura's intrusive comment. Laura lifted up her own worn pouch and continued, "I'm always sniffing it. It helps ground me, and I swear it helps me sleep."

Tom chimed in, "Yes, our little herbal goddess. Wait until she has you eating wild plantain seed. It's a good natural bug repellent, but it also gives me a bad case of the runs!"

They picked up the rest of the crew and some equipment from the VYCC headquarters and drove to the foot of Mt. Ascutney. Gracie maneuvered Van Go into the small trailhead parking lot, and as soon as they had unloaded all of their gear, she and Tom and the van left. The other roving crews needed transportation from project to project, but Emma was on a wilderness crew, which meant they'd be camping out, and staying at this one site for the entire eight-week session. Emma felt a little anxious that this was it; she'd be stuck in this one place with the same seven people for two months. In many ways, it seemed worse than juvy. Had she made the wrong choice?

They climbed the trail toward their home base. Branches tasseled with shadowy green filtered the sunshine along the rocky path. It wasn't very steep, but Emma's legs were used to flat sidewalks. Blue dots led to a clearing where the trees formed a fringed hem. Bags of gear had already been stacked in separate piles. Everyone dropped their packs and collapsed on the soft grass.

Before setting up camp, they had their first crew meeting. Laura and the other crew leader, Ryan, called the six corps members to gather in a circle. *Here we go again*, Emma thought. *More group therapy*. Laura introduced herself and asked everyone to take a turn telling their name and where they were from. She asked them all to keep it short and sweet, and she told them there'd be plenty of time to get to know each other better later. Right now they had to set up camp, get dinner ready, and agree on their chore system.

And that was it. Besides Emma from Lowell, Massachusetts, there was Rachel from Burlington, Vermont; Zoey from Jericho, Vermont; Lila from Albany, New York; Max from Hinesburg, Vermont; and Malik from New York City. No one pried into why each of them had ended up at this place. They checked each other out as best they could while Laura and Ryan went over the rules and routine. Rachel had been a corps member last summer, so she knew the ropes pretty well. She even volunteered to make the first night's dinner, and she turned toward Emma to ask her if she'd help. "We need two people on dinner, so you game?" Then she whispered to Emma, "And if we cook, we don't have to clean." Emma nodded okay.

They devised a rotating system for the corps members that would change every two days: two people in charge of planning and cooking dinner, two people to do the dinner dishes, one person to get bag lunches together, and one person in charge of drinking water. The crew leaders oversaw everything and made sure all equipment was handed out and returned, cleaned, sharpened (if need be), and in good condition.

Emma was assigned to share her tent with Rachel. She was used to sharing a bedroom with lots of other kids, but this seemed different, and she didn't know how she felt. The two of them set up their tent and then made dinner. Rachel really knew what she was doing, and soon Emma, too, was slicing and sautéing and boiling with the best of them. They made macaroni and cheese, but Rachel had some campground culinary tricks: she used three different cheeses and added caramelized onions and canned stewed tomatoes, topping the whole thing with their own homemade breadcrumbs. She managed to do all of this over a two-burner green metal camping stove.

The food was warm and creamy and filling, and one of the best things Emma had ever eaten. For dessert, they sliced apples and sprinkled them with cinnamon and brown sugar and butter, and warmed them in foil over the campfire. Everyone was very pleased with the first meal at work camp. They even applauded

Emma and Rachel. Rachel took a bow, then prodded Emma to stand for her own kudos: high fives all around. Ryan and Laura started clapping and began to sing a little song. Other than them, only Rachel knew the song, but everyone else quickly joined in. *Thank you thank you thank you and you and you, for what you did just dooooooooooooo. But the biggest thanks of all—from me to you—thank you just for being YOU!* The song got louder and louder and faster and faster, and everyone stomped around the campfire, pointing to each other. The laughter made it hard to sing the silly lyrics. Emma thought it was lame and annoying, and she didn't sing.

The best part was that they didn't have to clean up. After all, it wasn't their job. Emma watched Rachel pitch in anyway, and she figured she might as well help out, too. What else was she going to do out here in the wilderness? There was no TV, no radio, no computers, no cell phones, and even iPods weren't allowed. The whole crew ended up cleaning all the pots and pans and dishes. No complaints. Together.

After cleaning up, Emma went back to the tent. Lots to tell her journal. She jumped when Laura's giant shadow crept over the rain tarp. Emma covered her writing when Laura poked her head in.

"Hey, I have envelopes and stamps. We can mail letters home next week when we go into town for more provisions."

"No, thanks." Emma was surprised but relieved that they didn't know she had no family, no home. She thought the cops would have told them … everything.

Rachel unzipped the tent and crashed on her sleeping bag. "Malik and Max are arm wrestling. Guys think they're so tough. I'll give them a few days, and then I'll show them." She flexed her big, bad pipes, laughed, and began talking.

"I go to boarding school. Not the kind for troubled kids—the kind for rich, smart, privileged kids. Ha! My 'rents, they're big supporters of charitable foundations that work for the environment. Sent me here because they thought it would be 'good for me' and their other spawn to learn 'firsthand' about nature and conservation. I was into it anyway—I'm VP of our Ecology Club, and I've traveled a lot. A lot. Hiking in the Himalayas, whitewater rafting through the Grand Canyon ..."

The two girls were lying parallel to each other on their foam mats, both staring at the deep black night through the skylight, each star bisected by the mesh netting into a glowing grid. The infinite sky enveloped them as Rachel told Emma stories of her many adventures. At one point, Emma let out a big, loud yawn. Rachel apologized. "Oh, my God, I'm so sorry, I haven't shut up ... bad case of verbal diarrhea. You must be bored to death."

"No, no, it's incredible what you've done. I'm just wiped. I left Lowell on the 5 a.m. bus, and it's been a long day."

Rachel looked at the clock on her Swiss Army knife. "Shit, I had no idea it was so late. Momma Laura's gonna be in here any minute anyway telling us it's time for lights out. Better go brush our teeth before it's too late."

They barely made it back to the tent in time, but soon they were settled in for the night, and even though the tree peepers' high-pitched chorus was deafening, a noise so loud and irritating Emma was sure it would keep her up all night, before she knew it, it was 4:30 in the morning, and time to begin her first full day at Mt. Ascutney Wilderness VYCC camp. The nocturnal frogs were now silent. Emma woke up gradually, like a lazy sunrise emitting soft shades of coral and peach, taking its sweet time, teasing the mourning doves and ravens with its dawdling—is it time to coo and cackle yet? When she realized where she was and what time it was, she was astonished. This was the first uninterrupted night's sleep she'd had in eight years. No eyes open.

The day began with the gift of rest, and continued with a stream of offerings, there for the taking. Breakfast was simple. It was so early, and most of the corps members were not even fully awake yet, let alone hungry, but Ryan and Laura encouraged them to eat; it was going to be a long hike to their project site, and a lot of hard work on an empty stomach was not a good idea. Someone had brewed a big blue enamel pot of steaming coffee. It was received like liquid manna.

While the others were downing java and force-feeding themselves cornflakes, Malik packed bag lunches, and everyone found time to do the VYCC's daily education program. Emma didn't know that they'd be doing schoolwork in the back woods, but she liked learning, and didn't mind participating. They were supplied a stack of articles, short stories, and even poems, all with relevant—often controversial—topics. They were supposed to choose one, read it, and think about it during the morning work session so they'd be ready to discuss it over lunch.

Emma picked an article about poverty and education. The author felt that poverty would never be relieved if people didn't receive a good education. Emma had never heard of generational poverty, but it made sense. She knew lots of kids whose families were in the cycle of poverty the article talked about. And she knew it was hard to break out. Most of these VYCC kids wouldn't get it. She wasn't even going to discuss it at lunch. Why bother? What did any of them know—or care—anyway?

As soon as they had all finished up their readings, it was time for morning stretches. *What are we, in freaking kindergarten?* Emma thought. And it only got worse. Lila was asked to take her daily turn at leading the exercises. Choose a theme and make the stretches match, she was told. *What the hell?*

Lila turned herself into a saxophone and stretched herself into a jazz riff, and they all followed. All except Emma. Then Lila stretched her arms out as far as they could go, pretended to hug a tree, and became a bass drum—and they all became drums. Even Emma tried that stretch, reluctantly. Lila bent over and became a triangle, and they all became triangles. They stretched like this, an orchestra in the outback, expanding their muscles and ligaments and tendons, unfurling tissues, unleashing issues. Emma wouldn't admit it, but she felt good.

Ryan gathered them all around. "Alright, now that the exercise-induced serotonin has bathed your neurons and momentarily counteracted your other more moody adolescent hormones, it's time to get cracking!" He explained the project they'd be working on for the next few weeks: repairing one end of the bridge that

the CCC had built back in 1937. Ryan gave a brief talk about
the Civilian Conservation Corps and the young men who had
come here in the 1930s to 1940s, trying to make a better life for
themselves and their families, who were all being devastated by
the terrible economic conditions faced in the United States at
that time. He talked about Roosevelt and the New Deal, and the
dire need for conservation efforts back then. Even though Ryan
was enthusiastic and a great storyteller, most of the crew was only
half-listening. It was too early for a history lesson.

As soon as Ryan was done, the crew was directed to the tool
shed to gather what they'd need for the day's work. Laura had
given Emma the key, so she was the first one to the shed. As soon
as she entered, Emma stopped short. A wall of scent that was both
familiar and overwhelming hit her. She had no idea what it was.
Like the three stooges, Lila and Max walked right into Emma,
knocking each other over in the dark shed. It was a good thing
they weren't holding pitchforks. "What's that smell?" Emma asked.

Max answered, "Boiled linseed oil. To clean the wood handles.
We use it on the farm."

There were rows and rows of racks of tools, all labeled and
standing at attention, waiting to be used: timber carriers, hazel hoes, fire rakes, sledges, loppers, cutter mattocks. Then there
were small bins with wire brushes, handy claws, saw sharpeners.
Other racks held their uniforms and protective gear: the thigh
high rubber boots, hardhats, safety glasses, dark green work shirts,
backpacks, lanterns. Emma took an axe off the nearest rack and
brought it out into the daylight.

The wood grain formed rivulets, the veins mapping years of
growth and drought. Emma caressed the handle and brought it
up to her nose. She inhaled deeply and was back in her garage, her
dad fixing her bike chain. He'd used linseed oil to refinish all that
antique furniture strewn about—his side business to make ends
meet. She hadn't thought of that smell in a long time, but now she
savored its rich, full aroma. In an instant, she was holding Daddy's
hand, sniffing in how good he always smelled. Grease and oil and

the sweat of hard work combined with the soap and cologne he wore, just the way her mother liked. Her parents had always sniffed at each other like puppies, like teenagers in love. Emma would wiggle in between the two of them, and they'd shower her with kisses, safely swaddling her in their family cocoon.

Malik ran over to the tool shed and broke her concentration. Just as well. The smell—and the memory—were making her queasy. The guys said they'd carry not one, but two rock pry bars, one in each hand. Laura tried to dissuade them, but they were not about to be challenged. Zoey decided to join the competition; she was a tough kid from rural Vermont, and she knew a thing or two about heavy burdens. After hiking a mile uphill carrying the seven-foot-long steel bars, eighteen pounds each, the guys regretted their macho decision, and whined, "A little help here." Zoey was obviously hurting, too, but she didn't complain. By the end of the week, all three of them were carrying the rock bars uphill with ease.

The corps split into two groups. One would be repairing the seventy-year-old stone bridge, and the other would be doing trail work leading to and from the bridge, creating a variety of ways to keep water from crossing the trail. It was all about rocks and water. And leverage. When they weren't figuring out how to work as a group to move boulders safely, relying equally on physics and communication skills, they were digging ditches or retaining walls. Always, they were moving rocks and trying to keep water from moving where they did not want it to go. Divert. Divert. Divert.

For the first month, Emma was assigned the bridge work. A local stonemason was hired as the expert consultant on the project. He showed them the techniques that held the bridge up, and he brought them under the bridge to show them how well it had been built—which, he said, was remarkable, considering it had been completed in 1937. By hand.

Emma worked alongside Zoey and Malik. She found out that Zoey was from a small town in northern Vermont. Last year, when Zoey was on a field trip with her geography class, she had seen a VYCC roving crew building a boardwalk along the Missisquoi Wildlife Refuge. Wild blueberries and buttonbush grew all along the boardwalk. The new construction made it easier to walk through the nature trails, viewing great blue herons, cormorants, and wood ducks. Plus, it seemed like the crew members were not only working really hard, but also having a lot of fun, and they were doing important work, so she had decided to try it this year. Any excuse to get away from home for a while.

Malik was from Brooklyn, and this was the first time he'd ever been outside the city. He seemed like a tough guy with a big attitude who wasn't afraid of anything—until he saw an insect. No one—including the crew leaders—could contain their laughter at the way Malik screamed and ran around like a goofy toddler anytime a bug came near him. They couldn't imagine how he managed to survive in the capital of cockroaches and bedbugs. "Those are city bugs," he explained, and he and they had a mutual respect. "I know how they roll." It took him a week, but he finally accepted that most of the insects were harmless. He even learned to let a dragonfly land on him; he told the crew he was going to get a dragonfly "tatt" on his arm when he got back to the city.

One night after dinner, Ryan and Laura led them all on a short hike down to a small meadow nearby. As the sun set, they heard a strange sound. Laura hushed them and pointed to a spot in the meadow about 200 feet from where they were huddled. She directed them to sit silently and watch for the woodcock, which, of course, generated snickers from Malik and Max. In a moment, *peeent peeent* sounds came from the spot Laura had indicated. After a minute or so, the bird flew upward, creating a widening spiral that could still be seen in the deepening, dusk-filled sky. Emma was concerned about how high it was going. What if its wings melted?

As it flew higher and higher, the woodcock's twittering was followed by a chirping sound that intensified as the bird returned to earth in a high-speed zigzag dive. Silence for an instant, and then *peeent, peeent*—the mating display starting all over.

"Whoa," was all the crew could manage. Laura and Ryan smiled like proud parents who had just introduced their "kids" to one of nature's many marvels. They hiked back to the campground in silence, listening to the peepers revving up, led by the flashing lights of fireflies dancing. Could the night have ended on a more magical note?

As Emma entered her tent, she noticed a familiar *swooshing* noise. Ironically, her VYCC uniform was a pair of dark green coveralls, very much like the uniform she had worn in juvy. On both, the woven threads rubbed together as she walked, making a similar sound. How different the two uniforms made her feel. One, captive, dismissed, the other, worthwhile and free. She fell asleep with a grin on her face, to thoughts of wacky diving birds and horny bugs illuminating the sky, picturing herself as the empress with new clothes. No need for lavender tonight.

Emma could tell as soon as she saw his scowling face: Max had woken up in a bad mood. Though the girls were able to switch tent partners every week, the two boys had to remain roommates throughout the season. They came from very different backgrounds, and had strong, contrasting interests. Max was on his high school's baseball team; Malik played pick-up streetball in the projects. Max listened to *Top 20 Countdown*; Malik was into the beats and rhymes of alternative hip hop.

"Come on, that music you listen to is made by a bunch of superficial bullshit wannabees," Malik said.

"But that techno-crap and digital rap you listen to, it's so processed, you can't tell that it's even made by humans. Listen to the recordings of the old-time country singers ... you can actually hear them breathe."

Malik teased Max when he used New England expressions, like "I went acrosst the street" and "that's a good idear," and Max would throw it back it his face when Malik said "cawfee" and "yous guys."

Most of the time, they tolerated each other's differences and hardheaded opinions, and maybe even learned a little something from each other. On this particular morning, Malik was complaining to Ryan. Loudly.

"Man, why can't I wear them that way? Why?"

"Work clothes are not supposed to be worn down below your butt," Ryan said.

"Why not? That's how I wear my pants."

Max hadn't slept well. He was grumpy, and decided to side with Ryan for no reason other than to disagree with Malik.

Max said, "You look stupid trying to be all cool and gangstah in the boondocks of Verm—"

Ryan cut Max off. "Malik, it poses a danger to the other crew members if you trip over your sagging pants."

"Great, go ahead, gang up on me," Malik fumed as he pounded his fist in his other hand. Laura tried to calm him down, but that just made things worse. Malik slammed his fist harder and harder; his face beaded with sweat. Emma slowly walked to his side and just stood there. After a few moments, Malik stopped. He turned to Ryan.

"What if I wear them any way I want when we're not working on a project?"

"I'll consider that."

Max yelled, "There's no reason he should—"

"It's none of your business," Malik shouted back.

The arguing went on, getting louder and louder until the rest of the crew gathered around the testosterone pack. Knowing the boys, the females were ready for anything, but also concerned. A fight meant one or both of the guys would be kicked out of the program—grounds for immediate dismissal—and nobody wanted that to happen.

Chests were puffed, and Max and Malik were getting worked up, almost out of control. Both were spitting their words. Then, as quickly as the clash had started, Malik let out a long, slow exhale, and, grinding his teeth, said to Ryan, "Hey man, what if we solve this my way?"

Hesitantly, Ryan asked, "And how we will do that?"

Malik looked at Ryan and Max, took a step back, and jabbed his fist in the air. They both jumped back.

"You fools," Malik said. "I want to do rock, paper, scissors."

Malik knew damn well how to stay out of trouble if he needed to—and wanted to. Emma could relate.

She watched the guys play their little game, and broke out in a laugh that startled everyone, mostly herself. Here she was, on the side of a mountain in the middle of a freaking forest, surrounded by a motley crew, and the toughest guy she'd ever met was settling his business just like she had done when she was little. Before everything had gotten so complicated. She laughed so hard that tears streamed down her face. Overcome by emotion—and worried that she was going to pee in her pants—she ran away from them all, toward the latrine they had dug downhill from their tent site.

By the time Emma returned, it had begun to drizzle, the kind of forest shower that's more like standing droplets suspended between the trees than falling rain. She stood in the middle of the campsite, soaking wet and alone. Something had changed. She couldn't put her finger on it, but it seemed like maybe, just maybe, another thin layer had been shed, a veneer loosening in the mist.

They moved stones and dug ditches. They ate dinners of chili or pasta or stir-fry, often using wild edibles they gathered nearby after Laura taught them about the nutritional and medicinal properties of the local plants. They debated about anything and everything. They played soccer and they played cards and they swam in the frigid swimming hole. By the flickering light of the campfire, they took turns and told their stories. Each memoir contained tales of love, loss, fear, joy, hopelessness, and hope. Things that happened to them for no good reason, things that could never—and would never—be understood. In their short lifetimes, this crew of six summed up much of the human condition. Until she heard them, she had thought she was the only one.

One still evening, right before she fell asleep, Emma thought of a good theme for morning stretches. At breakfast, she asked to lead the group. They gathered in a circle and Emma stretched into a strange position. No one could figure out the shape or the theme. Unperturbed, she told them, "I am Malik's big old grin." Then she stretched into what appeared to be a heart. "I am Rachel's open heart." They took turns stretching into each other, into the gracious qualities they each gave freely. It was a warm way to start the workday. Emma got another thank you song from the group, and she smiled broadly, thanking them right back, singing at the top of her lungs.

Later that day, Emma took a break under the bridge. It was quiet there, and she liked to feel the cool, damp air trapped by the stone structure. She listened to the echo of the running waters as she ran her hand along the moss-covered rocks, caressing the softness, wondering what new shade of green was in the dark. She leaned close and breathed in, a lush sylvan smell, laden with water and life.

As she touched the stones with her fingers, she felt a jagged edge. She pulled away and sucked on her finger where she had cut herself. It was a fairly deep wound, and it hurt, but—like a tongue irrationally probing for the origin of sharp tooth pain—she was going to touch the stone again; she wanted to know what was there. She knelt down, turned on her lantern, and found the same spot. Behind the moss and cobwebs and fungus, there was definitely something. She scraped away part of the lichen, and there it was. Carved crudely into the stone, barely visible, were the words: *Tippy, The Prof, and Mac were here—October 1937.*

Emma didn't tell anyone about the inscription. She wanted to hold it for herself, just for a little while, to think about who these men were, what life was like for them, how they had ended up working on this bridge, the very bridge that was providing her passage, helping her to cross obstacles in her way, to reach the other side.

In 1937, he had to drop out of Lowell High to help his family by working, and, like so many of his buddies, he never found a job, and never learned to read or write very well. His parents warned him to stay away from certain kids, and not to fall in with the "wrong kind" of people. His gramma made him pray with her every time he visited. What'd they all think, he'd wind up in jail?

Month after month, he wandered the streets trying to find work—any work. Past bread lines, past friends' fathers trying to earn a living by selling apples for a nickel apiece, shining shoes, or waiting for their allotted dole. When Harry came across a big sign that said *Hiring!* he felt he'd hit the jackpot. In just a few minutes with the recruiter, he figured his best bet was to join the CCC, Roosevelt's Tree Army.

He knew about the CCC from the newsreels, but had never checked into it because it didn't seem like he'd do too well in the boonies. The rats and weeds in the back lot behind the grocery were all the wildlife he knew. The recruiter lured him in with that sign, making him think he was applying for a regular job, and then, when they explained what it was all about, it seemed to Harry like he should give the CCC a shot. And that was just what he did. No longer aimlessly hanging out in the streets, getting more and more frustrated by the lack of work, trying to stay out of trouble, hopeless spirits feeding the desperation of his plight and every other guy he knew. Soon, he'd be on his way to God-knows-where for six whole months, but they told him they'd put him to work, house him, feed him, fix his teeth, pay him, and—the best part—they'd pay his family, too.

May 15, 1937

deer mom and dad,

Im sorry I dint have a chance to say a proper gdby to you and Ozzie and Gramma Becky. Evrythins goin so fast. Firstall, Im fine. I dint no this was gnna hppen but I am leevin reel soon.

Il kawl yu on the tellafon when i get to the CCC camp.

I'm gonna miss howm and awl yu. Lots.
Salong 4 naw.
Yur boy,
Harry

Four hours after he had signed up, Harry was on a chartered Greyhound bus that was picking boys up from all over the region on the way to the base of Mt. Ascutney, near the little podunk town of Windsor, Vermont. Some of the boys were scared and quiet; others were bold and boisterous, and eventually able to get the more timid boys to join in singing—screeching—song after song, each one more raucous than the next. The bus driver had to quiet them down every so often. Mostly, he let them let loose; seemed like he knew there were a lot of anxious boys on board.

They'd been given brown bag lunches with a bologna sandwich, a hard-boiled egg, and an apple. It was the best meal many of them had had in months. They were told they would be fed well, and though the sack lunch was nothing great, the simple meal filled their bellies and satiated their spirits, both of which hadn't happened in a long time.

Right before the bus pulled in to the trailhead parking lot, they passed a field filled with dozens of big, ugly birds. "Wild turkeys," the bus driver told them. "Don't try to eat them, though—they're tough as boiled leather and taste real gamey, kind of like the grubs they eat."

Sitting right behind the driver was another old geezer, who introduced himself as the driver's co-pilot. Turned out he was his retired buddy who joined him on long rides, just for something to do. He told the boys, "Yeah, don't listen to him. Wild turkey has dark meat, moist and delicious. It's just that his wife is such a lousy cook, so's he thinks it's tough and tastes like crap—because that's the way she cooks it!" The young men laughed at the two old cronies' banter.

Harry stepped off the bus with nothing but the clothes on his back. A big lone mountain jutted out from a forest greener than

anything he'd ever seen before. As soon as they arrived, they we.
assigned into different groups—companies, they called them.
Harry was part of the 181st. As a company, they hiked up the
mountain, led by their crew leader and assistant leader. The trail
was steep, and most of the boys had never stepped foot on anything other than concrete and asphalt. During the hike, some of
them were silent, their eyes wide with wonder at the thick walls
of trees, their lungs full of shock at the fresh mountain air. Others
could not stop talking, noticing every detail, every moss-covered
boulder, every chipmunk, every tree root, exposed and curved into
unimaginable forms. These boys acted like they were on a sightseeing tour, the most interesting one they'd ever been on, seeing
vistas they hadn't known existed. *Gee, would you look at that! Did
you see that? What the heck was that? What a view!*

They ended at a clearing in the pines filled with a series of
tarpaper barracks they would call home. They were each issued
a folded iron army cot with a stiff canvas mattress, and an itchy
wool army-surplus blanket. Forty-eight to a crew, the cots were
placed head to foot. No soft bedding, but for many, it was better
than sleeping on the streets of Boston or Albany or New York
City.

Those early days flew by quickly. They were given physical
examinations and enough shots that at first, the boys' biggest
complaints were about their sore buttocks. One boy had so many
immunizations and such a bad reaction, he looked like he had
globs of peanut butter popping out of his left cheek. Not his face,
either. He didn't sleep so well—or sit so well—that whole first
week. They had their teeth examined—for most, the first time
ever in their lives. There were such screams and tears; you'd have
thought the dental assistants were extracting teeth without an-
esthesia, when all they were doing was checking for cavities and
cleaning off plaque.

The boys were furnished work clothes, all army surplus. They
were even issued dress woolens left over from the Great War.
Harry's pants were so short, he was embarrassed to show the rest

one's clothing fit well, and the choices were lim-
ll just stood there, staring at each other like a bunch
ks until the crew leader teased them, "What a motley
t the hell am I going to do with the likes of you?" Harry
hat none of the crews had that sharp, conformed look of
army. What difference did it make, anyway, out here in the
? They were supplied a toilet kit and a duffel bag to keep
thing organized, and sent off to find their sleeping quarters.

Harry's group was lucky. The crew leader told them that new
rivals usually ended up sleeping in squad tents for several weeks,
complete with mud, mosquitoes, leaky tarps, and bone-chilling
winds. One winter, the boys woke up in their tents to snow drifts
between the cots, compliments of blustery winds and unsecured
flaps. There happened to be a lull in the new arrivals that month,
and the permanent quarters were free, so the boys of the 181st
were able to move right into their new home without the usual
miserable transition. The best part of the barracks was that they
had actual doors, and two coal stoves, and—as long as the boys
kept up with their chores—the fires would be stoked. Despite the
black ash strewn everywhere, the room would stay warm, dry, and
comfortable.

There were separate buildings for the mess hall, headquarters,
infirmary, laundry, latrine, shower room, supplies and equipment,
blacksmith, and mechanical repair, and there was a small recreation hall with a canteen. There were even separate barracks for
the "colored" enrollees. "Segregation is not discrimination," they
were told. But this was no more true at the camp than it was back
home. Harry heard that even Native American recruits were sent
to their own camps, where tribal leaders were in charge of the
projects. What a world.

Their crew leader told them that the camp was modeled
after an army base. "It's our very own poor man's West Point,"
he joked. "It's got everything we need to keep you boys working, healthy, and happy." It even had two officers running things
who were part of the United States Army. Harry and the other

newcomers—"rookies," they were called—were a little nervous about having to report to, and act like, soldiers. The officers were decent guys, and they quickly made it clear that they did not expect these boys to be actual soldiers; they just wanted them to develop good habits and work hard. After being introduced to their "bosses," the boys were given work assignments. The army personnel ran the camp, but local experienced men—LEMs— came every day to impart the expertise needed to do the actual work, such as building bridges, quarrying stone, diverting water, moving earth, and felling trees.

When their LEM first showed them around, he pointed out that most of the parkland at Mt. Ascutney was comprised of forest or field, bisected by running water. Depending on the time of year, the stream would trickle by as a gentle, meandering creek, or become enraged, a roaring, frothy deluge. As Harry learned what they were going to be doing, and why, his excitement grew. In order to provide year-round safe passage up the trails, stable locations for scenic overlooks, and a way to cross over turbulent waters, the 181st were administered the jobs to create a series of hiking trails along Mt. Ascutney, to construct a lodge and a park entrance, and—their biggest goal—to build a stone bridge. All by hand.

May 20, 1937
deer mom and dad,

Im gnna have my new frend Jack rite the rest of this letter becawz hes tryn to spll it awl out ta me but its taken to long. Heer he is.

Hi folks, I am your son's new friend. He asked me to write this to you. We start classes next week so soon he'll be able to write you a proper letter by himself. For now, I will serve as his scribe. I hope that is okay. (I had two years at State Teachers' College so I am fortunate to have the benefit of a solid educational background.) He tried to reach you last week but the phone lines were very long and when he did reach the phones, he kept getting disconnected.

He just wanted me to tell you that he is safe and happy.
He (we) will keep you posted about how life is going in the
wilderness of Mt. Ascutney.
    Good thoughts to you all, especially to Grandma Becky.
    Your boy,
    Harry

Harry's bunk was smack between the two boys who would soon become his best buddies. It only took them a few sleepless nights of lying awake, trying to get used to the sounds of the forest and the other forty-five snorting, snoring guys, to trade their stories. They all got to know each other pretty quickly, and they learned to put up with each other—mostly, despite the tight quarters, and unavoidable smells.

Turned out Jack Donovan was twenty years old, from the suburbs of Albany, New York. His dad had a car dealership that had gone bust. At least Jack was lucky in that he had gone to college for a few years—he was one of the only literate boys in their barracks. Like Harry, when Jack couldn't find any work, he came to the CCC to help his family out. At first, he was rejected. Between odd jobs held by his mom, his dad, and the six kids, they earned twenty-five dollars per week; they were considered too rich!

Jack's father went to their minister to seek advice. Chaplain Macarlys pulled a few strings, and Jack was enlisted the next day. Jack said that ever since that miraculous intervention, the Donovan family had called him Chaplain Holy Mackerel! When Jack arrived at Mt. Ascutney, one of the officers nicknamed him "The Prof" ("on account of how smart you are") and paid him an extra three dollars per month to help tutor the rest of the company. Jack told Harry he would've done it for free, but his family could sure use the extra money.

Everett Hearn had grown up on a family farm outside of Topeka, which they were forced to abandon after it was ripped apart by the dust storms. Harry could hear Everett's voice crack when he described what their farm used to look like, and what it had meant to him. He ended up riding the rails. He said he was afraid at first, but then he found he craved the rush. Harry wished he'd been there, too: jumping on the high-speed trains, grabbing the ladders, climbing onto the catwalk, holding on for dear life. Everett told them that one morning was so cold, his hand became frigid and stuck fast against the iron rung as he clung on. The train jerked hard and a sharp edge caught the tip of his finger, slicing it clean through. He said he sure was lucky one of the other boxcar kids had some cloth to use as a tourniquet, otherwise he probably would've bled to death.

Everett would hop off the trains wherever he could, trying to find work in any town across the Midwest. Harry had never been to any of these places, and Everett's stories made his world larger. Everett told him it wasn't such a great life. To rest, he'd have to find a spot in the freight yard, and he always had to make sure to avoid the railroad dicks. He'd sleep in the boxcars, and described how they smelled real bad, like creosote and hobos. One night, he fell into a deep sleep, and before he knew it, the train whistle blew and woke him up; he had been on the Green Diamond run from St. Louis, and missed his stop.

The train continued from the Chicago Connect, ending up all the way in Buffalo, New York. At the Central Terminal, the cops pulled him in. When they realized he was "just another un-employed drifter," they told him they wouldn't press charges if he'd join the CCC. He didn't have much choice. When Everett arrived at CCC camp, the crew leader took one look at his hand, nicknamed him "Tippy," and told him he'd better not catch him trying to dig for gold with that little finger stump of his.

And that was how the three musketeers came to be.

Sometimes, Harry thought maybe they were more like the Three Stooges—the fun those boys had, and the trouble they'd get themselves into. For some reason, it was usually Harry who got the brunt of it. One day, Everett took out his Handy Twine pock-etknife, a special Christmas gift from his dad when their farm was still fertile and operating, bringing in a livable wage. He showed

Harry how to carve a piece of oak, how to shape it and whittle it smooth. Harry found a long, thick branch and was ready to carve. He reached for the knife, and it began to slip out of his hand. As he grabbed for the handle, Jack tried to help, but in the process, knocked Harry over. As Harry fell, the stick went flying—right into an officer's face. As usual, Harry wound up on the wrong end of the stick.

June 4, 1937

Dear Mom and Dad,

Hi there, this is still Jack writing for your son Harry. He still hopes someday to be able to write you his own decent letter. Here is what he wants me to write:

Well we are all settled in now and have a regular routine. They treat us kind of like an army, waking us up with reveille, inspecting our barracks to make sure we're keeping them clean, even eating in a mess hall and standing in formation for roll call. I'm not complaining cause I sure do look good in my buzz cut! Also, the way they treat us and what we do sure beats just hanging out on the front stoop or wandering around the lower Highlands trying to find work, or trying to avoid trouble. I'm not sure you know how many temptations are out on those streets, but keep your eye on Ozzie. I can't wait for him to be old enough to enlist in the CCC.

It feels real good to have something to do every day, something that is important. They have us moving rocks with this metal pry bar that must weight near thirty pound. And the rocks are more like boulders. We are either moving them or breaking them up into smaller rocks to stack and build the bridge.

And you should see my pipes! My biceps are getting so darn big, maybe when I get home I'll go up against Joe Louis. (Hi - This is Jack again, just imagine the scene: Laaaaaadies and Gentlemen, IIIIIINtroducing The World Heavyweight

Boxing Champeeeeeen, The Brown Bomber vs. the one, the
only, Harry "Mac"—the Lowell Lover!)

Anyway, they are still feeding us real good and everything
is fine. By the way, the crew leader nicknamed me "Mac"
and he said it wasn't even because of my last name. He said
it was because for such a scrawny kid, he never saw anyone
shovel in so much food, especially the macaroni and cheese. It's
real good. I actually like the custard pudding the best. Glad he
didn't nickname me "Puddin"!

How is everything at home? Did you get any money yet
from the CCC? They let me keep $5 each month, but you are
supposed to be getting the other $25 every month. And I have
hardly used my money so I will save most of that for you, too.

Well, give a hug to Grandma Becky and take care of each
other. I hope to see you soon. I miss you.

Your son,

Harry

P.S. I can't wait to be able to write you myself some day

After working hard all day, the boys ate dinner, and when they
weren't attending night classes to learn to read and write, they
were on their own. There were athletic competitions like basket-
ball, baseball, or football games. Lots of the guys played cards,
and—even though gambling wasn't allowed—poker tournaments,
with wagers, went on in all the barracks.

They also weren't allowed to drink alcohol, but Harry and the
other guys needed to blow off some steam. They could—and did—
partake when they went into town, but drinking was not tolerated
at camp. Even so, bootleggers would sneak onto base. On Mac's
eighteenth birthday, his bunkmates decided to throw him a little
party. If only it had remained little. Slowly, crewmembers from all
over camp heard and joined the birthday bash. Moonshine was
flowing and the coal stove was glowing. One joker decided to make
Mac a giant birthday candle, so he rolled up some tar paper and lit
the end on fire. The barracks filled up with thick black smoke and

everyone, in all stages of coughing, gagging, and inebriation, ran out onto the drill field, and smack into the crew leader.

Jack confessed to buying the moonshine, and he was docked one-month's teacher's pay. Everett got pneumonia after hiding behind the barracks all night, trying, successfully, to avoid getting caught. He ended up in the infirmary, and didn't have to do any work for a week. Poor Mac, because it was considered *his* party, ended up with latrine duty for two weeks, which included the annual cleaning—by shovel. That guy could fall in a barrel of nipples and come up sucking his thumb.

When they'd had enough of the R & R available at camp, they'd head into town for a little excitement. Or so they thought. The closest town of Windsor had a population of 878. Its one store did triple duty as post office, grocery, and hardware store. Another building across the road sold yard goods, housed the town library, and had an annex with a pool hall, a barbershop, and even a small restaurant.

Social events were held occasionally at the town hall, the church, and the grange, but folks didn't seem too keen on the CCC boys showing up in town. The one time Harry went into the library to look around, he smiled at the librarian and she chased him out, screaming, "We don't want the likes of you!" Then her husband showed up at camp to complain, something about not wanting "those unemployed, frustrated, sex-starved boys around." Harry didn't know what he had done—for goodness' sake, the librarian lady was old enough to be his mother.

Harry figured the locals must have caught on that the boys were spending money at their shops, because they began to warm up a bit. One kind family took Mac, Everett, and Jack in, on occasion; they'd make them home-cooked meals of brown bread, baked beans, and venison stew or roast wild turkey, which was delicious and made the boys laugh when they thought of the bus driver who had brought them to this mountain home. Seemed like a lifetime ago. After dinner, there would sometimes be apple cobbler or even a maple cream pie for dessert.

The boys were very appreciative; it didn't occur to them that the Quinns had six daughters they were trying to pawn off. At the end of their fourth weekly supper, the youngest Quinn girl—the sweet fifteen-year-old Millie—asked Mac to help with the dishes. He went back to the kitchen with her, oblivious to her flirtations and intentions. While Millie was cleaning up, Mac noticed a full sack of sugar. When he was a little kid, his gramma used to make him a special treat. Without thinking, he sat down in the middle of the pantry floor, took the corner of the cotton bag, twisted it, and started sucking on the sugar tit. Mr. Quinn walked in right then. That was the last meal in Windsor those boys were invited to attend. To top off the evening, the boys missed the last truck back to camp and had to walk the seven miles, all uphill.

October 1937
Dear mom and dad,
I am writing this letter to you all on my own this time. I've been working hard, out on the projects and in the classroom. I am sorry to hear gramma is sick. I wish I could visit. I hope its okay but Im thinking of re-enlisting for another six months. I hope that is okay with you.
They will keep sending you mony. They said I could probly get my high school diploma before I end my nex term. And then, who nos, maybe I'll enlist in the army. It feels good to serve, to have a purpose.
I would like to be able to work on more of Roosevelts programs like the CCC. It's a really good thing for our country. I no some peopel think its no better than one of Mussilini's fashist programs or even Hitlers Yuth Core, but I no it's a real good thing.
And then maybe I'll even try to get into college. I used to think I didn't have a prayer, but now, who nos? Wuldn't it be something if I could be the first MacNamara to go to college? Heck maybe I'll even becom a lawyer or something. Some day.
Ill call on Saturday. Your son, Harry

It took several months, but all the rocks they had been breaking down and piling up were at last starting to look like a bridge. They were making headway, and were anxious to keep going, especially because winter would soon wrap them in its frozen cape, slowing progress as it numbed fingers as well as spirits. One particularly beautiful autumn day, when the leaves on the trails were blazing colors the boys had never seen before, the crew decided to bring lunches in sacks so they could eat outside, eat quickly, and get right back to work. They broke for lunch, and headed to one of Ascutney's many granite outcroppings. The LEM told the boys that the Abenaki called the mountain Cas-Cad-Nac, *mountain of the rocky summit.* They understood that all too well.

As the crew reached the rock outcropping, they were stopped in their tracks. There, flying within arm's reach, was a bald eagle. The magnificent bird was circling out from the rock, its broad wings extended forever, its white head and tail reflecting the bright sunlight in the topaz sky. The details of its auburn-tinged, ebony feathers, deep golden hooked beak, and sharp talons were clear from this close proximity. Its eyes were the harvest moon, the deep coal pupil staring, piercing their hearts. These young men, usually so cocky and chatty, were silenced by the majesty of this bird. They had only seen its likeness on the back of a quarter, and here it was, first at eye level, now soaring higher and higher. Mac hoped it wouldn't fly too high. What if its wings melted?

If any one thing could represent the reason these boys were here, how they were serving their country, the strength, the freedom, the spirit, the boundless future, it was this bird. The eagle flew out of sight. All that remained were vibrant purples, flaming reds, whispering pinks, and screaming oranges framing the empty sky. "Whoa," was all they could manage. Jack took a long breath, then spoke softly, purposely: "E Pluribus Unum." *Out of many, one.*

Before they left the bridge that day, Everett pulled Harry and Jack over. "Hang back for a minute," he told them.

They volunteered to stay behind and straighten things up while the rest of the crew headed toward the camp. As soon as everyone else was out of sight, Everett dragged his buddies under the bridge. They had no idea what he was up to this time. He showed them an unusually flat rock, several stones down from the enormous keystone. Unlike most of the other rocks forming the bridge, this one was soft, not hard like granite or quartz.

Everett pulled out his pocket knife, and without saying a word, started carving. When he was done, he handed the knife to Jack, then to Harry. They took a step back and admired their handiwork, then carefully ran their fingers over the pristine carving, feeling how thick the marks were, how deep the lines went, how sharp the edges were. *This will last forever*, they thought. The air was dusty under the bridge; the broken rock surfaces were dry, and the mosses had not yet had a chance to stake their home. Everett had one more thing to add. He had found a feather after lunch, as white and stark as a virgin snowfall. "The eagle left it behind for us," he said. The highest honor, a gift from the master of the sky. He pushed the end of the feather's shaft into a crevice between the stones, right next to their inscription: *Tippy, The Prof, and Mac were here—October 1937.*

A little less than a month into the bridge repair, Emma was surprised when Ryan showed up at the work site in the middle of the chilly morning. They usually only saw him at noon, when both crews got together for lunch. Ryan was all enthused, and told them he'd just found out that one of the original CCC boys, who had worked on this very bridge, was staying at the campground nearby. Malik razzed Ryan, and told him he was acting so cheerful, he looked like he could piss rainbows.

Ryan ignored the bait, and continued. They were invited to meet him after lunch, so work was being suspended. Zoey and Malik were most fixated on the fact that they were off work for the rest of the day. Emma was intrigued; perhaps she'd get some of her questions answered, all she had been musing over for the past few weeks. Before she left work, she took another quick peek at the secret inscription under the bridge, even though she already knew exactly what it said. By heart. In her heart.

They headed back to camp to get cleaned up, then hiked down toward the stone lodge at the public campground. Emma and Rachel skipped down the trail, arm in arm. When they got to the bottom, they could see a man with a head of thick, smoky-grey hair sitting on a picnic bench with his back to them. Emma realized he'd have to be really old if he had worked here back in the thirties. She hoped he would still be able to think clearly, to remember.

It was a chilly afternoon, and the campfire was blazing, its shadows dancing on the stone structure, which had also been built by the CCC boys. As the crew approached, Laura gave them what little history of this man she had found out in her morning talk with him, after she had told him all about her crew, what they were doing, and how they were doing. She was all fired up. "He told me how much those years in the CCC had meant to him, that he found his way on this mountain." *To reach the other side*, Emma thought. "He told me how he firmly believed that the hard work and camaraderie saved his life." Emma's heart beat more quickly.

As they walked up behind the old man, Laura announced, "Okay, folks, it is my extreme privilege to introduce you to a former CCC boy, the Honorable Judge Harold MacNamara, known back in the day of the 181st as "Mac."

He slowly turned toward them, revealing the many deep creases in his face, vessels of untold insight and fond memories. Then Mac looked right at Emma, and smiled.

Chapter 2

As soon as it was an acceptable hour, I called my editor to tell her about my story, about the unique way I had approached the assignment. I was so grateful for Mac and Emma; they had been open and real, and wove a compelling tale, indeed. I was sure "Three Cs" was my best work. As usual, my editor's enthusiasm was underwhelming.

"Oh, Polly, you know we can't publish something like that. Have you started working on the manure runoff piece yet?"

It hadn't occurred to me before, but I'd picked an editor just like my mom. And why not? I'd picked a husband just like my dad, only not surprisingly, Gregg Harmon was now my ex-husband.

Gregg would be the only other person up this early—if he wasn't behind bars. He probably knew more about the CCC than I did, but surely, he'd think my article was a great idea. I bet he'd even throw me a *mazel tov* in his whiny, imitation-Jewish inflection, just to annoy me. The call went straight to voicemail. Gregg was out in the field. Some things never changed. There was always Mark, but I wouldn't give him the satisfaction of bringing me down.

It never used to be like that. Mark had been my biggest, most constant fan. Then Mom died, and he couldn't even look at me. It had actually started days before she died. I'd racked my brain to figure out what I had done. It was hard to make sense of it, since Mark wouldn't let me talk to him about it. I was just kind of floating out in the ether, trying to grasp at empyrean answers, getting bombarded by cosmic debris.

It couldn't have been the damned Victorian heirloom. An amputated lyrebird tail? That thing was repugnant. Mark knew that

Mom had specifically told me I was to take it. He'd even teased me about it, relieved he wasn't the one who'd have to be "keeper of the stub."

I sure as hell didn't want it. My insufferable inheritance was a salute to animal dismemberment. But Dad had bought it for Mom when I was born, so I guess her explicit bequest was some desperate, warped attempt at final absolution.

Dad would've been my first choice to call; he was always my first choice to share my latest success, even if he never paid any attention. *Dad, I made the honor roll. Dad, I got the lead in the play. Dad, I got the job. Daddy, look at me! Look at me!* But I didn't want another call like the last one. Besides, in reality, there was no more Dad around to impress.

And there was no more Mom. Not that it would have mattered if she had still been alive. I was sure there had been earlier moments, but the first time I could clearly remember her reaction to one of my accomplishments had been in seventh grade. I'd worked really hard in woodshop class to build a chessboard. Like all the other kids, I had carefully measured and cut and glued and sanded squares of mahogany and maple, alternating to form the playing surface. Then I went beyond the assignment, and created an intricate frame with routed edges. I'd worked for weeks, often going to the shop during my study hall periods and after school, carving a turned base on the wood lathe. I wanted to make a chess table, not just a board. Working the lathe became my first practice in meditation. The whir of the engine. The motion as the axle spun. The fresh, toasty smell of wood curls gently hitting my face and hands as they shed off the wood block, like layers of an onion, unraveling.

Mark had driven me home from school that day. He helped me lug the chess table up the stairs and into our family room. *General Hospital* was on, and we put the table in front of the TV. Mom was folding laundry. It was Thursday, after all. She looked up and squinted at my table. Her lips puckered, and she started to laugh. I stared at her. Mark said, "Mom, Polly made this in woodshop. Isn't it cool?" Mom kept laughing. Tears streamed down her face. She excused herself and headed toward the bathroom. I didn't move. On the TV, Audrey Hardy, R.N. was crying about something, accompanied by thick, melodramatic accordion bass chords. Mark came over and slapped me on the back. "You did great, Polly. Wanna play? You might be a better woodworker than me, but I can still whoop your little butt at chess."

Mom walked back in and gave me a stiff hug. "How in the world do you know how to do these things?" *How in the world? That was a good question.*

The bad question was the one currently bouncing around my brain. *Have you started working on the manure runoff piece yet?* I had less than no desire to work on the manure runoff piece. It was eight hours ahead in Madrid, so I tried to Skype Nebi, but as usual, my daughter wasn't online. Shit. I sat in front of the computer screen, ready to Facebook my writing breakthrough to all of my fb friends, and friends of friends, and friends of friends of friends. I was about to post about "Three Cs" to share my latest triumph, and my finger froze mid-keystroke. And that was when it dawned on me.

Just be. Just be with. Just be with it. Yourself. Find the accolades and kudos within. What difference does it make what anyone else thinks? Do you think they will love you any less if you don't star in the play, or win the contest, or score the goal, or get the grade? I wasn't sure what Emma and Mac had done to me, but there was a Pangaea-like shift as I thought about them and getting their story out. As I thought about why I wanted to do it. On that stone bridge high in the Green Mountains, I had finally cast off my inane need to seek external recognition and validation.

I just wished it hadn't taken me the better part of a half-century to figure that one out.

It usually does take time and deep mining to get to the best of finds. A few years ago, NASA had blown the side of a comet apart. The calculated impact was designed to allow them to find out what was inside. And they did retrieve some amazing finds in the interstellar dust: olivine, fool's gold, even the stuff of rubies. I had bought Nebi a ring with a tiny peridot cabochon, and told her to remember all the beauty that could be found inside a seemingly dull, rough exterior. She mocked me for my celestial lesson, but she never took the ring off.

I was a better teacher than student.

I did finally reach Nebi. When the video came on, we couldn't stop laughing. We were both wearing the same red flannel shirt, our hair was tied up in the same messy ponytail, bangs swept to the side, and we each had on a long necklace of turquoise beads. And large silver hoop earrings. She wanted to snap a screenshot of us, and we held pencils under our noses, squeezed in place with our upper lips. Snap. By the time we'd stopped laughing, she had already posted the picture on Facebook. A picture of my daughter and me enjoying each other's company. I didn't mind sharing that particular accomplishment with the world.

Nebi and I caught up, and I told her all about "Three Cs." I thought she was about to congratulate me, but instead, she paused. A still silence filled the cyberspace. I took pleasure in the time to reflect on my writing. I thought about my process, and my gratification in the end product.

"You seem so calm, Mom."

"You know I've been practicing mindfulness."

"No, really. It's like, normally, you're always fishing for a compliment. Like the entire point of your doing anything is to get someone to notice."

"Yeah, not very mindful."

"Usually, you're more like mind-full."

"Yuck, yuck. You're a funny girl."

"You know what Buddha said: *Peace comes from within. Do not seek it without.*"

"Yes, grasshopper. At least I should get a big congrats for how great I raised you."

I told her about my mini-epiphany, about no longer needing to look for admiration from anyone other than myself. It must've put a lot of pressure on my parents. I kept throwing myself at them—really, I was throwing my accomplishments at them—and I expected them to catch each one in a glove of enormous exaltation. Who could keep up with that?

"They probably got used to you, Mom. We all expect you to do a lot. You never stop."

"Yeah, but as a little kid, they could've given me a bit more praise."

"I know what I'd give you." And she gave me the finger, the one with the peridot ring on it.

All I could do was feign indignation.

"I miss Mema. And Pop-pop," Nebi said.

"I miss them, too. Every day."

"When're you going to see him?"

"I was going to head down there soon, but Mark said he'd go instead."

"Mom, Uncle Mark lives in Cali. You're so much closer."

"It's fine. Don't worry about it."

"Yeah, just hope I don't treat you like that when you're old."

It took all of my adult self-restraint to just smile and breathe. Nebi was distracted by some other chats she had going on at the same time—their generation should be the multitasking generation, not the millennial—so she didn't see my lip quiver ever so slightly.

"Mom, you really should get out of Vermont. You know, there's a whole world out there."

My dear daughter was right. In her few years as an adult, she'd traveled more than I had in my whole life. The manure runoff piece would have to wait. A quick Google search found me a super-cheap, last-minute redeye flight to the Dominican Republic. Only an overnight stay, but more than enough time for the interviews. Talk about a working vacation.

When I knocked on *Señor* Leon Haube's door, he accepted me as if I were an old friend, and insisted I call him Leon. I told him to call me Polly. I was struck by how much he looked like Mac. Two old men with grey hair and tender eyes. Add Dad to that list, except his eyes were more vacant than kind.

It was nice to feel welcomed, considering I wasn't in such a great place in my life: my mom had died, my dad was living in a nursing home, my daughter had moved to yet another country (my little Wandering Jewess), and my brother and I were barely on speaking terms. I hadn't had a romantic relationship in a long, long time, my ex was still sniffing around, and my creative juices were running low, sucked up by some kind of middle-aged sponge. And that wasn't the only part of me that was drying up.

I left out the pity-party details and explained only that I was the reporter from Vermont who had been communicating with him. I had called before I booked the flight, but I again apologized for the short notice, thanking him for accommodating me as I decided to take this unintended trip.

"That's how life goes, isn't it?" he said. "You map out a course, and as you head out, you find that the trail needs to be cleared. Or a different route leads you to a totally singular destination."

When *Señor* Leon Haube said those words, he inscribed me in his life's book. He opened his island home to me, opened his heart to me, and as he shared his story, I was smitten.

I'd initially found out about Leon when I'd started to research the possibility of getting a little place somewhere away from northern winters, somewhere outside of the United States that was not so developed. It was time for a fundamental transformation, and living a nice life on a steamy island sounded like a good idea for the home stretch.

What came up for me when I considered moving south should have been my first clue that I was in for an unexpected adventure. For some reason, I started thinking about whether there would be other Jews living in my new tropical refuge. I found it stunning that as a Jew who only attended services at the High Holy days and occasionally fried *latkes* or baked a *challah*, of all the is-sues—healthcare, transportation, making a living wage, language barriers, cultural barriers—the lack of Jews would even appear on my radar. But it did. So odd. You can take the Jew out of ...

I was intrigued when I learned that there was a well-estab-lished Jewish community in the tiny coastal town of Sosúa. How odd, indeed.

My research led me to find out about the fascinating history of this community "born of pain and nurtured in love," and how it came to be. And that was how I first heard of *Señor* Leon Haube. We'd been emailing ever since.

His foyer was covered floor-to-ceiling with framed art, each wall like a page out of a stamp collection. Curled fingers gin-gerly slid across the row of paintings hung at waist level, and I could almost see the trail left by years of comings and goings. Entering, I told Leon that I wasn't sure what I was going to do with his story—maybe turn it into a magazine piece or newspaper article—but I felt I needed to hear it directly from him. That his story needed to be told.

Without the least bit of hesitation, he shared the artifacts of his life of travel and intellectual and cultural curiosity. He offered me a glass of his precious Veterano, "the sun of Andalusia put into bottles," and we toasted, the first of several times that day, with a hearty "*¡Salud!*"

I followed him out to his garden, where he taught me about the history and botany of his different orchids, pointing out the way the sun hit the petals, how the changing light shifted every-thing. I watched the dappled shadows dance up my arm, and he smiled at me as if he knew they tickled my skin.

He proudly showed off his magnificent breadfruit tree, ex-plaining that it brought old-world fruit bats to his garden. "The old world pollinating the new!" he said, laughing. He told me he favored that tree because he could share with his neighbors the large quantities of fruit it produced. Then he quoted from Torah: "Don't harden your heart to those who are needy in your midst."

An early indication that each gesture throughout his life had been the embodiment of the commandment to give: the *mitzvah* of *tzedakah*.

Ninety-nine years old, and he had so much energy! We left his house and headed to a local pub. I was breathing heavily as I tried to keep up with his brisk pace. Even though it was early in the morning, all the expats were already there, sharing drinks and laughter. Between the cigarette smoke and a few emotional triggers, I'd never been particularly fond of bars, but something felt different at the Britannia. I felt a paradoxical comfort when I walked into this bar.

Perhaps it was the bartender.

As soon as we stepped into the Britannia Pub, I felt his eyes on me. He was tanned and tall, with bronze hair greying around his temples and in his scruffy beard—his look an alluring mix of distinguished and haphazard. A businessman turned surfer. He was across the room behind the bar, busy filling orders and chatting up the patrons. I saw him glance at me, and I blushed. He laughed.

Leon and I sat down, and the bartender brought over a tall glass of rum for Leon and a rum punch for me, complete with pink umbrella.

"What the striking woman ordered."

I didn't expect the American accent.

"Uh, I didn't order anything."

"You're welcome." And he walked away.

The fruit juice smelled luscious. I sipped. The drink was delicious, and I sipped again. And again.

Over many glasses of rum, Leon Haube told me the story of Sosúa, the story of his people. He also shared his own story, his memories switching back and forth through time. The bartender made sure we had whatever we needed.

Leon's face was a refugee's roadmap. Some lines cordoned off borders, others designated steep thresholds or shallow passes. The pockmarked roads from lips to eyes pulsed with each word as he recounted his tale. Or took another sip of rum. Each sunburned wrinkle traced his wayfaring spirit. Our travels couldn't have been more different, yet somehow, our lives intersected.

"They say I single-handedly cut the highway from Sosúa to Puerto Plata, with nothing but a machete," Leon began as I clicked on my digital recorder.

I took a quick peek at the bartender. He was ready to catch my glance. I wanted to linger, but I looked back toward Leon.

"I was alone, but it was just a footpath. And if you saw her river-green eyes …"

I was fully lost in Leon's words. His story was an essential stop along my route, a vital step in my serendipitous journey, the next chapter.

SHIBBOLETH

BY P.A. STERN

They say I single-handedly cut the highway from Sosúa to Puerto Plata with nothing but a machete. I was alone, but it was just a footpath. And if you saw her river-green eyes and smelled the coconut oil on her mahogany skin, you would have done it, too.

It was my Uncle Alfred who taught me that value, as an element of art, is not a monetary worth, but is based upon the degree of darkness or lightness. The different shades. The infinite variations of black and white. As an unfortunate element of humanity, hatred appears in shades so subtle it is often difficult to discern the inherent value placed on all the different greys. But it is there. Everywhere.

English-Canadians despise French-Canadians. Italians abhor the Irish. My wife's Catholic family said they'd rather her marry me—a Jew—than end up with a Protestant. Even though they are all Christians. American blacks reject African blacks, although they are all blacks, all originally African. The Sunnis and the Shiites fight to the death. Even though they are both Muslim. I am ninety-nine years old, and cannot recall a time when there haven't been two groups—no matter how close they seem—who have not become the target of each other's petty but powerful venom.

Sometimes, the animus made sense to me. Somewhat. My grandchildren in Southern California competed with recruited Korean students for the best grades, the finest college admissions. What right did the Asian imports have to take away their expected allotment? Their entitlement. The newer immigrants—Bosnian,

Honduran, Nicaraguan, Bhutanese refugees, desperate, hungry, willing—came along and took menial jobs from the established immigrant groups. Pakistani immigrants arriving in Britain are shunned and feared as terrorists. I don't agree with these attitudes and actions. Still, I can see where they originate.

What never made any sense to me was that Trujillo—the man who saved my life— could dictate systematic hatred based merely upon the degree of melanin in our skin. Skin dark as coal was thought ugly, intolerable compared to lighter tones, which were closer to Caucasian purity. The continuum of blackness was directly proportional to the revulsion, hostility, and bigotry spewed by the government. Embraced by the public. This was back in the thirties. Still, today, the Haitians, with their deeper, darker skin, are second-class citizens to what they consider the fairer-toned Dominicans.

Though the official ideology no longer contains *antihaitian-ismo*, the basic tenets are still present. Throughout the Dominican Republic, you'll hear repeatedly *no hay racismo aquí*. And that's true for us Jews. We've never had a problem, but that's not so for Haitians. Those who moved here to work, and even citizens of Haitian descent, have been intentionally denied the *cédulas de identidad*, the national identity card, for having Haitian-sounding surnames, or a certain color of skin. Without the *cédulas*, they cannot vote, work, or attend school. I knew many students over the years from good families who wanted to come to our *colegio* to learn. Even as founder and principal, I had to fight the *autoridades* to allow them to attend classes. More subtly, still damaging, you can see it on the streets. Lips puckered and eyes rolling, judging the potent stench of the cane-field workers. You can hear it in the comments. Snide. Soft-spoken, yet hard and sharp as an axe blade. Dirty, smelly monkey. Haitian devil sorcerer. The words *fuera Haitianos* scrawled in blood-red paint on a *mercado* wall.

Sssshwhoop. My machete sliced through the thick jungle foliage. Sweat poured from my head. I did not know there were so many sweat glands under my hair. I should have shaved my head. I couldn't see for the steam evaporating off my nose. The salt streams mingled with the salt air, and it was hard to distinguish which saline haze came from my skin, which dripped from my lashes, which rose from the sea.

The wet, heavy foliage produced its own sweat, rising from the tropical stomata like microscopic water spouts. I could almost feel the puffs of moist air particles hit me as they left the broad, lush leaves. Nothing back in Germany could have prepared me for this sweltering trek. The nice man who cleaned my father's Sabbath suits worked in such a place; scalding air scorched my lungs each time I entered the dry cleaner's establishment on *Magdeburger Allee* to pick up Papa's starched shirts. But those assaults were temporary, nothing like the oppressive, calescent path that seemed to have no end. I continued even as the heat blistered my skin.

I kept my machete passes as consistent as possible. I tried to remember what Jean-Jacques had taught me, how he showed me to respect the machete, with its powers like a beautiful woman. *Mujer seductora.* He handled his machete back in the cane fields like a *coup de femme dangereuse.* I needed to do the same. If I sped up, I would grow tired too quickly. If I slowed down, I would not arrive on time, before dark. I wanted nothing more than to rush, but fortunately, I knew that would be a mistake in the long run. This was the wisdom of a mature thirty-year-old man. I was beginning to feel older by the step, weaker by the stroke.

The *swoosh swoosh, hack hack* of my machete and the rush of air in and out of my lungs were mere hints of sound compared to the deafening din surrounding me. The jungle shouted so loudly. No streets back in Germany could compete with the volume and variety of noises here.

As a young boy in Erfurt, I'd often take rides with my Uncle Alfred on the Altentor Circular Line from the Bahnhof to the Kornmarkt, until they closed the northern section. The tram drivers would shout at the buggy drivers to move their stinking horse manure from the tracks. While we were stuck, the street vendors would take advantage of the delays and swoop in to sell their wares, and more shouting would occur. I loved these spirited exchanges, so entertaining, especially because no one was speaking the same language. The tram operators yelled in German, while the Gypsy vendors hawked in Romani and the buggy drivers bellowed in French and Spanish. How I soaked that all in!

After the arguing stopped, we'd get out and walk to the quieter neighborhoods to get away from the squeal of the tramcars and the blaring sounds of the main streets. I was most fascinated with the house in Schössergasse, where Dr. Faust purportedly made his pact with the devil and practiced his sorcery. Uncle Alfred told me not to tell my mother where we had gone. I suppose my interest with different cultures and religious practices had its early start here. We wouldn't stay long, because my concentration was usually broken by some noisy interference. Even with the fire sirens and hi-low air horns wailing in the mix with the bells from Dom St. Marien, the decibel levels of my hometown didn't approach the magnificent cacophony of the trail between Sosúa and Puerto Plata.

Competing with the loud, startling noises of the jungle was the ever-present song of the sea. A background meter to the island melody. Usually, the primordial rhythm was constant and comforting. The rush and lull, followed by rush and lull. But today, the waves were inconsistent, wrestling with themselves, a never-ending dance of struggle and surrender. Today, the sea did not whisper in my heart; it did not provide a calm and soothing song. Perhaps it was my own pulse I heard, an erratic aria, the excitement and rush of anticipation.

Noise and heat notwithstanding, it was all about the smells. Isn't it always? The most primordial sense. The good smells conjure comfort, become nostalgic triggers. The bad ones repulse, create visceral reactions of body and mind. Erfurt was a relatively civilized, clean city. Still, sanitation services were lacking, as they were all over Europe. Combined with the delicious smells of fresh-baked *stollen*, Thuringian *bratwurst*, and the perennial odors emanating from the *fischmarkt* was the fetor of a city filled with the refuse and excretions of thousands of people, houses, businesses, and industries, all crammed together in a few thousand hectares. The combinations of foul fumes and gases from the coal burning was, at best, annoying; at worst, it polluted our lungs, and after a week of winter smog episodes, became noxious and virulent— something I felt I could never forget. But in the jungle, faced with odors my body had never experienced, both ambrosial, like the almond blossoms and wild olive, and surprisingly offensive, like the vapors from the cocoa plant, the smells of my childhood were replaced by these powerful new stimulants.

With every slash of the blade, my head pounded. My arms ached from the constant swinging. Who would have thought a mere two kilograms would weigh so heavily? The knife's bugle insignia, with the words *Corneta Promedoca Rep Dom*, blurred with every stroke. The machete my Haitian friend had given to me, even though it was half of all his earthly belongings. It was an unlikely friendship. Jean-Jacques and I met in the batey when I was first learning about irrigation systems. He knew so much, and I so little. It was hard for me to imagine that only a year ago, only eighty kilometers away as the crow flies, on a path much like this, machetes had been the cause of so much misery. His people had been slaughtered. All because language was used as a political tool, an excuse for hate. All for the sound of an *r*.

Trujillo was a man of contradictions. When every other nation turned us away, only he offered refuge to the undesirable Jews of Europe. He saved me, and hundreds of other Jews. To the world, he appeared generous without rival. To us, he was a savior. He took us in when not even the Americans would. That was hard to understand. Shame on Roosevelt. Shame on the Americans. That was one of the reasons I never left here to move to the United States, like many of the other first settlers. I had a bitter taste. Besides, why leave paradise?

The other world leaders of wealthy, liberal, first-world countries did not allow us refuge. They turned away Jews wanting to flee the worsening conditions in Europe. There were no safe harbors. But Trujillo, this dictator who had three decades of horrendous violations of human rights, of oppression and murder, he was the only one to offer to resettle us, to open his doors and shores. We left one butcher in Germany, and arrived here at the hands of "The Butcher." He brought us to his island, welcomed us, and gave us a banana plantation. The United Fruit Company had abandoned it, so it was a fitting haven for us.

Some say he was trying to improve his international reputation. Just a year before the Évian Conference, the Parsley Massacre had taken place. Most people haven't heard of it, but it was another holocaust that must be remembered. Seventy years ago, on the week of my twenty-ninth birthday, Generalissimo Rafael Leonidas Trujillo Molina ordered the massacre of thousands of Haitians who lived here. He first created a mass revulsion for Haitians, then fed the frenzy with unfounded accusations of everything from degradations to thievery, telling his people, "I will fix this." An all-too-familiar solution.

He focused his murders on ethnic Haitians living in Dajabon, the area closest to our northwest border with Haiti. His troops and magistrates, *the alcaldes pedáneos*, along with overzealous civilians, massacred between 15,000 and 30,000 innocent people. We'll never know how many for certain. Many found their final resting place in the *Masacre del Río*. Another river of blood. Too many rivers of tears. It was so simple to identify those who were to be killed. As simple as making them wear a yellow star.

They'd hold up a sprig of parsley and ask, "¿Qué es esto?" *Perejil*, they should have responded *en español*. Native Dominicans trill their *r*. The Haitians, with their Kreyòl accents, could not. When the word was pronounced wrong, the offenders were brought to the forests and jungles, and hacked to death with machetes. People fear lions and bears and other animals in the wilderness. I've always felt the most dangerous animal on our planet is most certainly man.

Many of the slaughtered were trying to flee back to Haiti, and were told they were being deported as they were led instead to their mass graves. Most of the victims were actually born here, but still, that didn't matter. They were identified, rounded up, and caught up in Trujillo's state-induced hysteria of hatred. Dominicans refer to the slaughter as *el corte*, the cutting; Haitians call it *kout kouto-a*, the stabbing. In any language, it was an action of terror and injustice.

Giving us refuge was more than Trujillo trying to regain his regard in the international community, trying to erase the stain of parsley. Trujillo's supposed generosity was self-serving in another, more ironic way. It wasn't that he wanted to help us as much as he wanted our blood. Literally. Physically.

Since so much of Trujillo's motivation was his blind hatred of blacker skin, having us come here to interbreed, to whiten the bloodlines, was his reason to let us in. Back home, we Jews were shunned and looked upon as inferior. Here, the totalitarian ruler who'd committed countless atrocities against his own people looked at us as superior to his race. He wanted us to lighten things up. His motivation was wrong, but we were able to escape the concentration camps by coming here. We were full of gratitude.

When no one else wanted us, when "Jew" was an insult everywhere else—dirty Jew, Yid, kike—here, in Trujillo's Dominican Republic, that was not the case. And still, today, we have no problems, we aren't discriminated against. No one hates us here.

This blasted machete. The same tool that had caused so much unimaginable pain was bringing me closer to happiness. And as hard and fast as I worked, the birds mocked me with their childish chiding. The black-whiskered vireo whistled while the Hispaniolan woodpecker chattered noisily. They all thought my labors were a big joke. You call that work? *A paso de tortuga!* You are slow as a turtle!

All I wanted was to see her front porch, to know the beckoning rest of her *mecedoras*—the chairs where we would sit and rock and learn of one another. To see my Antonia. To see an opening in the shade.

Even though I have never considered myself to be white, there's really no category for the shade of the Semitic race. How hurtful this artificial concept of race, always changing, based on nothing more than how to use it against the other. There used to be an idea of a "racial angle" which classified people based on appearance, on the angle of their brow and nose. Then there was the "one-drop rule." It never ends. Have you seen the last census? Every country has their own definition of race! How is that even possible? In Brazil, you had to "Choose your race" from the following choices: White-*branca*, Black-*preta*, Yellow-*amarela*, Brown-*parda*, or Native, aboriginal-*indigena*. In Canada and the United States, they asked your race and then gave options, like Black, Arab, Filipino, White, Korean, Chinese. Totally subjective this idea of race, a false and dangerous idea, used so people are categorized in order to oppress.

On all the endless forms—travel documents, social security, health insurance—there's no place to check for "Semite," so I've always checked "Other" instead. Some experts say we are Semites based upon our language only. Perhaps that's true. To ignore the power of language is to be ignorant of one of the main causes of religious and cultural intolerance. It all starts in the beginning. In beginning.

The first words of the Torah—my Bible—begin, "be-re-SHIYT ba-RA eh-lo-HIYM." *Eh-lo-HIYM* means G-d. That part is easy. But the other phrase, *be-re-SHIYT*, comes from the

Hebrew root *resh* for *head* or *beginning*. And *bet*, translated as *at* or *in*, comes first, so it might be read as *at the head* or *in beginning*. This is a very important distinction, because read all together, it should be, "in beginning created G-d" instead of the common translation, "In the beginning G-d created …"

The implication of that one word in changing the way religions view G-d's role in the beginning of the universe is immense. Without the usual literal translation, it can be interpreted that THE beginning was not, in fact, five thousand-plus years ago, but that was only a retelling of what G-d did when "beginning," not "in THE beginning." Such subtlety. Such power. Placement of a simple "the" can alter the course of the history of the universe and humanity as perceived by billions. Death and persecution at the hands of the tongue. Pronunciation of an *r*.

Three thousand years ago, it was the Ephraimites' pronunciation of a *sh*, a torrent of water back in Gilead. In the 1300s, the Flemish identified and then slaughtered French residents of Bruges when they could not pronounce *schild ende vriend*, shield and friend. In the 1500s, ship crews were plundered and soldiers beheaded if they could not say *bûter, brea, en griene tsiis; wa't dat net sizze kin, is gjin oprjochte Fries*—butter, rye bread and green cheese, who cannot say that is not a genuine Frisian. And during World War II, Japanese spies posing as Filipinos were uncovered—and shot—when they tried to say "lollapalooza" and it came out "rorraparooza." *Perejil. Persil.* Parsley.

Catalunya in Barcelona. Politicians in India enforce schools to teach English or risk funding cuts. In the Quiet Revolution— *la Révolution tranquille*—the Québecois became *maîtres chez nous*. Masters of our own house. Bans against Ebonics. "Official English" legislation and English-only rules in American classrooms, where Spanish is often banned. I understand that soon there will be more native Spanish-speaking people in the United States than anywhere else in the world. *¿Habla usted español?*

With all the fear and bans surrounding who should or should not speak what where, perhaps anti-Semitism *is* mainly derived from the language—and the economic and social power associated with it. Whether a Semite, a Jew, a Caucasian, or Other, from my perspective, none of it made—nor makes—sense. But this very nonsense created my life. For the past seventy-three years. And for that, I truly give thanks. Even if I'm not thankful for the most current situation.

Though I travel less frequently now, I was recently in the States visiting my son. I was backing out of the market parking lot and clipped a bike. The bike got banged up a bit, but the rider was fine. Just a bruised shin. Two weeks later, the esteemed Department of Motor Vehicles of the City of Los Angeles revoked all my driving privileges. Now, when I go there, I must rely on Sebastian or the city buses. I don't think I can handle the public transportation. It's worse than the overcrowded *guaguas* back here. At least here, the worst that could happen is you'd get off at your stop smeared with the sweat of a hardworking cane-cutter. Back in L.A., they'll steal your belongings as soon as slit your throat. In Sosúa, I don't have to depend on anyone. I never have. Except, of course, for Antonia.

The dusk was landing on a field of biting, protesting insects. I suppose they didn't want me walking in their path. Why else would they need to attack so viciously? As the sun descended, millions of angry fungus gnats created a cloud of misery meant just for me. The only saving grace was the counter-attack by the Antillean siskin, swooping in and devouring the thick bug blanket.

Dominican animals are an interesting lot. I'd always imagined the overgrown wilds here would be filled with playful monkeys and other more threatening jungle wildlife. But there are no monkeys, no big cats, and no safari stalkers. Just some small rodents, vivacious birds, and many, many annoying insects. Even worse than the larger insects are the *mayes*, the ones you cannot see. Those nasty bloodsuckers, the *moscas de arena, chaquistíes*, and the *zancudos negros* cannot be avoided, especially if you're foolish enough to be out in the jungle when the sun is setting.

I was breathing hard and needed to pant, but I tried to remember to close my mouth or cover myself with a cloth so the
swarm wouldn't enter. It's a mixed blessing when they swarm, because that's the only time you can actually see them. Otherwise,
the attacks are as stealthy as they are torturous.

I thought the bites and the darkness would blind me before
I could reach her house. If that happened, I didn't know how I'd
find my way. Instead of fear, I felt absurdity. How could I have
managed to cross the globe, navigating busy roads and interconti-
nental waterways all the way from the bustling cities of Erfurt to
Ibiza to Paris to Santo Domingo, just to find myself lost on this
insignificant jungle path on this small Caribbean island? The reality was that my gift for languages, not my sense of direction, had
transported me and ultimately landed me on these shores.

I was born with an eager ear. Language was my passion. Other in-
fants take in their world in a physical fashion, chewing their own
toes, seeking whatever they can to suckle. I had no such propen-
sity. At first, there was worry that something was wrong with my
muscles, my brain. By eighteen months, I was still barely crawl-
ing. I was instead speaking full sentences in my native German
tongue.

How my mother loved to shock acquaintances and strangers
who cooed over her handsome toddler. "Leon," she'd say, "Please
tell Mr. Schwartz what you did yesterday." As I regaled our gro-
cer's assistant with tales of playgrounds and balls and baking, I'd
watch my mother watch the people's faces. Sometimes, there was
shock. Sometimes fear. Always, amazement and an unexpected
turn of their lips. Sometimes down, sometimes up.

We continued this game for many years. Shortly after my flu-
ency was established, I began gathering the other words in my
vicinity. Ripe for the picking. By kindergarten, I'd embraced the
colorful Yiddish of our neighborhood: a mixture of street German,
Hebrew, Polish, Slavic. Although we were Jews, and this was the

mame-loshn, the mother tongue of our Ashkenazi ancestors, my parents didn't want me to speak Yiddish. They considered it a bastardized, low-class language. Impure. By primary school, I'd learned many of the kosher butcher's lively Yiddish expressions—mostly the curses! One day, in a fit of frustration, the butcher yelled at a customer, "*Gay kaken oifen yom!*" I repeated the line at home, thinking it meant "Get lost!" I should've realized the literal translation was "Go shit in the ocean!" Mama was not very happy with either of us.

Sharing Hispaniola with Haitians, I came to realize that Yiddish was very similar to their Kreyòl. A fusion of French, African, Arabic, Spanish, Taíno, and English words, it's the language of the streets, of the people, considered unacceptable and lower-class by some. Impure. But just as earlier I couldn't resist the Yiddish philosophical horse sense couched in humor, I grew to love and respect the playful wisdom of my Haitian neighbors.

Once, when Jean-Jacques was giving me unsolicited advice on how to romance Antonia—which he did frequently—he said, "*Map kalonnen ak bel ti pawòl dous,*" and I was very upset with him, because I thought he was telling me to throw rocks at her. As I tried to express my concern over his *machismo* attitude, he started to giggle, which erupted into laughter so hard that his reaction only further infuriated me, and I'm not the type who angers easily. I didn't know what was going on until finally, he calmed down and explained that in Kreyòl, he was merely telling me how to whisper in her ear, "Let me tell you some sweet words." He was advising me to throw words, not rocks.

How my life took this path to all my teachers, to Uncle Alfred, to Jean-Jacques, to Miguel, to Antonia, is the biggest mystery of all. Turns out, in any language, it's all the same:

Man plan, Bondye ri.
Mentsch tracht, Gott lacht.
Man plans, G-d laughs.

By the time I was in grade three, I would buy French and Spanish books from the bookseller on *Meienbergstrasse* using money I had earned in local academic competitions, proving to my ignorant and jealous classmates that I did indeed have the power of language in my intellectual arsenal. Oddly, English was the last of my six languages. It was more difficult to learn without hearing it spoken.

Thank goodness for the cinema. I learned all I could from DeMille's *Old Wives for New*, which they showed at my favorite theater. I had to sneak in because I was only ten years old, and it was considered very racy for a romantic comedy. After watching it dozens of times, I was able to pick up some of the basics of the written English language. This continued for years as I devoured every silent foreign film—foreign to Germany!—that I could.

My English was fairly well established by the time I went to university. Any nuances I had yet to learn were solidified in the cinema as soon as sound arrived in the late 1920s. Ah, thank you again to Mr. Cecil B. DeMille, and to talkies. I thought you'd tantalized me all that was possible until I saw *The Sign of the Cross*.

That fall evening in 1929 was one that will stay with me until the last of my faculties fade. Even though it took a few years for me to realize that Americans did not truly speak like Romans in the time of Nero, I certainly learned much about the American culture. Watching the beautiful Miss Claudette Colbert bathing in ass's milk, wearing costumes that revealed her breasts, her nipples. Disrobing. And how could I ever forget the scene when those women danced together, so provocatively, nothing between them but sheer threads. Though of course we knew there were lesbians in our community and schools, we didn't speak of them openly, and this was certainly my first exposure to the intimate life of homosexuals. With all of those stimulating images, I'm surprised I was even able to focus on the language at all!

I also began to break down the essence of the Romance languages that I heard at my uncle's home. It was my Uncle Alfred who first formally exposed me to the wonders of culture, language, art, and the nuance of light. He was well-respected back in Erfurt because he ran the family-owned shoe factory—M. & L. Haube *Schuhfabrik*—that'd been started by my grandfather. Uncle Alfred was a very successful businessman, but his main interest in business was making money to fund his real passion—the arts. When the *Bauhaus* movement started, Uncle Alfred became enamored of the simplicity, the way the *Bauhaus* artists rejected flowery forms and typical painterly images, streamlining everything from furniture to architecture. He bought their paintings, he loaned them money. Anything he could do to support what he saw as the future of art in the world.

I learned from these great thinkers to be aware of light, to understand how value can weaken objects or strengthen a composition, how strong contrast can have a dramatic effect. I became aware of the power of black versus white. Aware of the role of shades. To respect luminosity, to know that if everything is of the same value, there's no interest, and light is lost. To get down to the essence, strip down to basic form and function, to streamline, to embrace rationality. Objectivity and harmony, balance. These were the thoughts of a new approach, an international style. Of the modern world.

Uncle Alfred and Aunt Thekla let the artists and writers stay at their house, Villa Haube, for weeks. Uncle helped them in any way he could. You should see his guest book. I have a copy of it. The visiting artists and intellectuals signed it, sometimes leaving messages of gratitude, sometimes drawings. Kandinsky, Klee, Dix, Kirchner. So many creative minds. Not only artists, but also the finest writers and musicians of the time. I was lucky to be able to visit and be surrounded by their energy, their insights. My uncle was a wise and innovative man at the forefront of the Golden Twenties.

He was also wise to the changing political climate and increasing anti-Semitism. He gave financial support and loans to the *Städtisches* Museum, yet because he was Jewish, there could be no public acknowledgement of his generosity. In the early 1920s, the Nationalistic groups were already leading anti-Semitic efforts and smear campaigns. They didn't want Jews, and they didn't want the new form of art. They began to lay the foundation of hate, and to enact laws to systemize anti-Semitism. They looked at expressionism and the *Bauhaus* movement as offensive to the sensibilities of traditional German values. The artists viewed their art as apolitical, but the Nazi regime didn't see it that way. State officials declared modern artists "anti-national cultural Bolsheviks" and the modern style to be unacceptable, degenerate art, clearly influenced by Jews and social liberals.

My uncle died in 1931. I've always felt that the stress of what was happening to his beloved Germany caused him to die of a broken heart. Aunt Thekla entrusted their vast art collection to my dear cousin Hans, and she fled to Bavaria and then London amidst growing anti-Semitic persecution.

It was around this time that I, too, thought it would be best to find another place to call home. Spain was my first destination. I visited Aunt Thekla years later, and she told me stories of how she and Hans, who had lost his well-paying job in 1933 due to "racial reasons," outsmarted the Nazi authorities—whose tax and foreign exchange laws were meant to further repress Jews—and kept Uncle Alfred's important collections from being confiscated, stolen, or destroyed. My aunt and cousin risked everything and lived on a meager subsistence, trying to hold the art collection together. Thanks to them, hundreds of expressionistic paintings, watercolors, and photographs continue to be exhibited, demonstrating that art can and will speak truth through the veils of politics, propaganda, and prejudice.

It was somewhat unusual for someone like me to just take up and leave the country on so many occasions. People were fleeing in anticipation of politics creating social unrest. But very few—especially Jews—left and returned, came and went as I did. In particular, some Jews—those who did not have their heads in the sand—sought asylum or attempted to be one step ahead of the impending doom.

For me, the act of travel did not arise from practicality, but from passion. The call of other countries was as comforting as my mama calling my name. Different languages, different cultures were my art. At bedtime, I'd even challenge myself to dream in alternate languages. To wake and discover where I'd gone that night was a journey in itself. Words and translations and dialects were the fuel for my mind; *wanderlust* was the food for my heart. I suppose I was just one of a long line of Wandering Jews!

In the early 1930s, I saw what was happening. Even though my family had been well-established and well-respected in Germany for hundreds of years, we were shunned, treated as strangers. It might as well have been 1349, when they rounded up the Jews in pogroms. The ignorance of the Middle Ages, yet it was happening again. Happening still. Germans weren't allowed to come to Jewish stores or see Jewish doctors or lawyers. The hardest part to accept was that most of the Germans agreed with Hitler's views. We could see what was coming.

In 1933, I left Germany and headed first to Spain, where I started my own bar. That was a fun time. At first. Unfortunate timing being what it was, the Spanish Civil War broke out, and I once again fled—this time to Paris, where I continued my language studies. But the French authorities were joining in the rising swell of anti-Semitism, and enacted a law that all of us Jews who had immigrated to France before a certain date had to leave or be thrown in jail.

Back in Germany, the Nuremberg Laws had already made Jews stateless refugees in our own country. I couldn't go back there. I tried to get a visa to stay and study and work in France. It wasn't allowed, and I feared what was to come. I went to consulate after consulate, and every embassy denied me a visa. Except the Dominican Republic. Even before Trujillo decided he wanted to lighten the population, the Dominican Republic had a long-standing tradition of being sympathetic to the Jews, beginning back in 1492 when Jews were forced out of Spain during the Inquisition. Several of Columbus' crewmembers, from the translator to the physician, were Jews. Some people even think Columbus himself was one of our tribe, a *Yehudim*. After Columbus landed, a strong Sephardic population remained on Hispaniola.

In June of 1937, I came by boat. It took three weeks. When I arrived on the shores of the Dominican Republic, I felt the breeze, I saw the smiles, I tasted freedom. It was primitive and it was hot, but there was no pollution, no noise, no prejudice. Like Columbus, I had discovered paradise. Unlike Columbus, I would honor it, and its people.

At first, I didn't know how I would support myself. I heard that in the nearby lake—*Lago Enriquillo*—there were alligators. I knew that in America, alligator handbags and shoes were all the rage. I had an idea that I could catch and skin alligators and export the skins to America. No big deal. After all, shoemaking was part of my family heritage. To make things even more encouraging, Bessie Smith had just died, and they kept showing her picture in the cinema reels and all over the newspapers. In most of the photographs, she was carrying her alligator handbag. Thank you, Empress of the Blues!

I found out *Lago Enriquillo* was a landlocked saltwater lake, and that they were actually crocodiles, not alligators. But these Dominican crocodiles were in great demand because they had the highest quality skins. I figured I could make a good living as the first Jewish crocodile hunter! I went to the lake, rented a boat, and hired a captain. We were out for seven hours. We saw turtles and crabs. I was so excited; what adventure in this new world! We saw the long burrows the crocs hide in, and we moved slowly through mangrove swamps, trying to track—or attract—*un gran cocodrilo*. Nothing. Finally, *el capitán* spotted the long, narrow snout. It was much more pointed than I had imagined. Green, silvery, calm. It didn't look so scary. Then I saw the teeth, erupted, coming straight out from the upper jaw. It opened its eye, and all the blood drained from my face.

El capitán responded with a bellowing laugh that both sealed my terror and signaled the capture to begin. *¡Vamos!* There was a flurry of activity, of which I was mostly a spectator. Then, in a flash, the croc was strapped up right next to us, not happy to be on board *Sin Miedo,* Fearless. It turned out to be a female, and though her scales were large, she was only about two meters long. I really didn't feel like killing her right then, so we took her with us to take care of the skinning later. When we got back to port, I decided I would take her to my apartment, which was right in the *Ens Quisqueia* district, between the marina and the city center. She lived in my bathtub for about a week before my landlord kicked us both out. I let "Bessie" go back in the lake, and I found a new apartment—and a new job teaching languages in Santo Domingo.

I suppose I was in the right place at the right time. In 1938, the Évian Conference was held to try to figure out what to do with the hundreds of thousands of Jewish refugees from Germany and Austria needing to flee Nazi persecution. For eight days, leaders from thirty-one countries and dozens of international volunteer organizations discussed the issue of the numbers and logistics; no mention was made of the cause of the "issue." No formal condemnation was made of Nazi philosophy or practices. In the end, many countries expressed sympathy, but only one leader offered the Jews refuge. Trujillo.

After the conference, representatives from the American Jewish Joint Distribution Committee came to Santo Domingo to negotiate the resettlement with the Trujillo government. One of the only reasons the Nazis allowed this emigration was because there was a condition that our families transfer our assets to the German authorities. Even with Trujillo's offer, the resettlement was funded mostly by Jewish families, and private donations from American Jewish organizations.

At the time, I was the only person around who spoke German, English, and Spanish, so I was hired to interpret. After about three weeks, they asked me if I was willing to move from the capital city to the small coastal town of Sosúa, where 11,000 hectares were being allotted for the Jewish refugees. So I came to Sosúa as an employee of the Dominican Republic Settlement Association—DORSA. I was the first settler, and helped transition the Jews who arrived. But more than the work I did, this land became my home, this community my heart.

The first Jews to arrive were mostly men. No single Jewish women. We didn't understand why that had happened until we realized it was intentional, that Trujillo had manipulated the visa process so he would have only men arrive. Lonely men. To assure we would intermarry and pass our seed to the local women.

It was like the old Taíno story, of how their men found women.

During the time of creation, the sun and moon lived in a cave called *Jovovava*. The sea did not exist at that time. The original inhabitants of the island were the Taíno. Humans lived in two caves in two different mountains, *Cacibajugua* and *Amayauna*. When they were in the *Cacibajugua* cave, a human named *Macocael* was in charge of keeping watch to see who left the cave, to make sure they were dispersed equally over the land. *Macocael* was late returning to the cave one day, and—being caught in the sun's rays—he was turned to stone. One person gathering herbs at sunrise was turned into a nightingale, and others were turned into jobos trees.

These events angered one Taíno named *Guaguyoa*, and he left the cave. He convinced all of the women to leave their husbands and follow him. They abandoned their children near a stream; the children called out in hunger, and were turned into frogs. Then the women were abandoned, as well; and in that manner, all the men were left without women. The men yearned for women and searched for footprints on rainy days, but to no avail. Eventually, a type of people—neither male nor female—was found, but couldn't be caught because they slipped away as if they were eels. Some Taíno had a mange-like disease called *caracaracol* that roughened their skin. It was up to them to use their coarse hands to catch these creatures. After being trapped, the creatures were bound and woodpeckers were placed on their bodies. The birds, thinking they were trees, pecked away at the spot where the female sex organs usually were. This is how the Indians obtained women, according to the old people.

The first fifty Jewish men who joined me in the Dominican Republic were faced with oppressive heat, primitive living conditions, language and cultural hurdles—but, oh we were so happy! We were free. And luckily for us, there were lots of young, healthy, unmarried Dominican women to keep us company. At thirty, I was still single, and now I was ready to settle down. A friend who lived in Puerto Plata told me there was a dance the following Sunday. He said he had a cousin he wanted to introduce me to. I knew Miguel was a fine man from a good Dominican family. He was smart and strong, and had a pleasant sense of humor and handsome looks, so I was hopeful his cousin would be just right for me.

I dressed up in an elegant suit and a Panama hat, and headed out on horseback. There were no trams here! It was difficult going, as there was no clear path to town. So many ruts and vines and roots. Too many potholes. As I got closer, I heard the alternating strains of *merengue* and American jazz standards coming from the dance hall. I arrived sweaty and smelling of horse, but I still looked dapper, and I was ready to meet my future bride. I came in behind a small crowd of singles. Across the hall, I saw my friend with his family, waiting to introduce me to his cousin. But *¡Dios mío!* She was not the girl for me. Her face was full of pock marks, but more than that, I could just feel she was not the one. Not wanting to hurt her feelings or disrespect my friend, I skirted around the perimeter of the hall, looking for someone else. I knew she was in there. I felt it.

Gathered nearby was a large family, laughing, telling stories, dancing. They were all talking at the same time, shouting *pssst,*

pssst, trying to get each other's attention, to get their turn. In the middle of the group, there she was. Antonia. Arm in arm with an older woman, who I later found out was her favorite aunt. Animated, so alive. Her skin was deep amber, and her jade eyes shot through me, body and soul. I was home.

I asked her to dance, and her family watched us every step, every moment. There was no judgment, no worry. No privacy. It is just the Dominican way. A way I grew to love as I grew to love Antonia and her family. We left that night, and we both knew. I had grown up a Jew in Germany, and she a Latina in Puerto Plata, but we were the same. It was *bershert*; she was my destiny.

And that was why I cut the trail from Sosúa to Puerto Plata. I courted Antonia for three weeks, and needed easy access!

Antonia and I were married with the blessings of both our families. I gave her a ring of larimar. This beautiful soft blue stone—the color of where sea meets sky—has only been found in one location in the world: the high mountainous region overlooking the Caribbean Sea. Only in our country. I felt our love was as rare as larimar, so no other stone would do.

I was the first to marry a non-Jew, a Dominican Catholic. Many felt it was a risk. Everything in my life seemed to be against the odds, and yet the odds paid off. As we were starting our new lives together, we were also helping the new settlers try to learn how to be farmers. Imagine a group of fifty urban, professional European Jews trying to till the land. Trujillo had determined that we would become "agricultural workers" in exchange for refuge. We were fine with that, but we had no idea what we were doing. Our first administrator was an agricultural economist who thought we should grow vegetables, as he had learned in Germany. Tomatoes. The land was arid, there was no irrigation, and the drainage was poor. On top of that, the Dominicans had no taste for our tomatoes. We had come so far and worked so hard, just to see our labors fail.

We did not give up. We had a specialist from the United States come and analyze our soil, our topography, the climate, the water. He concluded that the only kind of success we could have here would be raising cattle. We were very excited to become ranchers and cowboys. DORSA created many hectares of pastures, but they made one grave error. They tried to form small farming collectives of six to seven families to share the land and the labor. They figured if it was working for the Jews on the *kibbutzim* in Palestine, it would surely work here. Well, some of our farmers were lazy, others not as cooperative as needed. Most quarreled, and nothing got done. A bunch of Jews debating and arguing with each other? Who would have imagined?

As soon as they realized they had to change the system, they offered each of us private farms, and everything started to work. I applied for a farm myself, and for forty years, Antonia and I worked together. We created a good life for ourselves. We started with an allotment of twelve cows, but over time, I bought more and more, and in the end, we had eighty. There were cattle for meat and cows for dairy. We mixed the meat and the milk, and even though it was a Jewish settlement, the main product was pork. People have asked me if Antonia and I had a kosher home. The only kosher food we ate was pickles!

Together, we all built a factory called *Productos Sosúa* that made different cheeses and butter. Delicious. After all the years and all the changes, it's still today the Dominican Republic's main producer of dairy products. Jewish emigration ended in 1941, and at the final count, we were only able to take in about 600 settlers. After a while, many left to find family in America, or to help form the state of Israel. Most left because the tropical heat and conditions were too difficult. Only a few of us stayed to keep the factory and business going. I stayed because the Dominican Republic is my home.

With so few Jewish farmers, we relied heavily on the locals to work alongside us. It was a good working relationship, though there were a few minor glitches along the way: things we needed to learn, and things we needed to accept about and from each other. At first, the workers would leave at midday for their main meal, the *comida*, but it would last two hours, and we'd fall behind milking, making the cheese, slaughtering the cattle and pigs. The local workers had to change their ways, but they never seemed to mind. We closed early for *Shabbat*, and we never worked on Jewish holidays, so it seemed to make up for it. We worked together, merged our cultures.

Each *Pesach*, hundreds of Dominicans would join us for our community *Seder*. We'd all be together, elbow-high in *matzah* meal, creating an assembly line forming hundreds of *matzah* balls. We'd grind the local *bacalao* to make the *gefilte* fish. And since no one could prove biblically that *yuca* formed into *casabe* was not kosher for Passover, we enjoyed these little crisp cracker breads while we were not supposed to be eating anything leavened.

And together we'd dip our parsley—the *karpas*—in salt water and pray:

בָּרוּךְ אַתָּה יְ-יָ אֱ-לֹהֵינוּ מֶלֶךְ הָעוֹלָם בּוֹרֵא פְּרִי הָאֲדָמָה

B'oruch atah Adonai Eloheynu Melech ha-olam
borey pree ha- adamah.
Blessed art Thou, O Eternal, our G-d,
Creator of the fruits of the earth.

During the retelling of the Passover story, the *Haggadah* reveals to us that the parsley represents spring and a time of renewal, and the salt water represents the tears of our ancestors who were oppressed and persecuted. For many centuries, Jews used to dip the parsley in salt water mixed with red wine to symbolize not only tears, but also the blood that was smeared on the doorposts so the Lord would "pass over" the homes of those marked. But sometime during the twelfth century, we were accused of blood libel—using the blood of Christian children in our rituals. With no way to counter such an accusation, we stopped using the red wine. River of blood. River of tears. So together at our Sosúa *Seders*, the Jews and the Dominicans now dip the parsley in salt water only. At no *Seder* anywhere else on earth could that have more meaning.

We hold the *Seder* in German and Spanish, making the blessings and asking the four questions in Hebrew. This started back in

1940, and continues today. The same thing is true of other holidays and life-cycle events. We all celebrate the *bat* or *bar mitzvah* of our thirteen-year-old girls and boys, and we're invited for the *quinceañera*. Such a huge celebration for turning fifteen! It was always a good excuse for Antonia and me to dance our *merengue*—not that we needed any excuse. I must admit, for a Jew from Germany, I could *merengue* with the best of them.

And of course, as our people died, our new family would come sit *shiva* with us, and when our Dominican neighbors passed, we'd be there for the *velas*. My wife had worn her *Magen David* every day since our wedding, and it was her last wish that she be buried in our Jewish cemetery, which she was. Both Jews and Dominicans left pebbles on her headstone.

Antonia and I were married for sixty years. We had a good life together. We raised two incredible sons—a mixture of the two of us, of our bloodlines—and now their wives are our daughters, and we have four wonderful grandchildren to carry on our traditions. That is our legacy.

They called us "the human experiment" or "the Jewish experiment." Seems we have served in that role a lot throughout history. We were supposed to be a pilot program, a model for refugees heading to other parts of the world. I wish they had had a chance to learn from us. There was no time. Instead, the others—six million of them—headed to the gas chambers. Or were murdered by firing squads, by starvation, by torture … I'm still not sure what was learned from that experiment.

Maybe that we're a strong people, a people willing to work hard and get along with others, if we're accepted and given a chance. Maybe they learned that we're people who love culture. Even in the middle of the jungle, in these primitive conditions, we'd organize musical performances. In one barrack, we created a theater and performed plays. Writers wrote. Artists painted.

After being in Sosúa for a few years, we realized the need for formal education for the children, and I worked with some others to organize a school. I became a teacher, and later, the principal.

Antonia also taught at *Colegio Cristobel Colón*. We taught all the subjects in Spanish. We did have a teacher who taught Jewish religion, Jewish history, and Hebrew. The school was open to all, not just Jews. The school still operates today, I still visit, and I'm present at every graduation.

Maybe they learned that our values, our choices, our actions, are based upon *mitzvot*, our commandments. It's just who we are.

From this Jewish experiment, maybe they learned that we are survivors.

Chapter 3

And just like that, Leon Haube stopped. Three and a half hours had passed in an instant. He let out a low sigh and looked up; it was almost as if he'd forgotten I was there. His eyes were glazed, and he seemed exhausted.

As I checked my recorder, the bartender came over and helped Leon get up. They exchanged big hugs, and then the bartender gave me a warm, lingering embrace. A moment from my past swirled through me. I melted into him, and then clumsily let go. He grinned.

"Do you want me to join you?" he asked.

"Not now," I said. "But I'll be back."

"I know you will."

My mouth opened slightly, and out came a feeble attempt to utter anything remotely coherent. The bartender smiled and put his finger to my lips.

"Shhhh," he whispered.

My heart raced.

It took a long time to leave the pub; most of the patrons wanted to greet Leon. I snapped photos of him and his fans. What a rock star. When we arrived back at the house, his housekeeper stood in the doorway, ready to check on her employer and make sure her old friend was all right. She called him *Don* Haube, the ultimate sign of respect.

He laughed when the housekeeper suggested he take an afternoon nap. He said it was too late; if he took one now, he'd miss happy hour at the pub, where he spent every afternoon. I started to apologize. "I feel so bad that I messed up your daily routine …" Leon waved his hand as if to wipe away my guilt. The housekeeper's firm presence sent a clear message that it was time to leave.

Even though he was now a little shaky, he insisted on showing me the copy of his Uncle Alfred's guest book before I left. There were sketches and personal notes from the likes of Nina Kandinsky, Kurt Weill, and Erich Heckel. His eyes twinkled as he saw my jaw drop. While I looked through the book, he poured us both a drink. With a raise of his glass, he said, "Dark Dominican rum is the best rum in the world. Keeps you healthy and young." And a final "*¡Salud!*"

I didn't want to go. I took one last photo of him on his porch, in front of his warm, beautiful *casa*. He walked me out to the street, and a few children ran by. Without missing a beat, he shouted *¡Hola!* to them and they, too, gathered round. He reached in his pocket and passed out toffees—clearly a familiar routine—and a smile. Leon winked at me and said, "They love their *dulces*." After a moment, he murmured something else, more to himself than to me: "Just a small token of thanks."

He handed me a candy. We shook hands, and I asked if I could hug him. He smelled like a mix of rum and pipe smoke, and yes, coconut oil. He reminded me so much of my own father: his stature, his slightly slurred speech after a few "adult beverages," his generosity. Similar roots, different paths. I wondered what my dad's story would have been. If only I had taken the time to listen—while he still could remember.

I waved goodbye and called farewell to *Don* Haube and watched him go back inside. I hoped that he would collapse into a restful sleep, one filled with pleasant memories. Mostly, I hoped that our morning had not aroused too many bittersweet emotions.

I left the way we had come, down *Calle Pedro Clisante*, past the school, now named in honor of the great man who had founded it and the community. Its sign read:

Colegio Leon Haube
Fundada el en 1941
por la comunidad judae de sosúa

Underneath, it said:

Somos guardianes de los pasos que te conducen a un mundo mejor.
We are guardians of the steps that will lead to a better world.

I was lost in thought about all I'd just heard and felt. Instead of returning to the pub, which was straight ahead, I turned left at the corner. I needed some time to walk and think, my moving method of working through problems.

My earlier research had told me there were still a few of the other original settlers who had arrived shortly after Leon Haube had set up the transition. Besides him, only Mr. Reuben Katz, a car mechanic and salesman, still lived in Sosúa full-time, with an established business and extended family. Though I hadn't been able to reach him before I left Vermont, he was the other person I had hoped to interview that day. That interview would have to wait. I had too much on my mind, and I wanted to get a better feel for this town.

In the distance, there was the constant annoying buzz of the *motocicletas*, and even that far from the main road, the smell of gas fumes still consistently spewed from the *conchos* and *guaguas*. I passed the old original synagogue that had been turned into a Jewish museum commemorating the history of the town. The sign in front read:

Sosúa, a community born of pain and nurtured in love, must,
in the final analysis, represent the ultimate triumph of life.

I continued on, letting the ocean breeze guide me. I entered a neighborhood that consisted mostly of small shacks of plain cement blocks topped with zinc roofs, in classic Dominican

Republic style. The air was filled with the remnants of the cooling *arroz y frijoles*, rice and beans. I walked farther and farther, and down the road, I saw one compound quite different from the rest. The house rose above the others, with painted clapboards, a shingled roof intact, and a yard full of children's toys, yet neat and tidy. Beside the house was a garage—a rare commodity in small Dominican towns, never seen in the *barrios*—and the driveway was full of vehicles in different stages of repair. On one used car, a sign read *Coche usado para la venta Inf. 551-4299*.

I was drawn toward the compound, toward what I might find inside. As I approached, three typical young Dominican boys charged toward me, heading from the direction of *Colegio Leon Haube*, school books in their hands, backpacks swinging, a *futbal* at their feet. One child almost knocked me over, and, in the midst of his boyish escapades, he immediately turned back with a sincere, breathless *lo siento*. Such a sweet apology.

Kicking their *futbal* back and forth, they headed for home, past the colorful broken-down shacks. It could have been any small town on any Caribbean island, or in any African country. They were wearing the familiar bright yellow and navy school uniforms, laughing and teasing as they rushed by. Sweat beaded on their coal-black skin. These "burned Indians," *morenos, negros,* had their dark, coarse curls shorn short, avoiding the possibility of *pelo malo*. Bad hair. And on their heads, they wore *yarmulkes*.

Chapter 4

My head reeled from the cognitive dissonance, and from all Leon had shared. My stomach reeled from my liquid breakfast at the Britannia. After wandering around Sosúa a bit longer, I headed back to the pub to let my body settle, and to regroup. After all, I had told the bartender I'd be back.

He greeted me with another rum punch and a plate of *tostones.*

The waitress came over. "Hey, you keep that up, and I'm going to be out of a job," she chided. "He's just a big old flirt. And you're fresh meat. Don't worry about him."

I wasn't worried. I wasn't feeling much of anything. The rum had worked its magic, and my low tolerance made me very tolerant of this particular bar.

"You'll always have a job, Leta. How could I live without you?"

"See what I mean about him? Such a player," Leta said as she left to clean another table.

The warm, steaming fried plantains glistened with oily specks of salt and pepper. I nearly drooled, and shoved them in my mouth. Crisp, creamy bites played with my tongue. I hadn't realized how long it had been since my last meal: the cocktail peanuts I'd eaten on the plane.

"They'll soak up the booze," the bartender said. "You don't look too great."

"You look great," I slurred.

He grabbed my hand and pulled me to the bar. He introduced himself as Jamon, the J pronounced as in English, like in Joe. He spelled it Jamon, and then sounded it out: Juh-mihn.

fruit. The skin looked rotten, and when he scooped out the soft, brown pulp, I cringed.

"We call them *nispero*, but you might know them as medlars."

"Never heard of them. Not sure I want to taste them."

> *"I love to suck you out from your skins ...*
> *Wineskins of brown morbidity, ...*
> *Gods nude as blanched nut-kernels,*
> *Strangely, half-sinisterly flesh-fragrant*
> *As if with sweat,*
> *And drenched with mystery ...*
> *A kiss, and a vivid spasm of farewell, a moment's orgasm*
> *of rupture, ..."*

Hypnotized, I let him feed me. The custardy flesh was spicy, sweet, rich, and delicious. I groaned.

"D. H. Lawrence always has that effect." The tastes and smells Jamon offered were all intoxicating, but the true aphrodisiac was his mind.

My heart and brain were as full as my belly. We dozed off and on all night, swinging in his hammock. Jamon gently stroked my hair and rubbed my back. We never even kissed. In my frustrated contentment, I thought back many years ago to Ben, the boy I had met on the beach when I was still a virgin, and to Yakir, the first boy I ever loved. I met the two of them back-to-back when I was only sixteen. But now I was older—and clearly not a virgin—and I wanted to kiss this man. To be kissed. I wanted to be completely satiated.

"Not yet," he said.

It was still dark when the taxi arrived, with the same driver who had brought me to Sosúa. Just yesterday.

"Quick trip, *Señorita*," he said.

"Felt like a lifetime."

"I hope in a good way," Jamon said.

"In the best way possible."

We held hands through the window as the driver pulled away. A *merengue* blasted on the radio. I heard Jamon say one last thing before we had to let go.

"*Hasta luego.*"

Until then.

I was already smiling when I arrived at the airport, and saw that the first leg of my trip was on flight number 1937. Quite the year for Leon, and for Sosúa. When I boarded, I remembered the key to the Sosúa Palms Inn was still in my pocket; I'd grabbed my bag but forgotten to check out, and I hadn't even slept in the room. I also hadn't noticed that the room was number 37. The woman in the seat next to me gave me a polite nod when I laughed out loud. Hard to tell if I was giddy from the coincidence, from sleep deprivation, or from Jamon.

It didn't make sense that I could feel so at home at the Britannia. Bars had always held a negative association for me, and been a source of anguish. When I was a kid, Mom would drive me to the local bar, the one near the bus station, and send me in to find Daddy, to ask him to come home for dinner. Now. Please.

Middle-class Jewish dads were not supposed to be drunks. Good Jewish suburban moms didn't use their nice Jewish daughters to drag their inebriated fathers off their bar stools.

Sometimes, there'd be not one ounce of shame. He couldn't have cared less that I was there, leered at by his fellow derelicts, my innocent lungs filled with smoke, my ears filled with booze-induced grandiosity.

"Hi, Sweetie," Dad would gush. "This is my little girl. Isn't she the best?"

Other times, he'd bark at me, cheeks flushed, ire up. His eyes filled with disgust. All I wanted to do was cover my face and disappear: *see no evil*. I'd freeze, and then he'd turn on me.

"What the hell're you doing here? Can you believe this? Can't a man get some time to himself?"

I never knew which version of Daddy would show up.

I'd seen how much pain alcohol could cause, how out of control it made everyone. I know it sounds like something straight out of the Women's Christian Temperance Union, but that was my life. Because I was determined to get the upper hand, I made a conscious decision to walk into a club on my eighteenth birthday (which was still the drinking age), march up to the bar, and order a big tall glass of ... milk. I'd show them.

The fact that I was lactose intolerant—another Semitic affliction—and got sick to my stomach downing the milk, and the fact that no one else gave a shit about my so-called point, didn't make a difference to me. Long on principles, short on sagacity. I've avoided bars as much as possible since then. But yes, something felt different at the Britannia.

The trip back to Vermont took almost as long my entire stay in the DR. Like Vermonters say, "You can't get there from here."

It wasn't until I was an adult that I realized that my parents were pioneers of sorts. Instead of settling in the usual places that first generation Jewish Americans typically went—New York, New Jersey, Philadelphia, Los Angeles—Mom and Dad moved to Burlington, Vermont, not-so-affectionately referred to by the rest of our urban, ghettoized extended family as "Green Acres." The place to be.

I hated it that we lived so far from family. I missed my grandparents. We hardly ever visited. Mom was an only child, and Dad's younger sister Miriam was killed in a car crash when he was a high school senior, so he might as well have been an only child, as far as we were concerned. Not an uncle or aunt or cousin in sight, which just added to the disconnect. When we did visit the extended family, I never quite fit in. I had a deep pit in my gut when I saw my distant cousins hanging out; they seemed even closer than friends.

I didn't have the opportunity to develop those kinds of bonds. Jewish families are typically big on getting together for holidays. Lots of food, lots of affable arguing. But we'd never go see family, or even join other Jews in our community. If they didn't keep kosher—and hardly anyone we knew did—we couldn't eat at their house for holidays. Mom said it was "too much of a production" to have people over to our place.

She never admitted it was really about Dad. The *Haggadah* directs us: "Tonight, we drink four cups of wine." Nothing affable about Dad when he didn't stop at four. (The idea that the wine represents freedom, freedom that we seek in the four corners of the earth, freedom that must be guarded and shared, freedom to determine the course of our own lives, was an irony that did not escape my young mind.) So each *Rosh Hashana* or *Shabbat* or Passover, it was just the four of us. Crack open a jar of *gefilte* fish and call it a night.

Mom continued to insist that abiding by kosher laws was part of her covenant with G-d. It was okay to eat out at restaurants or bring pizza into the house. (*It's on paper plates.*) But we couldn't go to the Goldblatts for *Seder*, because they didn't keep kosher. Later, she wouldn't come to my place to be with Gregg and Nebi and me. And Dad just went along with her *mishugas*. No amount of arguing could convince Mom that it was better to share special occasions with loved ones than hold firm to hypocritical beliefs that left you alone and lonely. Guess everybody does what works for them.

I longed for family, but on the rare occasions we were together—mostly funerals—something was missing. Only I didn't know what.

I also longed to be to be in a real city, with other people like me. With big museums. With more than one newspaper. Maybe I just longed to feel like I belonged somewhere.

Whenever anyone asked Dad the equivalent of "What's a nice Jewish family like yours doing in a place like this?" he had his set, prepared explanation: that he had moved Mom up north so they could breathe fresh air and see the stars. So they could get away from horns and fumes.

Then he'd joke, "So now we get woken by honking geese, and we have to close our windows when they spread the cow shit." The first time I heard that line, I was confused by his words, by his tone.

"But Dad, I thought you wanted to be here."

"Oh, I do. About as much as I wanted you."

And then he'd laugh. I had no words to defend myself, only tears.

"Come on, Polly. You're so oversensitive."

I'd bite the inside of my cheek. I became accustomed to the iron taste that filled my mouth.

Dad loved his sarcasm. I knew it wasn't "just being funny." Miss Sullivan, my seventh-grade guidance counselor, explained that sarcasm comes from the Greek root *sarkasmos*, "to tear at the flesh." The next time Dad tried to dismiss me with his standard defense, I finally found the words.

"I'm not oversensitive. You're under-kind."

He didn't buy it. "What a bunch of psychobabble." One of his favorite expressions. And I never bought his cutting form of affection and his pat justification: "I'm your dad, for G-d's sake." Like that was enough.

Just because he was my dad didn't mean he liked me. Mom didn't, either. And I wasn't just being oversensitive. Well, maybe I was. Sensitive to the way they looked at me, and our family's isolation in Vermont. Something just wasn't right.

On my flight back from the Dominican Republic, what wasn't right was the coincidence/twisted fate/axiom that continued to bubble and spurt up, as if from an underground spring. I was reading a magazine piece about Lindbergh. Nothing out of the ordinary for an in-flight article. It started off with the usual descriptions of their horrific experience, the abduction, the botched police work. But then the article went on about the details of the kidnapping trial, how it had been such a mess of a media circus that Congress did all it could to create a ban on photography in courtrooms. The law finally went into effect five years after the kidnapping. In 1937.

"Come on!" I said out loud, a little too loudly.

The woman sitting next to me looked down, trying to pretend we weren't close enough to rub shoulders.

"No, you don't understand. Thirty-seven. It's everywhere: the CCC, Leon Haube ..." I tried to explain, but it was like I was in a bad *Twilight Zone* episode. The more emphatic I became, the more uncomfortable she seemed. I giggled just to let her know I wasn't entirely serious. She leaned over as far away from me as she could until she was dangling over the aisle. She finally excused herself and left, managing to vacate her seat for the remainder of the flight despite several warnings of "Please return to your seat and fasten your seatbelts." And despite lots of turbulence, I never did see her again.

Rudyard Kipling once said that the two most beautiful sunsets in the world were over Lake Tanganyika and Lake Champlain. As my flight from the Dominican Republic finally landed in Burlington, I was reminded how gorgeous the scenery was on the "west coast of New England." Something I could always count on.

I could also count on the fact that Gregg would be there to pick me up. He owed me.

Gregg was waiting at the baggage claim holding a sign. .

"Miss Shugenah? Car for Miss Shugenah," he shouted, pretending to be a driver looking for his passenger.

Mishugenah. Yiddish for crazy woman.

"Hysterical," I said, and rolled my eyes.

Then I smiled. Kind of adorable that he had gone to all that trouble.

I gave him a hug, and he held on a little longer than usual. It was awkward, but he did smell good. When I backed off, he had that same grin that I had seen on Jamon's face. Were my diminishing perimenopausal hormones a turn-on, sending a pheromonal message that there was no longer any chance of me getting pregnant? Sex for fun, not for profit. Who knows what motivates men?

Whatever Gregg and I had gone through, whatever had allowed us to drift apart, the sex—as infrequently as it happened—was always damn good. We might not have been able to connect on who should keep the checkbook balanced or whose turn it was to do the laundry, but we always connected on an intimate level, both sensually and philosophically. From that first debate on Sufism—mysticism or metabolism?—we were stellar at sharing an intellectual, rational worldview. And at sharing our primal passion. We just weren't so good at making breakfast together without someone's feelings getting hurt. Who knew toast could get so complicated?

It is said that when people say, "It's not about the money," it usually is about the money.

I suppose it wasn't really about the toast. I resented Gregg, and blamed him for messing up my plans.

When I was a kid, the first story I ever wrote was a fictional diary entry of how I dreamed my life would turn out. Every once in awhile, I would pull out the fading loose-leaf paper and reread it—a niggling memento of where I thought my path would lead me.

> *I'm on the muddy bank of the middle Zambezi, ankle-deep in the river's turbid waters, my body drenched in forest rains mixed with spray from the tumbling rapids. I'm not sure if my persistent chills are due to fear of what I cannot see below the surface or a fever from something that has bitten me ... or maybe from something I have bitten. I try to steady my hand to get that perfect shot of the tigerfish, a goliath with razor-sharp teeth, the one the Losi people call Mbilintu: frightful, unknown monster. The school is swimming so close, I can feel their ferocity through the water as they move together in a mercurial wave.*

I have to get the shot soon. Before the late-afternoon light fades and while the shadows are just right, allowing the sun to gently kiss the tigerfish's liquid sterling scales.

If it's too bright, the reflection will be blinding.

I can still hear the drumming that signals the Losi: time to leave the floodplain, time to retreat to the highlands. Every year, the Kuomboka ceremony takes place, but I'm the first one to have had the honor of capturing this ancient, awe-inspiring ritual.

When I'm done here, I'll pack up my equipment and head out, ready to trek past soaring vertical walls of basalt and arrive at Victoria Falls before the end of the month. If my blisters allow me. If my awful cramps let up. I've never been in so much discomfort. And I've never been happier.

I imagined and wrote many stories like that one. Not too shabby for a little kid. (I don't really remember, but I must have had our white and green, gold-embossed 1963 *World Book Encyclopedia* set handy.) The plan was that I'd grow up, go to school, and become an award-winning photojournalist—*National Geographic*, here I come.

I made my first pinhole camera when I was about eight. The cardboard inserts from Dad's dry-cleaned shirts were just the right size. We lived in a new suburban development, and I'd go into the nearby vacant lots, the ones that hadn't yet been covered with raised ranch style number three, brick siding instead of wood, and a lawn thick enough to erase the owner's memories of the grey urban past they thought they'd escaped. I'd take my notepad, invisible ink pen, and Dad's Leicaflex (he had bought me a Brownie Fiesta, but I quickly outgrew it) along with my pinhole. I took artsy shots of weeds growing out of the asphalt. Or action shots of our pet tabby stalking crickets.

I used to pretend my neighbor, Mr. Goldblatt, was a tribal chief. I wanted to enter the *LIFE* photography contest with the shot I got of Mr. Goldblatt kissing Mrs. Goldblatt in her floral muumuu—a real aboriginal moment. Mom wouldn't let me.

One evening, I hid behind the fence and took pictures of Chief Goldblatt grilling lamb chops in his low-slung cabana shorts. He caught me snapping the camera and chased after me, yelling, "Anna Stern! Get the hell out of here!" I tripped and broke my front tooth on the concrete curb and went home limping, proud to show off my hardcore field-correspondent wounds.

Mark was ready to go kick some butt, and I was ready to follow him—but Dad held him back. I couldn't tell if Dad was angrier with Mr. Goldblatt or me. Mark did a clumsy, juvenile war dance, and the harder Mom tried not to laugh, the louder her snorts became. She looked at him with complete adoration, and, as usual, he didn't seem to notice. Mom was oblivious that I was hurt, but it didn't bother me.

Blood was still dripping from my chin when I told them, "I'm glad it happened." And I was. That was when Mom started calling me Polly: short for Pollyanna, Anna being my real name. It wasn't until years later that I realized she was using the name of that sweet, optimistic little girl in a pejorative sense. Dad gave me a copy of the classic for my eleventh birthday, the year I was the same age as the fictional Pollyanna. That night, I braided my hair and put Mom's eyeliner on my face as freckles. Mom, Dad, and Mark were sitting at the table when I theatrically marched into the kitchen misquoting Porter: "When you look for the bad in mankind, expecting to find it, you surely will."

Right on cue, Mom replied, "When you look for the good in mankind, expecting to find it, you surely won't."

"Oh, Lainie, that's not nice," Dad said.

"It's true, though."

"Mom," Mark admonished. She'd listen to him.

In true Pollyanna fashion, I ran over and hugged Mom. "It's okay. I know you don't mean it."

She didn't hug me back.

The gate to international adventure opened when I saw Gregg Harmon sitting across the room munching on a branch of elderberries. It was the first day of Intro Anthro class. Freshman year. He was an archaeology major, and I knew at once that we'd travel the world together, Gregg working on digs in exotic locations while I wrote articles and took photographs, publishing scholarly pieces about undiscovered cultures and vanishing species.

Turned out Gregg and I did fall in love. It also turned out that he focused his studies on New England prehistory. The gate slammed shut; there'd be no Turkish ruins in our future.

Instead of exploring the world, we moved two towns over from where I had grown up in northern Vermont. I ended up writing for our community newspaper and local magazines. I wrote articles about the town's water treatment facility, the Walmart appeal process, and the high school grad who earned a perfect SAT score and was accepted to Harvard—the first in our town. Once in a while, I covered the harder news about drug busts and town clerks embezzling funds. Mostly, I contributed human interest stories: stories about other people's stories. About what lies behind the stories. I'd always preferred to fashion facts into a storytelling framework. Maybe that was considered soft news, but I found that it was the twisting tales, the truly personal ones, that readers could most relate to, that grabbed them and made them think. That made them feel.

Gregg and I got married, and I gave birth to our daughter. We named her Nebi. Nebi Lintowogan. Abenaki for *song of the water*.

I wanted to name her Miriam after the aunt I'd never known, but Gregg suggested we name her in honor of our Abenaki neighbors, the People of the Dawn.

"Come on. It's just like the Jewish 'Song of the Sea,' which was sung by Moses, and also sung by Miriam," he said.

"How nice. So we're really honoring my people, the People of the Desert."

After talking it through, we both were concerned that naming her Nebi could be considered an act of cultural appropriation.

But then I remembered that *Nebi'im* are the Jewish prophets, so I convinced myself it was okay to name her after them. Anyway, I'd always felt like a member of the lost tribe. Maybe because I'd always been drawn to Native American stories, particularly Abenaki stories, like the ones about Grandmother Woodchuck, who raised Gluskabe—the liar—after his mother's death. This wise old woodchuck giving her adopted grandson guidance was much more compelling than those old Jewish folklore stories of the *dybbuk*, a disembodied, clinging spirit.

Maybe it was because I related to what the Abenaki had gone through during the 1930s eugenics movement—which, unfortunately was far too similar to what the Jews had suffered at the same time.

Over time, I'd come to appreciate that, like Native American traditions, many Jewish rituals are also nature-based, and the Jewish calendar revolves around the phases of the moon. *Tu b'shevat* honors trees; *Sukkot* reminds us of our agricultural roots and the time of the harvest. I thought it was regrettable that these celebrations had changed into their modern American form. My disdain for attending services grew as I witnessed congregants using the holidays as an excuse to wear designer clothes to Temple. The further away we moved from nature, the more we forgot the origin of our prayer.

Thankfully, our rabbi focused the congregation on the deeper purpose of Judaism, from social justice to ethical behavior. Nebi would come home from Hebrew school excited about working in the community garden and raising crops for the food shelf. I was convinced she first caught the travel bug when the rabbi showed his Israeli slides, especially the one of him sandboarding the Negev dunes.

When my marriage to Gregg started to crumble, there was no defined break, but rather a series of sloughings-off, like neglected dry skin you forgot to moisturize. We decided to try therapy. Therapy wasn't going to help, but I figured it wouldn't hurt. And I knew I'd feel guilty ending our marriage if I hadn't at least made an effort.

It was pretty clear what the problems were. He was away on digs for weeks at a time, and I was so focused on Nebi that I forgot to focus on his needs—or my own, for that matter. As the joke goes, archaeologists make the best husbands, because the older you get, the more interested in you they become. In reality, archaeologists are the professionals with the second-highest rates of alcoholism, suicide, and divorce. (Dentists are the first.)

I must've looked like I'd had an instant brow lift when the therapist gave me a pencil and a handout—something along the lines of "Common Characteristics of Adult Children of Alcoholics (ACOAs)." I glared at Gregg, who had his arms crossed and a smirk on his face. That smirk.

"Why the hell are you looking at me like that?"

"I'm not looking at you any way, Polly. You're so oversensitive."

I'd been dealing with his passive-aggressive disdain for years. I turned to the therapist, expecting her to acknowledge that Gregg's grin was a vicious, arrogant attack, and waiting for backup. The two of them just sat there. The sun streamed in on the wood floors, highlighting the dust bunnies that had gotten caught on the bottoms of the chair legs. I realized it would probably be best if I did not bend over to pick up the muck, even though that was what I really felt the need to do at that moment. My teeth were buzzing as I looked down at the paper.

After checking eight out of ten of the self-assessed ACOA personality traits, I finally looked up. Gregg had unfolded his arms. He was looking down at his filthy work boots. His sneer had softened. The therapist suggested I go to a twelve-step meeting.

"You've got to be kidding me. I hardly even drink—maybe a little wine with dinner, but that's all. What do you mean that not everyone 'overreacts to changes over which they have no control' or 'constantly seeks approval and affirmations from other people' or 'is extremely loyal, even in the face of evidence that the loyalty is undeserved?'"

"Studies show that ACOAs are at increased risk for a whole host of negative outcomes, including depression, low self-esteem, self-destructive behavior, and relational difficulties," the therapist explained. "And having an alcoholic father often correlates to lower marital intimacy."

What a bunch of psychobabble.

"Pol, this is really good. It explains a lot. Just think about it."

And I did. As you've probably figured out, feelings are not my strong suit. But thinking, well ... that I am very good at.

Chapter 5

The carousel at the Burlington baggage claim spit my bag out. Gregg grabbed it, and we headed toward the parking garage. Such a good ex-husband. Even though I'd only been gone two days, he caught me up on the weather and the latest road repairs—two big topics in Vermont. There are only three seasons in Vermont: winter, mud season, and the very short season for getting road work done.

As we left the airport, I said, "It still cracks me up that it's called Burlington *International* Airport. It's not much larger than the tiny one I left in remote Puerto Plata."

"It's one of the busiest in New England, outside of Boston." Gregg, the voice of reason.

"I don't think any international flights actually land here."

"No, they do, from Canada."

"If you call that international."

We kept walking, and I pointed to the air traffic control tower.

"Are you even sure they have real air traffic controllers? It's probably just an empty old water tower. I bet the pilots have to wait to use the runways till the cows have crossed."

"I'm positive they have air traffic control, and real ground control, too."

Gregg was being as patient as possible. Then he told me the route he was about to take, to avoid the detours. I put on my best Yankee accent.

"I'm a Vermontah; I'll do what I wantah."

Gregg looked at me in a way only he could. It was a rare hot, steamy day in northern Vermont, but I shivered. He was the only

one besides our daughter Nebi who could so easily remind me
how much like my dad I had become.

Before taking me home, Gregg was adamant about getting me
the copy of an Alzheimer's study he had forgotten at his house.

"Can you drop it off later? Or email it?"

I just wanted to get home.

"It'll be quick."

I was too tired to argue.

His place was a two-room log cabin that he had first moved
into when we had separated. When it was his week, Nebi had
the bedroom, and Gregg slept on the futon in the combination
kitchen/living room. The bathroom was an outhouse. He would
have just gone in the woods if it hadn't been for Nebi. There was
an outside shower for warm weather, and a portable tub for bathing inside. At least he had put in running water and a backup
generator for electricity. I'd kept the family home, so Nebi was
able to ride bikes and play hoops with neighborhood friends in
her suburban life with me, and chop wood and forage fiddleheads
and mushrooms with her dad. The upside of joint custody. (I could
just hear Nebi: "Sure Ma, it was real fun for me.")

"Come in. I'll make tea." So much for being quick.

I lay down on the old slider in his screened-in porch, surrounded by shelves covered with pieces of driftwood, rocks,
arrowheads, bones, feathers, and bark.

"Remember your late notes?" I teased.

Gregg used to send Nebi to elementary school with notes
handwritten on sheets of birch bark. "*Please excuse Nebi for …*" We
laughed about the time the principal had called Gregg to tell him
how "unique" his notes were, and asked him to stop by her office.
Apparently, she had the hots for the mysterious *Indiana Jones* dad.
I could relate.

Gregg went to make us tea, and I must have fallen asleep.
When I woke up, he was rubbing my feet. I moaned because it felt
so good. Somehow, his hands moved up my leg, and we ended up
having sex. It had been a while for both of us. It was raw and fast,
and there was no kissing on the mouth. It felt like a perfunctory

act. A necessary outlet—nothing more, nothing less. I tried to convince myself. Gregg wasn't acting like he needed any convincing. The practical rationalization period lasted about as long as the sex before guilt set in. Even though I had just met Jamon, and we hadn't even kissed, I felt like I had been unfaithful. What an idiot. Any way you looked at it.

As Gregg drove me back to town, I told him about Sosúa and Leon Haube. I was surprised he hadn't known about the Évian Conference; Gregg was the smartest person I knew. I went on and on about my new 37 mindset. How now that I had that number on my mind, things kept appearing, referencing the number or the year.

"It's like that time we were going to buy a truck. Remember, we were thinking of a Toyota pickup? I wanted a red one. Everywhere we went, we saw Toyota pickups. Red ones. Someone even gave Nebi a onesie that had red 4Runners printed all over it."

"We have such cool, nonsexist friends."

"No, but really, you know what I mean? It's like all of a sudden, headlines and people keep mentioning 1937. But they're not coincidences."

"Okay, I thought you stopped smoking the *gange* when you got pregnant. Please tell me you didn't try some in the DR."

"Very funny."

"Polly, it's just your reticular activating system."

"Oooookay."

"We have a bundle of nerves in our brain stem that connects our subconscious from our conscious parts of the brain. It filters unnecessary things out and brings what we're looking for to light. Like red trucks. Also, has it occurred to you that this year is the seventieth anniversary of 1937?"

Count on Gregg to always point out the facts. Captain Blatant.

"So, my dear ex-wife who lives in fantasyland, maybe that's why it keeps coming up. Like there was just that HBO special about King Edward abdicating the throne in 1936 so he could marry Wally Simpson—in 1937."

"See, there's another one. So freakin' romantic."

"No way I would've given up my throne."

"And that, dear ex-husband, is why we're no longer married."

Gregg chuckled and I snorted, which made us both laugh even harder. It was moments like these, when witnessed by Nebi, that would prompt something like, "I don't understand. Why'd you and Daddy break up?"

Break down was more like it. Neither Gregg nor I had a good way to explain. Our different versions of why we had divorced were a mixture of fact, feelings, and fallacies. Mingled histories, self-imposed hurts, thoughtless words, and mostly inattention to each other and our different perspectives, all ending up in a Vermont Family Court Final Order and Decree of Divorce.

I was hoping Gregg would idle just long enough for me to get out. It had been a few long days of traveling and writing, and this afternoon of sex and latent regrets had only drained me more. Instead, he drove into my driveway and turned the car off.

"How's Mark doing?" he asked.

I grunted. As spent as I was, I didn't want to think about my brother, let alone talk about him.

"Still with Stephen?"

I nodded yes. Once.

"You two still on bad terms?"

I stared right through him.

He shook his head and asked, "Well, then, how's your dad doing?"

I shrugged my shoulders. I just wanted to get out of the car and into my fortress.

Again, he shook his head. This time, he added a derisive snort. "Okaaaaay, I guess I won't bother trying to talk about Nebi."

"What about Nebi?"

"Nothing, really. I just haven't talked to her in awhile."

"Maybe you should try a little harder."

"Whoa. I'm just going to chalk up that snarky comment to jet lag."

"I haven't changed time zones."

"You sure changed mood zones."

"Sorry. I'm just kind of wiped."

Gregg leaned over to give me a kiss goodbye, and must have noticed my eyes twitch as my moat became a little deeper, guarding myself from any more of his intimate intrusion.

"Well, Pol, I hope your 37 issues resolve themselves. Although maybe you have a few more than 37 …"

Hand on the door handle, I was ready to bolt when Gregg slapped the dashboard.

"What the fuck?" I shrieked, startled.

"Holy crap, now you have me doing it! You know that archaeology conference I went to in L.A. last month? One of the workshops was on findings from a dig of the Dani people of Papua New Guinea, and—"

"What, so *now* you're interested in foreign cultures?"

"Can you please just shut up for a minute? They described this place, this village, how they pieced together what happened there."

"What might have happened. Despite what all of you archaeologists believe, and what all of your artifacts point to, you can't be positive of what happened." I grinned my dismissive grin. There. Not in the mood for an anthropology lesson. Sex and academia. The only ways he knew how to communicate with me.

"Polly, do you want to hear it or not?" He exhaled and stared out the windshield.

I looked at his gloomy face and felt bad for snapping. "Look, if it's that important to you, tell me."

"The scenario … it took place in 1937."

"Okay. Now I'm listening."

TAIM BILONG TUMBUNA

BY P.A. STERN

The two naked children battled with ironwood sticks they had taken from the firewood pile. Their little arms could barely lift the larger branches; the boughs were as heavy and unwieldy as a squealing pig. As they played, the sticks collided in the sky, then struck the dry, compact, rocky ground. The clashes formed tiny mountains and scratched wild drawings of curling lines and sandy wisps in the earth. If the children had been flying above, like hawks, they would have looked down and seen the intricate patterns they had made, and they would have smiled.

Like the other villagers, these two cousins were born with bright smiles on their faces, filled with gladness for the first sights of the shining sun, broad leaves rustling in the winds, and high, distant mountain peaks. Joyous in the ways of their ancestors that they carried with them into this world.

The cousins left their stick battle and went to see what the Big Man was doing. When they found him, Chief Wamilik was sitting with nine of the ten men whose families lived together deep in the lush Baliem Valley. The Chief's brother, Guba, was at his right side. The men wore only their penis sheaths, made from gourds the women had grown. The Big Man's sheath was the largest one of the group. The men were also covered in a mixture of pig fat and black soot. Some adorned themselves with *cenderawasih* feathers, and others with cowrie-shell necklaces. Chief Wamilik had a very large, stark white boar tusk through his nose. When he let them, the village children would jump up and try to touch the tusk, giggling in the attempt. Now was not such a time; there was business to be done.

The men were sitting and telling stories when Yali entered the village gate, passed the watchtower, and headed toward the story circle. *Nayak lak,* they called, welcoming him. The cousins ran toward Yali and tried to grab his fishing gear. Yali swatted the children away like so many annoying fruit flies.

Carrying his bounty of nine piranhas and four bass along with his bamboo fishing spears, Yali walked proudly through the village. The other children ran toward him, trying to steal the fish, to nab the spears. They wanted to help present the catch, but Yali did not want their help. Yali laughed at them and pushed them onto the ground. They fell and bounced up, as only small children can do, covered with dust and full of happy shrieks, ready at once to continue their pesky chase.

The men watched the comical procession and laughed along. They were humored by the children's persistence, but mostly excited about the catch. Protein was always a rare commodity in their lives, and Yali was their best fisherman. The men and the children watched intently as Yali laid out his fish. He had been gone since before dawn, making the long trek down to the river. In a few years, the children would be old enough to accompany him on his fishing expeditions. A while ago, another of their tribe, Kardi, one of the elder males, had been their prized fisherman, but he had ventured far down the mountain to the lowland salt lakes. Eventually, his daring caught up with him, and he came down with the sickness. The bad mosquitoes did not fly as high as their high mountain valley, so their people were protected there. Kardi had wanted to provide for his village, and paid the ultimate price for his bravery.

When he died, his wife, in her grief, covered herself with ashes and yellow clay. She then did as her mother and mothers had done before her, and used a bamboo blade to cut off the first joint of one finger. She was already missing the tip of one finger, from when she lost her third baby from the sucking-dry that comes with diarrhea, and another from when her father had died. Like all women in her village, her hands were carved up—rough, irregular peaks like the mountain range that surrounded them.

The children liked to touch the females' smooth stubs. One child would run up behind a mother or grandmother or aunt and grab her hands. The woman would pretend to be unable to pull her hands away. In reality, these women were strong as cyclones from all the hard work they did: gathering ironwood, hoeing the soil, carrying babies and pigs and harvested sweet potatoes in the string net *nokens* they draped over their heads and hung down their backs. As one child held the woman captive, another child would then begin to pet the finger stub, tickling it around and around in mesmerizing circles.

Sometimes the cheekier children would suck on the stubs, like the piglets that often suckled on the women's dark brown nipples when a sow had died or been killed. The woman would giggle and tolerate the children for as long as she wanted, pretending to be annoyed; and then her face would open into a huge smile, and she would pull their hands away easily, swatting the playful imps away. The children would run off in joyful laughter, their happy song reflecting the women's cheerful cackles.

Once the children left their sides, the women continued their never-ending work. Today, they had already toiled in the sweet potato fields, bending over in the heat and humidity, hoeing the soil with stone blades, using the fire-hardened digging stick to harvest, and carrying heavy *nokens* full of potatoes back to the village. On top of all of that, tonight one of the girls would be honored with marriage. For this special occasion, a pig would be sacrificed and then cooked by the women. The sacred pig feast.

Before the big celebration, the fish Yali had caught needed to be prepared and cooked. The Big Man had already distributed them. Each of the nine families received one fish, and the Big Man kept the other three; one of his six wives would cook them up and make a stew for everyone in the village to share as part of the wedding feast. The other women wrapped their fish in banana leaves and steamed them. While the fish steamed, the pig roast preparations began.

The pit was dug, and filled with water and reeds and banana leaves. Then smooth stones that had been heated in the fire were laid on top. As this layer heated, the men appeared in full ceremonial warrior gear. They covered their naked bodies in pig fat and rubbed on black, tar-like patches. They wore headdresses and assorted penis gourds, some with feathers, others with tufts of fur. The Big Man's headgear was decorated with bird of paradise feathers, plumes so colorful and bright they seemed to sing as they danced in the breeze.

He also wore a wide panel made of cowrie shells that hung down the front of his chest. It had been given to him by the chief of a neighboring village, the same chief whose son was to marry one of their girls tonight, and who, along with his villagers, had just arrived here to join *bakar batu*, the underground baked-rock pig feast.

The men from the other village wore similar dress. The women wore nothing but short skirts woven from orchid fibers. Some had extra flaps of cloth braided from grasses and other leafy materials, or seeds strung on threads hung around their abdomens. The women from the other village carried their *nokens*, heavily laden with their own harvest and offerings for their neighbors. Everyone's teeth and lips were stained red from the *buai*—the betel nut they chewed constantly, both for the mind-altering effect of the nut and because it quelled their hunger.

Tonight, the visiting chief brought with him a dowry of three young pigs; their squeals were masked by the mocking, delighted squeals of the children. As soon as they arrived, the dancing and singing began, honoring the wedding couple and giving thanks to the pig spirit. Two strong warriors, one from each village, held up the biggest pig, and Yali, who was in good favor due to his recent catch, had the privilege of shooting the pig with an arrow through the heart. After it was killed, the pig was set on the fire to burn off its hair. It was then cut open, placed on the roasting pit, and covered with more leaves, many sweet potatoes, and more water.

When it was cooked, the Big Man distributed the meat, first to the other chief and then to the rest of the men. The women were given the intestines and other internal organs. Everyone filled their bellies with the roast pig and sweet potatoes. After they ate, Chief Wamilik was offered a special gift from the visiting villagers; they had gathered baskets of sago palm grubs and brought them for this auspicious occasion. The Big Man distributed the grubs to everyone's cries of *wah, wah, wah!* Thank you! The children screamed with glee as they chomped down on this rare, squishy, delicious treat.

The last time these two villages had been together was on the fighting grounds after the last battle. Out walking from the potato gardens, one of Guba's wives was abducted by the other tribe. The Big Man immediately called up his best warriors. Armed with spears and bows and arrows, the warriors covered themselves in clay and soot, a sign of ferocity. Invoking fear like living ghosts, they attacked the other village. The shouting and chanting began, and a short battle ensued. One warrior received a superficial wound and bled, red dripping over his grey-clay skin, tears forming paths over his soot-covered face.

Fortunately, there were no fatalities that time, and the battle ended quickly. The real reason was that a snake had been spotted in the field, the only thing that these brave warriors feared. Guba's wife was returned unharmed, and the victory singing began. Over the years, different villages would battle. Many warriors were lost. Sometimes, the battles were brutal; sometimes the dead were eaten along with the celebratory pigs. One month, the villages would socialize, the next month they would fight. The cycles of battles had carried on as long as time: to avenge the ghosts of slain villagers and to prove the warriors were complete as men. The battles were an important part of life in this sacred valley. They were the only time the children did not laugh or smile.

The wedding pig feast ended, and the chief's son left with his new bride, followed by the rest of their tribe. All headed through the jungle paths, lit by the clear, bright, blithe moon. After the guests were gone, the village men went into their *honai*, and the women and children went into their own *honai*.

The men sat in their hut around their fire, and played ancient melodies on their bamboo flutes as they beat their wooden *garamut* drums. They told stories of other feasts, of past wars, of the times before, and they joked about the visitors. The Big Man left the smoke-filled hut for a moment to walk around the village and make sure the lookout tower and fences were secure, that the women were all inside their huts, that the baked rocks were cooled off, and to look up at the sky. There, he spoke to the free wind, their Creator. He prayed for his people to have freedom from life's hardships: hunger, pain, illness. He spoke to the wind and he spoke to his ancestors, still living among them. He knew, because there is no air and no wind in Heaven, that the ancestors remained on Earth, together, forever. Spirits of the wind.

From the other *honai*, he heard the children's laughter and the women scolding them to go to sleep, then erupting into laughter themselves. The women worked hard from dawn to dark, and the children played hard. So much work and so much laughter throughout the day made sleep come easily; their hut soon filled with smoke and quiet.

As the combined merriment finally faded, the Big Man looked around one last time, and noticed the sparkling stars above reflected by the glow worms shimmering in the deep, dark rainforest surrounding the clearing that was their village, their home. He smiled. The last of the flute's notes dissolved into the dreams of the night, but the drummer's beat continued, as it would for a while longer, echoing the beating of their sleep breath, the rhythm of the jungle, transmitting secret codes to the other villages sharing this valley, and soothing the hearts of their ancestors. It was the beat of this valley, the heart of the island.

It had never occurred to them that there was more than this life they led, the same life their ancestors had led from before time. The Big Man—and all of his tribe—had never once been to the coast on this island they inhabited, the one known by others as *Papua New Guinea*; they had never seen the ocean surrounding them, or partaken in all of its bounty. They did not know that the largest butterfly in all the world lived not far from them, a butterfly so beautiful it would rival even their cherished bird of paradise, a bird with colors so intense it seemed to flicker and pulsate, wings as big as a warrior's head.

They did not know they used to be something called a *colony* of a land named *Germany*, but that they were now, in a time known as 1937, governed by someplace called *Australia*, under something called a *League of Nations Mandate*. From their vantage point, obscured by mountain walls, the Big Man—and all of his tribe—had heard unfamiliar, distant noises, but had never met the source of these mysterious sounds. They were unaware that a few months ago, their island had been the last place anyone had ever seen a woman named Amelia Earhart, and that in just a few months' time, they would hear the strange, frightening sounds of Richard Archbold's PBY-2 Catalina seaplane flying overhead, and they would look up, and he would look down, and everything would change.

They did not know that soon after, another man would fall out of the sky with a huge flapping cloth like a cloud to help him drift down, and come to their valley to teach and to preach the ways of others, or that people called the *Japanese* would soon occupy their lands, and then be defeated by another tribe called the *Americans*. Or that those people, as well as others from far away, would take what was not theirs, digging deep from within their mountains, their land.

It did not occur to the Big Man—or any of his tribe—that soon, there would no longer be just *mili*, black and grey and shades and dark colors, or *mola*, white and light colors, but they would be shown too many other names for how they were supposed to see their world. The smiles and the laughter would become less frequent. It would no longer be *Taim Bilong Tumbuna*, the time of the ways of their ancestors, the time before the white man came.

Chapter 6

By the time Gregg left, it was midnight. I had been up for thirty straight hours, other than the short, deep naps after sex—both times. I took a shower and fell asleep, and rose into dreams of fireflies and drums and castles, of Gregg and Jamon, of delightful laughter and mournful laments. When I awoke, my brain was in a sunrise fog, with bits of bright clarity softened in the haze. I lay in bed and tried to recollect the images and make sense of the stories, to discern what had been real from what I had dreamed. Before I opened my eyes, the last thing I saw, or maybe felt, was that the moat had dried up, and there were footprints in the dust.

I thought the ringing was the faint strains of bamboo flutes until I heard my voice. My outgoing message. "You've reached me. I'll call you back as soon as possible. There and back again …" And then my laughter—a little too shrill and a lot too forced, as Nebi liked to remark.

"Mom, are you seriously quoting Tolkien? On your answering machine?"

By the last trimester, Gregg had been halfway through reading *The Hobbit* out loud—to my belly. It was no surprise that Nebi had been born with pointy ears and hairy feet, like a little Bilbo Baggins. Fortunately, the hair fell off after a few weeks. We continued to read to her each night, all snuggled up, comfortable, belonging one to another. Until Gregg left.

My fog was lifting just as Gregg's voice imposed itself on the answering machine. "Hey Polly. Just wanted to check in on you. You seemed a little off last night. Maybe I filled your head with one too many thirty-sevens. Just to make it worse, you know what I thought of? The Green Monster is thirty-seven feet tall. Now that's important stuff. Oh, and listen, um, I kind of forgot to give you the article about that new Alzheimer's treatment out of Dartmouth. I'll just email it to you. I'll cc your dad's nurse. And Mark, too. Well, uh, give me a call if you want to … get together. And by the way, you do realize *The Hobbit* was written in 1937."

I hadn't realized. Of all the books and all the dates.

When the email arrived, it was nothing new. I already knew about the Dartmouth treatment. More false hope in a prescription bottle. It was nice of Gregg, though, to think of us, to try to help. He and Dad were close. I didn't like to admit it, but they had a lot in common. (Yeah, yeah, ACOAs are often attracted to men just like their daddies, to fulfill expectations that they are not worthy of love, *blah*, *blah*, *blah*. It was a lot simpler than that.) They bonded over baseball, even though Gregg was a die-hard member of the Red Sox nation, and Dad was a Mets fan. And, in their own ways, they had in common a pure dedication and devotion to their daughters. It just took me too long to figure that one out.

It was hard to accept, given our history. Also hard to accept what had happened to my dad. When Dad wasn't drinking, he was the sharpest one in the family. Even though I didn't have much interest in listening to him, I knew he had a keen mind. And now look at him. Ever since last summer, when Mom died, he'd gone deeper and deeper into a state somewhere between whimsy and bewilderment. As hard as it used to be to talk to him, I now had no idea what to do, what to make of him. Maybe he didn't mind what was happening to him. Maybe it was like being on a permanent high, something he used to seem to desire over anything else. Over anyone else.

Amazing what a screwed-up family we were.

Dad had been a successful businessman. He'd owned Selco's, the only department store in town that had an elevator. He was on the Chamber of Commerce, and respected in his trade. It wasn't just his associates who appreciated Dad. Waiters, in particular, loved to see Dad coming. When he'd had a few Seven and Sevens, he'd tip real big. It didn't take much to get the job done.

Mom had been the tightwad, and it killed her when he'd hand out twenties for a two-buck drink. They were both first-generation Americans who'd grown up in the shadow of the Holocaust, post-Depression, poor as dirt. Mom liked to remind us that she had to mix ketchup with water to make tomato soup for lunch.

Even after they moved up in the world and bought their nice house in the suburbs, she had kept that Depression-era mentality. She reused tea bags, folded tin foil, and gave us juice in those little glass jars that shrimp cocktail came in. (Because we kept kosher, she'd sneak down to the basement to eat the Sau-Sea shrimp when she was dieting. I suppose G-d doesn't check the cellar.)

Mom never got comfortable with her new status. They could afford costly jewelry and fine furnishings, but she always considered herself a peasant. Dad and Mark and I were the only ones who knew. Her transformation was flawless. She had a method I studied with utmost scrutiny, as if my life depended on it. Like our kitten learning to kill.

After baby animals imprint onto their mother, they learn survival behaviors in all sorts of ways. Even though predatory behavior is instinctual, when our cat was a kitten, she, along with her siblings, had learned to hunt by observing her mom, our neighbor's cat. First, the mother cat brought dead mice, kind of an appetizer to whet their appetites. Next, she brought prey that was still partially alive. Timid at first, the kittens learned to pounce and toss the practice mice around. It was revolting, but how could I get mad at them? The mom trained her kittens, who grew bolder and lunged at anything that moved, from a blade of grass to the dental floss hanging from my mouth. They soon acquired the skills and confidence to hunt and kill, their skills methodically prepped by their mother.

I watched my mother as she prepared to go to neighborhood cocktail parties. She'd put on a formal dress and stand in the mirror. A strand of genuine graduated pearls would come next. Then the thick cloud of lacquer hairspray, so no strawberry-blonde tresses could possibly fall out of place. The finishing touch. "Bet your ass I got class," she'd whisper, then she'd smile, and I knew she was ready to take the stage. She'd pretend to fit in, but she was intimidated around the doctors and lawyers who were our neighbors, embarrassed that she didn't have a college education, ashamed her husband was a drunk.

Mom would clean the house before the hired help came, just in case the housekeeper might gossip to her other bosses. I walked in one day and found Mom moving the piano, all 110 pounds of her versus the 500-pound Sohmer & Co upright. She must have done that every week, so she could vacuum under it. It was like cleaning was the only thing she could control other than her hair, which she dyed weekly with peroxide, trying to bleach away her roots.

Dad went in the other direction. Because he had "come from nothing" and worked hard to get ahead, he acted like he belonged. He bought the most expensive cars, stayed at the best hotels, sent us to pricey sleep-away camps, and had his suits custom-made at an exclusive tailor shop. (Mom also shopped exclusively—at the sale racks.) Dad gave away lots of money: to bartenders, to taxi drivers, to charities. Mom cringed when the bills flew. Each time he tipped big, I could hear her anxious breath tallying the losses. She once borrowed Mark's TI calculator to add up what Dad had spent on cigarettes and booze and gambling. It was one of the only times I saw her pour herself a drink. She sat at the kitchen table, crunching numbers, and alternated between crying and laughing as she sipped her Baileys on ice: "That's a shmoooooth drink!"

Dad sure liked his drink, too.

Family vacations consisted of junkets to Vegas or Puerto Rico, if you call gambling and showgirls and booze family friendly. I hated every moment of them. Dad drank and made bets and acted like a bigshot Mafioso. Mom window-shopped, sat poolside, and gossiped with the other wives. Mark and the friends he made as soon as we landed were always horsing around, jumping into the pool or meeting girls. It all seemed so superficial and frivolous. I wasn't old enough to go into the casino. Neither was Mark, but they let him in when he escorted Mom. Everyone seemed to be having a good time, except me. I was all alone. Once in a blue moon, Mark would spend time with me, but only if nobody else was around.

It was the same at home. At school, Mark was way too cool to hang out with me. Or so he pretended out in public. In the alcove between our bedrooms, we were inseparable confidants. We used to be able to sit together for hours, me writing and Mark sketching. When we were little, we'd be in our living room fort or the backyard tent (Dad said he'd build us a treehouse, and I kept waiting, but that never got done), silent, with nothing but a glance and three winks, alternating eyes—our covert club signal. We used a special notebook to send secret messages back and forth to each other, and each page would be folded and sealed with wax. *Gmar Chatimah Tova.* May you be inscribed in the Book of Life. For good.

When we weren't being quiet, we'd be on some sort of an adventure. Well, Mark would be on one, and I'd be chasing after him, whether he wanted me there or not.

"Mark, wait up!"

"Polly, get the hell out of here. I'm taking the sailboat out. Alone."

"I'm coming with you!"

"You're a real pain in my ass, you know that?"

"Yes, I do, brother bear."

I lost track of how many times I said, "Mark, wait up," only to have him leave me in his dust. But at home, we'd play Life, dress up and act out everything from musicals to sitcoms (with Mark always directing), escape to our magical castle, and complain about Mom and Dad. No, I'd complain; Mark would defend.

"Just give them a break, Pol. They're doing the best they can."

"She's such a hypocrite."

"They've had a hard life."

"Give me a break, oh perfect son who can do no wrong."

"Oh, I'll show you wrong."

And then he'd wrestle with me. Controlled, like a good big brother. I'd fight back like a feral pup with everything I had, which wasn't much. Mostly, I'd make lots of sounds. Then he'd make fun of my snorting or my ferocious growl, and I'd giggle until I had to pee in my pants.

It was like we had two different childhoods and two different sets of parents.

There's a story my family loves to tell, how there was a mix-up at the hospital, how I was almost taken home by another family, how one of the other family members lifted me up, all 7.4 pounds of me, and said, "She looks just like Uncle Vito," and they all laughed. I could never figure out why my mom watched them bundle me up and start to leave. Even though she thought it was me, she never bothered to question them. Thank goodness for the nurse, who had the wherewithal to check the hospital identification bracelet before I was taken away.

When Mark called me "Uncle Vito," or when he'd tease me with "Don't you know you're adopted?" it never seemed that funny. Maybe he was right, and I did go home with the wrong parents.

I learned quickly to stop confiding in Mark about Mom and Dad. It wasn't his fault that Mom thought her son walked on water. Maybe she was just being a typical Jewish mother. So what if Dad forgot my stupid tap recital? Missed my writing award assembly? Missed pretty much everything, because he was either at work or at the bar or feeling no pain, flat out on the rec room sofa? And Mom did nothing to help.

The more I complained to Mark, the more worthless I felt. Pathetic. What was wrong with me that I didn't have the every-thing-is-wonderful attitude? Maybe the reason they liked him better was because I was a little shit. Attitude turned to armor, candy-coated, which worked a whole lot better. Hello, Pollyanna.

The month before my sixteenth birthday, we took another family trip, this time to Puerto Rico. Mark didn't come with us because he had already left for college. When I called his dorm to say goodbye, to tell him I wished he were coming with us, when I heard his voice, all I could do was cry. It was a long-distance call, and "costing an arm and a leg!" Mom grabbed the phone, told Mark how much she missed him, and hung up before I had a chance to say anything.

When we got to San Juan, it was worse than I imagined. Mom and Dad expected me to join them at dinner, at the pool, in our claustrophobic hotel room; but it turned my stomach to be near them. After a few drinks, Dad was the center of attention, everyone was his best friend. Strangers who were more than happy to have him buy them drinks or throw some cash or chips their way. Waiters who played up to him. Cocktail waitresses who flirted shamelessly. And Mom stood by, jaws clenched, as he got drunker and drunker. She didn't touch a drop, but she blanked out and checked out—a dry drunk.

"You're the greatest!" he slurred to his latest best buddy, some acquaintance he barely knew. I couldn't stand him. And I couldn't stand Mom for her fake smile, and for selling out. As much as I wanted to tell them off, I said nothing. *Thou shalt speak no evil.*

It was a beautiful resort, with all-you-can-eat buffets and planned activities. We even had priority assigned poolside seating. I had everything anyone could ever want. I was surrounded by hundreds of families enjoying their vacations. I felt completely alone.

The gambling vacations were just one more place I didn't fit in. How could people waste so much time and money, so many brain cells? The only way I got through was to read a lot. The only way I made sense of it all was to write stories about the people I watched.

As long as I had books and notebooks, and as long as I had the beach and didn't have to witness the hypocrisy and greed, I was fine. Just fine. (At my first ACOA meeting, years later, I'd learn that "fine" stood for "fucked-up, insecure, neurotic, emotional." But what did they know?) I clicked off my contempt and went into numb mode. Trust me, denial is highly underrated. I left the resort and went for a walk. Maybe I could walk off my distracted, detached thoughts.

The sand was rough on my tender feet. Vermont winters don't allow toes to touch the ground for many months. I felt an odd satisfaction along my walk, enduring the minor pain of hot sandpaper biting at my soles, then being able to step into the cooling sea.

But this was the Atlantic. The sandy froth could be harsh, not healing. As the waves hit my legs and sent sharp needles into my ankles, I lost my footing, and was knocked over by something bobbing in the surf. I was struggling to get up when it licked my face. I screeched, and scrambled to get out of the water. As I flailed and stumbled, a pair of toes met my nose. Strong hands reached down and pulled me upright. I spit water and wiped snot from my nose. I rubbed my eyes, and I was face to face with a tall, muscular, soaking wet boy/man who was gorgeous and laughing. At me. I closed my eyes and hoped with all my might that the last few minutes had never happened. But they had.

"Are you okay?" He had a deep, kind voice.

I slowly opened my eyes as he picked up the biggest shell I had ever seen. A shiny pink conch.

"I think this is yours. Good find."

Somehow, I managed a weak smile. "Thanks. I thought it was trying to eat me."

I thought it was trying to eat me. Did I really just say that?

His name was Benjamin—he told me to call him Ben, and insisted on calling me Anna, my "real name"—and he was leaving the next day, first thing in the morning. He was twenty-two, and on vacation with a bunch of his grad school buddies. They were staying down the beach at a little bungalow. His friends came by just as we were cleaning the conch. At first, they were friendly. Flirtatious. They invited me to go surfing with them, and get drunk back at their place. A last hurrah. When they realized I was just fifteen, they backed right off, and strongly encouraged

Ben (*Dude, she's jailbait. Benny, what the hell you messing with this for?*) to do the same.

Ben didn't head back with them. We spent the rest of the day walking the beach, wading in the tidal pools, bodysurfing, and talking.

I understand that sun and surf excite hormones. That climate and conditions can create artificial feelings. Maybe that's what happened. I was alone and lonely, and sure had daddy issues. We can chalk it up to all that. But I connected with Ben in a way I had never connected with anyone else before.

He was the tall, great-looking guy with tawny, tousled hair, homecoming king in high school, who never would have noticed me then. And I would have felt I had nothing to offer. But Ben met me on an intellectual level, and I knew the more we talked, the more our mutual desire grew.

I could feel it in his fingertips as they played with mine. I could feel it in his arms as he held me high and threw me in the surf. As we fell asleep snuggled under a windswept palm, we whispered only about cerebral matters, but it was as if he was telling me about his raw sexual experiences and most intimate feelings. He listened to me like no one else had. Every story and joke and probing question felt real, and scary as hell.

The breeze on this deserted section of beach was light. He mumbled in his dreams, and his breath was steady as he held me tightly. His arms were strong; his eyes were kind and his mind keen. I was no longer pathetic. My body tingled, and my mind raced. I couldn't sleep as I thought about his lips over every part of my body.

Thankfully, he realized he was too old for me. If he had been less respectful and tried to take advantage of me, I have no doubt I would have done anything he wanted. It was almost dawn when Ben dropped me at the gate to our resort. I leaned up to kiss him, ready with mouth open and eyes closed. He gave only a gentle brush of his lips to my forehead. I stared at him as he started to stammer.

"Anna, I know, I know this is crazy, but let's meet again right here at midnight in five years—on your twenty-first birthday."

I couldn't speak.

"I'm serious," he said.

"Really?"

"I'll see you in five years."

"And one month," I added.

"I'll be here," Ben said.

I never went.

I have wondered—more than a few times over the years—what might have happened if I had gone, if Ben and I had reunited when I was twenty-one.

I wasn't sure if I fell in love that day, but just a few months later, in Israel, I did. His name was Yakir, but that's another story. What lovely Ben in Puerto Rico did for me was to allow me to fall in love with myself. For the first time. Hearing me through his ears, seeing me through his eyes, I felt smart and beautiful. And desirable.

My parents didn't even notice I had been gone all night. Dad was out cold on the hotel room sofa, and Mom was snoring. Probably took a sleeping pill from her portable pharmacy. I crept into my bed in the adjoining room and welcomed the first blush of the new day.

The only good thing that came out of our family vacations—other than Ben—was that I grew to love the ocean. As I was reminded in the DR, any trip to the beach is a good trip. Sea water coating my skin, salt air filling my lungs, sunshine warming my face made Pollyanna a happy girl.

But now, I was away from the ocean, back in Vermont, back to an empty house.

When Nebi first moved away, I fell to pieces. I'd sit on her bed in the dark, sobbing, my heart as vacant as her silent bedroom. Gregg, in his infinite male wisdom, told me how he was looking at this new phase of life.

"Polly, it's not an empty nest; it's a love nest."

Yeah, right.

I still didn't like the emptiness, but I made the best of it. What was hard was the emptiness I felt about Mark. He still wouldn't answer or return my calls. He still wouldn't explain what had torn us apart.

I couldn't imagine Chief Wamilik treating his brother like that. Who was smarter—the Dani, who lived simple lives, depending on each other, in tune with the natural order, or us, in our modern, disconnected, digital, stressed-out world? I didn't accept that a simple ACOA checklist could explain away my abandonment issues. Mom and Dad had never seemed to like me around. Then they had moved away, back to New York, as soon as I graduated high school. Supposedly to be closer to what little family we had left, the same family we had been so isolated from my whole childhood. And now, Mark would have nothing to do with me. So maybe, just maybe, my insecurities weren't all in my head. Maybe I had, in fact, been dumped. I wonder what the Big Man would do if Guba snubbed him? I had a new mantra: WWBMD? *What would Big Man do?*

I knew what he'd do, if he had a cell phone.

"Hey, Nebi, you up for a visit?"

"Really? Mom!"

Why not? The manure story wouldn't take long. Then I still had a few weeks to kill. I was on my way to *España*!

Nebi met me at the airport, and I was immediately struck by how right at home she looked. With her dark olive skin, almond-shaped, hazel eyes, and easy persona, she could fit in anywhere. I supposed now that I was in Spain, I'd be taken for Spanish, too. We shared that same chameleon quality. I was taken for a Greek in Greece, blended right in in any Little Italy, and, during my college years when I was a hostess at an Indian restaurant, diners often asked me what part of India I was from. My *sari* and bright red *bindi* might have added to the confusion. With my dark coloring, I'd even passed as Black Irish. Unlike Nebi, even if I looked like I fit in, I rarely felt it.

We hugged for a long, lovely time, then took the metro to Atocha Station. The intricate scaffolding of glass and wrought iron was mesmerizing. You could tell Gustave Eiffel had been one of the original architects. Travelers bustled by, but we strolled through the tropical gardens, Nebi pointing to her favorite spots in the light-filled arboretum. The terminal felt airy and uplifting. It was hard to wrap my head around the fact that just a few years ago, this same place had been ravaged by suicide bombers. A stark, minimalist memorial held constant vigil. We looked up at the hollow cylinder rising 40 feet high from a sea of blue light, and saw that it was filled with words, in all different tongues, and those words formed expressions of grief, thousands of messages of condolences and prayers, soaring to the skies. One at the very top read, "It takes a lot of imagination to deal with reality."

It took about fifteen minutes to walk to Nebi's apartment, a fifth-floor walk-up in the Lavapiés neighborhood. Nebi translated that Lavapiés means *wash feet*. Her landlord had told her it was probably a reference to the Jewish ritual washing of feet. For our ancestors traveling around the dusty desert in sandals, the washing of feet was a necessity of hygiene and comfort, and more. It was a sign of welcome. And it also had spiritual significance. Abraham offered water to wash the feet of angels. The Kohens, the priestly class, were to wash their feet prior to coming to the altar. A symbol of purity, to cleanse the soul. It was a status symbol—servants washed the feet of their masters. Until the most famous Jew came along and had the *chutzpah* to say that everyone should wash each other's feet—a lesson in humility.

Of course, Nebi had ended up living in Madrid's old Jewish Quarter, even though she was one of just a few Jews who now lived there. It had been a long time since Spanish Jews had enjoyed the good life under Muslim Moorish rule. After Catholic monarchs Ferdinand and Isabella married, *mierda* hit the fan. In 1492, they ordered the expulsion of all Muslims and Jews. Those who stayed could either convert or be put to death—without trial. The edict wasn't formally revoked until 1968.

By the time we arrived at Nebi's front door, I had traveled by car, plane, train, and foot. I was beat. I plopped down, my suitcase a makeshift seat. As I stopped to catch my breath before trudging up five flights, Nebi ran into the store across the alley. It was one of many Muslim-owned shops that now typified Lavapiés; though very few Jews had come back, it was apparent that a large population of Muslims had returned. Some shops sold Turkish carpets or Tunisian apparel; others, candy-colored beads and woven scarves blowing in the breeze like gentle rainbows. Conversations in Arabic mingled with Moroccan melodies. My stomach grumbled, excited by the smells of couscous and spicy fusions. I was so thirsty—for new flavors, for new cultures, and for something to drink.

Nebi returned with a water bottle, which I was about to grab when she kneeled down and gently removed my flip-flops. I had no idea what she was doing, but I was too bushed to protest. She looked up at me, those big hazel eyes sparkling, her smile soft. She unscrewed the bottle and poured the cool water on my feet.

"Welcome, Mom. Thanks for coming."

We snuggled on her bed like two childhood friends reunited after a too-long absence. So much to catch up on. Even though we phoned or g-chatted or Skyped almost daily, there was still so much more that could be shared in person.

"Let's go grab a bite before *siesta*," Nebi suggested.

I just wanted to sleep, but it would be better to stay awake. We headed out to *Mercado San Miguel*, Nebi's favorite bazaar. It was filled with a harmony of colors, aromas, and edible temptations, from wines to chocolates and every sort of *tapas* in between. Couples were everywhere, holding hands, kissing. Ubiquitous public displays of affection usually annoyed me, but not today. I was captivated by one couple. The man's sardine-grey hair looked like what I imagined Jamon's would in a few more years. We'd be nestled in a hammock, our grey hair flowing over the side, intertwined, swaying in the wind. Was I actually imagining Jamon in his old age? With me by his side? My belly warmed.

"Mom, hello? Are you in there?" Nebi's voice brought me back.

"Sorry, this place is overwhelming."

Since I didn't know where to start, Nebi ordered a plate of assorted olives, and suggested we sit down and relax. I'd never tasted an olive so fresh and flavorful. Each bite was filled with the essence of this special place. We each had a glass of Cava, although Nebi had to finish mine; I was already feeling a tad tipsy.

"This is nice, Neb."

"I thought you'd like it."

"Uncle Mark would love it here."

"I know. So how is he?"

"I'm not sure."

"What happened to you two? You used to be on the phone all the time. Or he was over at our place. It's the main reason I used to bug you for a brother or sister. I was jealous that you had a built-in best friend."

"I really don't know. Ever since Mema died, he's been avoiding me."

"You mean like moving to the other side of the country?"

"I know. I mean, I understand that San Francisco is a better place to be gay …"

"Mom. A better place to be gay? What the hell does that even mean?"

"I'm just saying, there are more options."

"Options?"

"Anyway, for whatever reason, he moved. Good thing he and Stephen can fit their work into bicoastal visits with Pop-pop. But the timing was so off. First we lose our mom, then our dad starts to slip away, and then Mark takes off."

"Hmm, and I moved, too. Maybe you should take it personally!"

"Shut up!"

"Mom!"

"You started."

"Now that's mature. So what about Uncle Marky?"

"There's nothing to tell. I can't get him to talk to me about anything, except a schedule for visiting Pop-pop."

"I'm sorry."

"Yeah, me too. It hurts like hell. I never understood why my mom … why she pushed me away. Now it's happening again."

"Let's hope it's not hereditary." Nebi laughed as she pulled me closer.

The vibe in Madrid was one of pure relaxation. *Madrileños* truly embrace the concept—and reality—of *siesta*. By the time we turned on to her *calle*, it was mid-afternoon, yet all of the shops were closed. Time for a nap. Nebi and I walked toward her apartment, arm in arm, same comfortable pace, same contented smile.

After *siesta*, Nebi had to go to work. That left me free for the first item on my tourist agenda: heading to the Reina Sofía and to *Guernica*. My elementary school art teacher had introduced me to Picasso. My classmates and I giggled at his funny faces, and then sat at long wooden tables and made blue cubist collages. She showed us a slideshow of his work, and something about the shapes and angles and style of *Guernica* struck me. I think it was my first awareness of the emotional impact art could have. Dad took me to buy a print at the mall poster shop and I hung it over my desk, right above my other favorite piece of art, a tiny replica of Myron's *Discobolus*—the discus thrower.

For years, I'd looked at *Guernica* when I was supposed to be doing homework, escaping into the hues of grey when I was stuck on some math problem, or tracing my fingers along the bull's thick black lines, perfecting the art of procrastination. My print was about eight inches wide and four inches tall.

When I entered the second floor of the Reina Sofia and turned the corner, there, covering the entire exhibit wall, was *Guernica*, all eleven by twenty-seven feet. It was like a bomb dropped. It had never occurred to me that it would be any bigger than the postcard-sized print I had stared at throughout my childhood. How could I have missed that one not-so-small detail?

I'd had the mindset that I had a unique, personal relationship with this diminutive piece of art. Seeing it in person, I grasped the magnitude of its size and the reaction it engendered: in just the few moments since I had arrived, hundreds of people had come to stand there, drawn to it, and also visibly in awe. I was struck with the constantly shifting boundaries between reality and fantasy, as generated by my point of view. Even though the masterpiece was enormous, even though I had had such an intimate bond with it, it was as if I had never seen it before. It boggled my mind that I could almost touch the brushstrokes, could see shadows of what was beneath the layers. I had goosebumps, and my heart danced as though I were meeting a new lover—but someone, on some level, I had always known.

I don't know how long I stood before a new tourist group jostled me away.

As I walked back toward Nebi's place, I formulated my next mini-quest. I was on a bit of a sugar high from the thick *chocolate y churros* I had devoured in the museum café, which, combined with my jet lag, had me vibrating. I was in Spain, and I realized that one of the most influential paintings in my life, and in the world, had been created in response to one of the world's most important international conflicts—the Spanish Civil War. In 1937. Yes; remarkable that I had also missed that fact.

I hadn't missed the fact that once again, I had to trudge five flights to get back to the apartment. But as I climbed, I was distracted by the smooth indentations and the deep, rich grain patterns on Nebi's stairs. I wanted to rush up to my computer to begin my research, but my body was not cooperating. I felt like a robot as I methodically lifted one leg at a time, step by step, for five flights. I looked down the entire time, to make sure I was landing on the narrow, irregular steps. With each step, I could feel the generations of feet that had touched the treads before me. The lopsided wooden boards were worn from hundreds of years of bodies climbing, heading home. Each time my sole touched the wood, a new connection was sealed.

Exhausted as I was, I had work to do. I knew there had been many battles in and around Madrid, and I decided I'd look into those and see what turned up. The story of *Guernica* had such a powerful impact, both from the actual bombing of the Basque town and the creation of the painting that revealed the horrors of war. I wondered what other stories I might find.

As it turned out, I didn't have to look further than a suburban town called Majadahonda, the very place where Nebi worked on sustainability issues. A few days later, Nebi accompanied me to Majadahonda to serve as my interpreter and guide. Her coworker had told us that there was a war monument in town, and because it was the seventieth anniversary, we were just in time for some kind of ceremony. Little did we know that the Majadahonda monument commemorated two Romanian Iron Guard volunteers who had fought for Franco. Little did we know that Ion Moța and Vasile Marin had been killed in Majadahonda on January 13, 1937, and died as martyrs. That their bodies had been transported across Europe by a funerary train, attracting hundreds of thousands of mourners and supporters. That Franco erected the monument in 1970 to honor the two heroes, men who believed that the enemies were capitalists, communists, and Jews.

Neither of us understood a word of the ceremony; it was all in Romanian. About two dozen people had gathered to listen to the speaker. He raised his fist, and the crowd was swept away in his fervor. Their seething rants needed no translation.

A small group of protesters tried to out-shout the Romanians. *Viva la libertad! Viva la revolución!* Two armed *policía* stood guard. Just in case. Nebi raised her eyebrows when I pulled her away from the crowd. That wasn't going to stop me from being a good mother.

The monument itself was worn and tired. Spray-painted graffiti covered much of the concrete arches. A dried-out old wreath leaned against the stone cross that stood on the location of the trench in which the two Francoists had been killed. Weeds rose from the cracks of the foundation. It didn't look as if too many visitors ever came to this site.

An elderly couple sat on an isolated bench. I couldn't make out any expression on their faces. Unlike the heated crowd, this pair was as stone cold as the granite courtyard.

The speech ended, the passion fizzled, and the small crowd dispersed. Thankfully, my fears were unfounded. Once the *policía* left, only the elderly couple remained.

It was a bright afternoon, and the distant mountains beyond the olive groves framed the couple's silhouettes. Nebi went to ask them if she could take their picture. I'd always been impressed with Nebi's good eye, but I was growing more awed with her confidence, the ease with which she was able to navigate different places and people. Nebi said *¡Hola!* and the man surprised us with an Anglo-accented *hi*. We introduced ourselves, and when I told him I was a writer, he pulled out a flask, patted down a spot on the bench next to them, and started talking.

By this point in time, I probably shouldn't have been surprised by anything. Across cultures, I'd been showered with coincidences. Call it kismet, karma, fate, destiny, or *bershert*, each meeting and occurrence seemed to spring from something more than chance. Stories had been presented to me like oblations. Actually, the stories themselves seemed to have their own ambitions and directives, as if they wanted to be heard. If the narratives longed to be chronicled, I was more than happy to be their scribe. The latest car in this steady, dependable train of thought shouldn't have surprised me, but these strangers' candid, meticulous account of what had happened here, in this lovely town of Majadahonda, left me breathless.

By the time the moon rose, the story had been told. I felt hungover. It wasn't entirely the *Orujo* I'd sipped from his flask, which tasted like something between lighter fluid and paint thinner. It was more of an emotional hangover. My mind was reeling from the sounds and smells of war, from what had happened right where we sat, mesmerized for hours on that rusty bench.

The couple slowly stood up. Nebi offered to escort them home. They politely refused.

"Thank you for bearing witness," the man said.

"I'm sure you'll do the story justice," the woman said.

With a silent hug, we parted ways. A slight nod of the man's head, and I felt I had made a pledge just by listening.

Back in the apartment, Nebi and I stayed up most of the rest of the night, recreating what we'd heard. I hadn't brought my recorder, but thankfully, Nebi's mind was still young and able to remember. Together, we pieced the details, fitting fragments as best we could, until Nebi drifted off to sleep. I was at the obsessive stage of immersion in a new undertaking, and rife with insomnia. Maniacally awake, I worked—new project, same year.

I had collected three authentic stories so far: the CCC story, the one about Leon Haube, and the one Gregg had told me. I hoped I could add this one, too. And I suppose I also hoped to get a fix; I was jonesing for 1937.

I spent the night meeting places and faces, sorting through contradictory data, taking notes, and noting potential leads. At this stage, the story was all possibility.

Nebi's apartment was the top floor of the building. If you stood on tippy toes, from the slanted skylights you could just make out the surrounding red tile roofs and the church steeple. Her stark white ceiling was lined with dark beams, the same aged wood as the stairwell. Only on these old timbers, no one had left their imprint.

I stared up at the beams and wished: *if only I could push a button and have all of my thoughts and words magically appear on paper.* My brain as a fax machine, and all I needed to do was scan my synapse activity, and the pages would print out. Already written.

I was confident that day would come. For now, I needed to press keys in order to transform mental ideas, crystal clear in my mind, into something concrete that others could read. I clicked away for hours, referring to our copious notes, taking breaks every now and then to sip coffee and stare at Nebi's Dali poster or watch the sun make its way across the ceiling, and the shadows dance across the beams.

Nebi moseyed out of bed around noon and slogged into the bathroom. She had sipped from the flask more than her fair share. She was probably not going to be in such a great mood, and I was prepared to give her a wide berth. I had the printout of "Windmills" in hand so I could proofread the finished piece, but I'd wait to let Nebi read their story. I was hopeful I had done it justice.

WINDMILLS

BY P.A. STERN

Until the sun came up, it was impossible to tell if the screams were out on the street or inside his head. As the sky turned from winter black to pale grey, he peeked out from the trench and saw the woman wandering through the town's wreckage. Her screams in the morning light sounded hollow as they filled the spaces among the rubble.

He watched her, and wondered if she had already gone mad before the bombing. Perhaps she was one of the rearguard *miliciana* who had just lost her way. It was frigid out, yet she wore nothing but a thin cotton calf-length dress. Her long dark hair was loose and matted. She was headed away from him, so he could not see her face, but he knew she was beautiful. She was half a kilometer away when Stephan Backler whispered to her, the breath barely making it past his chapped lips, "I'm here."

Stephan looked around. Just a few other soldiers were still alive. Some had already been dying from malnutrition before this last battle had begun. *Avitamosis*, they called it. Stephan jumped when two fat rats scurried across the trench. Somehow, the vermin always managed to find food. One rat dragged a ripped cloth, a piece of someone's shoddy uniform worn to mere threads. The soldiers whose bodies weren't frozen had minds that had become numb. Shell-shocked, like that poor kid from Barcelona who kept raving about the Fifth Column. "Get them, or they'll get us. Traitors! Death to the *Quinta Columna*. Death to the Fascist spies!" A declaration of delirium and truth.

When Stephan and his buddy had first arrived from Canada, it seemed that the Republicans were in good shape. Try as they might, the insurgents couldn't capture Madrid. The *Madrileños* believed in the cause, and General Miaga had been able to rally the troops. Supplies were plentiful, and there were lots of other volunteers who had come to support the International Brigade.

Madrid's buildings were pock-marked with shrapnel damage, strange carvings in patterns that made no sense. In the plazas, couples kissed, friends visited, *tapas* were served; the city was vibrant with activity, even though it was a constant target. The thick-walled buildings had huge holes filled with sandbags, and served as good refuge when the high, long whistles screeched, signaling incoming mortar.

On one patrol, Stephan saw wooden boxes piled near a military truck. He wasn't sure what they were. A man with olive skin and dark hair, wearing round tortoise-shell glasses, guarded the stack. Stephan assumed he was a Spanish soldier, and tried to ask him about the boxes *en español*. The soldier let Stephan struggle for a bit, then laughed, "Hey, I'm Sam. From Brooklyn. You evah heah of Ca-nah-sie?"

Sam was a writer, a Yiddish poet who loved words as much as he loved food. He told Stephan how excited he had been when he had first seen the wooden crates and thought they were filled with cheese, like the Home Relief boxes his dad would sneak into their apartment. The pine boxes here were filled with guns and bombs and other ammunition. A different kind of sustenance.

Stephan had come to Spain with Wilfred Felton, his closest childhood friend. Because the two Canadians were loggers and knew how to live off the land, they were accustomed to guns. Sam had arrived in Spain a few months before them and, although he was already fluent in Spanish, he still messed up when he loaded his rifle. Each time, he'd get his fingers caught in the latch, and howl, "*¡La madre que te parió!*" The mother who bore you!

Stephan also howled—with laughter. "Sammy, it's a damn good thing you know how to load your fountain pen."

Stephan's battalion consisted mostly of Serbs and Canadians, led by a Spaniard. There was no common language; even the volunteers from Argentina didn't seem to understand the locals. Over time, they all figured out basic ways to communicate. Their first night in Majadahonda, a stronghold on the northwest outskirts of Madrid, a young Chinese volunteer had shown up. The other volunteers didn't know how to talk to him, and everyone was so busy, they never tried. By the following noon, his legs were blown off and he bled out, and no one had even learned his name. Stephan found a jade pendant lying by the body, and he put it in his field pack.

After that, Stephan realized he might be the next. Another casualty, some foreigner buried in the Spanish earth. He thought about the deep woods back home, and wondered if he'd ever see them again.

Majadahonda felt strange, like a ghost town. Remnants of hanging laundry, left by fleeing refugees, fluttered in the frigid breezes. As other soldiers set up camp and dug trenches, Wilfred, Stephan, and Sam walked through the cobblestone streets, checking for anyone who had not evacuated, making sure the town was secure. Stephan kept reacting to wisps of movement—to that relentless scream—that neither of his companions seemed to notice. He wasn't sure if he was seeing things or hearing things, but everything was making him jumpy. Nothing was like he expected. Burned wagons, houses with no roofs, a child's toy with no child, the acrid smells of death. A donkey, half-alive, gazed up at him. How could one anticipate the sorrows of war?

They continued along *Calle Real*, and an emaciated dog ran out of the Church of Santa Catherine. As they passed the inn, Stephan saw something in the window—or what used to be a window—of what used to be a barbershop. He looked at his buddies, and this time, they did see it. Her. A fair young girl had been looking out at them, but she disappeared as quickly as she had come into sight. They entered the small building, and other than some broken mirrors, it was empty, completely empty, with no other exit. They stood for a while, uncertain what to do, then walked back out onto the vacant street without saying a word. Old sheets of newspaper blew across the silent road.

Sam began to sing softly, "*In mayne oygn bistu sheyn, sheyn vi di velt …*" And then he spoke, as he wandered off: "In my eyes, you are so beautiful, beautiful as all the world …"

"Where're you going, Sam?" Wilfred called.

"Gotta get back to the trucks for morning broadcast."

Alfonso, the stonemason from Galicia, would be waiting. Alfonso ran the equipment and read the announcements into the loudspeaker, and Sam translated the messages—loosely—into English, Serbian, French, and Yiddish. Sometimes, the brigade commander let them play record albums; sometimes Sam read from Lorca, Neruda, Hernandez, Cervantes, or Orwell, his rhythm syncopated with the battery of machine gun bullets.

Wilfred looked at Stephan. "What the hell just happened?"

"I have no idea."

They needed to clear their heads. They left town and walked toward the olive groves, passing the large sign that read *Junta de Defense Consejería de Evacuación* and explained the upturned baskets left on benches; the carts, half-filled, with broken wheels that rendered them unmovable; the metal bed frames left in the middle of the tree-lined roadway, probably dropped when they had become too heavy to carry, or when their carriers truly reckoned with how far they had to go.

The olive grove did not bring relief. The trees were destroyed, the branches ripped open and covered with soot. The sad sentinels stood as tall as they could. Stephan ran his fingers over the charred, grey-green bark. *They'll never bud in spring now.* Between the smoke and the fog, it was getting harder to see. The Soviet tanks had been there, and the machine guns blasted, blasted, blasted like a hailstorm. *Why did they have to aim at the trees?* Stephan smelled the air, and it wasn't vibrant like in the Kootenays, where fir and cedars grew thick, smelled sweet, and formed a welcoming fortress. The wind picked up, and Stephan heard its mournful cry.

He looked around the sparse olive grove and trembled. "Do you feel it? Their souls, they're slipping away."

"Whose?" Wilfred asked. He didn't press when no answer came.

The fog was getting thicker and thicker, and the temperature dropped, and the fog froze. Stephan had been born in a northern landscape, and he knew about snow. There was usually a stillness, a silence of snow when it first fell from the sky and landed on the spruce needles and the forest floor. A peaceful hush. But this fog snow was different; it created a deafening quiet with its blinding arrival. The skies opened, the snow fell, and everything stopped.

Stephan turned his ruddy face toward Wilfred, and through blue lips, said, "I thought it was going to be sunny in Spain."

"It's January."

"I know that, Wilfred, but how can it be so damn cold? There are palm trees growing here."

"Now you're an expert on Spanish forestry?"

"Aren't you cold?"

"Nah, I got the chamois shirt Ma gave me. You shoulda worn that Soviet fur hat. Even the beret. Here, take my helmet."

"No. Thanks."

"At least it's better than the 'slave camps' in B.C."

"You got that right."

"Better than Vancouver."

"Only place in Canada you can starve to death before you freeze to death."

They tried to find their way back to town, and they continued to tease each other, to joke their way through the fog and their fears, but they only made it as far as the stable. Because they were laughing, they missed the *baaing*, and were startled when they came upon a young shepherd. The boy, who couldn't have been more than ten, was crouched in the back of the barn, huddled with a dozen restless sheep. The soldiers aimed their guns at him, and he gasped. Even the sheep went silent.

The standstill felt like it lasted for hours, when really, just a few moments passed. Fear has its own timeline, measured by hearts beating loudly enough for your enemy to hear. Stephan's hands began to shake, and the rifle grew unsteady. The boy pointed toward an old sheepskin and Stephan grabbed it, then wrapped it around his thin cotton jacket. When Stephan stopped shivering, he nodded his head in a quiet *gracias*, and lowered his rifle. Wilfred still aimed right at the boy, but said nothing.

The shepherd tried to explain in a desperate stream of words that the two soldiers barely understood: "I would've fought. I wanted to. Grandpa told me to stay. We couldn't lose the sheep. But I wanted to join. The bastards. I would've fought. I would've ..."

The sheep were *baaing* so loudly that they muffled the sounds of the fighter plane. The soldiers finally heard shouts of *Avión! Avión!* and they motioned to the shepherd to follow them. The boy wouldn't leave. Stephan tried to drag him out, but the boy shook his head no and grabbed onto his sheep. Wilfred pulled Stephan away and ran out of the barn right before the bomb dove through its roof.

They ran through the frigid white screen, and soon, Stephan was separated from Wilfred, but he didn't notice. Shells blasted in an enormous counter attack. Shades of darkness accompanied the incessant machine-gun fire. Then the fighting ceased, and everything went silent for the briefest of moments, followed by the frantic noise of sirens and shouting. Stephan didn't know where he was, and he followed along the thin string of one scream that led him to the center of town. Out of the mist, he saw something red and blue. The scream called him, and he found himself in front of a collapsed building. The red roof tiles were shattered, the wooden doors in splinters. The crumbled sign, *Peluquería*, was lying on the ground next to the broken barber's pole: white for bandages, blue for veins, red for blood.

Stephan took off his sheepskin and gently lay his rifle on top of it, setting it next to the sign as a simple offering. He lit a cigarette and inhaled deeply, watching the ashes fall and the smoke swirl up and mingle with the sky, now thick with black. He continued to follow the scream, clinging to the invisible guide rope. Stephan took off his boots and socks and walked along the frigid cobblestones. He heard Sam's voice over the loudspeaker, shouting a hesitant declaration. "We got 'em. Moța and Marin are dead! Death to the Iron Guard! Down with our enemies. We will never stop." And then he heard it again and again and again, and in every language, it meant the same thing.

The scream was closer now, and Stephan felt it vibrate through the last length of thin filament. He walked toward her, the reluctant witness, her thin cotton shift beckoning. A white flag. She spoke to him in Spanish; still, he understood every word.

"We boiled cans, from condensed milk. We filled them with rocks and nails. With dynamite. The fuse was so short. So short. You must throw it very fast."

She shuddered, and he took off his shirt and handed it to her. She didn't take it.

"She wasn't fast enough," she whispered.

He wrapped his shirt around her. Her shoulder was bruised blue and dark, and he touched it gently.

"From firing my Mauser. Until it jammed."

There was a hush before she returned to her song of madness. He felt in his pocket until he found the jade pendant, and he placed it around her neck. She screamed her haunting cry, and he joined her as he tried to breathe through the frozen fog and the dust of war. They walked together, side by side, the defenders of Majadahonda.

Chapter 7

Incredible that we humans can build skyscrapers, plant orchards, compose operas, and also invent armaments—with the only purpose to maim and kill each other. It was hard to take it all in, what they told me, what I wrote, what had happened. What was happening still.

I went to wipe something off my chin. I hadn't realized my face was wet with tears.

While I was proofreading "Windmills" Nebi had gone back to her room. I looked in on her, and she had fallen asleep again. I always loved to watch her sleep, her grin a little goofy, one leg always pushed out from under the covers. How she had hated footie pajamas. It took months before we figured out that she had claustrophobic feet. After that infant stage, she slept deeply and well. Like a baby.

The coffee sang while I sat in Nebi's sun-drenched living room. I was flush with heat, and wondered whether I was feverish. A thermometer in the bathroom flashed my temperature: 37 degrees. Celsius. A quick Internet search gave me the conversion: 37 Celsius equals 98.6 Fahrenheit, the normal human temperature. Of course it did.

A chunk of baguette sat on the counter. So far, the Spanish bread hadn't been too impressive—the crust wasn't crusty enough, the insides not moist and chewy—but I needed something to soak up the leftover acid in my belly. As I smothered the bread with Nutella, the perfect antidote for dry crumb, my computer pinged. A quick check revealed the pinger: JamonMan. My heart pounded. The heat returned. I read his message:

Are you there? It's me, your long-lost tender.

Long-lost? Really? It had only been a few weeks.

Tender? I couldn't stop smiling at the thought of him tending to my every need. I paced fitfully back and forth from the kitchen to the living room. What the hell should I do?

Nebi made another appearance, slumped on the sofa, and grumbled, "What're you doing?"

Shit. I didn't want to have to explain. "Nothing."

Nebi rolled her eyes at me, a remaining affect from our intermittent parent/adolescent dance.

"Mom. Who is he?"

Can't hide anything from a daughter.

"I really like him. He lives in the DR, and, I don't know, he's ... he's ... he just is."

"Is what?" she said, that adorable, long-suffering tone now accompanying her faux-patient facial expression.

"Is who I've been waiting for."

"*En serio?* So why aren't you answering him?" Out of the mouths of babes.

Good afternoon, Jamon.

Good morning, sweet cheeks.

Sweet cheeks? That was intimate.

Sweet cheeks?

Could he hear the juvenile tone, the one Nebi had perfected and I had appropriated, through the keystrokes?

Your face. Your smile is a delectable confection.

Holy shit.

Hey, I didn't know you were a wordsmith.

Never before. But you are my muse.

"Awwwwww," Nebi sang.

"Stop reading."

"Mom, he's so romantic."

I slammed the laptop cover shut. "Nebi!"

"Why aren't you Skyping with him?"

"I can't. It's too hard. I'm more comfortable just with written words."

"What does he look like?"

"Like he sounds."

"Then he must be fantastic," she said. Fantastic didn't even begin to describe Jamon. "Guess I'll leave you alone with *Señor Fantástico.*"

Jamon was still there when I opened the laptop. We continued to flirt throughout our chat. Well, he flirted, and I stuck to chatter. I told him there were *jamón* shops on every street corner. He asked if that meant I kept thinking of him. I said he must be a big ham. He said he missed me. I agreed. He asked when I was coming back. I said I wasn't sure. He said all the expats asked about me. I told him to tell them hi. I asked him how Leon Haube was doing. He said Mr. Haube hadn't missed a happy hour since I'd been there. Then he wrote, *Mr. Haube says hi.*

Hi back.

I want to see you again.

Awww. Please tell Mr. Haube I want to see him again, too.

No, that's what I'm saying, not Mr. Haube.

Moment of truth.

Slight delay.

Uh, Polly? You still there? Did you read that last line? I want you to come back. I want to see you.

Press the goddamn key. Press it, you chicken shit. What the hell is wrong with y—

I want to see you, too.

But of course, I had to add the crazy-eyed animated emoticon. To lessen the import of my words. Way to go, Polly.

Glad to hear that.

Dear Jamon, I'm going to be on the road for a bit, but I hope to talk to you again soon.

Yes, dear Polly, let's talk soon. Where to now?

My daughter and I are going to chase windmills.

I had reserved a car for a weekend road trip to Toledo and Segovia. Nebi was still in a fog, but we managed to pack and get to the rental office just before they closed. We drove through the La Mancha region, past windmills: a few old ones that were used for grinding grain, and ridges filled with new ones that looked beautiful next to huge fields of solar panels, all generating clean energy. We passed thousands of acres of olive groves, and castle after castle in each little town along the way.

At a panoramic overlook we stopped to picnic on Manchego cheese and olives. Nebi asked me for the story, and I took a stroll through a nearby sheep field while she sat, back against an old olive tree, and read "Windmills." The sun beat down on her, and a gentle breeze rustled the leaves. I returned as she was on the last page.

"It all seems so surreal," she said.

"But war is too real."

"It's hard to understand why it's been such a constant part of human history."

"Therein lies the madness."

Nebi stood up and sighed. She reached over and gently stroked my arm.

"You did good, Mom. Real good."

I didn't correct her grammar.

As each town had a castle, each also had a monument to those killed during the civil war. Franco had left ruins intact throughout the countryside as a "live" memorial of the war. Maybe as a threat. Sites of battles and bombed-out villages were left to honor those who died. Who were killed. Along our route, civilian air-raid shelters had been tunneled into the rock, and there was even a field hospital set up in a cave, once used to service the wounded Republican forces and the International Brigade.

But most of the evidence was not in the hardscape. It seemed that the wounds had barely healed over. I thought of New York and

D.C. and 9/11. Much of the physical damage had been cleared up, but the emotional effects of the attacks were still an open trauma, still had an impact on relationships and politics. The national psyche has been wounded. Same in Spain. And in the Mid-East. In Asia. I thought about what Nebi had said. Was there any place, had there been any time untouched by the destruction of conflict?

It's the same with interpersonal wounds. Each harsh word and every act of mistrust creates a little fissure in your spirit. Like a laceration, the only way it can heal is when the rips fill up with scar tissue. The good news is that fibrous bridges make scars tough. Wounds hurt like hell, but in the long haul, if you can find forgiveness, your soul will be whole, your spirit strong.

The more I researched 1937, the more glaring it became that it was not a unique period in human history. In some ways, that's an unfortunate realization. In other ways, there is something comforting in human consistency. Are our acts a permanent battleground, or a foundation for absolution? It all depends which way you look at it.

Nebi taught me a new term, the Law of Historical Memory, *Ley de Memoria Histórica*, a Spanish law passed just that year. It was supposed to recognize the victims of both sides of the war. The law was criticized for opening old wounds, but maybe that was what was necessary for the wounds to scar over. Being able to confront the pain of the past and coming to terms with history seemed to be universal themes.

After I butchered the pronunciation of *Ley de Memoria Histórica*, Nebi tried once again to teach me Spanish. We thought it would be a good way to pass the time, a fun car ride game. She started simply enough:

"Let's try the verb *hablar*. To speak. Remember the pronouns?"

"I think."

"Mom, we've gone over this a gazillion times."

"I know. I'm just not good at this."

"Yes, you are. Try *I speak*."

"*Yo hablo*."

"*Bueno*. Now *you speak*."

"I am."

"Very funny. You cannot joke your way out of this."

"What a hardass."

"I learned from the best."

"Alright, um, *tú hablas?*"

"Stop saying it as a question. Have conviction. Now *we speak*."

"*Nosotros hablamos*."

"See how good you are. Let's do some past perfect."

"If only the past was perfect."

"Mom."

"Come on, I'm a writer, but I know grammar like a musician who plays by ear."

"Do it. The pluperfect: *I had spoken*."

"*Yo habré hablado?*"

"Close, but that's the future perfect."

"Again, if only."

"Mom. *¿Cómo se dice I had spoken?*"

"Forget it. I'm done."

"What do you mean?"

"I don't want to do this anymore."

"Give me a break. You always tell me not to be a quitter."

"Honey, you know me. As good as I am with English language, I'm pitiful with foreign languages. I'm just no good at it."

"You always say that about yourself."

"Because it's true."

"It's not true. You can learn if you want. It's just the story you tell about yourself. The story you've always told. It's like you have it stuck in your brain. Time to get the lube out. Time to change your story."

The Law of Historical Memory. It all depends on your perspective. The story you want to tell. And the one you want others to hear.

We did a whirlwind tour of Toledo, starting with the breathtaking overlook that revealed its medieval layout. Our goal was

to hit the cathedral, the mosque, and the synagogue. The Holy
Trifecta, which is why they call Toledo "Spain's Jerusalem." I
hadn't thought about Israel in a long time, but this city did remind
me of Jerusalem.

I hadn't been there since the summer I lived on a kibbutz.

When I was sixteen, I convinced my parents I wanted to find
out more about my roots, but really, I just wanted to get away
from them. I spent that summer weeding cotton, clearing apple
orchards, visiting historical sites, and learning about a Judaism
that was very different from my you-should-do-it-just-because-
you-should brand of religion. It was the first time I awakened to
the possibilities of the deep spiritual aspects of Judaism, based in
history but also founded on faith, as opposed to the dogmatic,
hypocritical, mandatory practice in which I had been raised.

And here I was, over thirty years later, still trying to sort out
what kind of Jew I was, and should be. It must be a hell of a lot
easier to have unquestioning faith. But aren't questions the foundation of Judaism? It's a whiplash religion. One day, do as I say
just because you should; the next day, time to wrestle with G-d,
with meaning, as the core of Jewish identity. If we are supposed to
argue with G-d, is it any wonder we argue with each other?

Once we were in the city itself, Toledo even had a similar
feel to Jerusalem, with its worn cobblestones, spicy smells, nar-
row-walled streets, markets, and three world religions trying to
co-exist, despite the odds.

Like the threads forming the arabesque tapestries that once
hung throughout the mosque, Muslims and Jews had once had
an interwoven relationship throughout Spain. Jews interpreted
for Muslims, Arabic was used for Jewish prayers, and there was
shared influence in the arts and literature, the sciences, and the
legal system. And depending on who was in charge at any particular period of history, both the Muslims and the Jews went in
and out of favor.

After learning that the Muslims had been forced out of
Toledo in 1502, shortly after the Jews, it was time to go find out

more about how both of our peoples had been persecuted by the Visigoths. Ah, the fun never stops. As we walked through the Jewish museum, it felt odd to see displays of familiar items, items that we used in our homes and at services—*mezuzahs*, *challah* plates, *matzoh* covers, *Shabbat* candelabra, a Torah—presented as artifacts of some lost culture, complete with written descriptions and accompanying audio recordings. I looked over at Nebi and knew she felt like I did: conspicuous and uncomfortable, as if we were on display. As if we might be found out.

When I saw the *shofar*, I thought of Mark, how he had practiced playing it at home, preparing for *Rosh Hashana* services, only he'd blast out great lyrical jazz riffs like some hipster trumpeter instead of the Biblical *T'qiah, sh'varim-t'ruah, t'qiah*.

When I tried to blow the *shofar*, it sounded like a dying animal moaning—maybe the ram whose horn had been turned into a ritual instrument. What was with my family and dead animal parts? The more frustrated I'd get, the more Mark would encourage me, always with warped wit.

"Shofar, sho good, little sister."

And I could always count on the obvious, the old one about why limousine drivers prefer Jewish bosses. "The pay is lousy, but once a year, they get to blow the shofar!"

Ba dum bum.

He'd get me laughing, which made it even harder to find the steady, powerful breath to get a decent sound.

"What're you smiling at, Mom?" Nebi had caught my nostalgic moment.

"Just how silly my brother used to be."

We walked by the museum Chanukah display, filled with *dreydls* of all sorts and shapes.

"Uncle Mark and I had an annual Chanukah tradition. We bought graham crackers and containers of ready-made frosting, and we built 'gingerbread' *dreydls*. We coated them with blue and white jellybeans."

"Why didn't we ever do that?"

I sort of heard Nebi's question, but I was still thinking of Mark. How his *dreydls* were always impeccable. How everything he did was accomplished with ultimate care and panache, from designing a set for the community theater production to making a tuna fish sandwich.

It was one of the reasons his coming out at eighteen hadn't been a big surprise to any of us. Sure, there are gay men who are slobs, and others who don't have that creative flair, but when it's your brother, your own flesh and blood, you just know.

What did surprise me was that Mark had never told me earlier. I thought we had shared all of our deepest secrets and longings. When Mark first came out, Mom's reaction was to hug and hover. Nothing out of the ordinary for her favored child. Dad opened a bottle of whiskey, and in the guise of acceptance and celebration, went to his happy place.

The only revelation Mark's news brought me was that we weren't as close as I had believed. The one person with whom I felt I most connected did not feel the same. I never thought Mark would be another family member to distance me, make me feel like I didn't belong. Why hadn't he told me first? Just me. I looked around at our little dysfunctional family unit, and then I stared at Mark, and the only thing he did was stare back. He tried to alternate three winks, but we both welled up and looked away. Then he tried to whistle the chickadee call, our other sibling code, but the notes wouldn't form. It wasn't clear what had upset him most. Our magical castle turned into a fortress that day and grew a little taller, the moat a little wider.

"Mom—why didn't we ever make *dreydls*?"

"Yeah, sorry, Neb. I don't know why we didn't."

"Probably Dad would've made us do it all authentic, dig up our own clay and build a fire pit."

"Probably."

Toledo was famous for its marzipan, and between each exceedingly depressing tourist stop, we frequented many of the candy shops. A sweet remedy. The windows were full of displays of almond paste molded into every shape and form: blush-tinged peaches, ornate fish with golden scales, saints' bones, and flawless architectural replicas. It was unimaginable how they had created buildings out of sugar. I joined the crowds to marvel at the details of the cathedral doors made to look like wood, the intricately carved archways, candy courtyards that mimicked stone. The annual celebrated gingerbread White House sculptures could not even come close to the *Santo Tome reproduccion en mazapán.*

A tourist pushed me away from one marzipan-filled window, and Nebi and I entered the shop. The sensory feast continued with roasted sugary aromas and bonbon delights. Nebi did not like the texture, and had never acquired a taste for marzipan—my one failing as her mother!—but that did not stop me. I couldn't decide between a pear, a swan, and a marzipan-stuffed fig that reminded me of my dinner with Jamon. So I bought them all, and ate until my teeth hurt. Woozy from almond intoxication, Nebi had to drag me away from the last shop. I looked back, longing for another sweet treat. A "delectable confection." I began to wobble and hum. Nebi shook her head and grabbed my arm; she must have assumed I was on yet another sugar high.

But this was a different kind of high.

We reached Segovia just as the sun was setting over the aqueduct. We rushed to the old city and had a quick self-guided tour. The plan was to find a cheap hotel and finish our sightseeing in the morning. As we approached our car, which we had hastily parked along the main road, the last bits of sunlight flickered, and we noticed a sign:

> *From the place we are standing, commonly known as El Pinarillo, you can see the Jewish quarter of Segovia, home to the Hebrew population of Segovia until 1492, the year they were expelled from the city. The quarter maintains its particular character and a number of original buildings, such as the wall protecting the quarter, the Jewish slaughterhouse, the palaces of Gensol and Abraham Seneor, the*

houses of Simuel Denán and Yaco Cahopo, the shop owned
by Ica Cohen, the Mesón del Espolón and three synagogues.
From these places, following the thousand-year-old ritual
of Jerusalem, the deceased Jew would be taken for burial
through a gateway (Puerta del Socorro), and then along a
river (El Clamores) and over a bridge (the Puente de La
Estrella) to be laid in this place, which was their cemetery.

We spun around like synchronized *dreydls*, and there, across the
paved roadway, was the Jewish cemetery. What was left of it. The
remaining clouds were on fire, magenta and tangerine, streaking
the walled city with shadow and flame. We ran across traffic and
stood at the edge of the archaeological excavation. If we hadn't
read the sign, we never would have seen it. We never would have
recognized the site for what it was. It looked like a pile of rubble,
just holes dug out of the hillside, left unattended, with litter-
strewn paths. It did not look like a sacred space. Darkness fell, and
passing headlights flashed the sight over and over. Like a crime
scene.

I said a little prayer, what I could remember of the Mourner's
Kaddish. *Yitgaddal veyitgaddash shmeh rabba* … As a Hebrew
school dropout, I'd developed a habit of replacing Hebrew with
imitation jabber. Mumble, mumble, then everyone's favorite *'oseh
shalom bimromav*—something about making peace—spoken
louder than the rest, then more mumbles fading into silence.

Nebi's mouth was moving, but I couldn't hear her over the car
engines as they blared by. I walked closer to listen, but she had
stopped speaking. Through the last bits of daylight, I saw a tear
wash down her face.

When we got back to Madrid, I took a few days to sort through
my notes and re-read what I'd already written. I wanted to organize
my work life, create a plan and timeline. Nebi went off to work and
I made lists, set up spreadsheets, and filled in my calendar. I jotted

down impressions of all the people I'd met, the places I'd visited, and the characters I'd collected. I wrote ideas for more research and formulated follow-up questions. I wasn't exactly sure where 1937 would lead me, but it appeared I was already on my way.

By the middle of the second day, though, I was feeling more scattered and less directed. I took a break and headed toward the Prado. In addition to walking, being surrounded by art had always helped me focus and inspired me to action. And I was in an action-oriented mode. Any motion, particularly forward motion, was my preferred state when I was feeling overwhelmed. Something about the blur of frenzy felt comfortable. Maybe familiar was a better description.

I passed a museum I hadn't heard of—Museo Thyssen-Bornemisza—and saw they were having a Piet Mondrian retrospective. I knew a little about Mondrian, mostly from the 1960s Yves Saint Laurent color-block dresses and the L'Oréal shampoo bottles inspired by his work. Plus, I noticed the exhibit was his work from the thirties. Background research. The display was called a "visual dialogue." I definitely talked to myself the entire time.

Mondrian's need to control his art, to control his life in an obsessive-compulsive way, shouted from his paintings. I felt myself tensing as I looked at painting after painting of stiff, structured lines. My mind felt as constricted as the black and white grids. I understood his anal need to bind in an attempt to manage. Many of his individual paintings were created as if they were fragments of another, larger piece. If you could put them all together, perhaps the whole picture would appear. I felt a little too connected to Mondrian's mind when I read one final description: *Mondrian stuck to black and white and primary colors; he avoided green because green represented nature, which was too unpredictable.* Mondrian did not like unpredictable.

I had no idea Mondrian and I had so much in common. All I could think of on the way back to Nebi's was how I had been avoiding any thoughts about my personal life. Making work "to do" lists was important. Scheduling deadlines was critical. But had I made a plan for how I'd deal with Dad and Mark? Had I listed the pros and cons of moving to the DR? Had I allowed myself thoughts of a real relationship with Jamon? I hated to admit that Jamon was my green.

I was wheezing at the fifth-floor landing. Nebi opened her door, and, without needing an explanation, urged me to go with her to a Jivamukti class. Maybe that would center me.

Nebi's extra yoga pants actually fit, which already put me in a good mood as we headed to the studio. As with every other yoga class I'd taken, we started with setting an intention. A right intention. I'd always used these moments to set goals. Basically, I used class to work through the problem *du jour*. (That was after my usual internal snarky retort: *Hey, isn't the road to hell paved with good intentions?*) Something Nebi's instructor said made me realize I had been misinterpreting all the other yoga instructors' directions. Setting an intention is not goal-oriented. It's not about a future outcome. According to Buddhist teachings, setting an intention is about being kind to yourself in the moment, about freeing yourself from clinging and grasping.

More likely, I hadn't been ready to hear until Mondrian shouted in my ear.

Certainly, goals were important, but figuring out a better way to handle finances, tweaking plot structure, or formulating a strongly worded letter to my brother were not what Buddha had in mind in his Fourth Noble Truth. For the next hour and a half, I followed my breath. I focused on the moment, on the breath, on the gap between each breath.

The intention I set was to not be attached to the outcome. I'd had a long life, with a lot of outcomes I'd imagined. A whole stack of them. I hadn't been using my right intentions, so it would probably take a while to develop them. I'd have to exercise my intentions like a muscle, build them up little by little. And I could start by letting go of expectations.

No sooner did I breathe into this new awareness than I was distracted by thoughts of Mark. I had tried to call him repeatedly, but he didn't answer. I had had enough. If Mark wouldn't meet me in New York as soon as I was finished visiting Dad, I was going to go see my brother. But before I went home, I had something to take care of, one more stop along the way.

Oh, shoot, what had the yoga instructor said?

"If thoughts come, let them come, watch them go. Be kind to yourself. Return to your intention."

Om sweet *om*. Oh my. Right intention is all about coming home to oneself. About letting go of demands. Hadn't I just embraced this new philosophy? Hadn't I just decided to exercise my intentions? Temporary amnesia must have taken over. It looked like I needed more practice.

Chapter 8

My time in Spain brought up a lot of feelings. Since I'd left Sosúa, I had been busy with research and writing, trying to figure out what was going on with Mark and Dad, traveling, and visiting Nebi. Obsessed with all things 37. In what little downtime I had, and at certain encroaching moments of my hyper-busy schedule, I was filled with thoughts of Jamon. When I allowed myself, I realized I was aching for him. How I longed to find out what his touch would feel like. To debate philosophical underpinnings of string theory. To laze about with him, saying nothing. It wouldn't be complicated, the way it had been with Gregg. Together, Jamon and I would make good toast.

It sounded naïve, and if Nebi had told me she felt this way about some guy she had just met, that was what I would have called her. There was just something so familiar about Jamon. I had spent most of my life feeling like I didn't fit in, but in Sosúa, in Jamon's presence, I finally felt like I belonged.

And I knew, if I gave in to his tender offerings, I would be in it for the long haul. Before I could even contemplate that kind of commitment, I had to find something out. I had been in love like this only once before, and it hadn't been with Gregg. I still loved Gregg very much; he was the father of my child, and for that gift and the special partnership that connected us through that, I was eternally grateful. But the kind of love you approach with full abandon, that makes you long not only for your partner, but for yourself, that love in which you trust not only the other person, but yourself—that is a rare find. Rare as butterfly milk.

If you're lucky, whole love comes along once in your life. I'd felt that kind of love the entire summer I was sixteen. I recognized the role of chemistry and lust in young love, but that was a limited definition of what I felt for Yakir.

He was a kibbutznik, born in England but raised on Kfar Blum after his family immigrated to their "homeland." The first time we met, he was driving the tractor that took the rest of the workers, including me, out to the fields. He glanced back at me when we left the kibbutz for the 5:30 a.m. shift. His profile was beautiful; he looked like a classical Greek sculpture. Like the discus thrower that sat on my desk below the tiny *Guernica*. I stared at the back of Yakir's shaven head as we bumped along the rocky farm road and crossed the Jordan River on our way to the cotton groves. Maybe the diesel fumes affected me, because I felt like he was sending me a message: *finally, you've come*. The thought was a song to my heart.

After six hours in the field, I was sweaty and dog tired. At our noontime break, I looked for him, but he was nowhere around. Shaina, a girl on my work crew, said, "My brother won't be back until the end of the day."

Mortified that my infatuation was so noticeable, I tried to be inconspicuous and walk away, but I tripped on a rock. I hopped without an ounce of grace, grabbing my stubbed toe. Shaina laughed, "He has that effect on girls. Poor thing. Should I call the *toe* truck?" That good-natured teasing began our friendship.

As we assembled for our last break of the day, pouring cool, clear water to drink away our thirst and wash away some of the dust from the fields, the tractor sputtered over the farm road. He jumped off and walked over to me.

"I'm Yakir."

"Hi, I'm Polly."

"Finally, you've come."

He took a bandana out of his pocket and gently wiped away the mud that was already drying on my forehead. It was the most comforting feeling I'd ever known.

That afternoon, after a long shower, I took my time getting ready. I felt like I was preparing for something special, like I was at a precipice, about to jump into a new beginning. Though I was anxious to go find him, I wanted to take each moment slowly, to savor these preparations as one luxuriates in putting the finishing touches on a gift box before presenting it to the recipient.

I stood naked in front of the mirror as I put on my favorite lotion, rubbing it in unhurried swirls. I splashed Jean Naté on top of the lotion, and methodically combed back my clean, wet hair into a tight ponytail. I put on a pair of small gold hoop earrings, and only then did I put on my simple white cotton panties and matching bra. I shimmied into a short white cotton dress. My arms and legs and shoulders gleamed from the day's exposure to the Middle Eastern sun. Just what my New England skin had been craving. When I finished witnessing the transformation, I went to the end of the hallway and dialed the payphone.

It would be ten o'clock in the morning back east. Mark was away at summer camp, hired to be their theater coach for the same camp we had both attended for many summers as campers. This was Mark's first summer as a counselor. Our first summer apart. Since the camp schedules were fairly regimented, I hoped he'd be in the main office for mid-morning break. I was right.

"Marky!" I shouted as soon as he picked up.

"Good timing, sissy. Just heading back to my bunk. How the hell are you? What's it like in the old country?"

"It's pretty great. My work crew's intense. I'm so wiped. But it feels good."

"You sound good."

"I am good."

It was silent, and before I let him talk, I continued.

"Marky, I think something's about to change for me. I wanted to tell you—"

"Who is he?"

"How'd you know?"

"Holy crap. You be careful, okay? Don't be stupid and bring home a little Sabra baby."

"Mark!"

"I'm serious. You still don't get it. Boys are only after one thing."

"What about you?"

"I'm just as bad."

In the distance, a group of kids called Mark's name. Then the voices got louder, and there was laughing and Mark trying to break up some friendly squabble.

"Sorry, Pol, I gotta go. Have fun, but not too much. Love you."

And as I said "love you" back, the phone clicked. I never even had a chance to ask him how he was doing.

I guess I had been looking for Mark's blessing, and with it, or close enough, I was ready to go meet the boy I knew would be my first love.

As I walked into the kibbutz's main dining hall, the fluorescent lights reflected off my rosy brown skin, highlighting the contrast of my pure white dress. Across the room, I saw the already familiar back of Yakir's head, his strong shoulders and V-shaped torso. The moment I stepped forward, he turned and looked straight at me. It was like that scene out of *West Side Story* when everyone is at a dance and all the faces and bodies blur except for Maria's and Tony's.

We walked toward each other, and as if we had rehearsed, simultaneously sat on a bench at the end of a long dining table.

"You clean up nice," he said. His accent was a perfect, compelling cross between adorable and provocative.

I blushed. "Thanks."

"You sure you're not a local? You look just like a Sabra."

"Nope. Just in spirit."

"Me, too. I'm like the desert cactus: tough on the outside, and delicate and sensitive on the inside."

I knew I had found my exact complement. Maybe he was the missing piece.

As each dawn broke for the next two months, we were together. Sometimes we woke early and met by the river, to watch the sun rise over Jordan. Sometimes we slept together.

I remained a virgin, but we explored every other way to enjoy our bodies. At first, Yakir was so sweet, much more considerate than the guys back home, who got pissed if you didn't give them a blowjob on the first date. I wasn't a prude, but I wanted my first time to be special. Something to remember. And with somebody to remember, not some jock who barely knew my name.

I knew I wasn't Yakir's first, and I didn't exactly know what I was doing, but he said he was satisfied. I felt like he cherished me, like he was content just kissing and touching. As the weeks went by, I could tell he was getting more and more frustrated. He kept taking things a little further, or deeper. He started saying that he wanted to take our physical relationship to the next level. I really wanted to, but I was nervous. Even though I wouldn't admit it, there was some part of me that was afraid to let go; I'd heard sex was about losing yourself, and I didn't know if that was a good thing.

Then one night, we skipped out of *Shabbat* dinner. We were napping under an apple tree when Yakir climbed on top of me. I loved the feel of his body pressing against mine. I reached over and grabbed an apple from the weeds. I held it up to Yakir's mouth and he bit it, then I took a bite. The mealy texture was disgusting, nothing like crisp, tart Vermont apples. I turned my head and spit. I felt Yakir laughing, sucking in air and breathing intensely.

His hard-on rubbed my groin with each breath. At first I was aroused, and returned his deep kisses. I was lost in the crickets' song and the stream running nearby. I was found in the sun beating down, and in Yakir's tender touch. When he pulled down my panties, it felt different from before. I wasn't sure what was happening. His movements were jerky, his body writhed and pumped with a frenetic energy. And then I saw the look on his face as the pain hit. He had entered me.

"Get off!" I screamed.

But he kept pumping. So hard, it hurt so much.

"Yakir! Stop!" I punched him on his side. "What're you doing?!" I kept punching until he rolled off of me.

"Shit. Shit. Fuck," he said, spitting.

I just lay there, panting and crying. Then he started crying.

"I'm so sorry. Please. I'm so sorry. I love you so much."

That was the first and last and only time he said he loved me.

I couldn't look at him. The crickets stopped, and clouds covered the sun. Only the steady stream carried on.

I avoided him for the next few weeks. I longed for him, but after what he had done, how could I trust him? Still, I couldn't help my feelings, that yearning. In my confusion, I did what felt most natural. I shut down. I wasn't angry. I wasn't hurt. I felt nothing, which was my family's legacy. A very useful trick I learned at an early age. Call me Cleo, queen of denial.

By the time the apples were ready to harvest, it was time for me to go home, only I felt homeless. I convinced myself that we lost touch because we lived thousands of miles apart. The Internet did not yet exist, and baby blue tissue-paper airmail envelopes were the only means of communication. His letter arrived in early September, and was filled with apology and explanations. I didn't write back. I ran home from school every day just to see if a new letter had arrived.

Mom would be cleaning or cooking and she'd look up at me as if I were a stranger. "You're always running. What are you are running away from?"

"I'm not running away from anything. I'm running to get the mail."

But she was right. I was running away.

"He's not going to keep writing. Long-distance relationships are tough. You might as well forget about him before you get hurt."

Her words weren't sarcastic, but they sure tore at the flesh.

"You know what? I'd rather live waiting for his next letter, not knowing what the future will bring, than live in your little pretend perfect bubble of fake superficial love."

I never told her the truth. I never apologized for being an ungrateful, nasty daughter. I never wrote Yakir back. And he never wrote me again.

Traveling to the Lavapiés and Toledo and Segovia and Sosúa had fueled my interest in my ancestry. Ance*story*. Maybe I had become yet another fleeing Jew, searching for refuge, for a homeland. Only I wasn't driven out by power and hate. I was moving forward freely, propelled by autonomy and love, Nebi's *modus operandi*.

The night I left Spain, we ate a disappointing meal—no *tapas* or *rioja* in the airport restaurant.

"Say hi to Daddy for me. And Pop-pop. And Uncle Mark."

"I will when I see them. But it'll be a while. I'm taking a detour before I head home."

"To the DR?" she said, teasing.

"As a matter of fact, I'm going to Israel. For research."

"Seriously? Nice of you to tell me. Maybe I would've come."

"Maybe I that's why I didn't tell you."

She winced.

"I'm sorry, sweetie. That wasn't very nice. I can't explain right now, but I need to do this alone."

A tearful kiss, a long, tight farewell hug, and I was through security. The flight to Tel Aviv was less than five hours long. After my visit there, I'd travel to Jerusalem and fly directly to New York from there. Gregg had agreed to check on my house. And yes, I'd already formulated a plot outline for a story about two teenagers who lived in Palestine. In 1937. I hadn't really lied to Nebi.

The Mandate would have been in effect for fifteen years. My characters would be too young to remember when the League of Nations split the weakening Ottoman territories, placing Palestine under British rule and TransJordan under Saudi rule. Or when British Foreign Minister Balfour declared his support for establishing a Jewish homeland in Palestine. But they would have heard stories of the riots that broke out as soon as word of the Mandate spread. Over the years, there were periodic violent clashes and revolts, resulting in much mayhem and so many deaths that in 1937, the Peel Commission recommended partitioning Palestine into two separate states.

I had a few ideas buzzing about in my brain, but my real reason for going to Israel was not to do research for a piece of historical fiction. My desire for Jamon was growing, and the prospect of an actual relationship was in the very scary realm of reality. The final step to accepting that certainty was to flex my right intention. To let go.

Or maybe I really wanted to see if I could rekindle another story, one that had taken place in my own personal history. I was going to find Yakir.

Chapter 9

I arrived at the hotel in Tel Aviv, showered, and went to the lobby. No use googling Yakir. I had done that many times throughout the years. With no luck. Instead, I was going to rely on a colleague from *The Jerusalem Post* I had met when we were both on the faculty for a writing retreat the previous summer. When I'd received the call about Mom's death, I immediately took off, and felt bad leaving her short-staffed. She was nice enough to check up on me, and we'd kept in touch over the past year. Fortunately, she was available to meet at Kfar Blum the following day. She would help track down Yakir.

The hired driver met me in the lobby with *As-salamu alaykum*. I smiled with a hearty hello. I knew better than to shake his hand.

"You're not Arab?" His eyes frowned in disbelief as I shook my head. "Oh, but I assure you, you must have Arab blood in you."

I half expected him to add, "You look just like Uncle Vito."

The fact that the driver had confused me for Arab was nothing new. No matter where I looked like I fit in, Israel was one of the places I felt most at home. I felt it the moment I landed when I was sixteen, and I felt it again, now, three-plus decades later. If you've ever scoffed at or wondered why anyone would walk off a plane and kiss the ground, you don't understand the illogical, fundamental desire to connect to a homeland. You either take your home for granted, or you're one of the lucky ones who feels at home in your own skin, no matter where you live.

We headed out of Tel Aviv and, after driving for awhile, what was new, what did not exist when I had last been in this part of the world, was unsettling in its stark prominence, the form clearly intentional for function—and intimidation factor. As we drove on, the wall came into view. The. Wall. Not the holy Western Wall, although much wailing has resulted from this wall. To Israelis, it was called a separation wall, or a security fence. To Palestinians, it was called a wall of apartheid. When the BBC or the *New York Times* referred to it, they used the term *barrier*. Built in response to the rampant violence during the Intifada, with the stated goal of eliminating "hostile infiltrations," the impact on Palestinians was malignant: severing communities, creating anxiety about the future, denying access to basic human rights. I had of course heard about it, and held all the complexities of its existence, but until you see it in person, it is difficult to explain what a visceral reaction the 25-foot-tall concrete wall provoked. My back spasmed. I couldn't breathe. I started salivating, and felt my blood pressure rise. Fight or flight response. Acute stress response. And this was my first time seeing it. What would it be like living with this wall fence barrier ever looming? Imagine if there was some sort of massive wall like this on our American borders. Like that would ever happen.

The driver checked on me, but it almost felt as if he were letting me alone, letting me get a tiny taste of what it felt like. I was glad he did. I didn't want to stuff, to erase, this new knowledge, and unless I really let myself feel the pain caused by this wall (what little I could), it would be easy to compartmentalize.

Through my tears, I noticed a sign pointed to Wadi Ara, which I had heard was a good place to learn more about the Arab culture in that part of the country. It was just a slight detour, after all. I had been waiting for years, so what were another few hours?

It was worth the stop. A large building and enormous gateway from the Ottoman period stood next to a couple of old stone houses, remnants of an Arab village from the late nineteenth century. Outside the village were burial caves dating back to the Bronze Age. We passed an information sign, and the driver shook his head in disgust.

"You see, plans are in the works to build an ultra-Orthodox Jewish settlement. Right here. Smack in the middle of the Wadi Ara. Probably just the beginning."

I pointed in the opposite direction, where another sign described the Hand in Hand School, a site for Arabs and Jews to come together, to learn from each other, to create equality and understanding.

"That's a good idea," the driver said. "We all have lots to learn."

"There's always hope," I said, softly. After seeing the wall, I'm not sure I believed my own words.

The history of the Middle East is even more convoluted and confusing than the current state of affairs. And therein lies the root of the problems. Shifting borders and alliances, layers of takeovers and defeats, competing causes in the name of religion. Hard to discern who and what is holy-inspired or power-hungry. And does it matter? Like many Jews, I had serious questions and grave concerns about the current government's actions. My mixed feelings about the State of Israel only fueled my insecurity about revealing my religion to strangers. Too many hard feelings. Too much misinformation. Continuing throughout history, there have been too many different sides to the story, too many different shades of truth. If only we could look at each person individually and value them for their humanity, instead of which tribe they were born into, or what tribe they have adopted.

My head was swirling from the historical tour and my conflicted emotions. Add to that my driver's own personal perspective—he seemed to think my vulnerable state meant it was a good time to proselytize—and I was in desperate need of a break. At his suggestion, we picnicked at Nahal Alexander while we watched the softshelled turtles on the shores of the river. It was a wonderful suggestion. The turtles were three feet long, and some frolicked in the water, creating a white foamy spray, while others lazed about in the sweetly scented eucalyptus grove.

Thank goodness there had been enough people with enough smarts to clean up the river pollution. Only twenty years earlier, most of the eggs wouldn't hatch, and those that did were born deformed. Preservation efforts changed all that. Now, if we could only remember to think before we did harm to rivers, to turtles, to our neighbors. Maybe there should be a fourth monkey: *do no evil*.

Down one side of the riverbank was an ancient ruin, which was used as a customs station to collect duty specifically for exporting watermelons, of all things. Or so the archaeologists believed. Where the river flowed into the Mediterranean, a beautiful beach stretched itself out in the afternoon sunshine. Remnants of another structure cast irregular shadows on the bank, and it was hard to make out what the original form might have been. My driver explained that it used to be a quay. When the British authorities had turned away ships filled with European Jews, this quay had been used for a clandestine operation, to help sneak the Jews in and enable them to flee from the Nazis. He joked that maybe they traded watermelons for Jews. I didn't laugh. He told me the quay had been built during the British Mandate. In 1937. And then I laughed out loud.

We drove north, but nothing looked familiar. The Kiryat Shmona bus station was now outside the lobby of a six-story building, and the small village had grown into a big urban center. Where was the rustic falafel stand Yakir and I used to visit? The rickety wooden tables shaded by palm trees? The dusty gravel roads? Had I imagined it all? Or had time just moved on?

We arrived at Kfar Blum at dusk. My colleague had left a message of apology: due to a family emergency, she couldn't join me. The kibbutz receptionist handed me a thin stack of papers; my colleague had faxed what little information she had. I bid farewell to my driver and started to pay him. He looked me in the eyes with grave intensity and spoke, as if in recitation:

"*Itha marra be yowmun wallam aktabes hudan wallam astafed ilman fama thak min omri.*"

"That's beautiful. It sounds like a song. What does it mean?"

"If a day passes that I do not do a good thing or learn a new thing, it is not part of my life."

"Thanks, that's good advice. I hope you have a safe trip home."

"*In šā'Allāh,*" he said. God willing.

I left my luxury room at the four-star Pastoral Kfar Blum Hotel—a far cry from the basic dorm-style housing we had when I'd worked here as a teenager. I wandered around the kibbutz as the sun settled in for the night and the stars came out to play. Nothing seemed like I remembered. There was a spa and Turkish baths, a zipline, a ropes course, a rock-climbing wall, and an outdoor amphitheatre. None of those existed when I had lived here. Tourism had evidently become an income-generating business for the kibbutz. Perhaps it was a draw for new kibbutzniks, since fewer and fewer young people were interested in living the collective lifestyle.

I'm not sure why I didn't realize this place would have changed over the decades. Just because something gets fixed in memory doesn't mean it gets fixed in time. It was oddly comforting that the bomb shelters were still where I remembered them. And the pool looked the same. The night sky was dazzling with stars so vivid, it was as if this place was in some way closer to the heavens. It was getting dark, and despite the twinkling guides I couldn't find the statue of the naked woman about to bathe, carved in stone. Our meeting place.

"*Look: thoughts and dreams are weaving*
their warp and woof; their wide camouflage-net,
and the reconnaissance planes and God
will never know
what we really want
and where we are going," Yakir recited.

"Did you write that?"

"Don't they teach you anything in America?" he said, laughing. "It's Yehuda Amichai."

"It's beautiful."

"You're beautiful."

Just then, Yakir snapped his camera. I still had the old Polaroid of me in front of that statue. In a bikini. Back when I had a waist.

I wished I could remember the last time we had met at the statue. But it was so long ago.

All night, gravity pulled on me, relentlessly. I felt like my world, the entire universe, had collapsed. No more light could get out. Like one of those stars that had been shouting so brightly last night, but had actually died millions of years before.

The restless sun rose over the Upper Galilee, and the reality of where I was and what I was doing finally sank in. I had fallen asleep reading through the faxed papers, trying to cross-reference facts on the Internet. I had little information, but what I did know was that I was not going to be able to reunite with Yakir.

My first love had died from cancer two years ago.

Loss upon loss filled me up like a black hole. And like a black hole, surrounding the enormous, overwhelming mass was the point of no return.

Yakir's sister Shaina still lived on the kibbutz. I had spent many days with her when we were kids. She was part of our gang, the American and British kids who came to Israel to find themselves, and, in addition, found each other. Over the years, I had tried to locate her, but she had married and changed her name. But now I knew her name, and her address.

Time to take a deep breath and go for another walk. If my legs would stop shaking. I crossed the lobby and saw another statue, one of the kibbutz's namesake, André Léon Blum, the first socialist and the first Jew to serve as Prime Minister of France—in 1937. A sign reminded me that Kfar Blum had not even existed in 1937. I passed the shiny sports complex next to the acres— hectares—of red grapefruit, and Mount Hermon loomed in the distance. Our group had hiked to the top and shouted songs in English and Hebrew, blaring our lungs as only irreverent teenagers can do. The audacity of youth. According to the Book of

Enoch (Noah's great-grandfather), Mount Hermon is where fallen angels descend to earth.

> *And it came to pass when the children of men had multiplied that in those days were born unto them beautiful and comely daughters. And the angels, the children of the heaven, saw and lusted after them, and said to one another: 'Come, let us choose us wives from among the children of men and beget us children.' And Semjâzâ, who was their leader, said unto them: 'I fear ye will not indeed agree to do this deed, and I alone shall have to pay the penalty of a great sin.' And they all answered him and said: 'Let us all swear an oath, and all bind ourselves by mutual imprecations not to abandon this plan but to do this thing.' Then sware they all together and bound themselves by mutual imprecations upon it. And they were in all two hundred; who descended in the days of Jared on the summit of Mount Hermon, and they called it Mount Hermon, because they had sworn and bound themselves by mutual imprecations upon it.*

I was pretty certain we hadn't thought about Enoch and "The Fall of the Angels: the Demoralisation of Mankind: the Intercession of the Angels on behalf of Mankind" when we made out near the clear mountain springs flowing from the summit. Maybe Israel does think about a great sin when it refers to Mount Hermon as "the eyes of the nation," a reference suggesting that its height—and location between Syria and Lebanon—makes it a perfect strategic early warning system. Could sin be in the eye of the beholder?

Mount Hermon left my line of sight as I headed for Shaina's house, set in a cluster of small residences behind the synagogue. When she opened the door, her face reflected the immediate recognition of my own, minus the anxiety.

Shaina grabbed my hand and pulled me to her as she whispered, "Finally, you've come."

Over tea and macaroons, we caught up. How had we gotten so old? How did our skin get as thin as tissue and dry as old cotton plant leaves? Her voice had deepened with age, and she laughed when I told her that now she sounded just like her brother. And she had the same hairy chin! We reminisced about that summer. Then she told me.

"He never stopped loving you."

Time is supposed to be linear, and move on. But that moment froze as time went backwards, flipping through memories and photographs, words scrawled on letters I never sent, emotion poured out onto pages of my diary. He had never stopped loving me?

"But he never told me. He only sent me one letter, and then I never heard from him again."

Without a word, Shaina moved gracefully across the room, like an apparition floating between worlds. She opened the bottom drawer of the simple white-lacquered buffet. She pulled out a box and walked toward me, her eyes never leaving mine, and presented it to me as a worshipper presents an offering.

Return to sender was printed in bold letters on envelope after envelope. Letters from the kibbutz. Letters from the army bases. Letters from college. Over and over. *Return to sender.*

In my mother's handwriting.

Shaina handed me one more letter. It was newer, and in a plain white envelope. Just my name was written, with no address, no return address, no stamp. No *return to sender.*

"He asked me to give this to you if—when—you arrived."

I held it like a child holds a cocoon they've found in the woods, wondering what will emerge.

As I cradled the letters, she told me about Yakir's death, and his life. Two years of struggle as the cancer cells defeated him. His wife was by his side the entire time. They had been married thirty years, and had no children. He wasn't able, and they chose not to adopt. He was the love of her life, but Shaina told me he did not feel the same. He loved his wife, but he never stopped thinking of me, his first and only love.

Thankfully, he'd never told his wife his true feelings. She had no idea there was another world going on inside his heart. She had been spared this other story. It would've been awful for her to feel unwanted, to feel like she was a second choice.

I stood up, wanting to flee. I fumbled with the letters, and Shaina gently put them all back in a neat pile. "Take them. They're yours."

We hugged as tightly as two sisters about to say a last goodbye. It was too much for me. My mind did flee, away from this new knowledge, from this moment. All I could think of was my dad, and how hard it must have been for him when Aunt Miriam died. He never had a chance to say a final goodbye to his sister.

I forced my mind back to this farewell, back to Shaina's arms, just as we let go of each other.

The only place to read the letters was the rocky farm road at the edge of the cotton fields, the spot where I had first met Yakir. I started with the most recent one.

> Dear Polly, dear, dear Polly,
>   If you are reading this, my old body has finally given out. Remember when I was young and strong? I'm glad you didn't see me as my muscles withered away and my skin sagged. I know you must still be beautiful. I can still smell your sweet scent, your lemony skin. You always smelled so good, even after a day pulling weeds!
>   Kissing your lips was like sipping from a cool waterfall.
>   I don't really want to die yet, but it doesn't matter. I've lived a full life. My only regret is that I did not spend it with you. I am so sorry I tore us apart.
>   You're the only one I ever truly loved. Our short but precious time together has lasted me until now. It will stay with me when this life has ceased. I'm not sure what comes next, but I am sure we will be together.
>   Remember Yehuda Amichai? I'm sorry I made fun of you for not knowing who he was. I really believe he wrote this for us:

'Once a great love cut my life in two.
The first part goes on twisting
at some other place like a snake cut in two.
The passing years have calmed me
and brought healing to my heart and rest to my eyes ...'
My dear Polly, thank you for coming back to me, for
bringing me calm. My last and only hope is that someday
you will join me for our second chance.
With great eternal love and deep sorrow,

Yakir

He had written it as he lay on his deathbed. I read every word carefully, under a palm tree. It was touching but it moved me only as a film manipulates emotions. Like a fictitious story. We had both shared that same story, a tether that we held on to. Yakir's sentiments resulted from a mixture of chemotherapy-induced confusion and false memories. All tinged with remorse. The clarity his letter brought was that we had both clung onto an imagined reality, and a profound but distorted loss we had chosen not to release.

The other letters moved me more. They were a yet-unopened account of a young man's life, an unintentional memoir. Page after page fluttered in the gentle breezes. I could hear the Jordan in the distance. Everything seemed distant. My summer in Israel, the conflicted longing I had felt for Yakir, and the false hope I had been resting on for too many years. What did not seem distant, what seemed too close to face at this moment, were Mom's actions. Her betrayal. Another act of unfaithfulness in a lifetime of detachment.

I would have kept the letters but the thought of carrying them with me, of making them part of my story, sickened me. The words of Yakir's life and my mother's ink stains left me as dry and parched as the eastern winds. I lit a match and watched the ashes drift in the withering hot drafts of the desert *hamsin*.

Just one more stop before heading home. Home. Whatever that meant.

I was relieved that, unlike Kfar Blum, Jerusalem hadn't changed a bit from the way I remembered it. In fact, the Old City hadn't changed much since King David ruled there three thousand years earlier. With its narrow alleys and vibrant markets, the whole place was at the same time enchanting and sacred. I had to remind myself it was real, and not some sort of Epcot recreation. It did feel like a Mid-East Magic Kingdom.

I picked up some trinkets at the Arab *suq*, and cried my eyes out at *Yad Vashem*. How can an entire room full of books contain the names of victims of the Holocaust? The sheer numbers were staggering. As I passed the Dome of the Rock, I felt and heard and smelled the hallowed building, and the next story I wanted to write formulated itself. The stories from '37 seemed to have a mind of their own. I jotted down notes until I realized I only had two hours before heading to the airport. Time for my last stop—the Western Wall.

When I was sixteen, this had also been my last stop before leaving Israel. I still have the tiny stone I took when I tucked my paper prayer into one of the crevices between the rough, sandy blocks. I had rolled my eyes at the old bearded men *davening*, with their stream of prayers that sounded more like droning horns than revered words, but I had carried that stone for years, and also carried the tradition. Wherever I'd traveled, I'd written on little slips of paper. Words had been my prayers, in any form: haikus, questions, lyrical wishes, or a special turn of phrase I thought was particularly brainy. I'd left these slips of paper—my apologies to the litter gods—every place I'd visited: in a knothole of a giant sequoia, squeezed into a clamshell on the Cape, tucked between stones at the 9/11 memorial. My messages and locales had been indiscriminate and interfaith.

But nowhere else felt like it felt at the Western Wall. One look and one listen to the wailing at the Wall, and all of my casual cleverness throughout the years was revealed as a series of faux-holy attempts. It's believed that the gate to Heaven is located near the Wall. That's why prayers made there transcend effortlessly to Heaven. You can see it in the stacks of weathered slips, thousands of wisps of hopes and pleas. Prayers formed out of paper steps, climbing up the cracks between the sun-drenched blocks to the skies. And you can feel it.

The drone of prayers faded as I walked toward the taxi stand. Around the plaza were men and women, painted all in white, wearing what looked like mummy wrappings. Was this some type of flash mob? I never expected buskers to be performing in such a holy place. Each person had transformed into a human version of strips of paper. They were holding signs written in quotes from the Psalms—the text, like the city itself, holy to all three religions. The music of the lyre, the songs of praise, cross all religions. One sign read:

> *"I praise You, for You have answered me, and have become my deliverance. The stone that the builders rejected has become the chief cornerstone. This is the Lord's doing; it is marvelous in our sight."*
> *~Psalms* 118:21-23

I stopped to write it down. Maybe something I'd use in my next story. Anything was fair game. Everything was material. As the taxi pulled out, heading to the airport, one of the street performers ran over and held her placard against the passenger window. I just barely made it out as we sped away.

> *"Consider the blameless, observe the upright; a future awaits those who seek peace."*
> *~Psalms* 37:37

As soon as I was settled in the airport lounge, I pulled out my laptop. Teenage voices—Palestinian teens—were speaking to me. Calling to me. From 1937.

I had a couple of hours before I boarded, and then it would be a ten-hour flight. I was running on adrenaline, and my fingers danced to tunes that came from some sacrosanct place. The intersection of right intention and divine intervention landed me in the middle of a village called Rosh Pinna.

AN OCCURRENCE
AT ROSH PINNA

BY P.A. STERN

They reached out for each other. All they wanted at this moment was to hold hands, like they had done so many times before throughout their seventeen years. It seemed that Channah and Asim had been together, best friends, since before birth. Their mothers found out a few days apart that they were pregnant. They even had the same due date. But Channah, never one for dawdling, was born early, with the smell of latkes *frying, on a mid-December day, the third day of the Festival of Lights. Asim waited another week; he was born with the need to catch up, always trying to find Channah, always wanting to be by her side. Asim, the protector. And this moment was no different.*

The town was covered with a thick dust that floated in the dry air. An unnatural cloud. They could not see each other, or anything else. Still, they knew they were within arm's reach. Channah could not feel the cobblestones against her back; she wasn't sure what to do. Asim would take care of this; he always did. There were crackling noises and the acrid smell of sulfur. Though there seemed to be much shouting, all the sounds were muffled, as if from a memory.

The tailor stood in front of his shop, yelling at the vendor. "You sold me yard goods last month, and they shredded into nothing more than threads. Such *schlock*! Useless! I want my money back, and I will never buy from you again."

"Well, if you will no longer be my customer, why then should I pay you back?" The vendor turned on his heels to walk down the cobblestone street, the wheels of his cart rising and falling on the irregular surface, a monkey grinding his organ.

The tailor barked and shouted until the vendor was out of sight. Asim and Channah ran past, hand in hand, giggling at his ruddy face and the Yiddish curses foaming from his grey-whiskered mouth. Just another day, and another argument on the streets of Rosh Pinna.

They were only five years old, and in a hurry to get their next adventure going. They had decided to be explorers that day, and map out their village from one end to the other. They had paper and pencils and Channah's mother's measuring tape—the one she used to sew her family's clothing and help the tailor, on occasion. They had asked their mothers to pack them snacks so they could stay out all day. There was important work to be done. Rosh Pinna—the cornerstone—was named for a verse from the Psalms: *I praise You for having answered me; You have become my deliverance. The stone that the builders rejected has become the cornerstone.* They would have to do it proud.

Asim's mother had insisted they leave only after a hearty lunch, and prepared them a traditional Arab stew made of lamb and lentils, Asim's favorite. The gamey scent steamed up the kitchen and made their tummies growl. A side dish of homemade yoghurt gave extra tanginess to the spicy stew, and also cooled the tongue. Asim's mother packed the explorers some fleshy apricots and kiwi she had picked that morning, and *ghoraibi*, the delicious cookies Asim helped make from fresh butter, before sending them on their way.

The day was magical, if not productive. They started out very seriously and industriously. Channah had her long, unruly hair pulled back into a tight ponytail, and she stood tall with a maturity that disguised her young age. She was clearly in charge, instructing Asim to help her count the number of steps from building to building, calculate the width of the roads, measure the size of courtyards and orchards and gardens. A pretend surveyor and her real assistant. As they stood next to each other, with their similar dark, almond-shaped eyes, wavy, dark brown hair, strong aquiline noses, and rosy cheeks, it was hard to believe they were not siblings. After less than an hour, they grew bored of the work and wanted instead to roam, not record. They stopped for a snack and a cool sip from the town spring. The sun shone down on their world; they saw each tree, they read each vein.

As they ate and plotted and teased, a few butterflies passed over their picnic. There were three two-tailed pashas and they fluttered a moment, hovering over some drips of ambrosial apricot nectar as if considering the risks, then took off. The children gathered up their snacks and ran after the grape-green butterflies, following in quick pursuit. Two of the prey disappeared, but the other was easy to keep track of, because this one had a chunk missing from one of its four tails. But two-tailed pashas fly high, way above the treetops, and soon the two friends could no longer see their pretty prey. Channah tried to chase it anyway, but Asim stopped her, afraid she'd stray too far.

At the spot it flew out of sight, there was a small sandy path down to the Rosh Pinna rivulet. They did not have to say anything; with just a glance, they were holding hands and on the trail as fast as their little legs could carry them. They threw rocks into the babbling stream. They splashed each other. They rested on the pebble bank, the strong Mediterranean sun beating down on their olive complexions. They finished what was left of their snack and the kiwi juice dribbled down their chins, sweet and sour.

Their memories of any day—especially holy days—included each other. Unique in their village as well as in other settler towns, the al-Kanani and Kohan families shared all of their festive meals, from the Passover S*eder* to *Eid Al-Fitr*. Channah had grown up so close to Asim's family and had acquired a taste for their foods, but

Channah's parents did not share her enthusiasm. They were happy they could use their *kashrut* laws as an excuse not to eat over at the al-Kanani house—other than on holidays.

During *Ramadan* in 1932, the year Asim was twelve, his father, Walid al-Kanani, announced that he would be leaving for Jerusalem for a few days. Asim wanted to travel with his father, and to fast just like him from dawn to sunset. When he was told he was not quite ready (for he had not yet reached puberty), Asim pouted and refused to eat. Channah finally cheered him up, and whet his appetite with apples and honey. She cut an apple in half and showed him the ten little holes inside and how it looked like a five-pointed star. She explained, "Since ten is the numerical value of the letter *Yud*, and five is the numerical value of *Hey*, together they spell out G-d's name, and remind us that if we look closely, we will discover G-d's hand in our lives. No matter how old we are." Asim knew Allah's hand was there as well.

Before he left for Jerusalem, Walid told Asim he could fast next year, and he could join him on another trip. This time, he was going to meet with some influential people, he told his son, who then told Channah. Channah's father Samuel thought it odd that his good friend Walid had neglected to mention this trip to him. If he had known he was going, Samuel would have accompanied him; he could always find business in Jerusalem.

Asim and his mother waited nervously for five days until Walid returned. Things had been relatively calm for a while, but it had still only been a few years since the bloody riots. The Mufti of Jerusalem had accused the Jews of plotting to destroy Muslim holy sites, which only fueled the fires of tension that had been brewing. *Izbah Al-Yahud!* "Slaughter the Jews!" was the call. Asim's mother knew that neither Jews nor Arabs were safe as long as the land acquisition disputes continued, as long as accusations were spewed, inciting revenge. For as long as time. As it always does, the vengeance bred violence with no boundaries; Jews, Arabs, and British all died in the aftermath. Poison cannot be directed into only one vein.

When the elder al-Kanani returned home, his wife and son felt great relief, which soon turned to surprise: traveling home with him were two strangers. While Walid was in the city, he had attended a lecture at the YMCA. There, two men spoke about their religions and how they related to the Muslim faith. They were a Christian and a Bahá'í. The two men were on their way to survey the villages in the Galilee, something to do with collecting land purchase data. Walid invited them to join his family for *Eid Al-Fitr*, the festive end of *Ramadan*. Since it was also *Rosh Hashanah*, the Jewish New Year, the Kohans invited all of them to come celebrate in their home.

So there they sat around their dining table, together with family and friends: Jews, Christians, Bahá'í, Muslims. Walid wore his white felt turban, Samuel wore his *yarmulke*. Asim's mother wore her beautiful, intricately embroidered headdress, and Channah's mother wore her plain linen headscarf. They waited for the call of the *shofar* and for the sun to set. Then, between prayers in Hebrew and Arabic, they offered and devoured full platters of both roast chicken and *maraq al dajaj*—chicken and potato stew—and rice, lentils, and dates. They broke the golden *challah*, always round on *Rosh Hashanah*, to signify the cycle of life. Of course, no pig was served.

They ate sweets until their teeth hurt: the al-Kananis brought *qatayef*, the sugary crepes that were another of Asim's favorite, and the Kohans served their sticky honey cake; they shared the wish for a New Year filled with sweetness. They made yet another blessing and broke open a fresh pomegranate, tasting the tart, sweet burgundy juice as the children tried to count the many seeds. Supposedly, there were 613, representing the 613 commandments of the Jews, the *mitzvot*, including good deeds to be done every day. Then Walid recited an Arabic poem, *Itha marra be yowmun wallam aktabes hudan wallam astafed ilman fama thak min omri.* "If a day passes that I do not do a good thing or learn a new thing, it is not part of my life." And they laughed and debated and learned about each other. Around that table—despite the many differences—they were joined together by their food, their hearts, and their humanity.

It was getting late. Asim and Channah were excused from the table so the adults could continue their chatter. Everyone shouted *Eid Mubārak!* and *L'shana tova!* as the children left and went out to the courtyard. They sat on the wooden bench and watched the stars come up as the sky darkened. The moon was turning from new to a slip of a crescent. Exhausted, they lay down in the stone-lined yard, side by side, staring up at the black sky lit with the thinnest slice of a moon, accompanied by flickering reminders of their place in the universe.

As the muffled shouts of the grown-ups filled the courtyard, wafting past the fluttering olive buds, gently tickling the palm fronds, landing softly on the glossy leaves of the pomegranate bush, Asim and Channah reached over and held hands, at peace on this day of awe. They did not know that a ripe pomegranate had fallen and cracked open, and was rolling toward them. The juices flowed through the rocky grid toward the resting children. When their parents discovered them there, fast asleep, they were at first startled to find their children's hands and clothes stained blood red. When they realized what had happened, there was nothing to do but laugh.

Channah heard her father the next day, whispering to her mother something about Walid. "Why does he always have to do things *be'shushu*? What does he think, he's some hotshot *shushuist* intelligence officer?" Asim's father, secretive? What did he mean? Why were they whispering? Channah walked in and her mother shushed her father. When she looked up at Channah, her mother's easy smile was as deceptive as a billowy cloud puff, its apparent lightness hiding the actual weight of the tons of water that comprise it. When the elders spoke of politics, which they did infrequently, and less as times and conflicts wore on, there was mostly shouting. Now, all the shouting faded like candle smoke drifting up, carrying prayers to Heaven.

As the memories stung, the stinging fog grew thicker. Channah and Asim were finding it harder to hold on. They searched for reason, they searched for each other as they tried to recall the past. The path to this moment.

"Our fathers sat in your kitchen and debated."

"It was not so long ago. My mother didn't think you should be there, but you stayed anyway. You pretended to stay to help serve tea, but I knew you were listening, using all of your self-control not to add your own thoughts. I waited outside, also listening to every word."

The tea water was boiling, and Walid was fuming. "Are you going to deny that the pioneering Zionists absolutely intended to conquer the country through the conquest of the soil? Why do you think your grandfather and the others came here other than to stake their place, to become firmly rooted in the land?"

"Trust me, when my ancestors came here in the late 1800s, they had no intention of taking over!" Samuel said, laughing.

Walid continued, in all seriousness, "And once the settlements are complete in the rural areas, what's next? At first your people wanted nothing of Jerusalem; there was no interest in it until twenty years ago. Now, all of a sudden, it's your spiritual homeland?"

"Those of us who were secular, sure, we didn't really care about Jerusalem, but the religious Zionists always wanted to return there, to the site of our temple, the Wailing Wall … You've been to our *Seders*, how do you not understand, we have always said *Le-shanah ha-ba-a b'Yerushalayim*, 'Next year in Jerusalem.' It's always been our dream. We just had to consider survival first, to find a place for all of our displaced people, so worrying about Jerusalem was not as pressing. Remember, even the Vatican was ready to oppose our presence in Jerusalem. One has to pick one's fights, and we decided to hold off on our claims to Jerusalem, our rightful claims."

"Your claims to *our* lands only began with your grandfather," Walid said.

Samuel turned toward his daughter to explain. "Your great-grandfather, from Russia, Papa Menachem, fled the pogroms in the 1880s and came here to help settle this village. He needed a place for his family, to work the land, to survive; at that moment, he was not so concerned with political happenings in Jerusalem. But Papa and the other *Hovevei Zion* soon realized that they had made a mistake. From then on, he preached to anyone who would listen, and even those who didn't: 'The land of Israel without Jerusalem is Palestine.'

"He worked hard with the Lovers of Zion, and they saved thousands of Jews, helping them find a new home here, settling the rural areas in our homeland." Aside, with a laugh, he added, "And besides, it was cheaper to buy this land than in the cities!"

Walid did not find the humor. "So at least you agree that your claims to this land only began in the past fifty years?"

"Still, in your mind, you see our claims as so recent? Even so, it shouldn't really matter. But how long do we need to go back? How long is long enough? Before the Ottoman rule? Before the Bronze Age when *your* Canaanite ancestors were conquered? Before the Greek Orthodox patriarch? Before the Crusaders—who conquered and ruled us all? Should we go as far back as those human remains they just found in Safed, of people who lived here over 600,000 years ago? Whose ancestor is this? Arab-Islamic rule only came about in the 600s. Because your people conquered the area then, does that dismiss our presence *before* that time? The conquerors become the conquered, and then it begins again. How far back do we need to go to make sense of this nonsense?"

The men were silent. The tea was still steeping in the pot, and was now as black as their mood; neither had taken the time to pour, and Channah did not have the nerve to intrude. She had become small, a spring wound tight by the kitchen door. She was coiled up, vibrating with her own arguments, her own confusions. If only Asim were by her now, he would guard her against the discord, make it all better. How could both sides make so much sense? Why did it matter? They were both here now. Their families were friends. So other Jews and Muslims could be, too.

"My friend, this is not nonsense. It's not about you, it's about your people stealing lands that do not belong to you, intending to conquer our land …"

Then Channah's father became furious; she'd seen him heated before, but she had never seen him erupt like this. "And when your father wanted to expand his shop, my father gave him money. 'It is not a loan, my friend,' he said. 'Use this to make your family prosper. If they prosper, our family, too, will be blessed.' Your father hugged my father, the two of them at a loss for mere words, the gesture enough of a statement. Finally, *In šā'Allāh*, he said. God willing. And now you accuse me, you accuse 'my people' of such malicious acts, such heinous intentions?"

Walid reached over and touched Samuel's shoulder. He handed him the hookah, offering hope that sharing the *sheesha* would bring them both calm. Passing the peace pipe. As Samuel lifted the brass base to take a smoke, Channah saw her father touch the elaborate pattern in the carving, lines within lines, lines crossing, lines crossing back, a labyrinth, hard to find the beginning or end, tracing the pattern that seemed to echo the complexity of their discussion. He exhaled, the scent of orange on his breath, his wrinkled brow revealing worries still in place.

"We'll keep arguing and arguing, forever," Samuel said. "You want we should keep going? It's *aroch kmo ha'galut*. Long like the diaspora."

The arguing had seethed to near-explosion, as it always had between these two hot-tempered Semites, but then friendship and respect overcame adrenaline. The cooling waters of the hookah tempered the fervent storm. Channah and Asim each took in a deep breath at the exact same moment, one in the house, the other outside.

The truth comes out in snippets. Love and friendship can suppress ancestral conflicts. Buried deep within, momentary flare-ups reveal true feelings kept in check out of necessity. But necessity, like alliances, can change in a flash.

> *Channah and Asim tried again to reach for each other. They knew their bodies were as close as the space between two heartbeats, but they could not see each other through the stinging smoke, and they could not feel where they tried to reach. It was best to keep going, to search their memories, hoping for a lifeline.*

When she first told him she was leaving to study at the Hebrew University in Jerusalem, he had joked about it. "Your papa had your application filled out the day they laid the cornerstone! You weren't even born yet! Did you have any other choice but to attend university next year?"

She had replied, "No, if they wouldn't let his grandfather or his father study in Russia, he was going to make sure I was able to get a college education in our new homeland."

"But I don't want you to leave Rosh Pinna," Asim had whined.

"I know, but you'll come visit me."

"Yeah, covered in dust from the fields, with calluses on my hands. Your new student friends won't understand why you cavort with the likes of me."

"Oh, Asim! Don't say that."

When he said, "It's too bad we Arabs don't have our own university. Maybe we will—someday," she didn't know what to say.

Perhaps that was where the seeds of discontent were sown. Another inequity between the cultures, widening the gap, testing the bonds. Channah hadn't realized it before, but now that she looked back, she was able to see transparency in the fog; it was back at that moment that Asim's veneer had begun to transform, to become unvarnished, tinged with bitterness.

Channah and Asim continued to reach out, to search for each other. As the dust grew thicker and their clarity began to drift away, they could not help but think back to the most recent argument, the last one, the one that had brought the truth to light.

"It was a beautiful fall day just two weeks ago, and my father was in the yard collecting the four species for our sukkah. *He had already gathered the date palm frond, the myrtle tree leaves, and the citron fruit."*

"He was trying to figure out how to cut the branches from the willow when my father entered your yard; I was close behind."

"Yes, when I realized I had left a basket of fresh eggs on the wooden bench in the courtyard, I looked up from baking. Then I saw you. I didn't like the look on your face."

"The riots had subsided for a few days, but we knew it was only time. Our peasants had been hurt economically. And now they were landless. Of course I was upset, of course there was unrest. You were comfortable in your warm kitchen. As usual, your head was in the clouds. How did you not know what was going on?"

"Of course I knew. It had been going on since we were toddlers. First the problems after the Mandate was announced. Then the '29 boycotts and riots. But it wouldn't stop. Now there were more strikes. And bombings."

"For good reason."

Asim could barely keep up as his father stormed into the Kohans' yard. Walid's accusations were flying as he moved toward Samuel. "You say you made the land good? You took sand and turned it into farmland, into orchards? You were able to do this because you stole our water. You couldn't have irrigated the land if you hadn't taken our resources."

Still looking up at the long willow branches, sharp saw in hand, Samuel spoke calmly, as if he'd been waiting for this moment, knowing it would eventually come. "It was the League of Nations who split the weakening Ottoman territories, who placed Palestine under British rule, who put TransJordan under Saudi rule. Your people didn't agree with Balfour, and you didn't accept the Mandate. And you still think my people caused all of this? You've been fed so much misinformation. You did not hear the truth. What, do you also believe that we committed blood libel?! Your people need to think. But instead, your answer is to riot and loot and kill. To punish us."

The floodgates opened as Walid spewed his own rhetoric. "All you *yishuvniks* complain that you gave money when you arrived, and now you do not get any services, no good medical care. Do you think we have good healthcare? We have nothing. No land, no doctors, no schools. You bring your people, you make demands. We're a poor country; now we're expected to provide services to two different communities. Your thousand pounds apiece cannot begin to pay for all that's needed to support you. What did you expect? To add insult to injury, you came here and took our jobs. You see what's happening in Jerusalem. Our people can't feed their families. We need the work. Now you want more jobs, and you want higher wages. And we all know you have secret funds coming in from your allies, your supporters. Yet still, you whine with greed."

There was a moment of quiet; neither man nor child could believe the depth of what they were hearing. Asim sank on the wooden bench. Walid did not let the moment last. "You and your Lovers of Zion should have gone to Uganda, like you originally intended."

A chill went up Channah's spine as she watched her papa grab his belly, and heard his next words, deeper, almost ... defeated. "How can you say such a thing? This is our home; this is where we belong. We escaped from Europe to come here. We bought land; we built a house, made a home. The British told us we should come, they set us up. Yes, it obviously was a setup. We are all, both of our people, just puppets—of Britain, France, Syria ... and now, now after we've lived here for years, built our lives here, we're told they want to put us under Arab rule, all of us Jews who moved here, assured the British would oversee our national home. The Peel Commission recommends to partition Palestine into two separate states—the wisdom of Solomon.

"There's so much antagonism now. So much violence. Who is there to defend our Jewish settlements? Your Grand Mufti incites more violence. He's collaborating with Hitler! Now they're talking about a land code, prohibiting Jews from buying land. They're blaming us for taking all the good land. They sold it to us—at ridiculous prices! When we bought the land, it *was* just sand, just swamps. We worked it, cultivated it. Now that it's fertile, they say we purchased all the good land from them. These orange groves would not be here if it wasn't for us. And now you won't let any more of us come here, to our homeland. You're as bad as America, who won't take us in. The Nazis continue to spread their hatred of us, to design ways to eliminate us. Our relatives back in Poland can't continue to live there. Their families will starve. And now we can't bring them here to join us."

Momentarily swallowing his fury, Samuel reached out. "My mother died when my little brother was born; he was nursed by a wet nurse, a Muslim wet nurse. And your own wife chose our daughter's name. 'She must be called Channah, child of grace,' she told us after she'd seen it in a dream. Can you not see how close we are? Don't let others dictate what you know in your heart."

The silence of distance grew. Channah stood motionless as her tears spattered the flour-covered counter. Asim sat tall on the bench and choked back his own sorrow. A reality formed slowly, achingly, like a bad dream unfolding, one you do not want to feel, one you have no way to stop.

You want us dead. You'll kill our children, you care nothing for us, both fathers thought, but didn't speak.

Holding back tears of sadness and rancor, Samuel asked, "My neighbor, my friend, what has provoked this wrath?"

"You killed al-Qassam. Our great martyr." The truth revealed, begun in Walid's simple response.

"No, not us, not us ... the British police killed him. A martyr? But he was training and arming peasants to destroy all our trees. To kill us. He preached the *jihād* against us. Just down the road, our neighbors were butchered, out on a walk to the gardens. I cannot believe you would support the actions of the Black Hand."

"And you tried to sneak in shipments of arms. At the port? Do you think we didn't know what those were for? You act like the innocent victims. Yet your *Haganah* defends your people. And what about your special night squads? One attack, then another. More torture, more Arabs dead. Your people are allowed to carry weapons; our people get executed for arming ourselves." Walid punched his fist on the wooden bench, startling Asim. The basket of eggs shook, and the shells cracked; the insides slowly leaked through the slats, down to the ground. Nothing could hold them back.

"Then your revenge. More Jews dead. A cycle of incessant destruction."

"The British come here to our village, they search our homes. They stole my mother's jewels, insulted my wife, tore our *Qur'an*. All in the name of stopping the violence, to find out who's rising up, where the arms are being hidden. Why shouldn't we join the revolt?"

"Walid? What are you saying? You must not follow the *Qassamiyun*. How could you, my friend, let Asim join the youth movement—whose entire goal is to destroy the Jews? Why don't you join up with your peace bands instead, to fight against these rebels?" To Asim, he implored, "My son, you were part of our family, your grandfather, what we did for him ... My neighbors, they told me not to let you in, not to trust you, please do not make them right, please, oh my G-d, no, please dear G-d."

Through his tears, Samuel noticed that Walid and Asim were now both wearing the white and black *keffiyeh*, a headdress worn as a symbol of Palestinian nationalism by the followers of al-Qassam. He gripped the saw in his hand tightly, but he could not even feel the deepening wounds.

"I was in the kitchen with my mother, making prep-arations for Sukkot. *My hands were full of flour and I heard the words our fathers were saying, felt the conflict, but I could only think of you as a sweet boy watching my grandmother, how she taught you to bake* challah, *making a mountain with her flour, scooping out a hole in the middle, gently placing the eggs and yeast and sugar and warm wa-ter, and swirling the mixture to form the dough."*

"Yes, I remember. When it came from the oven, I never smelled anything so good. And when you ripped a chunk of it, fresh-baked, still warm, and dipped it into honey, my tongue melted in the goodness."

"And then when I left that fond memory, and I un-derstood what was happening in our courtyard, I realized you just sat there, not even countering your father's argu-ments. As if you agreed with him, with his resentment, his hostility."

"I did—I do—agree with him."

"But Asim, you can't mean that. Asim? We've prayed together, we've eaten so many meals together, are we not from the same blood? How can you let the crowd mentality, the political forces tear us from your heart? I cannot bear to release you from my heart, it would be as if I had abandoned my own brother."

A week passed, and the two had not seen each other once. She missed her best friend. So, despite her parents' command not to leave the house, and specifically not to go see Asim, Channah went to see him anyway. She opened the al-Kanani gate slowly, halting just before the halfway point when the rusted metal hinge twisted ever so slightly, causing one short but loud squeak. If she stopped before that point and then quickly opened it the rest of the way, it would be silent, and she could enter undetected.

Asim was sitting on his stone throne. The limestone forma-tion, eroded into a perfect seat, had been here for eons, and his grandfather had built a beautiful garden with the stone as the centerpiece. Asim would sit and read, and write poetry evoking images of his surroundings, of his beloved *Qur'an*, of the lore of this ancient land. Sometimes, he'd sing his words, and the lyrical notes would drift over the olive blossoms or rest lightly in the myrtle boughs.

Channah snuck up behind him and put her hands over his eyes. He jumped and wrestled her to the ground forcefully. He grabbed a rock and was about to strike her face when he realized who it was. Her gleeful laughing ceased as soon as she saw the terror and aggression in his eyes. "Oh, my God, Channah, what're you doing? I almost crushed you!"

Channah was alarmed and confused. "We've played this game so many times before and always you've played along, in fun, with a light heart. Why now are you so defensive, so full of anger?"

"Channah, have you no idea what's going on? The British have come and torn through our home again; they all but accused me of being part of the gangs who are terrorizing the countryside. They didn't believe me, but my father reached our cleric, who intervened. The British bastards finally agreed to leave us."

Channah had never heard him speak like this.

Asim warned, "Sneaking up on me right now is not a good thing to do."

"I'm sorry. Do you want to go take a walk and play in the stream?" She reached for his hand, but he pulled away.

"It's not a good time. We're meeting with some people today. We have things to discuss."

"What people? What kinds of things?"

"Nothing to concern you."

Channah's eyes widened, became moist. Always, they had shared every detail of their lives, however small or insignificant. What book to read, which classmate to avoid, which place to explore. Soon, she'd be away at school, and they wouldn't have the daily contact. The details would be fewer, but she felt confident nothing else would change.

"Go. Just go off to your Hebrew University with all of your smart, privileged Jewish friends. Go figure out how to make things better for yourselves, and worse for us."

"Asim." She could say nothing more. Channah felt a depth of loss greater than she had ever known. Asim felt her loss, and his own. Channah tried to look at Asim, but he turned away. He would not look her in the eyes, eyes like his, so black there was no way to tell where the pupils began or ended. She ached, and could think of nothing else to do but walk away, past the myrtle trees, through the noisy gate. The sun was shining, but the sparkling reflections dancing along the cobblestones, the many shades of colors bursting from the autumn foliage, did nothing to lighten her heart.

Later that day, the riots began. Out of nowhere, hordes of young men stormed the streets in revolt. They threw rocks at buildings. They brandished daggers and clubs and pistols. The tailor ran out to see what was happening, and Channah saw him fall, a stone knocking him to the ground. They lit fire to the houses and stores. Channah screamed for her parents, ran toward her home. She knew she was supposed to crouch and hide, that was the drill—but she wanted to be home, so she ran as fast as she could down the middle of Rosh Pinna, the cornerstone.

The noise from the gangs and the flames was a deafening rumble, masking all other sound. No more stream flowing, no more rose finch melodies, no more gentle flapping of butterfly wings.

As she reached the town center, Channah heard yelling. Amaliyah istish'hadiyyah! *Die as Martyrs! So many voices shouting. In the midst of the cries, she heard Asim's voice calling for her. She turned to find him, and something struck her chest. She fell backward toward the ground in slow motion: first her head, then her body landing hard, flat on her back on the smooth cobblestones. Shots rang out and the sky filled with more acrid smoke. It was a sunny day, but the haze blocked out the sun, erasing the crystal blue sky.*

"Channah!" he yelled, panicked. "Channah!" his voice was getting closer. He would once again be her protector.

Then another muffled sound, an engine backfiring, a discordant chime. Asim stopped calling for Channah. He fell beside her, so close that their bodies, their hands, almost touched. But still, they could not find each other. They tried to reach out, and their arms would not move. With the last of their strength, they tried once more.

The insurgents continued their charge, trampling over Channah and Asim, whose bodies, for a brief moment, blocked their march as they advanced through the streets of Rosh Pinna.

You were my brother.   You were my sister.
I am a child of Palestine.   I am a child of Palestine.

When the dust settled, when their parents found them there, lying side by side on the cobblestones, holding hands, there was nothing to do but weep.

Chapter 10

I woke up shrouded in deep sadness, my face in a heavy frown, as if mourning for someone or something, but I didn't know who or what. Then I remembered Channah and Asim. It took me a few minutes to realize where I had been—what was real, and what I had created. Not easy to do in the most lucid of times.

My head was pounding. I went to rub the source of pain, and found a bump behind my ear. Had that always been there? There was one just like it on the other side. What was the pseudoscience that examined skull bumps to determine a person's disposition and inclinations? Cranioscopy? I thought it was phrenology. We had studied it in Physical Anthro class. Most of it was harmless, but during the 1930s, the Rwandan government had used this fringe science to prove the superiority of Tutsis over Hutus. The indentations and skull shape correlated to different personality traits and abilities—and disabilities. If I remembered correctly, the brain was broken down into different regions.

Thirty-seven of them.

I wasn't even out of bed yet, and I was already in a thirty-seven state of mind.

Coffee was perking, the neighbor was mowing, the cat was clawing my face. Time to get my day going.

I staggered into the closet and pulled down several old shoeboxes. I had to prop myself up on a suitcase to reach, but my hand finally touched smooth cedar. I sat on the closet floor among worn sneakers and hardly worn pumps, twenty-year-old cowboy boots and brand-new stilettos, my many personalities in the shape of practical and frivolous footwear. The Lane cedar mini hope chest was covered in a layer of thick dust; unlike my mom, I didn't clean what I could not see.

Beneath the mustiness was a ragged piece of cotton boll I had picked on the kibbutz over thirty years earlier. Underneath my old El Al boarding pass were a few photos, including the one Yakir had taken. Me in my white bikini, standing in front of the statue. And there was his letter, the only one I had received. I didn't even read it again. I had read it so many times throughout the years. The words were etched in my grey matter, and now they no longer mattered. I ripped up the letter and stacked all the tiny slips of paper. I threw away all of the other vestiges of that long-lost, serpentine love, and a distant past. So much for hope in a chest.

Pious Jews say there are ten levels of prayer, and then there is music. And so I sang and danced around my house, sending my off-key notes like smoke from a smudge stick, cleansing the old spirits and making room for the new. As long as I was mixing tribal metaphors, I started to dance a *hora* and I began singing *Hava Nagila, Hava Nagila, Hava Nagila* … Let us rejoice. I imagined Channah and Asim, dancing the *hora* together. I missed them. I missed who they could have been, the difference they could have made if things had turned out … another way. No. Not going down that road. If I had learned one thing from my journey to Israel, it was that there is no use living in the land of what ifs.

Hava Nagila … I was singing so loudly, I almost didn't hear the phone ring. Unknown caller. I let the machine answer, to see if the caller lasted through my annoying outgoing message. Telemarketers never did. "You've reached me …" *Beeeeeep.*

"Polly? I thought you'd be back by now."

The one voice that could bring me out of the what ifs of the past and into the what ifs of the future. I never knew I could move so quickly.

"Hi!"

"Hi, cutie. You are there. Hope I didn't wake you."

Wake me is exactly what you did, I thought. What I said was, "No."

"You sound out of breath."

"Just out of shape."

"Your shape is amazing."

"Thank you."

Faster than a speeding bullet! More powerful than a locomotive! Able to accept tall compliments at a single bound! Look! Up in the sky! It's Superwoman! Nice job, Polly.

"What're you up to?"

"Already working. Sort of."

"So early? Polly, you need to come down here and get into island mode."

"Yah, mon," I said.

"Yes?"

Huh?

"Get it? You said *Jamon*. Like they do down here, with the silent J. Never mind."

And then my jet lag lifted, and I got it. I snorted and held back giggles. One more snort, and my shoulders shook with silent, uncontrollable hysterics. I got it, all right. Time to let the last little slips of paper I'd been holding onto drift up and away. Time to send the prayers to Heaven.

The next time the phone rang, it was Mark. He was still in New York, and just wanted to let me know that everything with Dad was under control. He suggested I come at the end of the month. After he had gone back to California.

I was exhausted, but if I headed right down, I could catch him before he left; it would be my only opportunity to see him. I was also already thinking of my next 1937 story, and New York was the place to do that research. I packed an overnight bag, gassed up the Prius, checked the Tenement Museum tour hours, and headed south.

Mark had told me he was leaving on the weekend, so I hoped to be able to get him to myself for a couple of solid days. Maybe he'd even join me at the museum, so we could explore our ancestry together. We'd often talked about doing a genealogical search of our *mishugenah* family. It would be a great gift for Nebi.

Mark had been so masterful at avoiding me, then pretending it was just bad timing. Did he think I was that gullible? Maybe I was. Well, time to put an end to Gullible's travels.

I'd never had much trouble parking in the Lower East Side. There were so many side streets, so many people coming and going. If I timed it just right, when businesspeople were heading home and tourists hadn't yet arrived for dinner, there were usually plenty of spaces available. It was a finely honed skill, though—one I had perfected over the years.

Dad was living in Cabrini Eldercare Facility on East 5th. After Mom died, he had quickly gone downhill, and had to be moved from our family home. The social worker said that it was a fairly common phenomenon for a spouse to get ill, or even die, within a year of losing their loved one. It was particularly true if the husband was the survivor. They called it dying of a broken heart. You know all those married people's tombstones with death dates within a year of each other? What would it be like to have your life so intermeshed with another's, even to the final moments?

There was one space on a street that prohibited parking on Mondays and Wednesdays, 7 a.m. to 9:30 a.m., for street cleaning. It was Wednesday afternoon, so I was set for the next few days. Things were starting off well.

Cabrini's entire lobby was purple and full of violets, just like their sign and brochure. They explained their logo: "As a young child, St. Francis Xavier Cabrini loved violets, and imagined them to be bearers of God's love. She sent them forth in paper boats down the river. In our journey as a Cabrini community, we give shape to her vision."

They were sending Dad down the river in a paper boat? Not very comforting. I chuckled out loud as I went to the reception area. The smell hit me like a stone wall: a cocktail of must, disinfectant, overcooked meat, old skin, and pee. I felt nauseated, though it wasn't just the smells that were making me feel sick. Dad sat in the corner of the sunny lobby and Mark sat by his side, reading out loud.

I whistled the chickadee call, our secret song. Mark looked up, and his dumbfounded face made me beam, then hiccup. I ran over and sat on his lap, and he hugged me hard, like my old brother bear. He must have forgotten that he didn't like me anymore.

We wrestled and ribbed. It had been too long. An orderly smiled as he passed by.

"How's Stephen?" I asked.

"He's pretty terrific."

"Is the adoption still on? I can't wait to be an auntie."

Mark wriggled me off his lap. Gone was my momentarily playful, loving brother.

"Polly, what are you doing here?" He sounded as uncomfortable as he acted.

"Uh, nice to see you, too."

Dad had been staring into space. I thought I heard him mumble "Miriam, Miriam," but then he stopped and turned. His voice was confused when he asked, "Do you know when she'll be back?"

Mark turned to Dad. "Who, Dad?"

I whispered to Mark. "Is he waiting for his sister?"

"Where is she?" Dad sounded so befuddled.

"Who, Dad?" Mark tried to placate him.

"Lainie. Where's my wife?"

"Hey, Dad, it's me, Polly. I—"

"Lainie?" Dad turned and stroked my face, gently.

He thought I was Mom.

"Lainie." He smiled for a brief moment, then gritted his teeth and crumpled his brow.

"Are you Lainie? You're not Lainie!" His agitation escalated. The orderly was there in a flash. He calmed everyone down and wheeled Dad away.

I just stared at Mark.

"Yeah, this is what it's been like. Why'd you come?" More an accusation than a question.

"Why shouldn't I come?"

"Nothing. It's just, I told you I'd be here."

"So why can't we both be here? It's a lot easier to take together, isn't it?"

"Maybe." Then his briefly softened tune and tone changed. "Listen, Dad's going to nap. And then eat dinner. I have to do a few things. Why don't we meet back here in a couple of hours?"

"Seriously? You have to do a few things?" *What the fuck?*

"See you at seven."

"Screw that, big brother. I'm coming with you."

"No, Polly. Give it a rest."

And he walked away. It had been months since we'd last seen each other, and even then, he had been so distant.

It was a wonder I hadn't given myself whiplash from all the head shaking I'd been doing. Each step along the way, from Vermont to Spain to Israel, had left me wondering what the hell was going on, shaking my head in disbelief at the ironies and perplexities life had landed in my path. I imagined myself as a bobblehead, and snorted out loud. Then came more hiccups. Mark looked back. I could barely see his stunned expression as I wiped the tears from my eyes.

I tried to think WWBMD, but I came up empty. All Big Man needed was the wind.

Fine. Yes, in this case, fine was indeed fucked up, insecure, neurotic, emotional. I was not in the best of moods, but I had a few hours to kill, so off I went to the Tenement Museum. By myself. Time to give up the dream of Mark joining me. I'd just add that to my many lost realities.

Even before I entered the perfectly preserved tenement building, I was transported. The sights, the sounds, the smells of the Lower East Side were like bits of collective memories passed on from fading generations. Salty steam escaped street vents, landing as beaded sweat on my skin. The beats of the street left impressions in my eardrums. I saw children running, children in another time. Like Dad drifting between realities, I was swinging back and forth between then and now.

I wanted to learn more about my grandparents' neighborhood, where and how they had lived, and how the times shaped them. I didn't realize that an entire world, rich with unique inhabitants and their secret stories, would come alive the moment I stepped into the foyer at 97 Orchard Street.

By the time the tenement tour was over and I walked out into the moonlit night, I sure as hell needed a glass of *vino*. I couldn't stop thinking about this new story. About my main character. What it would be like to be inside his head. What it meant to feel so comfortable in your own world. To belong.

His name would be Teo.

I entered the closest bar, ordered a Chianti, and scribbled all over napkins, writing the story of the Scarpa family, the story of their two worlds. Even though it seemed self-indulgent, I was fixed on calling the mother Anna. I had no explanation; no other name seemed to work. I wasn't exactly sure what kind of man or father Vitale would be, but I knew he was faithful to his family. Constant. Like the moon. Perhaps the tenement would be its own character, breathing the soul of the city. Perhaps.

LA LUNA

BY P.A. STERN

Teodoro ran in circles and hummed like his favorite spinning top, the one painted with an animal parade led by the clarinet-playing monkey, and ending with the donkey banging the drums. When the tin toy spun round and round, there were no animal musicians, and there was no beginning or end—just a blur of colors. Vitale Scarpa watched his son to make sure he would not spin himself off the dock. His wife, Anna Rosa, rubbed her big belly, and—with eyes as fixed as the donkey drummer's—reminded him the baby would be there soon. After all those weeks of listening to how she did not want to get on board, to her *nervosismo*, Vitale was more than ready to get on with their voyage. Thank goodness he had his son's antics to entertain him while they waited. Every few twirls, Teo would stumble over and pat Anna's tummy, then zip away again. At least his son was in a good mood.

They waited on the crowded docks for hours in the damp, dark Naples morning, until, finally, it was his family's turn to step onto the wooden gangplank. Vitale made sure everything was in order: he organized the papers, counted their bags, directed Teo to settle down. He told his wife it was time, and Anna smoothed back her bushy black hair, picked up her things, gripped Teo's hand, and walked forward. Then she stopped. Vitale was right behind her and almost knocked her over. "*Scusa,*" he grinned as he leaned toward her, close enough to smell her sweat tinged with lavender, and he kissed her neck softly. He didn't want to anger his wife; she had more than enough to worry about. He was about to give her a gentle nudge to get her moving, but before he had the chance, Anna turned to look at him, her face as ashen as the smoky dawn, her dark brown eyes those of a wild mother boar about to charge. She faltered for a moment, and he thought she was about to pass out. He reached for her, but she turned and pulled Teo after her as she ran away from the boat, away from Vitale, through the thick throng of embarking passengers.

Vitale just stood there and watched his family disappear. His neck muscles became cables as he strained to see them, to figure out what was happening. Then his fight impulse kicked in, and he lowered his head, pushed his way out of line, and rushed toward them. His heart raced, yet it felt like he was running in slow motion, like he'd never reach them. Around him, in a blur, the crowds carried on their goodbyes, the crewmembers barked their orders, the Queen Frederica's huge blue funnel bellowed its coal-drenched steam, the engines growled, and the rope snakes clanged against the metal mast. The veins on his face bulged and his breath filled his ears, cushioning all other sounds. He could barely see them and did not know how he'd find them, but he knew somehow he would.

On the far end of the wharf, a row of timber posts lined the path to Harbour Station. Near the entrance, Teo stood still at Anna's side as she sat on their battered leather suitcase, her head between her knees, breathing heavily between sobs. When Vitale reached them, he bent over and hugged her, his wild black hair disappearing into his wife's dark mane. Then he lifted her chin and kissed every inch of her tear-covered face. Teo ran his fingers along the paisley pattern of her woolen shawl, trying to catch his breath—a humming top at last wound down. The three of them huddled together, their faces as tight as the pause between the ship's desperate horn blasts.

"*Amore mio*, if we miss this ship, we might not get another chance." She did not move. "We must go now." He stressed each word. Still, she did not move. Now he used a firmer voice, which came out more sharply than intended. "For Teodoro." Anna stood up and wiped her tears on the edge of her shawl. "*Scusami caro, va bene, va bene.*" All would be well. In their own silent parade, the Scarpa family made their way back to join the other travelers.

His baby daughter was born on the ship, somewhere between the Straits of Gibraltar and New York Harbor. Vitale held the newborn as she wept her first bittersweet lament. Anna needed rest, so he lifted Teo on his broad shoulders and carried his two children up on deck—their steadfast sentinel. The air was crisp and cool and wet; he felt his baby gasp, snort softly, then relax in his arms, lulled into the deep sleep of the sea. Vitale sat Teo on a bench and let him hold the baby. He told him to be careful, and he saw his son become a big, strong brother, his arms held tight around the tiny infant. When Teo leaned down to kiss the baby's soft face, Vitale was struck by the instant transformation. Compared to the baby's, Teo's ears looked enormous. And his hands. His head. Vitale realized he would never again be able to see his son as a little boy. With a sharp twist, a tourniquet compressed his heart.

> *Papa looks at us and he's smiling, but he seems so sad. I hope I didn't do anything wrong. The baby is warm in my arms, and her breath is the color of the soft sunrise. I thought it would sound red, but it's closer to the song of pink roses, velvet petals drifting, or like the flapping of dragonfly wings, flashing pale blue and clear. Flapping. Flapping. Flapping...*

Teo was fighting the lure of the ship's gentle sway. As Vitale watched his son's eyes grow drowsy, he knew he had only a few seconds. He turned from the bench and dashed across the deck, then leaned over the ship's skin and threw his St. Christopher's medal overboard. Vitale Scarpa whispered a quiet prayer to the seas, and abandoned his religion. Walking back toward his children, he felt a freedom whose conspirator was loss. The three of them melded together on the bench until the brackish spray picked up, the wind too frigid for the tender baby.

Back down in steerage, Teo hummed and the baby cooed as Vitale told Anna what he had done. He declared that they would call the infant Mia, the first of the Scarpa line not to be named after a patron saint.

Anna sank to the floor. "What does this mean?" First they had left their homeland, and now they were leaving their God behind. "Oh, Vitale," she cried, grabbing her children close to her breast. Teo's face was pressed against her as she shuddered and whispered, "The family back in Lazio, they will never find out, but Vitale, what about the family we're about to be reunited with in New York? What will they think?"

Vitale was full of hope and expectation, and it seemed the others on the boat were, too, yet his wife seemed full of fear. Maybe, he thought, for the health of the new baby, for the changes he was making, already begun—or for their Catholic upbringing, now forsaken. Maybe for the new life that lay ahead.

Every moment of the nine-day sea voyage seemed a relentless standstill of misery: one bathroom shared by hundreds, the stench of humanity, hard, narrow planks stacked three high masquerading as beds, paste-like boiled potatoes and stringy meat served by an irritable crew. A vomiting, jostling crowd covered each inch of the steerage-class level. Ants scurrying with nowhere to go.

When the storm cleared, Vitale took Teo to get some fresh air on the upper deck; Teo ran around and played dominoes with the second-class crew, who were more pleasant, and commented on his quick hands and quicker mind. Teo tilted his head at an odd angle so his rusty bangs flopped across his face, and he broke into an infectious smile, his teeth as bright as the blank ivory game tiles. Vitale tried to get Anna to come up with them, but she cried a lot, and wouldn't make the climb. Every minute was interminable, yet somehow, the days blurred into each other like the top's musical animal procession whirling yellow, red, and blue.

A few days before the boat was to dock, Vitale asked Teo to help gather the steerage passengers; he had some things he wanted to say. Vitale leapt up on a coil of thick rope and announced that a man named Fiorello La Guardia had just been elected New York's first *Italoamericano* mayor. He called it an auspicious sign. Teo could not contain his smile when the crowd applauded the prospect of 1933. Vitale flushed with pride as he watched his son pump his little fists with the rest of them, egging them on. He knew this was just the beginning, that his words could be a piston, reversing the tides, creating a wake in turbulent seas. The excitement grew and the crowd grew louder, until the ship's crew broke them all up. They had some harsh words for the Scarpas, father and son.

Anna did a little *tarantella* when they were finally off the boat. Teo spun alongside her. Even Vitale was relieved. No more nausea that came in currents, like the swells of the sea, the tides orchestrated by the waxing moon. Anna complained that her body was still sore from the labor and birth. The hours spent being poked and prodded on Ellis Island did not help, though she seemed placated when they all passed inspection. Some of the new friends they had made on board had their coat lapels marked with C for eye disease, or L for lameness, or X for mental defects, and they were turned away and had to return to *Italia*. The mainland was in their sight, less than two kilometers away. Wonder and wounds. Now they knew why it was called *Isola delle lacrime*. The island of tears.

They joined the rest of the travelers gathering in the great hall: some were beaten down and silent, others chattered and paced as they waited to get on the next boat to the city. Vitale watched Teo take it all in, and he wondered what his son was thinking. He was startled when his wife tried to lift Teo off the bench, but instead dropped him on the marble floor. She gasped when he fell, and then she froze, her eyes stretched and wet. Teo reached up and tried to touch her face, and she melted toward him. Vitale gave words to Teo's touch and let his wife know it was okay.

Vitale had a strong back from his work on the farm at home, and was able to carry Teodoro along with their bags and suitcases. Anna carried the baby Mia, so tiny and fragile, and the satchel of their most prized possessions: a few family photos, their saucepan, her rosary, and the piece of iron Vitale had held on their wedding day to ward off evil.

Once they reached the ferry, Vitale tried to contain Teo as he dragged them to the front. He couldn't believe his little boy was still so full of energy, but he imagined Teo would soon surrender to his fatigue. Teo's eyelids were almost frozen shut from the spray. He jumped up and down until Vitale hugged him to help him stay warm, so he could keep his eyes open and watch the majestic city grow in front of them. Vitale and Anna laughed for the first time in weeks, and Teo's face looked just like it had on the days right before *Carnevale*.

When they stepped off the ferry, the promise quickly faded. This new land offered new challenges to their senses, new physical assaults. The streets smelled like urine and fish and rotten vegetables and burning refuse. Not clean like the sea-bleached roads back home. Every few blocks, there were lines of people waiting to be given food. Bread lines. Vitale did not want to admit that he was a little disappointed that there really were no streets paved with gold. He knew that things had taken a bad turn in America, but still, he had felt it would be a better life for his family. Now he murmured that this was not what he had expected.

Even in their exhaustion, they tried to take in everything about this new city, but they were deep in a grotto, unable to see anything except what was right in front of them. It was hard to understand how such a place could exist. The buildings were so tall they blocked the sky. It was midday, and yet it seemed like dusk, a permanent haze created by the smoke and long shadows. Vitale wondered how they would be able to look up and tell the time. To see the stars. No bright blue Laziali skies here.

The mass of people, yelling, moving, buzzing, restricted their views even more. The papers Vitale clung to directed them to the corner of 1st Avenue and E 1st Street, right past Avenue A. 1st Street. 1st Avenue. Avenue A. A maze of confusion. The human river pushed them along, and they didn't know if they were headed the right way. Anna kept reassuring Teo that all would be fine. "*Andrà tutto bene, vedrai,*" she repeated, over and over, half aloud, stroking his hair. She told him here, they would find a new home. Here, things would be better.

> *Papa's holding me, but Mamma stays very close, so close I can smell where my new baby sister and Mamma's scents harmonize, creating swirls of pastels. The buildings soar like giant cypress trees. How does a person build something so high? What makes the skyscrapers stay up? Mamma rubs my head and speaks softly,* "Andrà tutto bene, vedrai," *though it seems like she is saying it more to herself than to me. I don't need to be reassured. I'm climbing on the tops of the buildings, touching the clouds. Swinging on the sides of the electric buses. Shwoosh. Steamy air rushes past my face. All the humming of the city, the vibrating energy, takes form, and the new aromas cast color combinations I hadn't known before. Each sound, each smell, brings a new image, a new shade, another tint. What I had seen only in dreams. New shapes, old forms come together, hues finally making sense. I'm not confused at all. No orange here.*

The sidewalks were wider than the ones in San Vittore, but they were packed with so many people, the width made no difference. The overflow ended up in the roads, and Vitale made sure his wife and children were not crushed as they were pushed off the sidewalks. They had to be careful to avoid being hit by a trolley or bus, or stepping in refuse, or worse. People rushed about, carried huge bundles of clothing, tended push-carts filled with strange fruits and vegetables. Vendors shouted to passersby to buy their newspapers, their pineapple nectar—only five cents, their Good Humor. Vitale's head spun from the movement and the people, hurrying everywhere all at once.

They walked down many streets; soon, they heard shouts in their language, only with different accents, different dialects.

First the Sicilians. Then the Sardinians. Each neighborhood had settled among their own, clusters from the original regions back home. Even here, separation existed. But really, now they were all *Italoamericani*. As his family turned up Broome Street heading toward Orchard Street, the familiar dialects of their Mezzogiorno neighbors blared out. Vitale could tell they were getting close.

A vision in black came at them. "*Mia sorella, la famiglia di mia sorella,*" she screamed. "*Siete qui!*" My sister, my sister's family, you are here!

They hadn't seen Aunt Josephine in two and a half years. She looked so different, so … fat. She grabbed them and hugged as only a southern Italian *zia* could do. She gave many kisses, all sloppy and wet, and all welcome. The tears flowed. The screeches woke Mia, and she added her own screams to the street-corner reunion. Grabbing the baby, Aunt Josephine noted playfully, "She looks just like Uncle Vito!"

"Especially the huge ears!" Anna agreed.

"How big Teodoro has grown. Such a head of ginger hair! And just who does *he* take after?" she teased. "*Che bello ragazzino!*"

They all laughed and cried, everyone but Teo—who stood there, not laughing, not crying, just looking up, taking it all in with eyes as wide as the manhole cover beneath his feet, one hand tracing lines in the air, his other holding tight to Vitale, who was not about to let go.

Josephine fed them *pignoli* cookies—a sweet taste from back home—as she led them halfway up the block to their new home at 47-½ E 1st Street. They had never had a home so tall. It was overwhelming, unfamiliar. But when they entered, there were paintings along the hallway walls that looked so much like their farm back home. *Could those be our chestnut trees?* No, these were paintings of trees from the local arbors, the ones that used to be here. Aunt Josephine joked, "The orchards that no longer exist anywhere along Orchard Street." Now just concrete and asphalt and stone. Still, the paintings were beautiful and colorful and comforting; the entry decorations boded well for what their apartment would look like. Teo was drawn to the oils on canvas and raised his hand, trying to taste them with his fingers, but he could barely reach the paintings. Vitale gave him a little lift, and Teo came face to face with the details, the textures, the tones and the smell of the paints. Vitale knew his son was home.

They walked up the five flights to the apartment they would share with the Nardos, Aunt Josephine's family. She told them that Uncle Giuseppe—or Joe, as he preferred to be called in America—was living upstate, working on the vineyards near the Finger Lakes. Aunt Josephine and the three boys, Dom, Leo, and Sal, had been living in a one-room place down on Mott Street. When they found out the Scarpas were finally coming, they applied for the larger apartment on E 1st Street; now it was moving day for them all.

They shifted around the tiny apartment like a school of sardines. The Nardos chirped happily about the amount of space in the three rooms. Vitale was shocked. The tenement's formal lobby belied the apartment's tired flooring and tattered wallpaper. Anna started crying as soon as they had the full tour of the entire 345 square feet they would call home. She apologized, and said she was very grateful and didn't know why she was so emotional. Vitale reminded her that she had acted like this—a little strange in the head—right after Teo had been born. He looked around their new home and just shook his head for the wonder of change, trying to hold back his own tears. Teo also looked at everything and touched everything, just once, in the center. He said nothing, as was his way.

The two mammas went to work and scoured the apartment from top to bottom. Vitale had the boys take turns filling the buckets, lugging the pails through the dark halls from the communal sink. The women kept the apartment swept and scrubbed clean, and gave the families a bit of privacy by hanging bed sheets from the ceiling tiles, dividing the rooms. Too many bodies in such a small space.

Vitale, Anna, and Mia slept in the front room, the one room with a window, the same room as Aunt Josephine and Uncle Joe, during his infrequent visits. The cousins slept on chairs in the middle room. They traded off who could put their feet up on the metal Coca-Cola tray table for the night. Teo always seemed to sleep better when he could stretch out like that. But not much. His dreams were so vivid that often he'd wake everyone as he cried out in his sleep, more a loud whimper than a call. Vitale needed his rest, so his wife would peek out from her room, whispering, "s*h, sh, sh,*" and Teo would snort himself back to sleep, the cousins half annoyed, half entertained. Something to tease about the next day.

Aunt Josephine was a seamstress in a factory nearby. Anna also sewed, but she did it from home. Vitale wanted her at home, to keep the children in line, to make the meals, to stay where she belonged. He allowed her to work, but behind closed doors, so they could still qualify for government assistance. And he didn't want her work to disrupt his family. Family came first. He made sure she knew that any money she brought in was appreciated, but only supplementary. No wife of his would need to work.

> *I like when the machine whirs on the kitchen table right next to me. Sometimes Mamma lets me climb on top of the smooth wooden cover and try the zigzag stitch. Then I draw the patterns it makes, and the motor's songs. Mamma keeps reminding me not to tell anyone about her sewing, that if anyone knows she makes extra money, we wouldn't get the welfare, a word that sounds like a good thing but that Mamma whispers every time she says. And then Papa gets that terrible look on his face. Welfare. I try to see it, but it has no color.*

Every Tuesday night, Vitale crossed 1st Street and carried home a box filled with cheese or other food or medicine or clothing. He held the box close to his chest, always with the label turned toward him. It was the only time Vitale walked with his head down, shoulders slumped, not talking to his neighbors. Most of the other men also walked this way when they brought their boxes home. When Anna met him at the door, she took the box while he took a deep breath. Anna said a prayer for President Roosevelt and his New Deal. Vitale laughed, but agreed that FDR was a hero and deserved thanks.

When the wooden cheese boxes were empty, Vitale removed the Home Relief labels, filled them with soil he had dug up near the train tracks, and planted sage and basil in them. He always tried to do something to brighten up their lives. The plants made the apartment smell good, and there was nothing like fresh sage and brown butter sauce. Sometimes, in early spring, he'd take Teo to gather dandelion greens, and *assenzio*—mugwort—from the vacant lots near the East River, to add to their cooking.

> *Papa tells me to stay away from the riverbank, because I don't pay attention when I look for the wild herbs. Before we left our country, my nonna told me that* assenzio *was so special it was named after the goddess of the moon, the goddess of the hunt, of childbirth. It smells peppery and it tastes tangy on my tongue, like yellow dancing with brown flecks.* Delizioso. *Mostly, I love the underneath of its leaves, the downy fuzz and its silvery sheen, just like the light of the moon. Nonna told me it was a powerful plant, made for traveling on the moon's rays. She told me to be careful because it would feed my soul, but if I ate too much, the real world would disappear. The stuff of dreams. She called me* piccolo assenzio—*her little mugwort—because my mouth was so full of the moon, nothing could get out. My head is so full of dreams. She worried the leaves would take me from the material world to a magical world. She did not know that already, the two worlds were no different to me.*
>
> *The herbs Papa grows smell fresh, a silky green ribbon surrounding my shoulders. But the cheese that originally came in those boxes we use as planters—Mamma mia! The cheese—it is disgusting. Mamma says she can't make a decent lasagna with government cheese. But her cooking is always*

delicious. And as Papa says, it's food in our mouths. Once in a great while, Papa comes home with a special treat, a block wrapped in shiny white paper. He's saved up enough to get a fresh piece of Parmigiano-Reggiano, *imported straight from* Italia. *Mamma is always so pleased; she kisses him and crosses herself, thanking the good Lord.* Grazie a Dio! *Papa laughs and reminds her that he brought the cheese home. Papa grates the cheese for our spaghetti, and—with so many people around—somehow he always manages to sneak me a big chunk from the end. I get lost in the brilliant blue saltiness, and can taste the copper vats, and the grass fields that fed the cows. I'm back on Nonna's farm, and it is midsummer, and I'm gone for hours, and Papa never knew where I went.*

Eventually, Vitale found work with the Journeymen Stonesetters, Local No. 84. He helped build the tall towers in the sky, stone by stone. He'd be gone for ten or twelve hours a day, and still, it wasn't enough pay. Even though they were already eight people living in three rooms, they brought in an extra boarder. The fifty cents a week helped.

Vitale worked hard and came home wearied and filthy, and yet he was always happy. Every day he'd run up the five flights, clomping in his heavy boots. He'd grab his *bellissima sposa*, give her a big, juicy kiss, and swing her around the room, careful not to knock over any of the children in the tiny space. Once, the picture of President Roosevelt went flying off the wall when Anna's hand accidentally banged it as she spun. The glass shattered, and the frame broke. Everyone was silent, waiting to see what would happen.

Mamma makes sure she didn't hit the painting of the good Lord Jesus, or the grandparents' portraits she carried so carefully across the sea. Papa picks through the broken pieces and lifts up the color photograph, pretending to be angry.

Carefully, silently, he folds the background behind the head,
then grabs one of Mia's paper dolls, and—beaming—he
makes them dance around the room like two farfalle, *butter-*
flies flitting up to the tin ceiling and down to the linoleum
floor. As he romps with his paper puppets, Papa sings, 'O
sole, 'o sole mio ... *and we all dance, and they sing along,*
shouting at the top of their lungs, until Mrs. Friedmann
downstairs comes pounding at our door, each beat an intense
splotch of burnt sienna, yelling at us to stop horsing around,
to quiet down and give her a little peace. So funny, because
she's the one making most of the noise.

    We all button our lips as Mamma motions us to do, and
then, in the deep silence, Papa turns the dancers into paper
airplanes, and with accompanying motor plane noises—
vroomvroomvroom—launches them at the door where Mrs.
Friedmann has been banging. Donna prepotente! *"Bossy*
woman," he whispers loudly. Another huge smile. They all
roar trying to hold in their laughter, and I cannot stop my
shoulders shaking. Sunset flowing on the surface of a soap
bubble. Everyone's rolling on the floor. Cousin Sal cuts him-
self on the broken picture glass, but as he bleeds, none of us
show him any real sympathy because we're too stunned with
giddiness. Oh, the tales he would tell about that scar. You'd
think he had received a shrapnel wound.

In the evenings, Vitale spent time at home, trying to make
life a little lighter in their dark tenement. His family meant everything to him; still, he usually left three to four nights a week to
attend union meetings. Vitale Scarpa had not come all this way,
fleeing Mussolini and fighting fascism, just to sit around and play
cards every night.

It was his obligation—his onus and his privilege—to be a
union organizer, to fight for the workers. Between the government and the church, the common man was not treated right.
Vitale was sick of the Catholics, the way the clergy kept asking

for more and more from the people when the people did not have any more to give. The fascists were worse. They were destroying the unions, keeping the working class weak. Denying individual thought. Suppressing opposing views. Mandating bigotry. If this year's Berlin Olympics were used as a political tool to champion the Nazi agenda the way Mussolini had used the World Cup to promote his fascist ideology two years ago, what was next? Cut from the same cloth. *Fascio*. A bundle of rods tied around an axe. Strength through unity, they believed. The unions would use the same philosophy, and strip the fascists of their power.

Vitale could not understand how so many of his neighbors and family back home could embrace *Il Duce*, cheer on his party and policies. Either they couldn't see what was happening to their beloved *Italia*, or they did not want to see. They knew how Vitale felt, what he believed in, why he had left his country. Still, they would write him, not asking for food or money, only asking him to send hunting guns. To fight alongside the fascists. To arm gangs of thugs. *Disgustoso*.

As a New York City union member, Vitale and his political views were finally accepted. He was no longer an outcast. When he entered the meeting hall, he'd hear respectful shouts of *Buona sera, Signore Scarpa! Come state?* His family missed Vitale all those nights away, but they knew his work was important, for him, for them, and for the world changing around them. Worth the sacrifice, they all convinced themselves.

> *I'm lucky, because Papa takes me to meetings with him whenever he can. There's one woman who's so loud and nosy that Papa does not take me if she's going to be there. "the* Chiacchierona," *they call her, though I think that isn't her real name, and we are told never to call her that. But she is a chatterbox and a busybody, so I do not understand why people cannot say what is true. She lives a few blocks away, and we don't see her very often, but sometimes, when Mamma is buying lemons at her favorite stand on Spring Street, we*

run into her and she asks all sorts of questions. She starts with something simple, like Mamma's recipe for meatloaf with the hard-boiled egg inside. Then she slowly works up to questions about me, about my "odd" behaviors. Why does the boy never speak? It seems like he lives in another world. Is he feebleminded? Have you had his head examined? Her words are a frothy foam, grey mixed with orange. Mamma tries to be as polite as she can, but "the Chiacchierona" is rude and has what mamma calls a mean spirit, just looking for dirt to spread—fertile ground for gossip. Mamma's face flushes, red as simmering sauce, and she grabs me and storms away. Better to say nothing, Mamma tells Papa when he comes home from work. I nod my head, agreeing.

There's a nice, quiet woman with a violet voice—she introduces herself to me as Miss Abbandonato—who takes the notes about everything that is said and voted on at the union meetings. She hands me blank pieces of paper and some pencils. This is my favorite time. People are shouting and arguing and making important-sounding speeches. There is clapping and laughing and yelling and pointing. A rainbow pulsing. I'm on the floor, listening as if the Roman gods are above me, debating the fate of mankind. Lost in the thunder, my mind wanders, and drawings pour out of my hands. Each week, the nice lady brings me one new color of wax crayon to use. Some I use with one hand; some work better in my other hand. At the end of each night, she coos and compliments me on my drawings, all very crude and rough to my mind's eye. Just sketches of what is to be. What could be.

One week, she brings me a whole new package of Binney & Smith Munsell-Perma crayons. Twelve new colors. Five Principal Hues at Middle Chroma, Five Principal Hues at Maximum Chroma with Middle Grey and Black. The colors of the moon glow. Brand new. I lift the lid of that cardboard box, and a floodgate opens. The smell is air to me. I do not know how I felt anything before I took that breath. The brilliant colors dance out of their neat rows, alive. The union meets and organizes. I blend yellow with red, form light, change value with the grey and carbon black, find strength in shades and tints, create worlds with the oily chalk, able at last to take the pictures in my mind and make them come out of my head and on to the page.

After one meeting, Miss Abbandonato asks me if she can take my drawings with her. She shows me how to sign my name at the bottom of each page. I think she thinks I draw very well, being that I am only six and three-quarters. But it's just what I do. My papa never sees what I draw because at the end of each meeting he's so busy. There are many private discussions to have, so many people to meet and talk to, big union work to get done.

Before the next monthly union leaders' meeting starts, Miss Abbandonato hurries over excited rushing her words telling me she knows a group of stonecutters who are not politically active, so they never come to the union meetings. They are artists, she tells me, and spend their free time "making art." When they aren't cutting and laying stones to build skyscrapers for $1.50 an hour, they're carving and making sculptures for love. One of the stonecutters, a Mr. Pollock, is an artist in the Work Relief Program, and she told him about me and he wants to meet me. I don't understand why she would do that. She's still talking in a stream of rushing purples when my papa abruptly asks her to hand out minutes. At home that night, Papa tells Mamma what happened. He knows about Mr. Pollock, who he says was originally a stonecutter but not very good. Papa tells Mamma Mr. Pollock is now just cleaning statues in Cooper Square. Papa does not look down on this man because of his station in life; he tells Mamma his only judgment is that people like Pollock benefit from the unions, yet do not put in the time or work to build something he calls solidarity.

One night, this Mr. Pollock appeared at the union meeting. Vitale was pleased to finally see him show up, until word spread that Mr. Pollock was only there to attend the meeting for research. He was about to paint a series of murals in public buildings, part of Roosevelt's Federal Art Project. Mr. Pollock introduced himself to Vitale, who shook his hand so hard, the artist's eyes watered. Undeterred, he told Vitale he had heard about Teodoro, and—in addition to his mural project—he was hoping to meet Vitale's son to see him work in person. Vitale didn't know what to make of this request.

Throughout the evening, Vitale was distracted as he kept his eye on Mr. Pollock. The artist made rough sketches of the meeting, but mostly watched Teo draw. Vitale was struck by the wondrous images his son produced. Mr. Pollock commented that it seemed as if Teo were illustrating the *sounds* he heard, creating fantastical, abstract visions from deep within his mind. Grasping the essence rather than the literal. Vitale didn't understand all that Mr. Pollock said, but he did understand that this *artista* was a bit too interested in his son.

Mr. Pollock asked Teo if he could draw something more realistic, perhaps what he actually saw in the meeting room, and Teo did as he was asked with exacting precision, replicating each specific line and detail, representing the people and furnishings, windows and architectural features in perfect proportion without once looking up, his mop of titian hair flopped in front of his eyes, as he switched his pencil from hand to hand. Mr. Pollock made odd clucks and grunts and sighs, shaking his head, first back and forth, then up and down. Clearly, he was astonished. Vitale was astonished, as well, and also saddened that he had never before taken time to know his son in this way. Mr. Pollock shook both of Teo's hands with great respect, then went over to Vitale, and, shored up this time, shook his hand, thanking him for his hard union work. Mr. Pollock told Vitale "they'd" be in touch.

One Saturday morning a few weeks later, Vitale was waiting for Teo to come home from the Gifkowitz's apartment, where he went to turn on their stove and turn off the lights, prepare the *gefilte* fish, and wash the dishes before the family returned from services at the Eldridge Street Synagogue. At age seven, Teo had earned the honor of becoming the Gifkowitz's *shabbos goy*. He also earned fifteen cents a week, and sometimes also a knish from Yonah Schimmel's, always presented before the Sabbath so they all could pretend it was a gift and not an actual payment. See how religion is a big game, Vitale liked to comment. Anna would gently smack him, wondering aloud, "What has become of my good *Cattolico* husband?"

As Vitale looked out toward the Gifkowitz's apartment, he saw a man coming down the hallway. It always made him nervous when strangers showed up. Usually, they brought word of a death or injury. Or the landlord sending his tough guys to complain, or ask for more money. Vitale's skin prickled, and he stood up a little taller, chest puffed up and jaw tightened.

And this man had on a suit—even more cause for concern. Maybe the visitor was from the Health Department, coming with bad news about Mr. Gifkowitz. When Mr. Gifkowitz, a kind, gentle tailor, came down with the cough, Vitale made it clear that he was not happy with Teo working for their neighbors. He was afraid they'd all get T.B., caused by everyone working so close together in the garment district, making the *schmatas*, as they called them. It was no wonder the garment workers were sick; they never got any fresh air like the stone workers.

Vitale was worried about Teo, and went to check on him. Teo had become distracted watching the mourning doves nesting on the Gifkowitz's windowsill. Vitale brought him back home, where the stranger was waiting at their door. He introduced himself and Vitale reluctantly invited him in. Teo sat down on the cool embossed floor to join Mia and the cousins playing with their toys. The man, who was not from the Department of Health, kept talking, and became very animated, and adamant. Vitale was not pleased he had come to his home. He was also concerned that Teo seemed to be listening intently, so he sent the children to play in the front room.

Mamma and Papa are listening to his words, but the man's thoughts, oh, there's more to the conversation than the words he speaks. More than my mamma and papa can grasp. Lines collide, shapes quarrel, threads tangle. The clashing colors are confusing.

Vitale was frustrated; he didn't want to spend his one day off with this man, this uninvited guest. Especially one who thought he knew what was right for Vitale's family. The discussion became a little heated until Anna politely offered some anise *taralli* and a glass of *vino*. As the old Italian saying goes, *tutto finisce a tarallucci e vino*. No matter what the argument, all can be resolved amiably.

After the words ran out, Vitale thanked the man and escorted him to the door. He told him they would consider his kind proposal. The man was about to leave, but had to present just one more argument, to plead his case one more time. Almost out of patience, Vitale and Anna listened.

"He could start this next school year," the man implored.

"*Si, si, bene.*"

The man finally left with a weak attempt at familiarity. "*Arrivederci! Grazie!*" Vitale nodded and Anna smiled, and they responded with *prego, prego* as they closed the door behind him.

After he left, Vitale grumbled, "So much talking, so little communication. I guess our little artist with the big ears is right, that silence truly is golden."

It is true, silence is golden. With streaks of platinum. Papa says nothing more. No one tells me who the man is, or exactly why he has been here. And I don't ask. I know it is something about me going to "study" art, which seems funny. How do you study how to breathe?

The children continued to play, and Anna began to peel onions for dinner. Vitale sat at the table, reading the latest issue of

Il Martello. The Hammer. Every once in a while, he muttered something about the fascists. Other than that, the room was heavy with silence.

Just then, Aunt Josephine came out from behind the sheet, looking like a bull. She had long, thick black hair, which she had just washed in hot soapy water and formed into two huge horns spiking out from her head. Something serious had been going on, and Vitale knew that Aunt Josephine did not like serious. She pretended to attack the children, chasing them around the end room, past the sheets, through the front room, and round and round. Mia was barely walking, so the sight of her toddling furiously with the big, scary bull in pursuit resulted in screams of glee from them all. Surely, they would be getting a visit from old Mrs. Friedmann. Any gravity in that home was soon lifted by the whirl of racing children, chased by *comico* Aunt Josephine, who Vitale called an Italian bull in a china shop.

In the middle of everything, Uncle Joe barged in. He wasn't expected until the next day, so along with many hugs, many questions flew. Everything was fine, the harvest had gone well; they had just finished early, and he missed his *famiglia* back in the city. And there they all were, in full, fine, breathless form. Uncle Joe mirrored Teo's crooked smile, and then turned to Aunt Josephine with a different type of smile. Vitale caught her look and winked at her, and she blushed rushing out of the room. Teo followed and watched her comb her hair, the wavy lines unraveling. Uncle Joe stood there, too. Watching. She pushed them both out. "*Dio mio,* let me make myself nice," she yelled.

Uncle Joe took Teo and the other boys to deliver the truckload of grape juice to a buyer over on the Bowery. Of course, before it was drained completely, he left a few barrels for the Scarpa/Nardo winery in the basement of 47-½ E 1st Street.

Like almost every Italian family in their neighborhood, they made their own wine. Vitale and Joe would get just the juice, or sometimes the grapes—which they'd press themselves—from upstate or from their few relatives who grew their own vines in

Brooklyn. They'd let the wine sit in barrels in their dark, locked cellars—just like cellars all across Little Italy and the Lower East Side. The wine was always red, always from their own family recipe. It was surprising that the other neighbors—the Irish, the Chinese, the Jews, and the *Merigans*—never complained when the leftover grape skins came pouring down the gutters, stinking up the hot city streets.

Vitale loved watching Teo on those days. His son would soak his fingers in the streams of dark burgundy pigment and draw on the pavement, monoprints in rich red. They'd go home, and Anna would grumble and glare at Vitale while scrubbing Teo clean with a hard brush and Boraxo and Fels Naptha. Vitale enjoyed getting a rise out of his wife; she'd steam up, and it would be more reason for kissing and teasing—a playful, cooling antidote. He never questioned Teodoro's actions; it was clear that both of them thought the repercussions were worth it.

Typical Italian papas, Vitale and Joe enjoyed their *vino*. The boys would take turns being sent down to the basement with the key and mason jars to fill their fathers up for the night. Vitale knew that the landlord would often be there right when they were unlocking the door. Teo told him that he would ask the boys to go run a little errand for him, like he was trying to get rid of them. On more than one occasion, Vitale caught the landlord leaving the cellar with a full jug, but he never said anything. Better to keep him happy and "relaxed" than to cause trouble.

Vitale noticed that little Dom would stay a little longer than the other boys, and he heard that he'd sometimes sneak sips from the spout. A lot of sips. Vitale listened as Anna fretted about Dom, worried that he was a little too fond of the spirits. She told Vitale that a habit like that could become a problem; he told her it was not her business. But he often sent Teo along whenever Dom volunteered to take trips to the cellar.

And life continued this way. Wine was made and consumed. Children played in the streets, cooling down in the fire hydrant spray or warming up in the steam from the El. Boarders came and left. Mr. Gifkowitz finally died, and Teo was sent to help the family as they sat *shiva*, for which he did not accept any payment. The mammas cooked and cleaned and listened to Italian soap operas on the radio, and helped the boys with schoolwork as much as they could. Everyone tried to learn English. "*In inglese!*" the boys would shout at their parents. And the strange, twisted-up words that came out made them all laugh—at themselves.

Vitale was now vice president of his union and busier than ever, trying to work with other branches to increase workers' wages. Still, work was scarce, and pay was not what they had expected; many of their neighbors left to go back home. Birds of passage, Vitale called them. Flitting to and fro, wherever it was the easier life. His brother back in the old country had become mayor of his town, and was prospering. Sometimes, when he was tired and forgot his hope, Vitale thought perhaps he, too, should have stayed in *Italia*. But then he'd stand up in the union hall and people would applaud his ideas, and Vitale would know he had made the right decision. Here, he could make a difference. Anything was possible in America. Things were changing. And as the world changed around him, Vitale watched his son create his own world full of light and color, shape and form, shades of his own design.

A few months passed, and one bright Sunday morning, Vitale and Teo were sitting on the front stoop, visiting with the neighbors. The streets were quiet but for the sounds of *bocce* balls clanging from the court nearby. Vitale chatted, and Teo got up and spun in circles while he hummed to himself, stopping every so often to watch a pigeon's dance or to study the rays of light and the shadows they cast, or to shake a neighbor's hand and gift them with his glorious sideways smile.

The landlord came out and posted a notice on the front door. He announced that they would all have to be gone by the next weekend. Gone? *Non capisco!* He told them he was closing up the building because the housing laws were putting him out of business. He didn't have the money to put in the required indoor toilets and windows and fire-retardant floors. He said he'd waited as long as he could, but now that they had started enforcing the law—they were already fining landlords down the street—he decided it was cheaper to evict them all, shut down the tenement, and walk away.

> *No more* tenerezza, *no place left to hold us here. No more vibrant pictures of the sounds of the city. It isn't a huge surprise. As soon as the landlord starts stammering, I know at once this means we are headed west, to live with relatives in the countryside. Mamma and Papa had already talked about the move. Someday, they said. I was in the alley, and heard the heather words bouncing back and forth between the laundry hanging above, falling down from the window, clanging against the iron fire escape, tumbling into my ears. When we move, we'll go over the singing bridge, the one with the vibrations that fill my brain full of colors. They said someday we would go where we can grow our own grapes and tomatoes. New Jersey tomatoes.*

Vitale had barely saved up enough money to move again. He had tried to make more money, the way they did in America. The union bosses encouraged him to support Roosevelt and buy war bonds, and they persuaded him to invest his meager savings in the stock market. At first, Vitale thought they were buying cattle and other livestock! He read all he could and learned about Black Tuesday and the crash of '29, and he knew the Depression, the losses from back then, were headed toward a strong recovery. But he was worried that the new Wall Street scandals and the war scares and the opposition from the new conservative coalition to Roosevelt's New Deal policies were affecting the market. He felt things weren't going to get any better. After all, it was still a struggle to afford a nine-cent loaf of Wonder Bread.

Mamma doesn't want to leave the street where all of her new friends and good neighbors are. But there are no afford-able tenements now, and Papa found work with the New Jersey Allied Stone Workers' Union. After cousin Sal snuck up and pulled the Chinaman's long braids and had to run like hell to get back to our side of the street, they were afraid I, too, would grow up and go down a bad road if I stayed in this area anymore. Too many temptations and bad influences, they said. Either that, or all the teasing would finally get to me, cause me to blow. Once again, for the children's sake, Mamma and Papa will pack up and move, carrying their old burdens and their new hopes. Time to leave again. Another new start.

I won't be able to study art uptown now, as planned, but I don't mind. As long as I can draw and paint, it doesn't matter to me if I do it in a fancy studio in Manhattan or on the family room floor in Garfield. They used words like gift-ed and prodigy and savant and said it was a shame, a real shame, and a waste, but my parents have other things to worry about and they don't really understand, and I don't really care. I have the sky and the moon. I have the colors I hear in my head. I will soon be eight, and old enough to join Uncle Joe transporting the grape juice, bringing home extra money per la mia famiglia. *I will help take care of Mia, who had the* buona fortuna *to begin her life on the high seas, floating between her two countries. She's already walking and singing and even drawing. And I will watch over Mamma, when Papa is busy at meetings. I will tend to the mulberry trees and the fig trees and the deep purple eggplants. I will go to school to learn to read and write English better, and maybe one day decide to speak, when there is a reason, and someday, hopefully, be a stonecutter just like Papa.*

Chapter 11

My fingers were cramping. I was driven, in a trance, as if I had partaken of some of Teo's mugwort.

It was like I had needed to create a new family, right then, like I needed to write one. Their story was scribbled over a stack of bar napkins.

I was forming the napkins into pages of a little book when the bartender asked me if I was ready to pay my tab. Shit. How many hours had passed? My cell phone showed it was already 7:30.

I was breathing hard as I rushed back to Cabrini. I passed evidence of the new immigrants who now inhabit Alphabet City: a Japanese restaurant, a Bangladeshi market, a Latino gallery, an Islamic Center. Upscale boutiques, microbreweries, and hipster lounges revealed gentrification and renewal. Some history was being preserved, but mostly, new had replaced old. The natural order of things.

The smells from Katz's Deli made my stomach protest. When was the last time I had eaten? Maybe Mark would come grab a nosh with me when we were done visiting Dad. No matter what the argument, it could all be resolved over a glass of Dr. Brown's Cel-Ray and a bowl of pickles. Thank you, Anna Scarpa.

I got to the lobby just as the orderly was rolling Dad back over to his corner, which was now lit by a blinking fluorescent fixture. Street signs flashed outside. Even in this relatively quiet section of the city, horns blared. The facility looked—and felt—much shabbier at night. An elderly woman sat across the room, slumped over, by herself. And Dad was in his pajamas. I needed to talk to Mark about Dad's care, about maybe moving him someplace closer to me.

The orderly told me Dad had spilled his dinner, a full bowl of minestrone. Luckily, he hadn't burned himself, but he was a mess, and had had to take a shower. That explained the pajamas. It seemed so sad that he'd be out in public like that.

Mark was waiting in the corner. He was playing solitaire, his face in the usual flat frown he'd worn since Mom died. First, Dad looked puzzled when he saw me. I guess a few hours could have been years to him. Decades. Then Dad looked past me, but spoke to me.

"Lainie."

Here we go again.

"Lainie," he said, a little more harshly.

I stayed silent, not sure what to do. When I had seen Dad in August, he was in and out of lucidity, but mostly, his mood was pleasant. Clearly, he'd gotten much worse. Mark should have warned me. The orderly nodded at me, as if I should just go along with the conversation. He left to tend the elderly woman in the opposite corner, who was now crying.

"I shouldn't have listened to you, Lainie."

"About what, Dad ... uh, Karl?"

"We should've told her."

"Told who what?"

"The liar's not enough," he said.

"Who's the liar?"

Dad lowered his head and sighed.

"I'm sorry, Lainie. You were wrong. We should've told her."

"Told who what?"

"Anna."

"Yes, Dad, it is me!" I looked at Mark but he just stood up and tried to move Dad's wheelchair away. I grabbed his hand, and he pushed back. Hard. Dad jerked forward and slumped, moaning.

"What the hell's wrong with you?" I snapped at Mark. "Dad? What do you mean? It's me, Anna."

"I'm so sorry," Dad kept repeating, head and shoulders drooped, tears streaming down his face.

"Shit. Goddamn you, Polly. Leave him the hell alone," my dear brother spat.

I froze, my thoughts, tumbleweed-messy, battling with a deep, primal fear. Something on some level I'd always known, but was never courageous enough to confront. And certainly not brave enough to allow myself to feel. Dad looked right at me. A fleeting moment of lucidity.

"We should've told you."

And then he was lost again, somewhere between the present reality and the shifting, leaky, impermanent truth.

They gave Dad something to help him sleep. An orderly sat with him until the medication took effect. Now he was snoring peacefully.

The orderly's name was Tsering, and he had a soothing, calm lilt and a gentle laugh. Poor thing. Now he had to comfort me in addition to his needy Alzheimer's patients. Only I was the biggest basket case in his caseload. Ship me down the river on a bed of violets.

When Tsering broke up our family feud, Mark looked at me with fiery eyes. I was hyperventilating, and full of rage. What in the world was wrong with everybody? With my brother?

He was livid, but he looked so confused. That same face he had worn as a kid, all the times he'd lashed out when he was just trying to cover up his inability to be himself. The anger that masked his deep hurt. It had taken Mark years to accept himself, and to allow others to do the same. To forgive himself for the time he lost. I hadn't seen that conflicted little boy in a very long time.

When he stormed out, we were back in middle school. My brother trying too hard to be the tough guy. "Tag, you're it. I'm outta here."

I knew I'd have to chase him down. On the playground. In the mall. At a family gathering. During a school dance. I'd run after him, wanting to be there for my big brother. To try to get him to open up and tell me what was the matter. Our little dance.

Dad's roommate was also fast asleep. Their snores, and the constant hum from some ancient motor, guided my breathing. Tsering stroked my hand, and soon I surrendered to the rhythm of my pulse. He asked me about myself, and I gave him the rote rundown: family composition, location, ethnicity, what I "did." I pulled out the napkin scribbles to give him a better picture of my work. When I mentioned my current fixation on 1937, his eyes lit up.

"That's an important year for my family," he said, laughing.

"Really," I replied. More of a statement than a question.

"Do you have any more napkins? It's kind of a long story."

"No need for napkins. I have a recorder."

As the moon made its way over Manhattan, with a brief, hazy appearance in Dad's bedroom window, I sat spellbound. Except for a slight interruption when the nurse made her rounds, I was 8,000 miles and seventy years away from 541 East 5th Street. Another lifetime away from Dad and Mark and whatever was tearing us apart. From the moment the recorder beeped, Tsering never let go of my hand as he told me the story of his great-grandfather and the Snow Lion.

THE SNOW LION

BY P.A. STERN

Tashi Yexe was born with the blessing of pure joy in his soul. Good fortune also gave him a keen mind, a kindhearted spirit, and natural athletic ability. Two years older than Tashi, his brother Ngompa, the hunter, possessed of similar gifts, was even more blessed. One single breath was all that separated him from the next life, and he lived every moment as if it were infinitely precious. One morning when Ngompa was seventeen, his butter lamp sputtered, then dissolved in coarse winds as he returned to the source of clear light. It was 1935. The Year of the Wood Pig. The year of the birth of His Holiness the Fourteenth Dalai Lama.

Tashi had woken up first so he could sort the horseshoes. He also wanted to help his mother haul water for the butter tea. It would be better to get out to the well without his brother, and before the Chinese kids. The last time, Ngompa had not been able to ignore the badgering. Jeers had turned into jabs, and Tashi had to pull Ngompa away. The brothers agreed not to tell their parents.

Today, Tashi and Ngompa were to leave early for a football match, but chores needed to be done first. Ngompa was going to be a starting player, and Tashi let him get a little more rest. When Tashi returned to their bedroom and found his brother still under the covers, he leapt on him, laughing, ready to wrestle him awake. But Ngompa was no longer asleep; he had passed into the next world.

The wail that came from Tashi's belly was heard throughout the village of Gurum. Immediately, it was joined by the woeful pitches of his mother and father, a disharmonious chorus. The bitter song brought goosebumps to the children playing in the

234

streets. Neighbors looked out from their homes, stopped caring for their animals, ceased cooking, and rushed to find Tashi and his parents in bed with Ngompa. A pile of sorrow, heaving.

Their house was built of strong wooden girders, flanked with a stone bounding wall, and covered with eight centimeters of Aga earth to keep out the rains, wet winds, and snow that pelted them throughout the changing seasons on the high plateau. The living quarters were upstairs, built above what used to be a barn for the highly valued Tibetan horses, now boarded at the bigger barns at the edge of town. As strong as it had been built, on that day, the house almost fell in on itself from the enormous weight of all the heavy hearts.

The entire Yexe family was devastated, as was the whole town. After the initial shock, emotions turned to action. The nuns and the monks came at once. As soon as they arrived, the monks prepared the body. Ngompa was bent into a sitting position, his head propped against his knees. Return to the womb. Tashi had seen others in this position, but they were older, and when they died, he had not felt the same about them. He smiled as he thought of Ngompa bending his upper body like that, right before he headed the ball into the net. Tashi was jarred by his fond memory as his brother's body slowly disappeared under the snow-white mourning cloth that was being wrapped around him, layers of gauzy petals engulfing his former self. When the cocoon was complete, they moved the swaddled body to the smooth earthen bank inside the door, on the right-hand side of the entry.

Soon, the *phowa* began with Tashi's and Ngompa's parents. Reading scripture aloud, chanting. Freeing Ngompa. Freeing them. As they invoked the presence of Buddha, they helped Ngompa enter the atmosphere in purity and truth. Not his body. His being. No longer constrained by the limitations and pains of flesh, *phowa* released Ngompa, bathing him in compassion, bringing him to the realm of rebirth, eventually allowing him to soar on rays of light where he would join with the enlightenment of the Buddhas and become one with them for eternity.

While Tashi truly believed as he had been raised and accepted that Ngompa was heading to his full liberation through *phowa*, he was still overcome with unbearable sadness. He left the others and entered his bedroom, the first time since the moment he realized Ngompa would not wake up. He looked around, but everything was blurry, as if the morning mist had entered their room. How could he carry on without Ngompa?

The more he felt the attachment to his brother's physical being, the more he forced himself to chant the mantras. But he did not want to chant. He wanted to lift stones with Ngompa, to compete against the other boys, to feel his brother's muscular grasp as together they tugged the heavy rocks, tied with yak hair rope, Ngompa as strong and fierce as the yak itself.

Tashi looked around their room. Through his fog, he reached out and grabbed a round white stone. Who would teach him to place the *rdel Bo* strategically, to master *mig mangs* and use the many eyes to perfect the killing rule, placing the smooth pebbles, creating the perfect tension between the black and white? Only Ngompa knew the spells and the value of the scarecrow stones, the oracles and symbolism of the ancient game taught to him by the old monk librarian, now also passed to the place of light.

He collapsed on their bedroom floor and rolled back and forth, side to side, wrestling with himself. All he wanted was his big brother to throw him in the stream, where they could wrestle together until the icy cold drove the loser to shore. Or they could become acrobats and practice *gnam bro thag rtsed* as they defied gravity and flew down the slippery yak-hair rope, spinning around and around in the rope game. Ngompa wasn't afraid of the dangerous sky dancing—he would try anything.

Through his tears, Tashi laughed when he thought of Ngompa chattering nonstop, everywhere, especially on the soccer field. Ngompa was comfortable talking with anyone, whether a visiting lama or a local schoolgirl. Not Tashi. Tashi was still young, still did not know how to speak to girls. He was hoping to soon approach Dekyi, the pretty girl with the laughing eyes who helped at the barns, but she still had only four pigtails, and was not yet old enough to court. He needed Ngompa to prod him, to show him the ways into manhood.

Tashi stood up and wiped the tears from his face. As his eyes cleared, he saw their football on the far side of the room. Which one of them had kicked it there last night, had had the last touch? How could he play with it anymore? He needed his brother to juggle the football and race from one goal to the other. Together.

But Tashi knew these thoughts of loss were preventing Ngompa from finding everlasting peace, that his own attachment to his brother's physical self kept Ngompa from dissolving into the light and wisdom of the Buddha. So Tashi buried his thoughts in prayer. He chanted without ceasing. Born of respect and the infinite love of a brother for his older brother, his only brother, a fever grew. Through his hard work and determined effort, he would free his brother. He would let him go, as he knew he should.

Om Mani Padme Hum Hrih
Om Mani Padme Hum Hrih
Om Mani Padme Hum Hrih

Tashi's chants were joined by many voices, from home to home across the village. As the day progressed, townspeople, family, and friends came to the house and presented *hada*. White silk cloths were draped over every open space, as if the loosely-woven fabric, the nubbiness of the raw silk, could somehow fill the emptiness of their hearts. Hundreds of *kha-tha-thags*, fairies' streamers, floated in the sad winds.

Word spread, and more friends and family arrived from nearby villages. The Yexe house was too small to accommodate all the mourners, so some went up to the nearby monastery. Tashi could see them heading past the monastery's blood-red stone walls, toward the protector's shrine built into the steep rocky slope. There, the mourners prayed for Ngompa, chanting while circling the monastery's compound. The high hills and the village valley were soon connected by vocal vibrations.

When Ngompa's best friend Kalsang came to the Yexe home, he lifted up over his head the *hada* he had brought, bowed forward slightly, and placed the long piece of silk at the feet of Ngompa's parents. Although they had very little strength left, and they had not returned *hadas* to any of the other visitors, for Kalsang, they made an exception. The Yexes had saved a *hada*, two meters in length, for Ngompa's favorite friend. Kalsang's eyes grew wide as he accepted such an honor.

Tashi agreed with his parents: Ngompa's friend from infancy was their third son, and he would feel the loss as deeply as they. Kalsang showed his thanks and respect by accepting the *hada* with both of his hands, raising it over his head, and placing it on his shoulders, which shook as he tried to hold back his tears.

Draped in his own *hada*, Kalsang then hung another around Tashi's neck. This *hada* was not white, but a special five-colored *hada*. Blue for sky. White for cloud. Yellow for land. Green for river. Red for the god of protection. With its five colors, this cloth was the cloth of the Buddha. Brothers in life. Brothers for life. Nothing else would do.

As the visitors arrived and left, the nuns and monks continued to pray. The juniper incense was lit, and the chanting continued throughout the day, into the night. The jewel in the lotus.

> *Om amarani jiwantiye svaha*
> *Om amarani jiwantiye svaha*
> *Om amarani jiwantiye svaha*

Ngompa's body was to be carried to the charnel grounds in the morning, before the light of dawn began to take form. He had died the day before a lucky day, and therefore, the family wanted the burial to take place right away instead of waiting the customary three days. There was a sky burial ground on the hilltop right outside of their village, but a few towns away were the Drikung charnel grounds, which a rainbow joined with the Sitavana grounds in India. It was a five-hour walk, but Tashi's parents felt strongly that the number of this day and the nature and proximity of the other auspicious burial ground meant it should be the last resting place for the body of their elder son.

Even though the Yexe family had felt, from the moment Tashi had found Ngompa's body without breath, that time had stalled in a permanent state of surreal numbness, the day awakened anyway, insisting on moving ahead regardless of their perception of its halted temporal condition.

The procession left by the light of a butter lamp. The yawning sky grew apricot over the high ridge, the chilling mist catching much of the hue, so it faded as a dream fades upon waking. Mothers carried babies on their backs and the elderly stumbled on the uneven paths as the long procession walked toward the burial grounds. They passed piles of rocks, some left by glacial movement, some dropped from high cliffs by forces of erosion, and others placed purposely, the acts of mourners honoring those who had died before. Tashi was focused on the shredded prayer flags that lined the rough paths like faded fingers fluttering in the winds. Threads unraveled and were carried away in the breeze. He found comfort that, with each thread, another prayer was released, carrying compassion as far as the traveling winds blew.

Tashi had helped lift Ngompa's body so it could be carried out of the village by their paternal uncle. He had never before been able to lift his bigger, stronger brother so high. As they came closer to the charnel grounds, Tashi helped transfer the body to a professional carrier, who would transport it the rest of the way. When they reached the sky burial grounds, they were all weary from the long walk, but they rested for a mere moment to catch their breath, and began their prayers. Over and over, they bowed to the ground, raised their arms to the skies, and clasped hands, ready to release Ngompa. Tashi completed these actions as though they were a daily routine, rote, staring at the circle of large boulders arranged before them—a *mandala* for Chakrasamvara, the Mother Tantra deity.

In the dull light, he saw the body placed on the large flat rock on the highest point of the hillside. The celestial burial master came and prepared it. He lit the *su*, and the smoke rose to the skies. With a deep breath, he blew one long, high note from the *kangling*, a human thigh-bone trumpet. Tashi skated on that note, fixated until the chanting began. He joined in and chanted, and watched the master raise the two-sided *damaru* drum to the skies and play, the red brocade tail and turquoise beads flapping along with the rhythm that also accompanied the hypnotic chants. The drum was made from the tops of two human skulls; both instruments had been created from remnants of past sky burials, as it was meant to be. A reminder to let go of the flesh.

And then Tashi and his family left. They were not to be present for the remainder of the funeral. Kalsang and a few other friends stayed behind, but the ritual was left to the *rogyapa* to fulfill his role as body-breaker. Only he and his assistant, the burial master, a few onlookers, and the vultures would witness the rest of the sky burial.

Tashi took one last look back at the body of his brother, and left in the same numb haze that had transported him to the charnel grounds. The clouds covered the peaks of the surrounding mountains. There was no clear indication of a separation between earth and sky, only a path that left the rocky ledges and continued into the soft, comforting clouds. His parents followed, weak from the long walk, empty from their long sadness.

As Tashi took each step toward home, steps that took him farther from Drikung, his mind stayed behind as he pictured every step of his brother's burial. Tashi had been to other burials and knew the ritual, knew it was time for *jhator*, the giving of alms to the birds. With an easy manner, the assistant would lift the cloth. Chatting and relaxed, he and the *rogyapa* would proceed to cut up the body. Lighthearted in their work. If Tashi were there, he, too, would be light, not solemn. The levity would allow his brother to pass to the next life with ease and certainty.

As if on cue, Tashi could see the first few small dots in the larger sky. One by one, the condors came, growing in size and number, attracted by the scent of the *su* smoke and fresh flesh. He watched them descend until they disappeared from view. The rest he saw in his mind's-eye.

The big birds would land near the body, line up, sit, and wait. In some odd ritual of nature, in their delay, they seemed to show respect for the master, for the family, for the dead. When the initial preparations were complete and the body was cut into manageable pieces, the *rogyapa* would back off and the holy birds would begin their feast. Tashi knew in his heart that the white vultures would eat first, and this, too, was an auspicious sign that his brother had indeed died without sin.

In less than an hour, the birds would devour most of the flesh and perch back, bellies full, waiting for what they knew would come next. The remaining bones would be crushed with sledge-hammers and ground up against the large, flat stone. The fine powder would be swept up, then mixed with *tsampa*, roasted high-land barley and yak milk. This mixture would be fed to the birds, ensuring that no part of the flesh remained on earth. And Tashi knew that the birds would fly up and away, and Ngompa would merge with the sky, his soul ascending to Heaven.

Though their firm beliefs affirmed that all life is transitory, the sudden departure of their son was initially devastating to his mother and father. Back home, they had to wrestle with their emotions, but with the perspective that comes with age and their faith in the way of the Buddha, his parents were able to move on and find the blessings in the death of their eldest son. Within a few weeks, his father was back tending the horses, getting ready for the next trade on the Tea Horse Trail. Tashi's mother prepared the meals, wove the cloth, gathered dung for heat, and kept the family intact.

Tashi was not so capable of accepting his loss and moving on. His grieving continued for months and months. To Tashi's mourning eyes, all color drained from the roof of the world, leaving it only as shades of grey and beige, a limited buttermilk sky. In his sadness, Tashi's favorite foods lost their flavors and appeal. He found no comfort as he cared for their horses. And he no longer had any romantic interest in Dekyi.

Even his beloved football brought him hollow relief. Running, kicking, passing—all used to be physical expressions of elation, approaching the perfect joy of the Buddha. Now they were silly, meaningless acts with the ball, and did little to free Tashi from his mournful state or, more importantly, to release Ngompa from his perpetual state of *bardo*, intermediate death.

As the months turned into a year, it was clear that Tashi was still not ready to find his solo path living on the earth without his brother. Like the interminable monsoon rains preceding *Vassa*, it seemed that Tashi's grief would never end. All too aware of his extended mourning period, the townspeople complained to him that Ngompa would return as a hungry ghost to wander about the village during the continuing bereavement, and they urged Tashi to seek advice from the monks.

For the one-year anniversary ceremony, a group of nuns came to Gurum to pray with Tashi, to pray for Ngompa's soul. Behind the monastery, a field of poppies bloomed alongside the wild roses. The path to town filled with the throng of orange robes, and as they passed, the flowers waved in unison: a chanting, flowing stream of saffron praying to bring release to the two brothers.

The day of the memorial felt to Tashi like all others since the day Ngompa had stopped breathing: endless and numb, and no different from every other day. Tashi chanted and grieved; it made no difference to him that a whole year had come and gone. When the memorial was complete, the nuns returned up the hill. Their robes, glowing red in the light of dusk, climbed the path like flames, merging with the blaze of the setting sun. One of the nuns remained behind, approached Tashi, and made him a unique offering.

In the folds of her *chuba*, between the golden gown and her outer robe, the nun had wrapped in her shawl a six-week-old mastiff *paga*, a gift of hope in a ball of fur. Still numb from the many months of grief, Tashi felt the first flutters of awakening. When the last layer of the nun's outer *zhen* was peeled back, the puppy unfurled his tail with a tentative wag, stretched his nose to take in Tashi's scent, and let out a yelp—as ferocious as possible for such a tiny dog—insisting on his place. Tashi's heart instantly turned as soft as the puppy's belly, and his natural uplifted spirit returned.

When the nun presented the puppy to Tashi, she told him it was the most recent mastiff born at the Tsurphu Monastery, and the only one in the litter. The puppy looked like the whitest snow, like the pure snow on the highest peaks, not the trail snow always dirtied by the fine dust of the rocky moraine. She told Tashi that such a rare creature was known in ancient times as a Snow Lion— the embodiment of playfulness and joy, thought to represent pure harmony. She also told Tashi that the monks felt it was in the best interest of the village to share this single offspring with him, another single offspring. The monks believed Tashi would be the perfect recipient and caretaker of Buddha's guardian. It was an honor of which Tashi did not feel worthy, but which he accepted nonetheless.

It was as if the gift of the "heavenly dog" freed him to carry on without his brother, and allowed Ngompa's soul to ascend to its rightful place. By embracing this new life, Tashi was able to let go of his grief. Now Tashi's view upward was endless once more, and returned to *Gyu*, the brilliant turquoise of Heaven. Now the mouthwatering *momos* and warm mutton stew smelled delicious and tasted savory and good, especially served with the fresh, tangy yoghurt atop roasted sheep intestines. Once again, he found comfort as he tended the horses. Once again, Tashi flushed with excitement as he thought of courting Dekyi. And football again became a joyous extension of Tashi's physical being, a constant source of his infectious smile.

Tashi called the Tibetan mastiff Kang-ri, short for Ngompa kang-ri khyi—Hunter's Snow Lion Dog. In honor of his brother.

There had not been a mastiff puppy in their village in a long time, since packs of mastiffs had roamed the high pastures, guarding herds from attacks by snow leopards and wolves. In Tashi's town, the dogs used to keep intruders from their masters' homes. Over the years, fewer and fewer mastiffs were raised. Limited food supplies in their rough mountain region made it difficult to feed both families and the huge dogs. More than that, the Tibetan mastiffs could be loyal to a fault, attacking not only strangers, but also their own family when members returned home in the dark of night. Too often, leaving these nocturnal sentries unchained had proven fatal.

Kang-ri was one of the *Tsang-khyi* breed of mastiff that Tashi had first met when his brother took him up to the monastery. Ngompa had been an apprentice with the librarian, and helped him preserve the sacred scrolls, coating the *thangkas'* pigments—malachite and cinnabar—with yak glue, ox bile, and an occasional misting with ice water so the images remained bright and vivid. Whenever they could, Tashi and his brother had visited with the monks, who still raised and kept mastiffs in their high monastery, primarily to protect the sacred scrolls; the monks and the mastiffs worked together to safeguard the ancient teachings.

While Ngompa had worked, Tashi had been allowed to sit and watch. To learn. He was also allowed to play with the dogs. Once, the librarian had shown Tashi and Ngompa a picture book of dogs. The monastery mastiffs were larger, and had longer manes and more wrinkles than their cousins raised by nomads. Ngompa had whispered to Tashi that the dogs looked like the sage old lamas who cared for them.

Kang-ri's fur was softer than the fuzziest yak calf, fluffier than the down of a tundra swan, and the village children vied for turns holding him, petting him. Tashi welcomed the help with the endless task of grooming the soft fur of Kang-ri's double coat with an ox-horn comb. As the puppy reached adolescence, he grew a long, shaggy mane surrounding his enormous head. The mane was copper fur tinged with white, an unusual coloration for this unusual dog. The rest of the fur on his torso and haunches remained the rarest pearl white. The reddish-orange ruff surrounding his snowy neck made him look even more like a lion. Tashi knew the celestial Snow Lion of myth had a mane of turquoise. He joked that perhaps the copper in Kang-ri's fur had not yet turned to green!

But the best part about Kang-ri was his wrinkles. Despite the sad look from his droopy ears and expressive eyebrows, the way his many wrinkled folds hugged his face and gathered near his eyes made Kang-ri seem like he was always smiling. Just like his master.

Those were good days, days of hard work and harder play. Tashi returned to his football, training and playing with his team, which had become known as Gurum United—GU. Frequent practices, games against other teams that had formed throughout Tibet, and spirited matches versus the chesty British Mission Marmots—the MM—kept Tashi too active to hold onto thoughts of Ngompa.

And Kang-ri was right there at every game; he became their mascot and ran drills with them at practices. Tashi could not afford a real football, so he made one out of old paper and string. When it fell apart, he made another one. Tashi would kick the ragged ball and the large white beast would bound across the makeshift pitch, trapping the ball by plopping his massive, furry body on top of it. Then he'd get up, bow in a downward-facing dog position, and make a powerful pass back to Tashi by propelling the ball with his snout. Onlookers loved to watch this captivating display. It was clear that Kang-ri was helping Tashi become the best player on GU.

Kang-ri also pranced around the pitch before and after each game—when he wasn't barking at some perceived threat. The British players and spectators in particular coveted this unusual dog. Tashi was constantly being offered money and other gifts in exchange for the "dandy white beast," but nothing could replace Kang-ri; it would be like trading in his mother. When the propositions didn't let up, Kang-ri's hackles would rise. He'd bare his teeth and let out a deep growl, as if sensing Tashi's discomfort.

Tashi would grab the dog by his scruff and run as fast as he could away from the Brits. They were a pretty fast duo. The first time this happened, the Brits were stupefied.

"I can't see their arses for dust!" the British wing joshed.

The MM striker replied, "Well, can you just bloody well beat that?"

As he pulled Kang-ri away, Tashi could hear the Brits bantering on, wondering what they had done. He could tell they thought he was strange, but he also knew they had no idea of the possible danger they were actually in.

Several months later, early in the morning of a game day, Tashi was at home, pacing and muttering to himself. His mother sent him down to the barn to do chores, to burn off some nervous energy. Tashi was feeding the foals when he heard an unfamiliar voice. He looked out of the stall and saw a Chinese boy about his age standing very close to Dekyi, who had an odd look on her face: lips pinched, eyes lowered, cheeks flushed. It was the kid with the bad limp, the one who hung around the football field, always watching but never playing. Because Tashi figured the visitor was looking for him, he put down his shovel and walked toward them.

Kang-ri bounded ahead of Tashi. The stranger flinched when the dog came close. When the visitor saw that Tashi was also in the barn, he turned red and backed up, almost falling over a pitchfork. Without saying anything, the young Chinese man ran from the stable. Tashi watched him flee, surprised at how quickly he moved, considering he had such a severe limp.

Tashi tried to make Dekyi feel better. As he walked alongside her, he began to imitate his good friend Tenzin, their team's striker, who was the poorest of the players and the most spiritual. Tenzin wrapped his braids into a topknot and kept a charm box inside it, which made it difficult to head the ball in the net. Tashi pranced about, lowered his head, and stumbled, pretending to be Tenzin scoring a goal. Tashi and Dekyi—dog in tow—giggled about Tashi's silly impersonation. As they left the barn, they looked up and noticed that the Chinese youth had stopped down the path. He was watching them, his chest heaving, his face full of anger and bitterness. Tashi hoped he had not been the cause of the distress.

An older man walked up the road and approached the youth. Tashi recognized the Chinese dignitary, and realized the boy was his son. As Tashi and Dekyi watched, it was clear the man was not happy with what his son was telling him. The father gave him a strong scolding, insulting him with *tshig-gi*—words meant to hit at the heart. Tashi and Dekyi could barely make out what was being said as the dignitary spat, "What do you mean you were flirting with the Tibetan peasant? And the boy saw you? He may be poor, but at least he can run." Then the father gave his son a cruel beating that brought more pain to his already deformed leg. Tashi and Dekyi lowered their eyes and said a prayer for his suffering. Kang-ri moaned. The young Chinese man did not attend the game that afternoon.

It was a misty day, but the boys played with unusual crispness and focus. In the final seconds, Tenzin passed the ball to Tashi, who kicked it with such force that bits of feathers and yak hair flew out through the split seams, deflating the ball ever so slightly but resulting in a boot that flew past the defenders, just barely missing the bamboo posts and ending up in the back right corner of the net. The goalie never saw it coming. Even if he had, there was nothing he could have done to stop the conviction of that kick, to block the arc of the ball. Still, he fell to the ground in disgust.

Tashi also dropped to the ground, but his was a champion's dive. His teammates leapt on top of him, and together they rolled in the high plateau dust, celebrating the beauty of the moment, of that perfect goal.

Tense and concerned, Kang-ri lurched up, let out his ferocious bark, and landed his huge paws high on the pile of boys. At less than one year old and seventy kilograms, the lion-maned mastiff was as formidable as the high peaks from which his breed originated. He was Tashi's steadfast guardian, just as his ancestors had been loyal protectors for Genghis Khan and Marco Polo centuries before.

The team knew this was just Kang-ri's way of protecting Tashi. Despite his colossal size, the boys pushed the dog, wrestling the beast off of them. When they stood up, they were all covered with bits of barley along with the dried, broken soil left over from the pigs who had been there foraging hours before.

The game was over, and both sides headed back toward town—the dog, as usual, fixed at Tashi's heels. This could have been just any day, any game. On any other day, Tashi and his teammates would simply be pleased with their winning performance. On any other day, their rivals would nurse their disappointment with the outcome, but still be content with the fun of the play. The lighthearted teasing would continue until the next game, the next defeat. But today was different. The final team was being selected, and Tashi had just secured himself a spot on the roster, the last opening. His ever-present grin was now impossible to contain. His parents would be filled with pride for their son—and for all of the other boys. It was the last lunar cycle of 1937, the Year of the Fire Ox, and at sixteen, Tashi would be the youngest member of the first official Tibetan soccer team.

No matter whom Tashi's team played, before each game, the boys would chant their prayers. They would pray for all players to do well, for everyone to win. Then they would present *hadas* to the opposing team's players. The first time they played, the British marveled at the odd rituals. The Marmots beat them seven-nil. It was hard to beat a team of players who all wore their army field boots. The second time they played, one of the MM defensive players snickered, "No wonder they never win; they're too damned polite!" One British spectator was quite rude, imitating their prayer stance, mocking the mantras, carrying on with a constant stream of insults. Finally, mid-run, the Brits' team captain stopped dead in the middle of the pitch, trapped the ball, booted it as hard as he could straight at the loudmouth, and shouted, "Stop it right now, you old wanker!" and that was the last of the cultural clash.

Tashi enjoyed the British, and it seemed the Brits enjoyed being in Tibet. Even though they had established themselves in Tibet through force, which had led to the deaths of thousands of Tibetans, relations with the British had grown cordial over the years. Instead of trying to conquer the Tibetans, to master their culture and change their ways, the British formed sincere friendships and seemed to respect the pure beauty of the sur-roundings, the "mystical ways." The Marmots' keeper, Basil Gould, said they had found their earthly paradise, their Shangri-la in the *Shambhala*. And he often teased Tashi and his teammates that the Brits were, in fact, the ones who had introduced football to Tibet, after their conquest of Lhasa.

The GU would also play against a team made up of the Chinese, who were now living mostly in Lhasa, but also in their village. Tashi wished it wasn't so, but it was clear that the two nations living in close proximity for centuries had resulted in a mixture of conflicts and a strange relationship stemming from trade routes and necessity.

Several Chinese dignitaries had built nice homes in the hills overlooking Gurum. Just a few years ago, the government of the Republic of China had established an agency to oversee Tibetan affairs. These denizens were administering and monitoring the lo-cal governments, insinuating their voices in subtle but growing ways. Some locals were alarmed; others, like Tashi's parents, were less concerned. They trusted in the will of the Buddha.

With the Brits, all remained cordial; with the Chinese, negativity grew and apprehension mounted. To counteract the tension, the lamas increased their mantras. Still, antagonistic in-teractions arose. No one complained, but they knew that even the Chinese football team's name, the Imperialist Warriors, or

IW, indicated the depth and extent of the issues. The perceived historical prerogative.

Unfortunately, relations with the Chinese were strained off and on the field. The lamas advised the followers and footballers to increase their focus on the positive light of the Buddha. Spreading compassion. But nothing seemed to help. Often, on his way to the barns, Tashi would run into Chinese kids heading to or from their private school. They'd tease him for his clothes, his cheekbones, the angle of his eyes. When Ngompa was alive, they had each other to temper the wrath. Mostly, they learned to avoid the Chinese whenever possible. And, of course, to pray for them.

Tashi's neighbors even had a strained relationship with the Chinese Muslims, especially after a Muslim warlord took control of the birthplace of the Fourteenth Dalai Lama. Many townspeople would not forgive them; mistrust and antagonism was cemented between the two cultures. Tashi accepted that they had to rely on Muslim butchers and tanners to do their slaughtering. They were Buddhists, but they needed to eat meat, to wear furs. And at least the Muslim butchers would give Tashi's mother extra bones for Kang-ri. The other Chinese certainly did not show Kang-ri that kind of respect.

The townspeople also respected Kang-ri, and the Brits were infatuated with him. Tenzin, the GU striker, had taught Basil Gould the Tibetan word *tuchi che*, thank you, and Gould would say it—and mean it—every time he saw Kang-ri. He would also pronounce it incorrectly most of the time, much to their mutual amusement.

The unusual heat wave experienced in the high plateau did not help anyone's mood. At one very close game in which GU tied the Chinese IW, both teams were getting ready to take penalty kicks to determine the winner. Usually, Kang-ri sat next to Tashi, or, when Tashi was busy playing, another team member would sit with the dog—as a precaution. Because of the tie, it became a little chaotic, as all of the players were lining up, stretching, and preparing themselves for the kicks in case they were selected. Kang-ri was fast asleep, drained from the high temperatures combined with the intense practices three days prior to the game. He was all alone on the rocky sidelines.

In the midst of the activity, Tashi noticed a Chinese spectator hobbling in the direction of Kang-ri. Tashi thought nothing of it until he saw the young man stir up the attention of some of the Chinese onlookers, point toward Kang-ri, and encourage them to cheer him on. The other players on the field responded as if they thought the spectators were cheering for the game.

Tashi realized it was the kid from the barn, the one who had made Dekyi uncomfortable, the one whose father had beat him. He watched in disbelief as the Chinese kid quickly crept up behind Kang-ri and threw himself on top of him, as though he were capturing the sleeping beast. The shock of the assault threw Kang-ri into immediate instinctual aggression. He gripped the young man's arm with his powerful jaw, canines clamped down. The blood-curdling yell from the sidelines caused everyone in the makeshift stadium to freeze.

Tashi was already rushing to his dog, screaming for him to let go.

Blood was everywhere. Onlookers held their breath, then did the only thing they could do to help: chant, furiously. The Chinese kid threw up all over himself, and then alternated between whimpering and shrieking. The audience was both disgusted and delighted at the turn of events.

Tashi had to whip his beloved pet with the yak-hair rope to get his attention. Tashi yelled and whipped, yelled and whipped, tears streaming as he did. It took five teammates to tear the jaws apart and pull the dog off. Bleeding, whining, the boy turned and kicked Kang-ri in the head, as if it were somehow the dog's fault. Then he fled, limping away as fast as he could.

The game was over. It was the only game on record that ended in a tie.

Tashi was visibly shaken. He had had to hurt Kang-ri, who had been bred to be fierce and protective, but who was mostly loving and gentle. His cherished dog was suffering, yet his dog had tried to harm someone. The dog looked up at him with sad, confused eyes and retreated home, his majestic tail curled between his legs. Kang-ri had been forced to act against his nature, and it seemed as if he felt the disgrace deep in his large heart.

Some neighbors were concerned for Tashi and his dog, expressing sympathy and condolences; others were upset that he had been the cause of any contention with the Chinese. No one wanted to increase the already-growing animosity between the two nations, no matter who had started it. Tashi hoped they could find some way to coexist, to live in harmony.

Tashi liked the Brits, but not the way some of them mocked the Tibetans' rituals. At least the Chinese shared the Buddhist practices. Like others in Gurum, Tashi was growing concerned that a sense of arrogance and entitlement had appeared among the Chinese, not only in attitude, but also more and more in the practical governance of the town and the country. Very few Tibetans had close interactions with the Chinese, yet they knew the Chinese nationals considered Tibet to be part of China, not an independent nation. The Yexe family was one of the few who had befriended the Chinese, albeit cautiously, over the course of many decades of business dealings.

Tashi and his father raised and cared for Tibetan horses. When the horses were ready, father and son would travel along the Tea Horse Trail, meeting Chinese traders and exchanging horses for tea, the commodity so revered for its nutritional, medicinal, and spiritual qualities that it sometimes seemed as if their entire culture revolved around the making and drinking of butter tea, delicious *po cha*. Made from black tea boiled in water for hours and hours, then mixed with yak butter and salt, tangy and brackish, the savory, hot drink was part of everyday life: for rituals, business, and socializing. It provided much-needed calories and warmth.

Watching locals offer *po cha* to foreign visitors was quite fun. A cup of tea would be poured, and they would await the first sip. The unexpected saltiness and bitterness of the butter tea made for a wide range of reactions, from polite grimaces to spitting to an uncontrollable gag reflex—embarrassing for the guest, but all in good fun. The locals found it odd that their beloved beverage was actually an acquired taste.

Tashi had learned about trading horses for tea from his father's stories, passed down from his Yexe ancestors, and what Ngompa had learned from the old librarian. Since the topography and climate did not allow tea crops to flourish, their people had to get tea from China. For the Chinese, being able to acquire the prized warhorses was worth their weight in … tea. From living at high altitude and selective breeding, Tibetan horses had the desirable features of large lungs and hearts. They were powerful, even if they were small in stature, and they could maneuver steadily over high mountain passes deep with snow as well as steep, stony terrain. The Chinese valued these characteristics, and coveted the animals as draft horses for both commerce and war. Their own cavalry stock was not able to perform in the harsh topography against nomadic populations. The discovery of the Tibetan horses enabled the Chinese to have a successful mounted infantry. The Tea Horse Trail had been built to get these horses across the high Tibetan plateau.

Tashi's father told stories of how porters from China traveled the high, risky trails, carrying impossibly heavy loads of tea bricks on their backs, walking thousands of kilometers, bringing the tea to trade for horses. Ngompa had pointed out what the monk had told him: that the trades had continued for centuries, until Chinese needs changed. As the cavalry no longer relied on horses for anything more than pomp, the wearing of ceremonial armor, and the provision of status for the royal guard—hopefully to inspire loyalty from the masses—they had lost their value.

Tashi thought it was funny that the old monk knew so much about war.

The librarian believed that the Tea Horse Trail was still open because the monks required a constant source of tea. Tashi's father believed it was because the townspeople and the people of the high plateau were sick of drinking nothing but boiled water, their tasteless "white tea." Tashi was proud that they were one of the few families left who still earned their living on the Tea Horse Trail by providing some of the last of the Tibetan horses desired by the Chinese, trading them for medicinal herbs and other staples.

A new foal was to be born any day, and his father needed to stay and care for the mare. Tashi was to make the trek on his own. His first time. Of course, now Kang-ri would be there as Tashi's companion and guardian. Tashi was to travel three days out along the trail's southern route, accompanied by the latest horse requested for purchase. The horse would fulfill his role perfectly, looking regal with his wide, open nostrils, ready to become part of the imperial guard. Tashi was to meet Cheung Jian Chieng, the Chinese tea porter who had traded with his father and grandfather before him.

Kang-ri seemed particularly excited as they set out; this was his first trip outside the village since his arrival as a puppy. The new smells overwhelmed his highly sensitive nose. He could barely contain himself. His normally placid personality was replaced by playful exuberance. Tashi had to calm him down with his familiar low whistle.

"*Shwoo, shwoo, shwoo,*" Tashi kept repeating as they began the walk away from their home. A dog-owner's mantra. As they were about to leave the village gate, Kang-ri stopped and sniffed the air, turned his head, and moaned. Tashi followed his dog's snout and saw a figure down the lonely alley. It was that boy, the boy who had hurt Kang-ri. He was kicking a soccer ball up the stony path, and when the ball rolled back down to him, he hobbled over and trapped it, and kicked it back up again. A solitary practice. Kang-ri's moan began to turn into a howl, but Tashi yanked the yak-hair leash and left before the boy could see them.

Eventually, Kang-ri calmed down and fell into the rhythm of the trek, pacing right alongside his master. Tashi carried a yak bladder sack filled with water. Every so often, he would stop and pour some into his wooden cup and let the dog drink. Tashi also carried *tsampa* in a leather sack that had been waterproofed with yak fat. These provisions were to be shared with the horse and Kang-ri. Each night, Tashi tethered the horse and put a rope on the mastiff before dinner began.

Besides the staples, Tashi had with him his precious football, a real one Kalsang had given him at the New Year. He'd spend hours kicking the ball toward Kang-ri, who would nose it back, the way he did at home. On this trek, they were both very careful to keep the ball from plunging thousands of meters off the trail. Kang-ri liked to take turns licking the ball, then licking Tashi's face. The ball's stickiness helped keep the passes controlled. And the kisses helped keep Tashi's loneliness at bay.

Tashi had spent many nights of his youth camping out on the plains in their black yak felt tent, looking at the deep blackness of the night sky, the absence of light and color on the roof of the world. At all of these other times, he had been with Ngompa. He did not realize how different it would be without his brother to trick him out of his fears, or sing him into irrepressible laughter.

Ngompa had been the master at singing the *gzas-tshig*, songs filled with puns and sarcasm. He would start softly, singing traditional love songs, teasing his little brother with temptations and flirtations, pretending to be the pretty Dekyi. As the night grew darker and the *chhaang* barley beer flowed faster, Ngompa would get louder. The nectar of the gods would help his voice grow more off-key as he shouted the lyrics of off-color songs he had heard from traders or on the back streets of their village.

When the Tibetans are happy, they don themselves in
    festive Chinese attire;
When the Chinese are desperate, they start to speak
    Tibetan.
Bod skyid rgyags na sku lus rgya chas byed
rgya 'u thug na gsun bod skad la byon
When food is placed in the hands of people,
It decreases more and more;
When talk passes through other people's mouths,
It increases more and more.
Zas mi laf bzag na je nyun
gtam mi kha brgyud na je man
Beer that is tasty to the mouth is nectar.
Words that are pleasant to the ear are truths.
Chan kha la zim po bdud rtsi yin
tshig ma bar snan po gtam dpe yin

Tashi couldn't remember the whole song, but he was no longer afraid; he just missed his brother. Now it was only Tashi and
the horse and the dog. He did not really need the companionship.
He had to become a man on his own. The Buddha would guide
him, and Kang-ri would guard him.

At his campsite, Tashi kept his *threng wa* close, fingering and
counting the 108 rosary beads over and over. Like an abacus, the
wooden beads were divided by three larger coral beads and counting beads. Tashi rolled the beads one at a time throughout the
long darkness of night to count to 10,800 prayers, repeating his
mantras, chanting for peace for all people, praying to overcome
his worry.

On the third day, Tashi approached the meeting place. Though
he was growing tired, he wished they had agreed upon a spot
twenty kilometers further east. That way, he could have stopped at
one of his favorite places, the startling emerald waters of Basum
Tso Lake. Before his brother had passed, his family would take
the semi-annual trek to the Tsodzong Monastery on the banks

of this holy lake. Together with thousands of other pilgrims, they would wander the circumference of the lake, burning incense, pouring yak butter for the lamps, spinning the prayer wheels at the temple. Worshippers would give money and tea to beggars along the route. Always, Ngompa would end up throwing Tashi in the lake as their parents howled with laughter, and Tashi would pretend to be angry, even though he loved the feel of the cool green waters and the freedom he felt while floating, looking up at the tall cypresses silhouetted in the bright azure sky. He wondered if they would ever again visit this special place.

Tashi and Kang-ri had passed very few travelers along the trail, and none on this day. Even the winds were not moving, and neither were the many prayer flags along the route. A little apprehensive of the solitude and stillness, Tashi chose to walk with feigned confidence and absolute awareness. Kang-ri also seemed on edge, panting more than usual and barking at the quiet air. After waiting at the designated spot for several hours, Tashi began to worry. He knew that Mr. Chieng was one of the lucky tea porters. Through the years, Mr. Chieng had never fallen off any portion of the rough and unstable trail, landing thousands of meters below. Other porters had been stranded or drowned in torrential downpours and landslides; or worse, found themselves in a sudden snow squall that obscured their vision and made the trek even more treacherous than usual. Others had been attacked by bandits. Tashi hoped Mr. Chieng's luck had not run out.

Despite severe weather on many occasions, Tashi and his father had always been on time to rendezvous with tea porters. The few times they had run a little late weren't because they were irresponsible traders—the horses had refused to move at a steady pace. Even though their work route consisted of steep rocky crags, icy steppes, and wind-scoured networks barely visible at times, they were usually punctual. They had earned a good reputation, which helped keep their family in business all these years.

His father hadn't advised him what to do if Mr. Chieng did not arrive; it was unprecedented. And Ngompa wasn't here to counsel him, either. Tashi sat and scratched the thick undercoat on Kang-ri's haunches, waiting. It was molting season, and Kang-ri's coat was in full shed. With each stroke, Tashi pulled out another handful of thick fur, letting the tufts go with abandon. He watched the white puffs float upwards, little clouds drifting across the cerulean summer sky. The winds were picking up, and despite the fact that it was mid-July, the air was frigid. Kang-ri's hot breath and long coat kept them both warm.

Lost in the mindless motions of grooming, Tashi was startled when Kang-ri began barking ferociously, jumping up and down. Tashi quickly grabbed the end of the rope to restrain him. He looked at Kang-ri's face to read what he was trying to communicate. Fear, warning, anger? Thin brown membranes—haws—rose diagonally across Kang-ri's eyes, concealing most of the white and cloaking them like a sudden storm cloud. Tashi wasn't sure what this meant; his own mood had become as dark as the haw.

Mr. Chieng came running along the path from the west, shouting. Panic. Even though he knew it was the young Yexe boy he'd met many times before, he still shouted: *Are you Tashi? Khye-rang Ta-shi yin-pe?* The tea porter was moving along as fast as he could, his metal-spiked canes digging in before him like a cat clawing its way up a tree. In his frenetic rush, he didn't even need to watch where he ran; as for all the elders, each step of the trail was embedded in the muscle memory of decades of walking the same routes.

A group of men was right behind him. Tashi's heart pounded.

"Bandits! They're trying to get me. Keep away, you miserable bandits! Tashi? Help an old man!" Mr. Chieng shouted frantically.

The porter had bowed legs and a severely humped back from carrying hundreds of kilograms of tea bricks over thousands of kilometers up and down the mountainous passes for many years. Like Kang-ri, his face was wrinkled, but these wrinkles were from a harsh life lived in a harsher environment. Tashi could see the general agonizing toll in Mr. Chieng's walk. As he came closer, Tashi could also see how cloudy Mr. Chieng's left eye had become. Would his own eyes end up like that?

Mr. Chieng fell into Tashi's arms, more from grave fear than the weight of the enormous pack. The group behind him appeared to consist of three Sherpas and five other men who did not seem to be Asian.

At once, Kang-ri became very still. His thunderous barking ceased, and he was on high alert. As the guard dog watched the party of eight men draw near, he took a position of attack, stared down the path, and made a long, low, chill-producing growl. The horse reared up and whinnied with his head held high, then exhaled and let out a deep blow, adding his threatening stare to the menace directed at the approaching men. Up until then, the group had advanced jovially, talking and joking, pretending to chase the old porter, turning his rightful fear into buffoonery. But now, it looked as though the men were experiencing their own mortal fright, which stopped them in their tracks. Their fear produced a cold sweat—an instinctual response as cold as the icy peaks surrounding this unlikely coterie.

High on this harsh passageway at the top of the world, they were at a standoff. The raw silence was deafening. Bravely, a man from the group of eight walked forward. He wore a broad smile and spoke with an easy manner. "Hello. We'd like to introduce ourselves. Would that be okay?" The man seemed so polite, but Tashi heard Mr. Chieng muttering and felt his terrified grip on his shoulder. Kang-ri's snarl confused Tashi even further.

"*Bsdad!*" Tashi firmly commanded Kang-ri to sit, and he did as he was told. Tashi knew that mastiffs' behavior could be unpredictable, especially when the dogs sensed their owner's mood, so he had spent many hours in proper training to keep his dog obedient and safe. While Tashi often acted as Kang-ri's brother and friend instead of his master, when it was necessary, he could and would assume the role of leader. Firm. Strong.

"It's now safe to approach," Tashi told the strangers. He uttered his sacred mantras and felt their calming effect.

The men moved forward with caution as Mr. Chieng moved backward, also with caution. He did not trust that this was not, indeed, a team of bandits. When the group was close, the leader put his two hands together and bowed in a traditional Tibetan greeting. "*Tashi delek.*" Tashi's name came from the same origins: to be lucky. Fortunate greetings. May all be well. Impressed and comforted by their manners, Tashi introduced himself, and explained what he and Mr. Chieng and the horse and the dog were doing. In exchange, Dr. Bruno Beger, a man not much older than Tashi, came forward, blue eyes flashing. As the stranger took off his hat to show respect, the wind unexpectedly picked up and blew his long hair around like shafts of golden wheat swaying in a field. Dr. Beger gave an account of their expedition by way of one of the Tibetans, who turned out to be an interpreter, not a porter.

The group had come all the way from Germany, and was traveling throughout Tibet to gather scientific information about this little-explored region. In addition to the one man whose job it was to guide them through the technical difficulties of the formidable trek, the team was composed of a geologist, a zoologist, an anthropologist, and an entomologist, who was also a filmmaker. Tashi had been schooled at the monastery as a young boy and had a little knowledge about other countries and scientific disciplines, but it took a bit of explaining for him to understand the complexity and depth of these men and their mission.

Mr. Chieng had no interest in these foreigners, and made it clear that he wanted to make his trade and be gone. As soon as they finished their transactions, he pulled Tashi aside. In hushed tones, he warned him that his countrymen were engaged in a civil war back home, and cautioned that more Chinese were expressing interest in taking over Tibet. Mr. Chieng wanted Tashi to pass this information on to his father. Tashi listened with respect, but decided that a lot of the worry was just the irrational ravings of an old man. Tashi was distracted, and anxious to get back to the Germans.

After Mr. Chieng parted, horse in tow, Tashi was left to carry the tea bricks, as he had expected. The Germans insisted that their porters help, and Tashi certainly appreciated the lightened load. They set up camp and spent the rest of the evening together. The

Germans regaled Tashi with stories of their mountaineering adventures in the wilderness of Tibet, places Tashi could not even imagine existed in his own country. They alluded to the fact that this was primarily a zoological expedition. They even showed him specimens of insects they had collected, explaining the importance to the scientific community. The more he talked, the less Dr. Beger could contain himself. At last, he ordered a porter to bring over a small suitcase. He took out one of the *thangkas* they had acquired from their visit to Lhasa, and Dr. Beger showed Tashi how similar their swastika was to his own spiritual symbol.

Kang-ri had settled down by now, and became particularly fond of the expedition leader, Herr Ernst Schäfer. The Germans were all fascinated by this unique Snow Lion, and reveled in hearing all about the dog and his ancestors. Like all of the other foreigners, they offered money and other bribes for Kang-ri. They promised Tashi they would provide the dog with the best care possible. Of course, Tashi refused, much to their dismay. They took many photos and measurements of the great beast, treating Kang-ri like the mere specimen he was to them, just like the rare white Tibetan butterfly, *Parnassius charitonius*, they called it. They showed the beautiful butterfly to Tashi, its white wings tinged with copper as it lay dead, labeled, pinned to a specimen board.

Together, these odd travel companions trekked back to Gurum. When they arrived, word spread quickly. Soon, the Germans had met with the British and Chinese dignitaries as well as the aristocratic Tibetan families. The monastery was leery of these outsiders, and would not allow them entry until they had gotten permission from the high lama.

Tashi served as the Germans' local guide, and he could see that they already knew how things worked, how to infiltrate the community in the most efficient way. That they were more interested in finding out about the people of Tibet than the animal populations. Whenever he could, Dr. Beger took photographs and ran physical tests on the locals. The most invasive were the cranial measurements and facial casts. Very few villagers agreed to participate. Tashi considered it, but his parents refused to allow him unless the monks approved. His father was shocked when the Germans were blessed by Reting Rinpoche, the regent who had been placed in charge of Tibet from the time of the death of the Thirteenth Dalai Lama until the Fourteenth Dalai Lama was of age to rule. When the regent was seen playing soccer with the explorers, Tashi's father voiced concern over his actions. "He behaves not as a revered holy monk, but as a frivolous, irresponsible adolescent. Something must change."

After four days, the German expedition was ready to go explore the region to the east. On their way out of Gurum, they stopped by the barns one last time to try and convince Tashi to let them take Kang-ri. They left without their mastiff specimen, but with more research and data to prove scientifically the origins of the Aryan race.

Because Tashi had arrived with the Germans, and because of all the attention he was getting, the local Chinese officials acted more and more suspicious of the young Tibetan. The Chinese kids had always harassed him, but now he felt that even the adults were keeping a close eye on him. Tashi did not participate in the domestic affairs in his own little village; he could not understand why or how he would pose any threat.

The Germans had left; the Chinese and Brits stayed. Disquiet with the Chinese continued. Tashi's life in Gurum also continued as usual. There were horses to tend to, household chores to complete, tea to drink, girls to woo, festivals to celebrate, prayers to be made. And, of course, there was Kang-ri—and football. Tashi's dribbling skills were improving with every practice. His performance at games was consistent; he played hard, was precise at passing, had good foot skills, communicated well with his teammates, and was a respected leader. Kang-ri continued to be Tashi's best practice partner, and they could often be seen at the edge of the village—the only flat area nearby—in their unique version of football.

Tashi and the other footballers around the country played matches whenever they could find the time, resources, ability to travel to each other. Football fever grew, starting in Lhasa and spreading throughout the country. One huge fan of football was the regent. He was a young monk who had little experience with politics, and Tashi's father again expressed unease that Reting Rinpoche had tastes for secular pleasures, even the material luxuries provided by the Chinese. Tashi thought it was great good fortune that the regent played football every day.

It seemed that everywhere Tashi went, villagers, nomads, and monks were debating strategy and the different teams' virtues over cups of steaming butter tea. There was even talk of selecting a national team to travel outside the country, to play a match versus another nation's team. All of the players could barely contain themselves with that prospect. They were thrilled when the regent passionately came out in support of the national team.

Unfortunately, the regent's passions did not stop at football. When he was accused of corruption and adultery, it made the religious hierarchy look bad. As Tashi's father had predicted, something had to change. The cabinet ministers, together with senior clerics, took the only action they could against the regent. They banned football throughout Tibet, stating, "kicking a football is as bad as kicking the head of the Lord Buddha." It was then that it was declared a crime against their nation—and against their religion—to play football.

Tashi and his teammates were crushed. They had already been dreaming up strategies for an international match, teasing each other about who would make the team, spinning the prayer wheels, and chanting mantras so that they all could make it.

Tashi went into a deep depression. Kang-ri, too, seemed saddened that they could no longer play their usual game. In a bold move out of character Tashi went up to the monastery and tried to convince the monks to help lift the ban. After all, the monks and nuns from Tsurphu Monastery were GU's biggest supporters, cheering them on during matches, sending special prayers for their safe travel, and providing them with thermoses of hot tea. And of course, they had provided GU with their very own prized mascot.

Tashi's pleas were not well received. He was reminded of the
Buddha's teachings and reprimanded for finding such joy in secular activities. Tashi returned to town defeated. He spent much of
the next two weeks at the barn, speaking to no one. Dekyi tried
to engage him in conversation and even flirtations, but Tashi had
no interest in anything or anyone. Even Kang-ri moped about as
though he felt abandoned.

One morning, Tenzin, the team's striker, came running to the
barn. Usually reserved when off the field, today Tenzin was bursting with words.

"Tashi, you have to go!" he shouted. Tashi was mindlessly
grooming a horse and looked up in surprise.

"Tashi, you can do it. We all decided," Tenzin continued.

"What are you talking about, you crazy fool? *Smyon pa,*" he
admonished.

His words rushing as furiously as migrating antelopes, Tenzin
explained that the people of British India had sent word that they
would let Tibetan footballers come to play on their teams. Word
of mouth had spread the news around Gurum in no time flat.

"A telegraph came from India to Lhasa, and when the chaps
from the MM received the message, they invited some football
fans in for tea and told them the big news, and then we just found
out," Tenzin spouted.

Tashi was shocked. He did not have to think about it. He
would do this. He would leave Tibet and go to India to play football. Ngompa would have been brave enough. He would do this
for his brother.

His parents were concerned, but knew the trip was necessary
to lift Tashi's spirits. They also knew their Lord Buddha would
protect Tashi. Their preparations consisted of spending a week at
the temple lighting incense, making many mantras, spinning the
scroll inside the prayer wheel, and bringing positive energy, just
like the energies swirling around the heart chakra. His parents
had little time to bring Tashi good karma before he left, and they
wanted him to have as much protection as possible.

Om Mani Padme Hum

Their mantra's vibrations harmonized with the resonance of the universe, leading to spiritual transformation. Every aspect of the 84,000 sections of the Buddha's teachings was summed up in these six simple syllables.

Om Mani Padme Hum

The more they repeated the mantra—aloud or through spinning—the more they would remove suffering, and bring enlightenment and compassion. What more would parents want for their only son as he journeyed across the Himalayas?

Tashi also took time to pray, but he had to attend to many physical preparations before leaving. The barn was put in the care of his dear friend Kalsang, who would do anything for Ngompa's family. There were so many things Tashi did automatically that he was finding it difficult to remember everything he needed to tell Kalsang. Grooming, feeding, inspecting horseshoes, caring for wounds, training. Tashi had only a few days to pass on his horse sense.

He did not explain life on the Tea Horse Trail, because he expected to return before the next trade. In the middle of mucking the stable, Tashi threw down the shovel in exasperation and began to furiously pick the poisonous weeds that were sprouting at its corners. Yew. Sorghum. Laurel. He had just cleared the barn of these harmful plants last week.

"*Lkugs pa shing tshal!*" he shouted. Stupid plants!

Kang-ri, with his uncanny sense of Tashi's mood, paced, perturbed, in front of the stall. Dekyi was watching both of them as the anxiety grew. In her typical gentle, unassuming way, she walked over to Tashi.

"Please do not worry. We will take care of everything," she said.

Tashi shook his head, agreeing. His usual irrepressible smile started to form, but contorted. His eyes twitched, and his mouth

was somewhere between a frown and a grimace. He was staring at Dekyi, and she back, their eyes fixed on each other like a
safety rope. And then the tears came. Tashi and Dekyi fell to the
floor, sitting as close as they possibly could. Kang-ri came over
and joined them, all three a pile of puppies looking for warmth
and comfort in the loose hay. Kang-ri, acting like a lap dog, forgot
his enormous size and massive weight, and climbed up on the
two sniveling friends, licking their faces with his rough, spotted
tongue. Kang-ri soon had them laughing uncontrollably in between the tears. Such ferocious behavior from the big guard dog.

There they sat for hours. Tashi opened up to Dekyi, telling her
of his fears, revealing the confusion he felt. Up until now, Tashi
had acted so confident, so single-minded in his decision to leave.
She had no idea he was conflicted. She, too, shared her apprehension. Was he doing the right thing? Neither of them could say
for sure. What they could say was how they felt for each other.
There, on that frigid barn floor, surrounded by the warmth of their
cherished dog, Tashi and Dekyi shared their first kiss. Soft and
tender, lips brushed against each other, breath mingled in a moment that would last forever, throughout this life and into the
next. Unexpected, yet destined. Karma.

Tashi promised Dekyi to return to her so they could become
husband and wife. By the time he came back to Gurum, Dekyi
would be wearing more than ten braids, the sign that she was now
available for marriage. When he returned, she would be adorned
with earrings, necklaces, bracelets, and a heavy ornamental headdress. Wearing the head of the sky. Her plaits would be entwined
with coral, turquoise, and *dzi* beads, yak bones, and silver. And she
would gain the privilege of wearing the brightly-colored striped
apron. Then she would be eligible to marry Tashi.

The sky was just turning from coal black to the blue of the deepest waters of the Tsangpo River. It was time. Tashi carried with
him the same staples he had when heading out to trade, but much

more of each. This trek would take him across the familiar Tea Horse Trail, then on the unknown path over the mighty mountains to the south, leading through Nepal into India. He had been told there would be respites along the way where he could stop and be fed. Warmed with butter tea. One distant cousin lived as a lama's apprentice in a cave dwelling halfway to India. There, he could rest, get blankets, and find more supplies for the rest of the trip.

He hoped the path would be marked as well as he had been told. Just follow the prayer flags, they had said. The subtle signposts made of rock piles. He had heard of others losing toes to frostbite, so he had extra yak fur to protect his feet. At times, he would be traveling through knee-deep snow. He would have to watch out for loose scree hidden beneath the drifts, avoid treacherous crevasses and perilous ice holes, and conquer the formidable rock outcroppings. Combat the altitude. Kang-ri would keep him warm and safe. His Snow Lion would dominate over the mountains, protecting Buddha, who, in turn, would provide him protection. Tashi was expecting a brutal trip on a violent landscape. Anything less would be a gift from Buddha.

He was glad he had listened well to the Germans' cautionary tales of their grueling mountaineering expeditions. He wished he had fancy crampons like those explorers, or even rustic ones like Mr. Chieng. Tashi was young and strong and smart. As long as he had Kang-ri, they would be fine. In three weeks, he was to meet his contact from the British Mission across the first border in Luka. He just needed to get over the Nangpa La pass. After that, he needn't worry about supplies or directions; his hosts would get him from Nepal to Kanpur. Then he could finally play football.

With incense burning and a new *hada* across his antelope wool *chuba*, Tashi left his town to the sounds of chanting and the ringing of *dorje* bells and singing bowls. The sacred tones came from high in the monastery and down across the village channels. The only other sounds Tashi heard were his teammates' cheers and his parents' cries merging with the whipping winds. He took in a deep breath to hold the smells of Gurum and forged ahead, laden with sustenance. Even though it took up valuable room, he carried with him a handheld prayer wheel, so he could pray as he walked.

Tashi arrived at Basum Tso Lake in just three days' time. He was already ahead of schedule. He had planned this side trip without telling anyone. He wanted to stop here, to visit the Tsodzong Monastery, to remember. The familiar smells of the yak butter lamps and the juniper incense were intoxicating. Hundreds of people were already gathered at the alpine lake. Most were praying, circumambulating the shores, completing the rituals.

A dozen or so people were not participating in the walking prayers. At closer inspection, they were a group of Chinese dignitaries and their families picnicking on the scenic shores. He recognized a few from football matches and official duties in Gurum. And how could the picnickers miss the renowned Tibetan footballer with his conspicuous companion? They looked up and pointed at him as he passed. He heard them laugh, and thought he heard jeers. Some of the Chinese wore uniforms. Ominous. Others looked less intimidating. They, too, were Buddhists, yet they seemed oblivious to the sacred nature of this place as they chattered noisily and shot off loud fireworks, the smoky sulfur smells defiling the pleasing sweetness of the incense. Oblivious or purposely offensive, it was hard to tell.

Tashi remembered a line from *The Tibetan Book of the Dead*: "Be not fond of the dull smoke-colored light from hell." He shook his head and said a prayer for the Chinese souls. A *chorten* was in his sight; the unexpected vision of this prayer shrine at this moment of prayer was a good sign. Tashi and Kang-ri headed past the picnickers onto a small field, then down a short path through dense foliage that ended on a secluded beach. As Tashi began to disrobe, Kang-ri took long laps of the cool water, quenching his thirst from the three-day walk. Then Kang-ri went to explore, first startled by several grey-green frogs jumping into the water, then scratching his back on the scrub rhododendron branches, all the while inhaling the new smells of this piece of earth. Kang-ri pranced about, a dog happy to be free in such a place.

An *abra*—a plateau pika—emerged from its burrow to nibble a piece of grass. Its silky light brown fur glistened in the sunlight. Kang-ri caught its scent, then saw its plump, round body. Very slowly, he approached, and the pika stood still as stone. Tashi was shocked as he watched them actually sniff each other, the dog's nose the size of the furry rock rabbit. The chase was on!

"Kang-ri!" Tashi yelled. A few Chinese onlookers noticed the unusual sight. This pure white mammoth bounding after the tiny mammal, followed by the half-dressed Tibetan. Clearly, the gentle giant had no intention of catching the pika, or it would have been devoured by now. Up the path they raced to the grassy knoll. There, the pika dove into another entrance leading to his burrow.

"Kang-ri! Stop. Come back!" Tashi called out even louder, his voice booming as if he were on the pitch, directing his fellow players. More heads turned. Tashi was annoyed that he had to traipse back up the path where he realized his dog was just playing. So, apparently, was the pika. Kang-ri circled a few times, then settled down in the soft grass above the path, his white coat reflecting the bright sun. Though Tashi wanted him to stay close, Kang-ri began to breathe deeply, then snore and bark in his sleep, running and chasing something in his dreams. His sleeping life seemed as happy as his waking one. Reluctantly, Tashi left him there to rest, and he returned down to the water's edge alone.

The butter lamps reflected on the still surface. As Tashi entered the clear lake, the water certainly felt holy. His body caused ripples, the reflections now moving and changing shape with each swell. Tashi submerged, rinsing away all of his sins. He then lay back, floating. The sun was so bright that at first, he could not even see the towering cypress trees. He shut his eyes, expecting darkness, but instead saw crimson, sunlight coursing through closed eyelids. His floating breath was muffled but steady, and he drifted, allowing the calm rhythm of the waters and the gentle breeze to lull him into deep meditation.

It is nighttime. The full glaring moon lights their way as the two of them run behind the houses, giggling. Ngompa is chasing him. He knows his brother can easily catch him, and is about to. But Ngompa pretends to trip, and then the hysteria begins again. A mother calls down from an open second-story window; the boys are waking her baby. "Smon lam rgyag!" she whispers. "Go pray!" The boys run away, hands covering their mouths to keep them silent. They stop and say a mantra, then run even faster into the yard behind the barns. There, they take turns throwing loose stones, seeing who will get the tail stone, the middle stone, or the head stone closest to the target. Though Ngompa can outrun Tashi, in this game, the younger brother is the champion. He does a silly winner's dance. They try to suppress their laughter, but the harder they try, the louder they get. Soon, the horses are neighing, and a yak lamp is coming toward them; someone wants to find out who is causing such a commotion.

The wind picked up slightly, and small waves washed over Tashi as he floated. Chilling at first, the snow-melted waters brought quick relief from the intense heat. They also brought Tashi out of his deep, peaceful thoughts into the realm somewhere between meditation and awareness. There, he said good-by to Ngompa. To regrets. He prayed for his parents, for Dekyi, for his village, and for all people. He released his suffering, acknowledging all that we endure in this life. The human condition. No longer would he let the eight worldly concerns dominate his life. He prayed for his safe journey in anticipation of all that lay ahead, a new beginning. Breath. In. Out. Deeply. Gentle ripples spreading out, touching, being touched. All connected. Stillness.

A high-pitched call sounded. The pika. A warning scream. A firework exploded in a flash of light so bright Tashi saw it with his eyes closed. Startled, Tashi felt his head go under, and when he arose, he was choking from the water he had swallowed. He stood up, coughing, water dripping from his nose, his eyelashes.

He had to wipe his eyes to see, but even then, he was blinded by the bright sun.

Something was not right. It was silent but for the wind. His heart felt it before his mind knew. He tumbled to shore and looked up toward the grassy ridge. It had not been a firework. It had been a gunshot. A man limped away quickly, and the life drained from Tashi's Snow Lion, pure white turning to red.

The sound of the shot continued to echo off the high peaks, pounding back and forth between the rock walls and Tashi's skull. He collapsed onto Kang-ri's body and deeply inhaled his sweet scent. At the same moment, Kang-ri let out a weak whimper, and Tashi felt his dog's last breath whisper as it climbed up and out the roof of the world. He buried his face in the thick fur, still warm from the sun. He knew Kang-ri was already gone, returned to his master. Tashi dug his fingers into the shaggy mane and held on as tightly as he could, his voice muffled as he prayed to join them. The sun beat down and Tashi drifted to sleep, hoping that he, too, would awaken in a new life.

Chapter 12

Tsering finished his story and excused himself to take care of another patient. My hand was sweaty and numb, but I hadn't dared move it until he let go. Why was he smiling? I was a blubbering mess, and almost wiped my face with my tenement napkins. I had to stifle my sobs so I wouldn't wake Dad. But I couldn't stifle my sadness.

If you believe life is suffering and death brings relief, I suppose "The Snow Lion" has a happy ending. This was a different kind of faith. A deep acceptance. I needed time to absorb the intricacies of the perspective with which I had been presented. When Tsering returned, he was still smiling. I tried to smile back, but I must have looked odd, a sad clown with an awkward grin painted across my face. One glance at the shiny bed tray confirmed my suspicion. I didn't want to be stuck in that façade.

Tsering's shift was up. When he left, I felt like I was losing a long-lost friend. And gaining one. Intimacy can be reached in the most unexpected ways. Like Leon Haube, my teachers had just shown up, within the forest, outside the barn, overlooking the olive groves. Even in a depressing nursing home. When I was open and allowed myself to be vulnerable. When I was ready to listen.

Dad woke up and didn't recognize me. According to his caseworker, he'd reached middle dementia. At first, I laughed, because I thought of Dad on a quest to Middle-earth. I could picture the maps delineating the Blue Mountains and Mordor, east of the Great River Anduin. But Dad's was an uncharted destination. Stage six on the seven-stage Global Deterioration Scale. Think Locally, Deteriorate Globally. The reality was that, if we were lucky, we'd have about two more years to watch him reach the failure-to-thrive stage. In the meantime, we needed to learn our own coping strategies. Like dealing with the loss. Like forgiving myself for dismissing Dad long before he disappeared.

Mark never came back to Cabrini's. He sent a text:

Going home. Ttys

The new relationship for the new millennium: intimacy and rejection by cell. I sure couldn't envision Tashi and Ngompa disrespecting each other like this. Even a tweet would have had more characters. Yes, everyone in our family seemed to be lacking some character.

If Mark thought I was going to let him get away with an electronic brush-off, he could think again. I said goodbye to Dad and managed to book a last-minute reservation on a flight from JFK to SFO.

On the way to the airport, I stopped by the cemetery so I could place a pebble on Mom's headstone. At the unveiling a few months earlier, we had all been somewhat taken aback when we saw Dad's full name and birthdate already engraved next to Mom's. There was a hyphen and a blank. Waiting for the date of expiration. Like a container of soured cream.

This time, when I examined the gravestone, something else struck me. It hadn't occurred to me before, but now that I realized, it just confirmed that there truly were no coincidences. Dad had been born in 1937.

I did the only thing that made sense in the moment: muddled through the Kaddish prayer, just as I had back in Segovia. At this point in my life, how did I still not know all the words? A few mourners were visiting gravesites nearby. I quietly mumbled, and hoped I hadn't botched it too much. If I feigned confidence, added a little sway to my *davening*, maybe no one would notice that I was faking it. I was quite sure Mom would, though I hoped death would have softened her, and she'd give me a break. I'd come all this way to visit, after all, like a good daughter. Wasn't that enough? Was it ever?

I also hoped she'd give me some answers. What had Dad been saying last night? What did he mean? Mom died, Dad lost his mind, and Mark banished me. Not the right ingredients to get any kind of closure. And still, graveside, I hoped some clarity would come. There was a good reason they called me Pollyanna.

The Prius was now running in gas mode, leaving me torn between honoring Mom and honoring Mother Earth. The idling engine won out. I did have a plane to catch, after all.

My flight was supposed to have a two-hour layover in Chicago. Or so I thought. *Mentsch tracht, Gott lacht.* Man plans, G-d laughs. The Windy City lived up to its name. During our landing, I almost threw up the bagel with Tofutti creamless cream cheese I had brought with me from the Big Apple. Because of the potential for wind shear, our outgoing flight was delayed. Though I didn't want to spend the night in Chicago, what I wanted less was to get back on another plane in these high winds.

The airline paid for my airport transfer and hotel room. They even gave me a voucher for dinner. Quite generous, but I planned to order in and spend the evening zoned out in front of reality TV, my escapist drug of choice. After just a few minutes, I couldn't stomach the nasty housewives, and the toddlers in tiaras were as disturbing as their parents were disturbed. My own reality had trumped their pseudo-scripted lives. If only I could edit my own storyline.

I went to my next go-to diversion, distracting myself with this old pet fantasy: *What would have happened on my twenty-first birthday if I had actually gone to Puerto Rico to meet Ben?* He was so gorgeous and smart and I felt like … We had connected deeply on so many levels. Playing out that fantasy was such a nice way to avoid trying to be comfortable with uncertainty. After that luscious imaginary reunion ended, I was once again alone. With me. With my thoughts. Now that is scary.

On to my next favorite detour out of current reality: research. The laptop hum was a pacifier, except when it led me to
digital overload. Let's see, Chicago, 1937. Web search "all" results:
Memorial Day Massacre. Bears, Cubs, Sox. Chicago Cardinals.
IMDb *In Old Chicago*.

Chicago, 1937. Web search "images" results: black-and-white
photos of movie posters and buildings and fire trucks and big
bands. All very interesting, but nothing was drawing me in. I was
lightheaded from the flight and from my hunger. Time for a practical search, someplace to get some food. I added "restaurant," but
forgot to delete "1937," and there it was. The Pump Room. On its
website, one reviewer wrote, "So much history." And then I read
the menu page. It said, "At night, the restaurant's bar transforms
into a supper club, recapturing the glamour of the '30s and '40s
with a modern twist." Another incident of *bershert*?

This story had to be told in real time, because that was how
I experienced it. I sat only a few feet away from them. At first, I
thought they were just a typical couple on a night out. It quickly
became apparent that they were fitting right into my thematic
journey, as if I had been invited here specifically to witness their
performance. I pressed my recorder on as quickly as possible, but
I had to recreate the first few minutes when I had just been eaves-
dropping. I filled in the gaps with what I imagined as truth, how
I perceived each person's perspective, and bits of history I learned
from the hotel's concierge and the books I bought in the gift shop
before heading back to the airport for my final leg. You know, you
just can't make this stuff up.

PUMP ROOM

BY P.A. STERN

They sit at a table overlooking the lake. The ornate crystal chandeliers reflect on the many-mirrored walls. Lights from the skyscrapers flicker through the windows. Old black-and-white photographs adorn the intricately carved wood panels. In their own way, they each take notice of their surroundings. He was born into this world. She was not.

"Quite a view, isn't it?" he remarks.

"Yeah, but I'm still not happy with the Trump Tower. It's the perfect example of wretched excess."

He's admiring how the candlelight glows on her shiny hair, and is caught off guard by her statement. He is not sure what she means, but decides not to ask.

She looks around the room. "This whole place is pretty old-school Chicago. I kind of expect a gangster to walk in any minute."

"Yes, I heard Kanye is doing a gig here this weekend." He tries to be hip and funny.

"I didn't mean that type of gang*stah*," she says.

He touches her hair and comments on how soft it is. She blushes from his touch and tells him she uses natural, organic avocados and bananas as conditioner.

"Oooh," he says, "that makes you good enough to eat." They slide closer on the booth, enjoying the romantic semantics.

"Sooo, what's your favorite color?" She doesn't really care what his answer will be.

"Uh, not really sure. Kind of like blue, I guess." He, too, couldn't care less.

They giggle as if "blue" is some type of secret mating code, and he has got it right. It's a first date, and they're both being quite flirtatious. She feeds him a piece of bread, and laughs when he frantically wipes the crumbs off his charcoal Valenti suit. She likes the way his broad shoulders fill out the jacket. She leans back against the white booth.

"Do you think this is real leather?" she says, concerned. She's about to go into a tirade about the social and environmental impacts of the leather industry.

"Not sure." He's oblivious to the reason she asks about the seat cover. "You've never been here before? I figured everyone from Chicago had been here."

"Just not my thing."

"It's a great place, steeped in Chi-town history ... the views, the woodwork, the style. Pretty darn romantic." She's finishing his sentence in her head, thinking, *Pretty darn decadent.*

He leans in for a bit of affection. She lets down her guard for a moment, responding to the ambience. Her mind squashes her emotions.

She throws him a bone. Sort of. "Well, I appreciate you bringing me here to expose me to the finer things in life."

He's not quite sure how to take that last comment. There's an awkward moment, and the two of them look away from each other, scoping out the room.

"Such an incredible setting: mahogany panels, that bar—so glamorous, the extraordinary view. All the celebrities and dignitaries who made this place famous ..."

"Come on, those bar stools are pretty tacky," she says. "And the patterned wall-to-wall carpeting? Maybe it was once *de rigueur*, but it's so shabby. Look at the threads unraveling."

"It's a moment of history caught in time."

"Time has moved on, and thankfully, left an era behind."

He takes a deep breath. "Where one person sees pollution, another can see poetry."

They both pick up their menus. Their waiter comes to the table.

"And have you two *ado*rable lovebirds decided yet?" He's wearing a scarlet red hunting coat, and clearly, his personality is as flamboyant as his attire.

"Tweet, tweet," the man says, and leans over to give his date a peck on the cheek. He's trying too hard.

She tells the waiter, "I think I'd like the Whale of a Salad." He starts to write her order as she asks, "But wait—there's not really whale in it, is there?"

The waiter chortles, "No, it just means it's a gi*nor*mous sala—"

She cuts him off. "Because whales are an endangered species. Very. If we destroy those beautiful creatures, we deplete a significant part of the food web, and our entire ecosystem will be out of whack. The whole equilibrium of life could get out of balance."

Speaking of unbalanced, the waiter thinks to himself. "No, at the Pump Room, we never serve whale meat. Only the blow holes."

She finds no humor in this. The man does, and starts to laugh, but holds back when he realizes she's not playing along.

"And your lettuce? Is it approved by the USDA? Do you know that they found perchlorate, the nasty toxic chemical from rocket fuel, in lettuce samples grown near the Colorado River? Thirty parts per billion! The EPA says only one ppb is safe! It can cause thyroid problems and birth defects, and—"

The waiter cuts her off. "Oh, goodness, I guess you don't want our Honeymoon Salad, then."

"What's that?"

"Lettuce alone!"

He cracks himself up. The man joins in, and again realizes his date is not laughing. He buries his head in his menu.

She tells the waiter, "I'll take the local, sustainable, farm-grown mixed greens."

Her date adds, "I'll have the steak, rare."

She is shocked. "You. Eat. Meat?"

He's not sure what he has done wrong. "Um, yes. Why?"

"Well, the environmental impacts of raising beef are so well documented. The impact on global warming, deforestation, biodiversity ... I could go on and on ..." And she does.

The waiter is still standing at the table, witnessing this sanctimonious prattle. He cannot fight back a snide interjection. "Wouldn't that be some sort of *noise* pollution?" He leaves with their menus, shaking his head.

She continues, "Producing just one pound of meat emits the same amount of greenhouse gases as driving an SUV forty miles. It takes 2,500 gallons of water to produce one pound of meat, while growing one pound of grain only requires twenty-five gallons. Not to mention the health effects of—"

Her date sees an opening—and a solution. "You know, you are absolutely right. I've been thinking of taking up hunting anyway, so maybe from now on, I'll eat only animals I kill myself."

She gets all dewy-eyed and affectionate. She puts her hand on his thigh and gives him a gentle squeeze. He flashes his perfect white smile. She grins back.

He's feeling the mood of the place. "*We'll meet at the Pump Room-Ambassador East, to say the least, on shish kebab and breast of squab we will feast, and get fleeced,*" he sings, slightly off-key. She looks at him with a questioning half grin. She doesn't recognize the song.

"It's an old Fred Fisher song from the twenties ...? *Chicago?* Sinatra recorded it," he explains. "For someone who grew up in this town, you don't seem to know much about it." He pauses. "This place was really something in its heyday. It opened after Prohibition ended. Everyone who was anyone came here."

The waiter has returned with another basket of bread and rolls. He overhears their conversation, and can't refrain from chiming in; he loves to talk about the Pump Room.

"Oh, yes, Bogey and Bacall came here, and even Miss Judy Garland with the fabulous Liza with a Z—as a mere toddler," he says with reverence. "And over there is the famous Booth Number One. If you were the 'it' person, you'd sit there and host all the actors and singers and artists and bigwigs who came to visit. Everyone from Cary Grant to JFK. We opened in thirty-eight, and it was non-stop glam from that moment on."

He leaves, still caught up in his visions of icons of American history, and waiters in satin jackets with velvet epaulets and feathered caps, skewers aflame. It is a good thing he doesn't stay for her next diatribe.

"I have no idea why people are so obsessed with celebrities. I mean, they're just people who happen to be famous. So they have tons of money. Does that make them better than everyone else? What were those rich, famous people doing back then? It was the thirties, the world was going to war, there was terrible poverty, the environment was going to hell, and these people—the supposed giants of society—sat here drinking martinis up in this ivory tower."

She pauses for a moment. "You know, the main reason I never came here before was that my great-grandfather helped build this restaurant back in thirty-seven. He was a master woodworker, and he hand-carved most of the ornamentation that's still here. Look at the curves and details in this leaf. You can see the veins. He told stories of how hard he worked, and how much he got shafted. He worked for pennies so the rich owners of this hotel could get richer. So I have kind of a sour taste in my mouth about this place."

Again, he tries to turn things to a more positive, optimistic note. "It's astonishing that you have a personal story about the Pump Room. I'd think you would feel even more connected. You can literally see your ancestor's handiwork here."

She touches the wall and explores the smooth indentations of the carvings of berries and birds. She gets nostalgic for a moment, but doesn't allow herself to go down that road.

"No, he wanted to be an artist, a photographer, really—I suppose that's where I got it from—but he had to work three jobs to support his family, and times were tough, so he never did get to do what he wanted. If he had, he might've been able to actually *become* a celebrity, instead of breaking his back to build this watering hole for all of those spoiled rich folks who never did a damn thing to make the world a better place."

"Whoooa, there. You do not know that. Many celebrities and wealthy people do a lot of good. Who do you think funds most of the big charitable foundations, now and back then? And you don't know what those people did to end the war, or help the planet. Coincidentally, my great-aunt Mags—who *was* well-to-do—was actually one of the women who photographed the devastating environmental and economic effects of the Dust Bowl. Her photographs helped change people's attitudes about farm practices, and even brought attention to the need for maintaining ecological balance. It was photos like hers that actually inspired FDR to enact some of the first environmental legislation and establish organizations like the Soil Conservation Service and the Civilian Conservation Corps. Her sister—my other great-aunt—was a hotshot lawyer in Chicago, and great-aunt Mags spent a lot of time here, including eating at the Pump Room. Your grandfather worked here, and my great-aunt ate and socialized here. What're the odds?"

There is a moment of silence. They are both thinking of this room and their connection to it, to each other. He realizes things may have gotten a bit heavy-handed, and believes the chance for romance has been crushed. Just as he's thinking that their date is a lost cause, she flips a switch and gets them back on track.

"Sooo, what's your favorite vacation you ever took?" she asks, sweet and flirty.

He's unsure of her new coyness. "Last year I took a great cruise to Alaska—"

"Are you serious?" She's no longer demure.

Here we go again, he thinks. "Don't worry, we didn't drill for oil or anything."

"Don't you know that cruise ships are like floating cities that just dump all their waste—that's raw sewage—right into the oceans, with no regulation? They severely threaten the coral reefs, not to mention all of the CO2 emissions from the ridiculous amounts of fossil fuels they use." There's yet another awkward pause. His turn to revive the deteriorating date.

"Uh, what about you?" he asks with trepidation.

"Me? What?"

"Best vacation?"

She brightens. "Well, I just went on an eco-trek in *Chile* (she pronounces it emphatically *en español*). We explored the rainforest canopy and helped create conservation areas to protect the endangered pumas."

Once again, he tries to be funny. "Don't *they* eat meat?" She is not amused.

He thinks her flushed face is a sign she's aroused. He decides to change the subject to something that might impress her. "Oh, did I mention that I just completed a big reno on my country house?"

Now that is something she can sink her teeth into. "Really? That's so exciting! How'd it go? What was your LEED rating?"

"Uh, well, it wasn't that easy to get rated, to be so …"

"To be so what?"

"To be so green with every single choice. It was a big addition, a new master *en suite* with all the amenities … a soaking tub, steam shower for two …" He attempts to be seductive. She pulls away. His jaw tightens. "I tried. Truly, whenever I could, I—"

She begins to chastise, "If you *really* wanted to, you—"

"I put in low-flow shower heads."

"Sure, in your environmentally-friendly shower with *two* shower heads."

"And I put in all LED lighting in my wine cellar."

She cannot contain her sarcasm. "Impressive."

This conversation—and this date—is not going very well. He tries to explain his conundrum, to appeal to her softer, kinder side. If it exists.

"No, really. It isn't as clear-cut as you'd think. I mean I did everything I could, like recycle materials and be as energy-efficient as possible. I even put in a wood-pellet stove. You don't know how confusing so many of the choices are. Sometimes, in life, it is not all black and white; there are shades of grey."

Her retort is dismissive. "Whatever. My friend just built a sunroom and a sweat lodge, and she made sure that everything, every nail, every board, was reused or reclaimed, or—"

He's had enough. He cuts her off, finally, frustrated at having to defend his every move.

"For instance, I went to buy flooring. I would've gotten bamboo, but my dog, well, she would've scratched it up in a day."

She claps her hands together. "You have a dog? That's so sweet. I love dogs! What kind?" He is silent. She persists. "Do you have pictures of her? What kind of a mutt is she?"

He smiles at her sheepishly. He knows right where this is all going.

She continues on one of her pet subjects. "I volunteer at the Humane Society on Fourth Street."

"Of course you do."

Still intrigued by him being a dog lover, she asks, "Where did you rescue her from?"

He lets out a big sigh. He knows all too well that he cannot win this one. She finally understands, and blisters, "Don't tell me—a purebred. From a puppy mill. Let me guess … pit bull?"

He's getting sick of this. "Not even close," he sputters with pride. "Standard poodle. And she is spectacular." He pulls out some pictures from his wallet.

She doesn't even feign interest in the photographs, and cannot get the sermon out fast enough. "Can you say genetic mutations, over-bred unnatural traits, hip dysplasia, progressive renal atrophy? Wait; have you no concern about the hundreds of thousands of lovable mixed breeds who have no homes? I backpacked through Central America last year, and you would not believe how many dogs are there, abused, looking for forever homes."

He's full out irritated, and responds with an edge, "Somehow, I don't see me adopting a pooch from Honduras. Wouldn't transporting it be a big waste of plane fuel?"

The waiter walks over with bottles of water. She puts her hand up and refuses. "Please bring us tap water. How can this restaurant serve plastic bottles? Around the world, we use 200 *billion* bottles every year. That's *so* much plastic, and it'll just stay in our land-fills—or in our oceans—for a long, long time. Like an eternity."

Her annoyed companion remarks under his breath, "Like this date."

The waiter starts to walk away, and sees the dog pictures. He's aware of the mood at the table, but still he blurts out, "She is *so* adorable! I know it's not soft and furry like your cutie patootie, but I have a *fab*ulous six-foot red-tailed boa …"

The man shoots the waiter a look, like, *oh, boy, you have no idea what you've gotten yourself into*. And he is correct.

She rants back, "I cannot believe you think it's okay to own a wild animal and hold it in captivity! Exotic pets are just awful on so many levels. When you get tired of it or it becomes too scary, what're you going to do with it? Do you even comprehend how many boa constrictors and Burmese pythons—former pets—have been released into places like the Everglades, and have created total environmental havoc as they devour indigenous species?"

The waiter tries to back away from the table to quietly avert more conflict. "Alright, then, I'll be right back with your tap wa-ter." When he says the word "tap," he makes a gagging sound, to try to lighten things up.

She impedes his swift departure. "Excuse me, while you're at it, please bring this seafood selector list of acceptable fish put out by the Environmental Defense Fund to your head chef. It will help him be a bit more knowledgeable in the future about which sea animals are good to serve people—and will be least harmful to the ocean habitats." She hands him a pamphlet out of a huge stack she keeps in her purse. She offers one to her date, too. He's not sure what to do, but takes it and stuffs it in his wallet.

She's oblivious that she has come across as an argumenta-tive, cynical pessimist during this date. She is quite capable of separating her socio-eco-political self from her sociable self. Now that she's done lecturing, she's back in dating mode. As if nothing negative has occurred, she perks up and resumes their conversation. "You were telling me about your reno." She parts her lips as if hungry—for something.

He's suffering from wooing whiplash, and has no idea what to make of this woman. He doesn't understand how she can change from an authoritarian, antagonistic zealot into a tender, tolerant admirer in the blink of an eye. He's unsure of her motivation, but realizes two things about this date that go hand in hand: save the planet, and get some action.

He goes with the flow. "So since I couldn't use bamboo, hardwoods were my next choice, but there was no way to tell if the hardwoods were being illegally imported from ancient rainforests. Then I looked into carpets, and I wanted to go with something more eco-friendly, so I started with wool, but the wool comes from New Zealand, so then you have to consider the transport and what they're feeding the sheep and spraying on the fields. And it was like $50 a square foot, and even though it lasts so much longer, I'm sure I am going to want to change my carpeting in another ten years, so it really doesn't matter how long it lasts, anyway. And then I looked into the carpets made from corn ..."

"Now we're talking." His story is turning her on. As he becomes more animated, she becomes more and more intimate. She stretches her arms over her head and takes in a deep breath—on purpose. She's well aware that he notices her ample, heaving breasts.

He's enjoying her sensual advances, but feels a need to finish his retail eco-saga. "... But I started thinking, if they're using so much acreage growing corn for carpets, isn't that ultimately bad for the environment? It's not like they're growing it organically, so there are all of those negative effects of pesticides, and agrochemicals, not to mention how much water is wasted, and ..."

"You sound like my sister when she was trying to decide whether to use cloth diapers or disposable ones. I was so adamant about cloth, and I gave her *such* a hard time—"

He interrupts in mock surprise. "No, really? You?"

Without missing a beat, or taking a breath, she continues, "And then she told me about washing the cloth diapers, and about how much water and detergent and energy it takes to heat the water, and how much chlorine you use, and how many phosphates go into our rivers and cause algal blooms in our lakes, and then she said the kids wear the plastic diapers longer, so they use fewer of them, and now they're making them with these better biodegradable materials, and … well, she just didn't have any definitive evidence about which had the least environmental impact. Guess in this case, it just depends."

"Yeah, when I'm on a long road trip or watching the game and I just do not want to get up, I'm a big fan of Depends." She grants him the faintest of smiles. "And speaking of that …" He excuses himself to go to the restroom.

As soon as he leaves, she pulls out her cell phone and dials. She whispers into the phone, "Hey, it's me. Uh huh, it's going *great*!" She arranges the sugar packets in a happy face. "I'm pretty sure he totally likes me. And—oh, my God—he is so adorable." She reads the back of the mustard jar and shakes her head in disgust. "He's a bit stuffy in some of his views, but nothing I can't change." She puts the sugar packs back into their holder and laughs. "Come on, remember my mantra: if you want to change the world, do it one unsuspecting hot guy at a time. You know what they say about a man with a big carbon footprint!" Forced laughter as she looks around the room, and then touches one of the wall carvings. "All those awful stories Grandpa told about his dad working here … I had no idea, but this place is really incredible. Kind of like being in another time. You get a really good feel for what it was like in the thirties. Not too many places like this left. I don't know, it makes you think. What if we were born back then? I wonder what I would've been like? What would have been my cause in 1937? It's just interesting to think about how the times we live in shape us." She sighs, then starts to hum *Chicago*. "Oh, okay. No problem. I should probably get off anyway … hey, hey, make sure Mom puts the recycling bin out."

He returns, and she picks up right where she left off. "Please tell me at least that you used low-VOC paints, didn't you?"

"Yes, I did."

She gives him a big smooch. He likes it. Very much. Not thinking, he adds, "But my painter said they covered so poorly that he had to use about twice as much to get the coats to look good."

The drilling resumes. "Energy Star appliances?"

"Well, I happen to be a gourmet cook …"

She purrs, "Oh, I love a guy who knows his way around a sushi knife. I'd like to see you in the kitchen, barefoot, in an apron—and nothing else."

He's uncomfortable, but definitely aroused. "So I decided to get the professional-quality appliances, and they're not necessarily the most energy efficient." Trying to save himself, he adds, "But on the positive side, I do make a mean tofu roast."

"Yeah, sorry, I'm not a big fan of tofu."

His exasperation palpable, he shakes his head and throws up his hands: *I give up*. He just can't win. Still, he continues sharing his journey into eco-decorating. "To me, the worst was when I tried to get local stone countertops and the only granite was from Brazil, and the marble—which is what I prefer—was imported from Italy."

She coos, "Oooh, Carrara marble. I bet it's gorgeous."

He finds a rare opportunity to give her a taste of her own medicine and confront her with her political incorrectness. "But instead of trucking it from the quarries just a hundred miles away, they have to transport the blocks from another continent, on ships, wasting all of that fuel. Can *you* say climate change? Not to mention how the quarry workers may or may not be treated under the country's regulations. So many potential human rights violations."

The waiter approaches. He's hesitant, but presents a platter to them. "The maitre d' wanted me to bring you this appetizer, compliments of the chef."

She's stimulated by the pampering. "That's so nice. What is it?"

"He calls it Second City Surprise."

Her date chimes in. "If you don't mind, I think I've had enough surprises for one night. Maybe you should tell this lovely woman what it's made of. Please."

The waiter gets the picture. "It's our newest organic, plant-based, raw, wheatgrass-infused, gluten-free, flax-seed brûlée."

The man cannot contain his pseudo-excitement. "Yummy."

She, on the other hand, truly is enthralled. She grabs a spoon and begins to dig in. "I'm so excited … here, you go first, yes you, you …" She baby-talks her date, attempting to get him to take a bite. She tries to spoon-feed him as he resists. He finally gives in. The waiter is watching the whole thing, and distracts her long enough for the man to spit the food out into his napkin without her seeing. She's duly impressed with her date's apparently open attitude and her delectable dish. It warms her up, and she gets *very* affectionate again. She's about to offer him one more bite, but the waiter plucks the plate from her hand and leaves.

They sit there for a moment in silence. The moon and stars are peeking in from the hazy city sky. The room is their third companion, and is now doing the talking. It conjures up the past: visions of guests, images of staff, thoughts of what it was like outside on the city streets, in the surrounding countryside. The man finally says, "I wonder what I would've been up to back in the thirties, what I would have been like if I had grown up then instead of now."

She's about to make a snarky comment, but stops herself. "Yeah, me too." She reaches over and brushes his bangs across his forehead. "Guess we'll never know."

The waiter returns with a giant salad for her and a big juicy steak for him, but he "accidentally" mixes up the plates. She gets very upset. She says to no one in particular, "I think I'm going to barf … oh, my God, I cannot even eat this now. That is so gross. I feel faint."

The waiter responds drolly, "Maybe if you had some more red meat in your diet, you wouldn't be so anemic." She shoots the waiter a toxic look. The man catches the waiter's facial expression, and it takes all of his concentration to suppress a laugh.

She continues her whine. "Please just wrap this up. And no Styrofoam. Unless it's at least twenty-five percent post-consumer recycled materials." He starts to leave with her food, but she is not done. She pulls out a big metal bucket from her enormous woven Peruvian satchel, and hands it to the waiter, directing. "And make sure you put the vegetable scraps from your kitchen in this so I can compost it at our community garden."

He also hands the waiter his plate. "You can just put mine in a doggy bag. I kind of lost my appetite, too." Still, he tries to keep the evening light. Using a fake French accent, he continues, "I am sure my *little Madame Bush* will be happy to devour a nice piece of beef."

"Uh, I make my cats homemade organic vegetarian pâté fresh every day instead of buying artificial store-bought kibble."

"Lucky them."

The waiter interrupts, "May I get you anything else?"

Quickly, desperately, the man states, "Just the check, please. And I'll take a coffee—to go."

"Make sure his coffee is fair-trade. And I'll have an organic, water-pure decaffeinated green tea to go. With just a smidge of some natural sweetener. Please." The waiter starts to leave, and she quickly rifles through her satchel and hands him a huge glass mason jar to put the tea in. He heads toward the kitchen.

When the waiter is gone, the man asks her, "You know, I'm just curious … when we first met at the bar at the conference center last week, weren't you there right after we heard the same keynote speaker? At the Young Conservative Republican Convention?"

She shakes her head no.

He persists, "May I ask, then … what convention *were* you attending?"

"PETA."

The waiter walks across the elegant dining room and passes impeccably dressed patrons, the lustrous grand piano, and photographs of the many celebrities, starlets, and socialites who have frequented this fine establishment for seventy-plus years. Never before in the history of this world-class restaurant has a compost pail crossed the Pump Room, adding a bit of agrarian aesthetic to the cultured grandeur. Heads turn to watch the unusual sight. He hands the woman her kitchen scraps. He hands the man his doggy bag and the bill. He returns with a paper cup of coffee for the man and the mason jar of tea for the woman. Then he theatrically hands her a three-foot long piece of sugar cane, asking acerbically, "Natural enough for you?"

"Well, I appreciate the gesture, but are you aware that most sugar cane is grown on sensitive habitats like former wetlands, and burning the fields and the processing cause emissions of soot and ash and ammonia? And cane workers are exploited all over the world by the plantations that *our* government started, and ..."

The man puts cash on the table. In classic Pump Room polite form, the waiter states with utmost civility, "It's been a pleasure. Thank you for dining with us. Please join us again." He turns to the man and adds in his real voice, "Good luck, man."

The waiter leaves, and the couple starts to get up from the booth. The man points to a photograph on the wall right behind them. "My great-aunt Mags took that one of Brando."

She kneels on the booth to take a closer look at the photograph. It's signed *Margaret Bourke-White*. The first female war correspondent. The photographer who documented the Holocaust. The woman who had the first cover for *LIFE* magazine. Who photographed Gandhi. And Stalin. And here was one of her celebrity photos.

"It's incredible," she says with utmost respect as she throws her arms around him. "And I know her other photos made a real difference in the world. You ought to be very proud."

He's about to go in for a kiss, but she releases her hug and starts to back up. He takes a deep breath as he gestures around the Pump Room. "And you ought to be very proud of the fine

craftsmanship your great-grandfather did. He certainly contributed a lot to the world, too." She smiles. They share a gentle, silent
moment of personal reflection.

He says, "So, I'm guessing I can't give you a ride home?"

"I think I'll take the CTA, public transportation you know—
to do my part."

He shrugs, smiles, waves a meek goodbye, and heads out. She
sits there while he walks away. She calls to him with a bit of an
attitude, "Hey, just out of curiosity, what do you drive, anyway?"

His response is nonchalant. "Oh, I have that new rechargeable
electric hybrid convertible sports car. It's rainforest green with recycled hemp cloth seats, and I hook it into my solar panels up at
the lake house, which is, incidentally, off the grid."

She takes barely a moment, grabs her jacket and satchel, and
runs to him. Together, they walk past the gleaming bar, down the
marble stairs, and out the Ambassador Hotel lobby, arm in arm.

Chapter 13

Ah, thank you, Pump Room, for the comic relief. It couldn't have come at a better time. It'd been quite the journey—up and down and back up again, like a rollercoaster time machine through a wormhole. Across the miles and in my own mind. By the time I landed at SFO, I had transcribed all of the conversation and added my two cents—let's say eighty cents, allowing for inflation since '37. "Pump Room" read sort of like a theatrical script, but that made sense. The restaurant had a phenomenal stage set, two lead players, authentic costuming, a fine actor in a witty supporting role, and I was the audience with a front-row seat. Curtain up, and the story progressed until the standing ovation.

As we rolled onto the tarmac, I clicked *send*. "Pump Room" was on its way to Nebi, deconstructed into binary patterns and groups of ones and zeros, then somehow reconstructed into nineteen pages of 164 paragraphs made up of 433 lines, which equaled 5,342 words, which equaled 24,521 characters (no spaces) or 29,862 characters (with spaces). In whatever form it was received, it didn't matter what her response would be. I had written it, and I was happy with it. I could just see Nebi's incredulous smile and hear her loving admonition about my newfound confidence: "It's about freaking time, Mom!"

It suddenly occurred to me that I had enough stories linked by the same year for a collection. An unintentional collection. How was I going to put all of them together? Maybe I should just call the collection *1937*. Or *Thirty-Seven*. No, wait: *37*. We were stuck on the runway, so I jotted down a synopsis:

The U.S. economy is tanking, average families are trying to make ends meet, Palestinians and Jews continue their age-old conflict, Tibetan culture is threatened, oppressive dictators massacre their citizens, and the world is in an environmental crisis. Unfortunately, this was the reality of what life was like seventy years ago—in 1937.

37 is a collection of stories linked by this significant year in which they occur. Set against the backdrop of tense international affairs, simple lives carry on. People struggle, people rejoice and love, and friendships are made and strained, whether on a stone bridge high in the Green Mountains of Vermont, on a kosher farm carved out of the jungle in the Dominican Republic, near a remote hut in uncharted Papua New Guinea, in a tenement on the Lower East Side of Manhattan, or in the Himalayas, as a boy and his snow-white Tibetan mastiff make a dangerous trek. Diverse cultures. Distant locations. Different, yet universal challenges. *37* explores the question: *How can the events of one year capture the whole of the human condition?*

The seatbelt lights finally went off. We all grabbed our overhead baggage and disembarked, each passenger headed to his or her different, yet universal challenges. Time to see if my productive trip would continue. Hopefully, there would be a constructive outcome in my personal life, as well.

Dear big brother, here I come. I've always been good at chasing you and tracking you down. Ready, get set, go.

Mark hadn't answered my calls. I refused to return his curt communication via text. I went through the courtyard behind his building to get to his door. He didn't answer his buzzer. I could wait on his front stoop, wait to find the courage, but after the long flight, I needed to move. It was a gorgeous San Francisco day: the fog had just burned off, the sun was reflecting off the white stucco buildings and pastel painted ladies, and palm trees danced in the light breezes. Such a sharp contrast from New York and Chicago.

I decided to take a walk and think about what I wanted to say. How I could reconnect with Mark.

Walking had always been my way to solve problems. If I got stuck, personally or professionally, I walked. On the street, through the woods, on the beach. Walk and think, walk and think. My method was probably counterproductive to the mindfulness practice I'd been trying to embrace. Instead of falling into the frenetic energy of walking, it would be better to be in the moment as I walked, to feel the wind caress my face and my feet touch the earth. To listen to the pattern of my breath. It would be better just to notice my emotions, and not get caught up in trying to fix everything and everyone.

And that, for me, was not a proverbial walk in the park.

Maybe I could mindfully walk *and* work through some dilemmas. So many issues, so little time, after all. Was multitasking mindful? I needed to figure out a few things, and the hilly streets of the Mission District seemed the perfect route.

I thought of all of the people I'd recently met, how their challenges and my own were different, yet universal. How they summed up the whole of the human condition. Our shared humanity. That famous, haunting line, "Oh, the humanity!" came to mind, immediately followed by another thought plucked from my brain's recesses, of when the Hindenburg disaster had happened: in 1937. At that point, nothing surprised me.

Clearly, during this walk, my mind preferred chaos to quiescence. An effective delay tactic, but it was not helping me focus on Mark, on how to resolve our complex story. How the hell had we ended up like a Dickensian serial?

I thought about Jamon. About how I didn't really have a question about him. I just had a smile and a longing. He felt like hope and home. And just as I pictured his tempting lips, my phone rang. I expected Mark, and was about to answer in my toughest voice, "Yo, wassup, bro?" to try to lighten a pretty gloomy situation. I saw the call was from Jamon. In my excitement, I thought it'd be funny to keep the same greeting.

"Oh, sorry, I must have the wrong number." Jamon sounded so cute when he was flustered.

"No, Jamon, it's me."

"Whoa. You getting all street on me?"

"Where are you?"

"At the pub, where else? The real question is, where are you?"

"Actually, in San Francisco."

"Really?"

"Yup. Trying to track down my brother. We have some talking to do."

"Weren't you just together in New York?"

"It's a long story," I said.

"I can't wait to hear it, every detail, while I hold you tight and we watch the sun set on Sosúa."

No amount of walking or mindfulness could have brought me more calm.

"That sounds perfect."

"That's a lot of pressure. There is no perfect, you know," he said.

"Yeah, but some things, and some people, are pretty close."

"Alright, get back down here as quick as you can, okay? I have a yen for that beautiful smile."

"I'll see what I can do. I have to take care of few things first."

"Well, just let me know when you're heading this way. I'll shave. And get a haircut."

"Which one?"

He laughed. "You're adorable." And I laughed. I was pretty adorable.

I continued walking, and we just chatted, as if he were right by my side.

"I always wanted to see the Golden Gate Bridge," he said.

"It's about to come into view. Just a sec."

The splendor of the mountains and the sea and the magnificent orange structure left me speechless. I thought I could even see whales in the distance. He had to have heard my breathing.

"Polly?"

"Just soaking it all in."

"Wish I was there."

"You are."

I felt like I was floating, but also as grounded as I'd ever been. That same feeling of purpose and pure intention I'd had when I became a mother. I wish I had asked Mom if she had felt the same when I was born. But I felt good. Hopeful. Like I belonged. At last.

Jamon and I hung up, and I turned a corner. Literally and figuratively. I had completely lost track of where I was, and there in front of me was a huge mural. At first, I thought it was graffiti. The colors were bright, the style fantastical. A woman's face merged with waves and whales leapt, as if flying. An impressionistic version of the paprika bridge loomed over the entire painting. A sign explained that this was the first "page" of a commissioned piece. It was described as a wall-art novella, a combination of visual images, written text, and audio recordings, all telling the story called *At last, the mighty task is done.* Like a walking meditation, the story continued from one block to the next, one scene per block. Motion detectors cued the audio, timed perfectly so that you could walk along and hear the narrator while you read the words and saw the paintings. It was a literary scavenger hunt, complete with clues and answers and a treasure map. Descriptions mirrored the actual surroundings, only they had taken place in another time, decades ago, when the Golden Gate Bridge was built.

AT LAST,
THE MIGHTY TASK IS DONE

BY P.A. STERN

The call came in late at night that her husband was needed in early for his four-day shift, something about an escape. She thought the news would set him off, but when he hung up the phone, he laughed.

"Why the hell would anyone try to escape in December? The idjuts'll freeze to death before their asses hit the Bay. Hell, it'll just shorten my rounds, so fine with me."

He got real quiet and she got real still, expecting a blow.

Sometimes, if she'd get tiny small, he didn't notice her, and he didn't take out on her whatever it was storming round in his head. She started to shrink, and then she realized he was fast asleep.

She was still awake, one eye open, when he woke at 5 a.m., and she heard him cursing to himself about the long walk down to the pier. But he'd never spring a nickel for the trolley. The first time she'd pulled him toward a ticket booth, he'd stopped and stood as hard as the cobblestones beneath their feet, and yanked his hand away.

"The pinko cable car companies are in the hole, and we're sup-posed to pay out of our pockets to bail them out?" She figured he was just joshing, but when she tried to hop on board, he barked, "What are you, huh? Part of this city of gimps, too lazy to get off their asses and walk?" He instantly broke into a seductive grin, and a phantom smile formed on her flushed face as they contin-ued walking down Mason Street.

Today, when he left in the pitch dark of morning to catch the first ferry out, there was no smile on her face. He didn't even say goodbye.

In some strange way, she missed him when he was at work, even though it was the only time she could stop wincing. Why, she didn't know. When he was away on his overnight shifts, it gave the bruises time to disappear. The worst ones, the ones that took the longest to heal and stayed the most tender, were the ones layered on top of each other like a stack of old grey slate, so many different shades. After the blotches turned inky blue, they faded into what looked like coffee stains. That was when she got the most stares. As if she had some birthmark—a defect painted across her skin. Maybe she did.

When he was at work, she could remember to breathe. And it was the only time she felt safe to wander.

Still, they had been together for thirteen years, and even though it wasn't so good, it was something.

Many of the other guards actually lived at Alcatraz with their families. She and her husband lived on the mainland, in a decent cottage, but the jail would've been better. The residential apartments were isolated, which meant she'd be living in a prison; even so, she wished they were there. At least then there would be other women around, people to talk to. And there would be children. It had been so long since he'd allowed her to see her nieces and nephews.

A few years ago, after she'd found out some of the other guards and their families had left, it had seemed odd that they hadn't heard about an opening. When she'd gotten up the nerve to ask, her husband made it clear—very clear—that it was not her place to question, that he liked things just the way they were.

It hadn't even been twenty-four hours since he'd left for work on short notice, and her husband had already called home twice. When he had phoned last night, after the routine drilling, he told her that two inmates—Cole and Roe—had indeed tried to escape.

"We haven't found them yet, but I'm sure they already froze to death. One of them used a five-gallon can as a float. A guard saw it shoot straight up into the air as the stupid-ass shit was sucked beneath the surface. The other chump was carried out toward the bridge by the rapid current. Must've drowned. Nobody gets off the rock." Her husband was livid that he'd had to spend time outside in the freezing spray. She thought about the prisoners, what it must have felt like to hit the cold water.

She was grateful he had been called in early. She had planned for today, in hopes he'd be working. She felt the tiniest flutter of excitement, the first in seven months. For four and a half years, she had watched while they built the bridge, her attention riveted from the moment the house began to shake as they blasted the rock away. She watched the access trestle being built, the huge concrete pier going in, and the south tower rising from its base, the zigzag framework fitting together like her nephew's Tinkertoys.

She couldn't tell her husband about her pastime. Shortly after the bridge construction had begun, he'd landed the job at Alcatraz, and was relieved that they could finally get off public charity. He'd just gotten his first paycheck, ending months of embarrassing unemployment assistance from the Citizens' Advisory Relief Committee, and then he found out his taxes were going up. All because they were levying a three-cent fee to build the bridge.

"What the hell do we need the goddamn thing for, anyways? Nobody wants another Bloody Thursday," he fumed. "But I'm sure ready to strike—hell, I'll even fight—so's I don't have to line the pockets of those crooks. Damn politicians."

She asked him what he meant, and he just glared at her, then smiled through gritted teeth.

After so many years together, she knew better than to tell him about anything she found beautiful. When they'd first started courting, he had spoken to her gently and touched her softly. He treated her real nice: he took her on walks along the beach, they collected shells, they went fishing at the wharf, they rented boats and sailed with friends. Out on the broad, open ocean, they watched whales swim and feed. She grew more and more interested in the sea, and she brought home books from the library to learn about the tides and marine life. She became fascinated with whales, and watched for them from the state beach. She hoped to see a greyback someday, but they were being hunted into extinction. When she saw the whaling ships with their harpoon cannons, her heart hurt.

She told her husband about how the German and Japanese whalers and the Unilever and Kyokuyo companies wouldn't support a ban on hunting grey whales. She thought he would agree about the terrible conservation practices and corrupt corporations. She thought he'd respect her passion. She thought he'd encourage her. He had to believe as she did, be in awe of the whales' great beauty and concerned for their plight.

But that was when it started. He said sure, the Japanese won't agree with America, what'd she expect? He yelled about the filthy Japs and the worthless spics and the lousy Jews moving into the neighborhood, at least the Germans had the right idea about that. They'd just gotten married, and he made them move out of the neighborhood and away from the friends who sailed, away from all her friends and family. He didn't allow her to visit the beach. He took away her library card. And she received the first of many lessons to teach her that she better shut her trap, her role was not to express her stupid opinion. Not to think. Not to feel. Not to know beauty.

At first, she had climbed the old oak in their side yard. From a low branch, she could make out most of the bay. Hours would pass as the salty breezes brushed her face, the faithful waves her only companion. One afternoon, her husband found her up there. (He had come home from work a day early.) He yanked her down and dislocated her shoulder.

"What in God's name are you doing climbing trees like some stinkin' critter?" Possum pussy, he called her that night when he had his way with her.

The next time he caught her up there, he spoke real sweet. "C'mon, baby, just jump to me. I'll catch you." She wasn't sure, but she melted a little when he smiled like that. And he had apologized about her shoulder. Even brought her a jar of Ingram's Milkweed Cream. Her favorite.

She jumped, he stepped back, and she landed on the garbage cans. That time, she needed stitches across her forehead. When they got home from the hospital, he made her apologize for the humiliation and pay for all the money it had cost. The "payment" ripped out the stitches. She started wearing finger waves so no one ever saw the scar.

He cut down the low branch.

But her husband had an old wooden ladder in the garage that he had taken when he lost his job with the fire department.

"It weren't stealing," he said. "I deserve it. Earned it. My bosses have enough goddamn money to buy new fancy aluminum ladders, but not enough to let me keep my job. Fuck 'em." So the ladder was hidden in the back of the garage, a justified trophy.

While he was at work, she'd bring the ladder to the yard, prop it up against the tree, and climb to the top to see the bridge construction. She was always very careful to return the ladder to its exact position. He never caught on, and she was able to watch the progress throughout the years.

When the bridge had finally been finished back in May, she'd made sure to be one of the first to walk across. The newspaper headlines called it "Span O' Beauty." The *Call Bulletin* wrote, "Cleft Heart of California Bound Together by Sutures of Steel." She knew all about stitches and broken hearts. She wanted to know about beauty.

The day of the fiesta had been brilliant, with blue skies and bright green leaves, the young, undeveloped buds still bursting forth in late spring—the late bloomers. When the last swirls of morning fog lifted, the reflections off the orange steel nearly blinded her as she approached the bridge. Tall, startling shadows were cast along the vibrant glow of its vertical surfaces. The collective excitement was unlike anything she had ever witnessed. The crowds and the lighthearted chatter were an intimidating revelation; it had been such a long time since she had been around people. She could not remember when she had been around joy.

The foghorn blasted, the ribbon was cut, and the bridge was open. She was pushed along with the mass of people. Thousands and thousands. Women dressed in fine linen outfits stopped to pose for photographs. Little children jumped as high as they could to see if they could touch the cables while their parents grabbed them tightly to keep them from being carried off by the wind. Police were on horseback, high school students were on roller skates; politicians, wearing their best suits and hats, shouted accolades and instigated cheers. People rode unicycles, played tubas, walked across on stilts. Small planes flew overhead. The crowd pressed on.

A few men had stopped mid-path and stood still as the rest pushed their way past. She could make out tears in these men's eyes. The only time she'd ever seen a man cry was when her husband had dropped on his knees and begged forgiveness for his latest cruelty. But those were fake, temporary tears. These men's faces held no such falsehood, no manipulation. Perhaps these men shed tears for the majesty surrounding them; she could certainly understand how they would be overcome with deep emotion. Perhaps these men had worked on the bridge. Maybe they were members of that halfway-to-hell club, the lucky ones caught in the safety net. The survivors. Perhaps they knew one of the workers who hadn't been so lucky. She swam in their tears until she was rescued by the high-pitched laughter and gleeful screeches of other people passing by.

She found it hard to believe she could be standing so high above the water. She had never felt so safe before, not even in her own bed. She wasn't afraid when the bridge swayed ever so slightly; she knew her footing was firm. She also wasn't scared when she looked down. She could see the tops of what looked like toy boats—shrimp junks, ferries, barges. The whitecaps were bits of cotton wool. And what were those huge bumps? She knew there weren't any rocks jutting out of the strait, or clusters of tiny islands. "Oh, my," she spoke aloud. Humpbacks! She'd never seen whales from this vantage point or angle.

She leaned farther over the railing to get a better look. She realized that one of the whales was actually a huge greyback, and her tears dropped into the water. She stared down at the whales' graceful parade, laughing every time their blowholes spouted, trying to see each movement through her wet eyes. Had they, too, come to celebrate this manmade wonder? The greyback jumped, and she gasped. There was a bright glimmer, and for a moment, she thought she could look in the magnificent creature's eyes. They stared at each other, and her heart pounded. Her body shuddered, and then she was whisked away by the crowd.

She reached the center of the bridge, where the cables were at the lowest points in their downward swoop. Large tables had been set up, covered with crisp white cloths and celebratory beverages. She wove her way through the crowd until she was close enough to touch the massive cable. As her hand brushed the cool, smooth surface, she felt a powerful surge pass through the solid steel and jolt her hand away. She looked around at the hundreds of people also patting the thick cable; it didn't seem as if anyone else had felt what she had. Hesitantly, she touched it again, and her hand clenched onto the cylinder as if an electrical current was constricting her muscles. But there was no shock, no pain. Only pure calm, and then flight as she was transported up to the highest peak, where she floated, suspended over the bridge, the strait, the frolicking whales and sea lions.

In the distance, she could barely make out the roof of her house and where her oak branch used to be. She turned slightly and saw the imposing shape of Alcatraz, and wondered what her husband was doing, and what he'd say if he saw her flying on top of the water, on top of the world. She pictured him beating down one of the inmates, his eyes dark and darting, all the while complaining about her—his crazy, stupid wife. She tried to stop thoughts of him, but it was too late; she was back in the middle of the road, pushed away from the cable by the excited walkers.

Jostled, she held her ground at the very center of the bridge. Now she looked up, and this time, her eyes climbed the cables to the peak. How had this astounding structure come to be? Even though she had witnessed every step of the construction—placing the catwalks, spinning the cables, joining the two sections of the main span, even the last details of the rivets and paint as she watched the bridge unfurl before her eyes over the many, many months—still, it was as if it had magically appeared one day. All at once. Complete. As though a mighty redwood had sprouted overnight. She was startled by the simple complexity as she breathed it all in, so close she could smell the fumes coming off the orange steel, warmed by the intense spring sunshine.

Memories of that glorious sun-filled day kept her going, a tether to hope.

On this December day, it was frigid and foggy, and from her perch on the top tread of the ladder, she could not see the bridge. She could barely make out the sounds of the choppy waves over the frantic winds. She wrapped her wool shawl around herself tightly and decided to go back in the house, an unlikely refuge.

She returned the ladder to its precise spot, and as she stepped underneath the lintel, she heard a sound. Penetrating, but songlike. She backed up and stood outside to see if it was just her imagination, but sure enough, she heard it again. A song. Calling to her. She had never heard anything like it before, yet it seemed like it was part of her. Her pulse was the metronome for the mythic voice. The beautiful music lasted just a few moments before the whipping winds picked up and their icy whistle merged with the melodic call, eventually erasing it altogether. She shook her head to clear the vibrations from her ears and went inside.

She hadn't realized how cold she had become, or how much warm air she had let out of the house, until she saw the white breath puff from her mouth as she entered the chilly kitchen. She stoked the fire and stood quietly, wondering what had just happened.

She needed to get going in order to be back in time, in case her husband called again, like he had this morning, checking up on her and still griping about Cole and Roe.

"Like we can see anything in this intense fog. If we do find them alive, there'll be hell to pay for all the trouble." He went on and on about Al Capone and Machine Gun Kelly, how those were prisoners he actually respected. "Ya gotta give them credit for at least being smart enough to know their place. They got it pretty good here, so's they don't even try to escape."

She was glad he wasn't there to hear her heart pounding, or to see the look of disgust on her face.

"Yeah, Cole and Roe, they're just two-bit criminals, not even real high-class public enemies. Sure as hell not worth saving their sorry asses. No one will miss them anyways."

She was silent as she wondered if anyone would miss her when she was gone.

Then she heard a click, and realized her husband had hung up. She remembered to breathe.

It was a long walk to South Point. Today, they were breaking ground for a statue of Joseph Strauss, the chief engineer, and she hoped to get a glimpse of him. To her, Strauss was a genius. She often imagined what it'd be like to be an engineer, or a scientist, or maybe a marine biologist—something to make a mark. Look at Amelia Earhart, God rest her soul. Or that woman, the architect she had seen when they opened the YWCA on Clay Street back in '31. Julia Morgan, strong and confident and leading all those men around, those reporters and bigshots, showing off the building that she had designed.

The wind picked up and she picked up her pace, trying to leave behind a disappointment with every step. She had been born at the wrong time, in the wrong place, and she could never go to school. Even if she was smart enough and had the money, her husband wouldn't let her, so why bother thinking about it?

She could see, though, and she could feel, and she could believe. She wanted to be there to honor Strauss, the man who had not doubted, despite all the naysayers and obstacles, that the Golden Gate Bridge could and would be built. And he had built it. He had built grace. She was going to the park, and then she'd walk across the bridge one more time. She had saved—and hidden—enough for the coin turnstile. She thought the pedestrian toll was a fine idea, that the extra money would help keep her bridge strong and shiny. The news of the sidewalk fee had brought yet another rage, another bruise.

The fog was thick, and she could barely see anything in the park. When she got near, she asked the attendant if he knew where the dedication was going to be held. He motioned behind him, but also said that it had been cancelled due to weather. That was the official reason. Really, he confided, it was because Strauss was in "one of his moods." Besides, he had pissed off so many people that the powers that be were thinking of putting the statue on hold.

She let out a big sigh and continued onto the bridge. The fog lifted enough to create a cloud ceiling, dense and grey and tinged with lavender as it hung over the roadway, obscuring the cables and peaks as if the wires holding up the bridge were just threads disappearing into the thick air. No one else was out walking on such a miserable day. Cars zipped by. She walked along as she had dozens of times since last May. She knew exactly how many steps it took to reach the other side. She stopped at the midpoint, her favorite place where she could rest and touch the cable, feel the energy of her bridge.

The fog continued to lift, and she looked down and watched the Chrysopolis and Redwood Empire ferryboats as they came and went on their hourly trip. Three whales followed the steamers, two black, and one—could it be the grey again? She shouted hello and waved wildly to them. The whales seemed to be having a great time of it as they jumped; their dives sprayed the ferries and shocked the passengers. She watched them as they played with the ferries to and from the San Francisco run. The two humpbacks followed the ships as they headed to port, but the one lone grey whale separated from the pod. As it turned, it almost hit a small bay craft. She was shocked to see it was headed under the bridge.

She'd never seen whales in that part of the shallow harbor. As she leaned over to watch the greyback go under the bridge, it jumped straight into the air and looked right at her, its eye reflecting a single sun ray escaped from the thick cloud cover. She saw its mottled skin, slate grey, covered with scars and oddly-shaped patches like coffee stains. She heard its song, the same song that had called to her in her yard and in her dreams. The bridge was a lyre and the wires its strings, and the strong winds played along with the music of the sea. The whale submerged and went under the bridge. Without thinking, she ran across the slippery road, across the traffic to watch it enter the bay. Horns honked and people shouted at her, but she did not stop.

By the time she got there, the whale had already surfaced and was starting a shallow dive. She saw something, something that looked like a man, riding on its back. The man wore a ragged uniform, his head was lifted to the skies, and he was laughing. The whale turned, on course straight out to the ocean. Before it went back under the bridge, both whale and passenger sunk out of sight. The last thing she saw was the grey's tale as it soared high and waved to her.

She ran across traffic again, with horns blaring and brakes squealing. She could barely breathe as she sprinted toward the ocean side. The sun broke through the fog and lit the swelling waves. She saw the grey giant jump out of the sea and heard the man gasp for air. She, too, gasped as she continued, running and running, then jumping up and over the rail of her exquisite bridge. The gale winds picked her up and she glided until she gently landed on the back of the great beast, right behind the man. They shared a quick glance, their eyes alive, their smiles wide with the taste of salt and freedom. Soaring through the remnants of fog, a surprising calm overcame them before they each took a deep breath, at the very same moment, right before the whale dove and headed out to the open sea.

Chapter 14

As I read the final sentence, I took in a deep breath. The last panel was situated in such a way that when you looked at it, it melded with the actual scene of the living bay. The natural inclination for anyone reading was to continue one's gaze and picture the man and the woman and the whale. A fresh breeze lifted, and for a moment, I, too, was soaring out to sea. A few other participants came to the story's end, and it seemed their experience had been just like mine. Some cried. Some gasped. Some clapped. No matter what the initial reaction, the last thing each person did was to stand still and exhale. We were a pensive, breathing assembly.

The artists who had created this interactive art piece were a clever lot. I had become part of the story. It was an extraordinary way to navigate through this picturesque City by the Bay. The fact that Joseph Strauss had completed the bridge and written the poem "The Mighty Task Is Done" in 1937, well, what more could I expect? Sometimes, you need to just let go and realize there are forces at work greater than yourself. Thirty-seven had become my *bershert*.

Of all the characters—real or imagined—I had met over these few months, the female protagonist in *At last* was probably my favorite. No, that wasn't the right sentiment. As far as favorites went, I had particularly enjoyed Dekyi. Leon Haube had been inspirational. And since I was still thinking *WWBMD?*, I'd probably have to add Chief Wamilik to the list of my favorites. Oh, and I was also quite fond of Teo and his mom; and Mac, with his sagacious, twinkling persona, would also be a top choice.

The tree-climbing, whale-riding, freedom-seeking, unnamed woman was the person with whom I most related. I'd never been beaten, and I'd never floated above a bridge, but I knew her. Aren't we all looking for a sense of who we really are? Don't each of us long to connect to something, to someone, in a meaningful way? Aren't we all searching for freedom, longing to soar on the back of a whale? And don't we all have forces working against us, internally or externally, that get in our way? Usually, it's the self that is the biggest obstacle.

I turned my back to the bridge, but its power and strength propelled me. By the time I returned to Mark's, his living room light was on, and through the window, I could see him on his sofa. I couldn't help myself. I stood for many minutes, just watching, taking it all in. Mark with his partner, Mark in his new home, in his own life.

Stephen kissed Mark's forehead and left the apartment. He worked at a nearby club, and would probably be gone for a while. Mark's shoulders were slumped, and when Stephen passed right by me, his face was crumpled, like someone who didn't know how to help his loved one feel better. My reflection in the lobby window had that same look.

I buzzed. Mark met me at the door, his face full of resignation. His lips and eyes and chin held the same confused tension I felt. When I looked at my brother, my expression softened. His expression mirrored mine. I smiled, and then he smiled. I snorted, and then he snorted. Our snorts joined, turning us into some spastic horn section in a wild boar band. We were on the stoop hugging our bellies. Tears streamed down our faces.

A neighbor walked by and spoke to Mark.

"That must be your sister!"

We looked up at him, then at each other, and the geyser of laughter erupted again. Mark tried to apologize to the man, but it was no use.

"Want to go for a walk?" Mark finally had breath to ask.

"Not really. I'm kind of walked out." *At last* had walked the fight out of me.

"I really don't want to either." Mark seemed drained, too. We were a good match.

Round one.

"I'm sorry. Pol. I'm so sorry."

"For what?"

"For not telling you."

We sat sole-to-sole on his futon and pushed each other's feet.

"When Mom was about to pass—"

"Pass? Since when do you call it passing? She died ..."

"Let me just get this out, okay?"

"Mom and Dad sat me down and told me. They told me that you ..."

Mark stopped mid-sentence, and just sat there.

A San Francisco earthquake rumbled across my gut. "Mark!"

"Polly, you're adopted." The words rushed out.

"That's real funny, Mark. What's next? Is Uncle Vito stopping by?"

"Pol, I'm serious. Mom couldn't have any more kids after me. Dad didn't want me to go through what he did after he lost his sister. I don't think he ever got over Aunt Miriam dying like that. He wanted me to have a sister. One of their cleaning ladies worked for a family whose teenager was pregnant. Mom and Dad found out, and made the arrangements. They adopted the baby. They adopted you."

Have you ever looked through a pair of binoculars the wrong way? Everything in your vision narrows down to a tiny dot; everything in your line of sight shrinks. My whole world zoomed down to the freckle on the bottom of Mark's big toe.

I'm not sure how long I stared at what was left of my life. My hearing must have had the same reaction as my vision.

"Pol Pol Pol Pol **Pol!**"

When I looked up, Mark was on the floor next to the futon, his hands on my hands. His face was wet and flushed.

"Hey, Mark." I smiled as my focus returned. "Don't cry, Marky."

"Are you okay?"

"I think I had an out-of-body experience. I was like that woman, flying over the Golden Gate Bridge."

"Pol, maybe we should take you to see somebody, maybe go to the hospital."

"No, I'm okay. Really."

I felt like Vitale when he first saw Teo next to the new baby, how Teo's ears looked enormous. And his hands. His head. Vitale realized he would never again be able to see his son as a little boy. With a sharp twist, a tourniquet compressed his heart. I felt that same clutching ache. When the blood gets shut off, all that's left is numbness.

"At least now you know you weren't crazy for always feeling like you didn't fit in."

I didn't know what to say or what to feel. Aftershocks rippled up and down my spine.

"Why did they adopt me and then keep pushing me away?"

"I don't know, Pol. Who the hell knows why people do what they do?"

"Who are my parents?"

"What do you mean? Mom and Dad …"

"No. My real parents."

"That's the thing. Mom wouldn't tell me, and now Dad doesn't remember anything. All Mom said was to make sure you had the lyrebird. 'The lyre will explain.' As if that gross taxidermy would have the answer."

"The lyrebird?"

"The lyrebird."

We looked at each other.

"That's what Dad was saying. *Li, er.* Lyre. He wasn't calling anyone a liar. Although they were. The whole lot of them. And you, too."

"Polly, I'm really sorry. I didn't want to be the one to tell you, but the further and further Dad got lost in his dementia, the more

I realized it was up to me to tell you. I couldn't stand to be near you, not because I don't love you, but because I love you too much to cause you any pain."

"Goddamn."

"Pol, wha …?"

"You jerk."

"That's it? That's all you've got? I tell you you're adopted. I tell you Mom and Dad lied to you, to us, all these years, and that I covered for them, and 'you jerk' is the best you got?"

You know that feeling, when your foot has fallen asleep? And then the blood starts to return, and with it comes the stinging jabs of pins and needles? Numbness turns to excruciating pain before normalcy can return.

Some sort of peace settled in. That watery barrier that kept forming throughout my life, the one that I thought was protecting me, turned into a different kind of moat—a soul moat. I walked through it, and each step cleansed.

"I love you, Marky."

Forgiveness has its own story. In journalistic terms, forgiveness has its own *who what where when how*. Because I am the writer, I get to choose.

Chapter 15

Gregg picked me up at BTV again (another practical use for ex-husbands), but now I didn't have the heart to give him a hard time. About anything. I had already told him about the adoption. I wanted him on board when I told Nebi. Now she had her own legacy of not knowing half of her genetic story. Her grandparents had written her biological fiction. Gregg met me with a gentle hug and kind eyes. It was the first time in a long time he didn't try to seduce me.

We headed down to Burlington's waterfront and sat on a bench swing. A great blue heron soared over the calm lake. It landed in the still, perse water and when the graceful bird bent down to search for food, the reflection of its neck and body—joined to its real body—looked like a big, wispy heart. Reflections are like that, bringing to focus what we often can't see for ourselves, what makes us up: our history, our biology, our mythology, and our spiritual essence.

Gregg pointed to a small island in the distance, bare rock jutting from the lake.

"Remember when Mark, you, and I sailed past that for the first time?"

"Yes. He tried to flip us. To see how you'd react. Your initiation into my family."

"Guess I passed the test."

"It's Rock Dunder, right?"

"Not to the Abenaki. To them, it's Odzihozo, the Creator, who made himself from nothing, then created the lake and mountains, and then turned himself into that rock. His name means *he makes himself from something unknown.* The more common translation is *the man who made himself from nothing.*"

"I thought that was Gluskabe."

"It's confusing. There're a lot of stories about Gluskabe, mostly how he created good in the world. Sometimes, Gluskabe is also referred to as the man who made himself from nothing. He's the trickster, but in a positive way, and he—"

"I know, I know—he's a virtuous caretaker. But he's also the liar."

"Yes, he is. But Grandmother Woodchuck took him in, and … Pol, he was adopted, too!"

"Gee, thanks for reminding me. For a moment, I was lost in your creation myth." The sunset joined us, soft and subtle. Pale greys and tints of lilac streaked the sky.

"In some ways, I can't believe this at all. In other ways, it makes total sense."

"Pol, it also makes sense about us. I always felt we were right, but I also felt you were looking for something else, like you were searching for a missing piece, and I just wasn't fitting."

"That's just all my ACOA shit."

"No, I think on some level, you always knew there was … more. I'm sorry I wasn't enough."

"It wasn't that you weren't enough. You were, you are."

"It explains a lot about her," he said.

"You mean my mother, the ice queen?"

"She was one pretty cold lady."

"Frigid," I said.

"Frigid as a brass bra on a witch's tit."

"Quite the metaphor," I said, laughing.

We watched the sunset in quiet comfort, my breath in tune with the gentle swing of the bench. Waves lapped the shore.

"You know, Pol, she probably didn't know how to bond with you. How to love you."

"That's pretty screwed up. Don't you think?"

That was one of the saddest realities I now faced. One of the many things I didn't understand. How do you not love a child? Any child, no matter whose it is?

When Nebi was about three years old, I watched her ride on a merry-go-round at the county fair. She had cute face paint on—I think it was a kitty cat—that emphasized her bright eyes and button nose and pursed, pink lips. I was admiring her, thinking how incredible she was, how extraordinary in her innocent beauty. How lucky I was. I turned to smile at the other parents standing nearby (maybe with just a little hubris in the back of my mind), and I realized that they, too, were staring at their own little beauties. Each parent had the same look of wonder and awe for the child in their sight. I became conscious that every child was worthy and deserving of admiration. Each one was beautiful. I knew at that moment that I could love any child.

"Maybe your parents just wanted to protect you from being labeled."

"Labeled?"

"How would you like to be known as Polly, that adopted kid?"

"It wouldn't matter. I'm more than ready to be Auntie to Mark's 'adopted kid.'"

"'Once you label me, you negate me.'"

"Yes, Kierkegaard."

Labels are part of who we are. Mark was gay. Gregg was smart. But did I want to be known as the funny one, or the one who was good with words, or the one with the tender heart? Or the ACOA? I was many things. I wore many labels. I was a woman. I was Jewish. I was …

Right then, it dawned on me. Was I even Jewish? Did it matter if I didn't have the hereditary trait? Identity is tough without a bloodline as a tether. I felt sort of like those people who were sterilized and weren't even aware of what the physicians had done to them, who no longer had a future—only I no longer had a past.

How would Nebi take all this?

Gregg asked if I wanted him to stay while I Skyped with Nebi. I decided to go it alone.

"Did you ever read that article I sent, about memory?"

"The Dartmouth Alzheimer's study?"

"No, the one about thresholds. Turns out there's a reason we forget why we've walked into a room. *Was I looking for my keys? What was I supposed to be doing?*"

"It's so frustrating."

"I know, but there's an evolutionary reason. We're designed to put all of our focus into the space we currently occupy. Let's say you're a hunter. You need to be fully aware of your surroundings. In the moment. Or you won't survive."

"I'm not a hunter."

"But it's still embedded in your DNA. So when the hunter moves from the forest to a field, he—"

"Or she."

Gregg cleared his throat. "The hunter needs to be able to switch gears completely. They can't be thinking about what happened back in the forest. All of their attention, all their senses, need to be on the field. So if you move from the bedroom to the living room, once you pass the threshold between one location and another, what you were doing or thinking or needing in the former area goes out of your memory."

I was passing over a threshold. We kissed goodbye, and I knew this was a true goodbye. "Thank you, dear ex. You are a wonderful dad, and you were the best husband anyone could've been to me."

When I reached Nebi on Skype, she was on her way out to protest in Plaza del Sol with *Democracia Real Ya*.

"Have to run, Mom. Everyone's fed up with being unemployed, with the economy, with the disconnect between the policies and the people, and—"

"Honey, I need to tell you something."

"Right now?"

"Yes."

"Okay."

"It's … Uncle Mark finally told me what was going on."

"Good. What?"

"Just that the fabric of what I believed about myself has unraveled."

"Mom? Are you okay?"

"I'm upset, but I am okay."

"Tell me!"

"Turns out, right before Mema died, she told Mark I was … I was adopted."

"Adopted? *En serio*?"

"*Si.*"

"Mom." Her voice cracked.

"Unreal, huh?"

"You're adopted. And they never told you. That's incredible. And harsh. But it's also kind of fascinating, in a warped, surreal way. Do you know anything more? What happened? Why didn't they tell you?"

"Nebi, I don't know anything. Not why they did this, not who my birth parents were, not a goddamn thing. And now there's no way to find out."

"Wow, Mom. That must be a lot to take in."

"Ain't that the truth. I mean, how could—"

"Mom, I really do need to get to the *Plaza*."

I was stunned. Didn't anyone care that my whole world had been turned upside down? Not even my own daughter, my own flesh and blood?

"Alright," I said. "Let me know when you want to talk more about the adoption."

"Mom, it's terrible you had to find out like you did. I can't even imagine how hard it must be to wrap your head around this new reality. Well, I kind of can, because I'm feeling that right now. Seems like the universe is forcing you to do something you couldn't do for yourself. That's a good thing. Time to let go."

"Sounds simple enough."

"If you want it to be. Mom, I have no idea what they were thinking. It was just so stupid of them. But it's your life, so, like you always tell me, just deal with it. The only thing any of us can control is our own reactions. The past is the past."

Nebi was right. I wanted someone else to massage my knotted emotions, to make everything better. But there was no changing the past. If I held onto resentment, my bitter thoughts and regretful feelings would just continue to be re-sent over and over, and that wouldn't do me any good. It wasn't going to change what had already happened.

That didn't mean it was easy to do.

I thanked her and told her to be careful, and I reminded her to urge the protesters and politicians to listen to each other's stories. After all, our stories are what connect us. Nebi signed off with "I love you, *Mamacita*," her watery song.

The last thing I saw was the Dali print hanging behind her, over her living room sofa. The Spanish sun was streaming in like a spotlight on *Persistence of Memory*, warming the blue and yellow sky and the barren landscape. Surreal watches melted in a dream state, an ode to the relativity between space and time. I didn't know what, exactly, Dali had in his sublimely mad mind, but at that moment, the painting made me think of the irrelevance of time. Of how memories are products of distortion, which render them meaningless. Of how the only moment is the current moment. And ultimately, I thought of human fragility. The screen went black, and I closed my eyes. In the darkness of the instant, I felt a deep sense of compassion and forgiveness.

I felt.

I was born with a mind that preferred the world of imagination to the world everyone else seemed to consider real. In general, it's hard to recount a story, any story, with complete accuracy, because images and perspectives change, like when you try to solve a sliding-tile puzzle. Our story changes with newfound knowledge: how I felt before I found out. How I felt before I wrote it down. How my perceptions and lens changed the story, and the retelling of it. I had always loved hearing other people's stories. As it turned out, I didn't even know my own. As it turned out, everyone else's stories provided the clues to who I was.

And why focus on 1937? I couldn't be sure. Maybe that period of time spoke to me. Maybe it was just a mindset, and nothing more. Some people use ritual, some religion; a friend uses medicine cards and finds wisdom in animals. I guess we can find answers anywhere we look for them. In a field of fireflies, in the warm embrace of baking bread, in someone's story that may or may not be real.

I was thinking of these lofty notions as I passed through the archway leading into my living room. I stood for a moment, wondering why I was in there. I didn't need to find my wallet or water the ficus. Another threshold of forgetfulness. Time to be mindful. I would be still, and pay attention to my breath and feel the light breeze on my face coming in from the bay window. I was trying to be quiet and present in the moment, but there was something gnawing at me, something I needed to take care of. My mindful mind was chattering away, and instead of tranquility, I was anxiously surveying the room. As soon as I saw it, I remembered exactly what I was supposed to do.

In the corner, hidden as well as possible behind some potted plants, stood the obnoxious Victorian lyrebird tail. The one Mom had left to me. I picked up the dusty DVD on top and read the label:

> *The lyrebird is from Australia. It lays and raises one lone egg. This magical bird is very shy and wary. It is also difficult to approach, and therefore, not much is known about their behaviors or the reasons for their behaviors. The one thing we do know is that their mating song is the envy of other birds.*

I popped in the disc and watched the episode from BBC Worldwide. The "superb lyrebird" appeared center stage with his magnificent plumage as Sir David Attenborough narrated:

The lyrebird clears a space in the forest to serve as his concert platform ... he sings the most complex song he can manage. And he does that by copying the songs of all the other birds around him ... it's a very convincing impersonation. Even the original is fooled ... he also, in his attempt to out-sing his rivals, incorporates other sounds that he hears in the forest ... a camera with a motor drive ... a car alarm, and now the sounds of foresters and their chainsaws working nearby.

My inheritance was a stuffed impersonator. A mimic. A trickster. How appropriate. How fucking appropriate. Looked like the joke was on me. Goddamn them all. I went to wipe a smudge off the glass casing, but instead, I grabbed the whole abhorrent heirloom and lifted it as high as I could. Forget the understanding calm I had embraced since I left Mark's apartment. Forget being fucking mindful. With every ounce of raw emotion I had suppressed throughout the years, I screamed from deep within and smashed my birthright to the floor.

Glass shot out in every direction. Feathers flew, and bamboo splintered into sharp little picks. The lyrebird tail was twisted and split in half; it no longer looked like a musical instrument. The bottom of the frame was now upside down. There, taped to the underbelly of the beast, was a white business envelope.

Familiar bold letters beckoned. My trembling hands could barely open it. Inside was a handwritten letter from my mother. I couldn't wait to hear the song of the lousy lying lyrebird.

Dearest Anna,

We are so sorry. Daddy wanted to tell you when you were still a small child, but I kept saying we should wait. And then you were a pre-teen, and I was worried you wouldn't understand. And then you became a teenager, and by then, we didn't know how best to broach the subject. And the years flew by.

I told Mark just last week. Please, please don't be mad at him. He's your brother, after all.

I wanted to tell him, since I don't have much longer to be with Daddy and you, my dear, beloved children. I'm so sorry I was a chicken all these years. I hope you can forgive us. Forgive me.

Anna, I love you more than I was ever able to express. All I ever wanted was to protect you, to keep you safe. And honestly, I felt inferior to be the one to raise someone as special and amazing as you.

L'Chaim!

Love,
Mom

P.S. Daddy wanted to give you some cash. You know him!

In the bottom of the envelope were twenty one-hundred dollar bills.

Holy … simply, holy.

I sat for many moments, not thinking. It wasn't a choice. How does one create deep understanding through thought? My breath quickened, then calmed. My skin tingled, and then the nervous energy subsided. I sat with the sensations. Crimson turned to light rose. Pounding became gentle beats. It felt like I was floating in a sensory deprivation tank, only there was no deprivation. All my senses were there. They were just … neutral. Just being.

Another breath.

Thanks, Daddy. I'm sorry I never appreciated you, the way you showed me love. In your own way.

His gift was to provide for me.

And thanks, Mom, for your apology. I'm sorry I mistook your humility for indifference. It was hard to read you. Maybe it was hard for you to read me.

Like Nebi said, it was my life. I could tell the story any way I wanted. Once, there was a little girl who needed a home. My parents—my mom and dad—gave me that home, and a family. What greater gifts? Like all of us, they did the best they could.

Chapter 16

Luckily, the late-season storm hit after my plane had landed in Puerto Plata. It was pouring when the taxi pulled up to the sidewalk. The canopies on the nearby cafés were flapping with panic in the violent winds. Over the Britannia Pub, the awning was still, then moved slowly, erratically, then convulsed and was still again. *Whomp, whoosh, whomp.* It looked like sails on a boat caught "in irons," when there's not enough drive to maintain forward momentum and the boat eventually coasts to a stop. Dead in the water.

I laughed when the pub's awning caught a gust and started flapping. It's a fine art to know when you're truly in irons, and must wait it out and let nature take its course, or when you can manipulate the tiller and maneuver your way out. Patience is required, and calm but keen attention. Everyone does get out of irons, though not always in the direction intended.

The tropical winter storms are more frequent on the northern coast of the Dominican Republic. The rest of the island is drier. But the rains are warm and keep Sosúa lush, the land good for farming.

The rain beat against the taxi and I waited, taking a moment before moving forward. I wanted to set an intention, a right intention, like I did at the beginning of my yoga practice. I was thinking about what was across the next threshold. And then I remembered a different type of intention, *kavanah,* the mindset necessary before Jewish prayer. This intention, which directs the duties of the mind and heart, is, at its root, about introspection. The intention is to become more deeply in touch with who we are.

A soaking wet dog ran down the sidewalk. His white fur was thick and matted to his body. He stopped for a moment and shook, and the water shot off like a burst of comets. For a second, his fur fluffed up, and I thought of Kang-ri, that sweet, loyal mastiff. The shaggy, drenched dog looked up at me and smiled, then scampered away.

I jumped out of the taxi and dashed across the street toward the Britannia. The pub's glass doors were condensed with fog and *cerveza*; my hand left an imprint when I pushed them open. The bartender looked up. And then I knew. *¡Dios mío! Dio mio.* Oh my ...

I wanted to dive into his shiny smile. As promised, he had shaved, and gotten a haircut.

I walked toward the bar. My hair was dripping, and my clothes were as transparent as my feelings.

"Welcome home, Anna," he said.

How in the world had I not recognized him? *How in the world?*

Leta, that delightful waitress, ran over with a towel and dried me like I was a wet baby.

"I thought your name was Pollyanna," she said.

"No, that's the name of a little girl, a fictional orphan. She's from Vermont, too." I smiled at the bartender. "I'd like to order a drink."

"A glass of *la leche*?"

"Well, it's kind of a special day."

"How about a glass of champagne?"

"Thanks, Ben."

Leta looked confused. "Ben? I've never heard anyone call you that. Is Ben your real name?!"

"Benjamin."

Ben, that kind and soul-stirring boy/man who had made my body tingle and my mind race on that beach in Puerto Rico, when I was still a girl. Back then, my inexperienced mind had imagined his lips over every part of my body. I still do. Only now he is a man, and I am a woman. And not so inexperienced.

"Ben. Benjamin. Ben-juh, Juh-mihn … oh, now I get the Jamon!" Leta giggled.

"Happy birthday, Anna. Glad you finally made it," said Ben Benjamin Ben-ja … Jamon.

"Me, too. Not sure what took so long."

"You know what they say around here: *Planes del hombre, Dios se ríe.*"

"Man plans, G-d laughs." My Spanish was getting better.

"Women's plans get messed up, too," he said.

"Ben, I'm so sorry I stood you up."

"What's thirty-seven years between lovers?"

"We have a whole lot of making up to do," I said.

"And a whole lot of stories to tell."

<hr />

Ben and I came back to the states to visit Dad, and then we headed north to spend a month in Vermont. I couldn't miss the painted forests of autumn, the pulsating northern lights, and the farewell parade of the geese. No tropical sun or ocean or sand could make up for fall in New England. Luckily, Ben agreed.

Yesterday, Nebi and I had immersed ourselves in a private pond out near the foothills of the Green Mountains. Since there wasn't any way to tell if I had Jewish ancestry, I decided to have a *mikveh*, as a convert would, to achieve ritual purification. The *mikveh* is a private rite, often passed down from mother to daughter. Nebi flew in to join me, and we submerged together in the chilly, spring-fed pool.

Just a few close friends were there to witness as our rabbi guided us through the steps. Gregg came and watched it all as an anthropological encounter. Mark had to stay in the city with Dad, but Stephen and the new baby were there. They named her Elaine, after Mom. Ben wept when he heard Nebi and me recite the *she'hecheyanu,* offering our prayer of thanks to celebrate the joyous moment. I looked past him, and on the bank, a woodchuck was standing on its hind legs. Wise old Grandmother Woodchuck was there to protect and guide us.

There are many layers of meaning for the *mikveh*. It's thought to be like passing over a spiritual threshold. *Mikveh* and the Hebrew word for *hope* share their root letters, and the immersion is full of hope. Mostly, the *mikveh* is like a womb. I felt like a newborn, calm, floating, suspended in the water, momentarily without breath. The moment between life and death. As I emerged, desperate to gasp for air, I came face to face with Nebi, and we each took in a deep breath, as full and powerful as the first time.

The rabbi cheered when we surfaced, even though we splashed him, soaking his peppered beard. As we dried off, he spoke.

"I know you've been on a journey, Anna, and I understand thirty-seven has been a recurring theme. For those of you who don't know, the Hebrew alphabet uses letters to represent numbers. We have an ancient mystical system called Gematria in which we sum all of the letter values of words to get a numerical value, and then we can find symbolic meaning for the word or phrase. Probably the most familiar is the number eighteen, which is significant because the two letters in *chai*—Hebrew for *life*— add up to eighteen.

"Thirty-seven has a supremely important symbolic association. One of the words that adds up to thirty-seven is *pure*, which is appropriate for today's ritual. The Hebrew words for *to exhale* and *to knit* or *twist together* also add up to thirty-seven. I thought they would have particular meaning for you.

"But Anna, thirty-seven is also the value of the word for *heart*. Its reverse, seventy-three, is the value of the word *wisdom*. They are both known as star numbers. If you multiply that palindromic pair of primes, 37 x 73, the sum coordinates with the value of the first seven words of Genesis 1.1. In beginning ... And that numerical intersection, where wisdom meets the heart, is a rare occurrence that can only be divided by itself."

Everyone had left by morning, each loved one heading to his or her respective home. Ben and I slept in, then took a midday hike followed by a picnic of hot cocoa and warm cider donuts. We came home and spent the early afternoon making love, sweet and tender, by the roaring fire. Ben fell into a deep sleep, and I decided to run some errands while he napped. I kissed his chestnut-streaked grey bangs, and drove into town to mail my finished manuscript to a prospective literary agent. I'd finally gotten rid of my detached, taciturn editor.

I headed to the post office in Swanton, a tiny Vermont town right near the Canadian border. I passed the village green, where the resident namesake swans live. Both swans were drifting on their artificial pond, and, as usual, the two of them were inseparable. It's true that swans mate for life, but what's also true is that if there's a nesting failure, the couple will split up. Their complete dedication ends if they can't produce offspring. There's a lot to be said for alternative approaches to nesting success.

It was time to clean the pond, so the animal control officer was getting ready to move the swans out of their enclosure. How do you catch a swan? You put your arm around the wing, and wait. If it trusts you, it'll wrap its neck around your neck. You need to be patient and surrender to the scary beak and muscular neck. If you don't want to get your eyes pecked out.

While he moved the male swan, the female spread her enormous white wings, and as she hissed and flapped, splashing the shallow waters, I noticed something behind the pond. An elderly man was standing in front of an old house covered top to bottom with cast iron pans, rusting black dots in place of siding. I had passed the house many times, but had never seen anyone outside. I pulled over and asked if I could take his photograph. I had always planned to do a photojournalism piece on the unusual aspects of this quirky town: the marble mill with its eight-million-dollar Ponzi scheme, the controversial excavation of Abenaki burial grounds, and the endangered spiny softshelled turtles inhabiting the Missisquoi National Wildlife Refuge.

The man was excited to hear about my writing. He spoke as quickly as his aged lips could manage. He used to work in the old Barney Marble Mill, quarrying the infamous Swanton Red, and boy, did he have stories to tell. His grandfather was half-Abenaki, and had arrived in Swanton by canoe from Canada. He told me that it had been his wife's former husband who had covered their house with cast iron pans. When he married her after she became a widow, he hadn't had the heart to take them down. He wasn't really sure why the late husband had done it in the first place.

Sometimes, you never do find out why people do what they do.

I wanted to get to the post office before they closed, but his stories were captivating. Children were gathering by the swans, and the three-car rush hour traffic was backing up along Route 7N. By the time the old man finished his stream of stories, it was too late to get the mail out. There'd be another chance tomorrow. And tomorrow, with luck, someone else would share his or her story with me. Everyone has a tale to tell.

Acknowledgments

It is a mosaic of experiences and relationships that forms a piece of art. It's not possible for me to pinpoint each person who has contributed a phrase here, an image there, a thought like a timeworn whisper, materializing into a sentence. Still, specific acknowledgements are possible. I offer sincere thanks to ...

Mildred and Harold Cohen, my parents, both long gone, but ever in my heart as my first and most consistent fans. It's not really clear to me why—there was no specific encouragement or recognition—but I knew in my core that they believed in me. And with that vital base, I was able to grow into a woman who believes in herself.

Dylana Dillon and Ezra Dillon, my daughter and son, for the most beautiful bond of love, unbreakable and everlasting—no matter what life has presented us. Thank you for bringing JW and Alexis and Damian into our family. You all fill my heart. I constantly learn from each of you, and my world is enriched with your presence.

Ronni Kremberg and Debra Cohen Levine, my sisters, for being my guides through childhood, my constant companions through adulthood, holders of my memory and curators of my past. Thank you for being beacons of strength, paving the way to understanding how this wacky thing called life works.

And to the rest of my family, for the love and laughter, the lineage connection to the stories of our family, the ones that are true, the ones we lost, the ones we made up, and the ones yet to be.

So many dear friends I've known and kept since kindergarten, since high school, since college, through childrearing, through marriages, through divorces, old friends and new, for providing me with the knowledge and comfort that they were always there. I thank all of you, and the many ways you have shown up throughout the years. I know you are rooting me on, as I always do for you.

I have not named each special person who has come into my life by chance or choice. As a way to thank you for your invaluable gifts of friendship and support, I hope you will find bits of yourselves and your families throughout this novel.

All of my students, from kindergarteners to graduate students, who have been the true teachers. And to all of the teachers—and librarians—out there who open hearts and minds.

Those who generously shared their knowledge of writing and publishing, culture and language, and their stories and support: Amanda Amend, Sonam Chophel, President, Tibetan Association of Vermont, Rita Scarpa Dillon, Joseph Ferdinand, Professor Emeritus, Saint Michael's College, Thomas Hark, Founder, Past President, Vermont Youth Conservation Corps, Jimmy Karlan, Stephen P. Kiernan, Ali Mahdi, Agostino Masecchia, Kathryn Mason, Mark Pendergrast, Rabbi Jan Salzman, Congregation Ruach haMaqom, Bill Schubart, Vince Sgambati, Bojana Skrt, Rabbi Amy Small, Ohavi Zedek Synagogue, JoEllen Tarallo, the late Mary and Joseph Tarallo, and the late Luis Hess, whose conversations with me in Sosúa, a small coastal town in the Dominican Republic, moved me, and his words really were the initial spark of this entire endeavor.

The Lower East Side Tenement Museum, which I visited years before I began this novel, (followed, of course, by a knish at Yonah Schimmel) for providing many authentic sensory details of 1937.

Allen Jomoc Jr. for capturing the essence of my novel in his beautiful book cover design.

Two stellar editors: Katherine Quimby Johnson, who joined me at the beginning stages of this process, and whose early encouragement stayed with me until now; and Julie Roorda who edited the final pass, for her attention to detail, and caring and careful touch.

My publisher, Michael Mirolla, for patiently answering my many questions, and for believing in my work. Guernica Editions publicist Margo LaPierre and marketing and sales assistant Dylan Curran for taking on the task of making sure my book gets out into spaces where readers can access it.

University of California Press Books for granting permission to use the Yehuda Amichai poem, "Look: Thoughts and Dreams," from *The Selected Poetry of Yehuda Amichai*. Harper Collins for granting permission to use the Yehuda Amichai poem, "Once a Great Love," from *Amen*. The British Broadcasting Corporation for granting permission to quote Sir David Attenborough from BBC's *Life of Birds*.

Nature, for offering expansiveness, and for softening my heart. I highly recommend everyone make time often to listen to bird-song, feel earth beneath shoeless feet, get lost in Orion's belt, and, whenever possible, dance naked under a full moon.

About the Author

Joy Cohen is an award-winning writer and educator. Her plays include *Anna's Journal*, *Respite*, and *Of the Better Kind*. Joy taught Art and Science in public schools, and was an adjunct at the University of Vermont where she developed and led graduate courses on The Creative Process, and Teaching for Social Justice and Equity. Born in Brooklyn and back often, Joy now lives in rural Vermont, along the shores of beautiful Lake Champlain. *37* is her debut novel.

Printed in June 2021
by Gauvin Press,
Gatineau, Québec